DEREK VASCONI

KAI

Derek Vasconi was educated at Penn State University.
He lives in Los Angeles, but his heart and mind
are perpetually someplace else.

KAI

A NOVEL

DEREK VASCONI

ISBN: 978-0692422120

Book Cover Design by Anna Fong

Interior Layout by Rania Meng

Printed in the United States of America

For Yoko. This book simply couldn't have been written without you.

All my thanks to Hiroko, Dominic, Frankie, Gina, Marleen, and Gachi. Your support during the past five years while I wrote KAI means more to me than a stupid mention on a thank you page. I write these words for you.

For Mom, I owe you my passion for horror because you were nice enough to let me watch terrible, fucked up movies when I was a young kid. I always respected you for trusting me to not end up bringing a knife or worse to school and murdering my classmates because of what you allowed me to watch in my formative years.

A huge thanks to Miyuki for teaching me that it's never too late to hope in this life.

Thank you also to Gordon Warnock for his tireless efforts in editing this book, and to Rania Meng, who is the most gifted graphic designer I've ever had to coax into working way more than anyone ever should on a book cover and book interior layout. I owe her so much for putting up with my bullshit.

Thanks to Rachel Yoo for helping me understand the wonderfully complicated world of Korean names. And to Mary, Morris, Sarah, Dan, Dr. Howard Gardner, Kalin, and of course, Nick (one of the only people in this world I can truly call my "best friend"), I thank you all as well.

Finally, I owe enormous thanks to everyone I met while living in Hiroshima. They helped me wash the white off this book. They also proved to me that starting over isn't just for fairy tales, but something to be cherished when given the chance to do so.

PART ONE

Her brain floods the world.
Her skin has Saran-Wrapped an entire nation of nonbelievers.
Cognition exists only to satisfy a lustful apparition that has been sent
forth to answer the divine vituperations against her.
Against the choice to forget.
Against the choice to reincarnate as a timid expression of life.
Instead, she assaults the despondent with voracious fingertips
and hungry hands in a wave of purification.

Satsuki wanted a holocaust.

It was almost too much for her to bear. The Hiroshimakanon High School *kumidaiko*[1] group pounded on their *taiko*[2] drums in consistent, violent intervals. The *bachi*[3] sticks made from Japanese white oak trees carried memories of war from hundreds, even thousands of years ago. They screamed in every thud and pummel shot to the stretched out skin over the tops of wine-barrel-shaped *nagado-daiko*[4] drums, releasing the sounds of battles fought to the very last man. A cloud of steam floated above the performers, mingling with the invoked spirits of the dead.

Satsuki's head swelled from the rhythmic thumping, which had gone on for nearly an hour. She sat with her hands over both her knees on the gymnasium floor of Nakahiro Junior High School. She was a first-year student, thirteen years old, who sat near the back of her homeroom, but today, her class and the entire student body were front and center, forming neat rows to watch the guest high school perform for them. The songs were meant to "instill a fighting spirit into the hearts of the courageous students," who must take the sixth and final exam of the first school term. Or so said Mr. Kobayashi, their stoic principal. It was one week before July 19th, and summer break would last until the end of August.

The *taiko* drums reminded Satsuki of Rie Wakayama, her best friend for seven years. Both of them grew up together in Musashino City in Western Tokyo (Satsuki had moved there a year after her birth in Hiroshima) and spent many days riding bikes and chasing the dog-sized crows that hopped around on their dirt playgrounds. One day Rie's family invited Satsuki to go

---

1. *kumidaiko*—a taiko ensemble that consists of various taikos.
2. *taiko*—Japanese barrel-shaped drum that range in various sizes.
3. *bachi*—a type of wooden drumstick used to play taiko.
4. *nagado-daiko*—elongated drum roughly shaped like a wine barrel and varying in size.

with them to Shinagawa and see a new aquarium that had just opened up. Satsuki remembered the dolphin show clearly: a young female trainer zipped in a tight, blue wetsuit shot through the air on the bottle-nosed tip of a dolphin. Its lambent body was like a sprung metal coil, flinging upwards the girl who was trying to hit a *taiko* drum that hung suspended high above the water tank. The performance was the last time Rie and Satsuki spent together. The week after the trip, Satsuki's father was offered a job at the Mazda Motor Corporation as an international sales consultant. Satsuki moved back to Hiroshima and never saw Rie or her family again. Satsuki was ten at the time and had begged her father and mother to let them stay in Musashino City so she could be with Rie. She had even considered running away to live with her, but it soon became obvious that Rie had moved on from their friendship. Satsuki called Rie's cell phone and wrote to her every month for six months straight but never got a response back. Not even once.

For the last part of the drum ensemble, an *odaiko*[5] drum was rolled out on a moveable platform. All the students gasped with awe. The drum looked pregnant, its engorged sides arcing in wide directions before joining at the top of a massive, five-foot-wide head. Two students stood on either side, each holding *hinoki-odaiko bachi*[6] sticks, and assumed striking positions. A new song began with their choreographed swinging, and the slow "ma" spaces between hits were nearly drowned out by the reverberation of the strikes. The smell of cedar was everywhere.

Satsuki remembered that a smaller version of this drum had also played at the Shinagawa Aquarium. A dolphin trainer had pounded on it somewhere just above the highest row in the amphi-theater-style seating. Satsuki had loved the solemn feeling of awe she had felt when she had heard the pulsing drums and watched the dolphins fly through hoops and splash gallons of water into the audience. Now that sound was death. It was a war cry.

Since she had moved to Hirose Kitamachi, the northern area of Hiroshima's Naka-ku business district, only a few students

5. *odaiko*—a very large drum that is often the centerpiece drum in a taiko drum group.
6. *hinoki-odaiko bachi*—the drum sticks made of Cypress and used to play the odaiko drum.

dared to speak to her. In fact, most of the thirty-five children in her homeroom shunned her or didn't even notice her presence at all. To them, she was nothing more than a *mojyo*[7]. She had tried to make friends, but between adjusting to her new school surroundings and helping out at home, her social life was a vacuum. It had been easier to just stop trying. Satsuki had wanted to be part of the class, but the class hadn't wanted to be part of her.

Satsuki peeked at everyone from underneath her black hair burqa. Her perfectly straight locks, which normally rested just above her bony shoulders, were wrapped around her face in a clammy paste. The rest of her stayed completely still. The air in the gymnasium was more humid than outside, making Satsuki sweat in the folds of her crisp button-up shirt. Underneath her knees felt soaked with perspiration, too. Moving around meant sweat would drip into other unwelcome places on her body, so while doing her best not to move a muscle, she searched the room with her big brown eyes for anyone who wanted to defect and come to her side, to share, maybe, the annoyance she felt about the already way-too-long drum performance. She wondered if even one boy or girl would make eye contact with her, but they all sat captured in the war song rapture of what sounded like the concluding measures of the set. The drums were so loud now that cars driving by slowed down to hear the thunderous roar bursting through the school walls.

Izumi Kano, a fellow classmate who was popular with all the boys, smiled for just a moment in Satsuki's direction, but it was meant for Kazuya Nakamura, the captain of the Nakahiro Junior High baseball team. He slightly arched his upper lip in response, sending a shockwave of giggles through Izumi and her friends.

Future slut. You would be the first to burn, Satsuki thought, as she smiled anyway at Izumi, but Izumi pretended not to see it. *That's right, don't acknowledge me. In a few months, everything is going to change, and I won't need anyone at this damn school!*

Nine sets of three beats. Speed them up. Advance towards the enemy.

7. *mojyo*—creepy girl, unpopular or antisocial woman.

Satsuki almost didn't hear the squawking crossing signal as she stood by the large crosswalk near her school. She pulled her cell phone out of her purse and stared at the picture she had snapped of her mother's belly. Her mother was seven months pregnant. *Cute. Soooo soooo cute,* Satsuki thought to herself. *I can't wait to meet you, my imouto*[8].

Kids from her grade filed past her, some giving her a cocked-head look, but most of them ignored her completely. They were just excited to be going home and starting their week-end fun. It was another infernal summer Friday, the kind that baked the heads of every Nakahiro Junior High School student who walked home.

To Satsuki, however, it was one more day closer to having her very own sister. She forgot about the heat for a moment, locked in a projected reverie of life with a younger sibling. Oh, how they would run around in Otemachi Park near the Motoyasu River and fly kites there in the fall season. They would go shopping at the Pacela department store together, eat strawberry Walky Walky and Jagabee treats after splurging on *okonomiyaki*[9] with all its yummy layers of cabbage and fried squid. They would protect each other, share secrets, play jokes on Mom and Dad, and listen to Perfume on repeat while dancing around in their room. Her little sister would make things even in the world.

Satsuki stopped by the Lawson near her family's apartment. She bought a peach *aisunomi*[10] dessert and a Junsui Anzui fruit drink, her favorite after-school snacks. Afterwards, she continued heading towards home, only stopping at a housing complex with a blue-shingled roof (the only one of its kind in the entire Naka-Ku business district). Satsuki's favorite neighbors, Mrs.

8. *imouto*—little sister.
9. *okonomiyaki*—a Japanese style pancake that is widely associated with Hiroshima. Ingredients for the Hiroshima style include layers of batter, cabbage, pork, and noodles, with optional ingredients like squid or cheese added for extra flavor.
10. *aisunomi*—a small shaped ice cream treat sold in Japan.

Sato and her pet duck, lived there. Satsuki peeked over the chest-high bushes lining Mrs. Sato's home and watched as the old lady whispered something into the duck's face. It waddled around but didn't quack when Mrs. Sato pet it. Satsuki laughed. Mrs. Sato sat up and noticing she had an audience, quickly waddled out of view herself.

"*Tadaima*[11]!"

Satsuki stood in the *genkan*[12] and caught her breath. The elevator in the housing complex had been broken for a week, and she had to climb three flights of stairs to reach her front door. A wooden plaque above the door read:

(Takamoto)
~~(3 people)~~   (4 people)

Immediately after her mother had announced she was pregnant, Satsuki had dashed outside and scribbled over the number 3 so she could be reminded of her sister's arrival in less than a year's time.

"*Okaeri*[13]. What are you doing home so early?"

---

11. *tadaima*— "I'm home."
12. *genkan*—a traditional Japanese entryway for a house or apartment. This is usually where a person would take their shoes off before entering any part of the home and put on a pair of inside slippers.
13. *okaeri*—"welcome home."

Yoshiko spotted her daughter leaning against the *genkan's* shoe cabinet. She rubbed her lower back and offered a meek wave to Satsuki. Yoshiko had just spent the whole day cleaning the apartment and doing laundry. She was tired but happy to see her daughter home from school so early. She could prepare dinner way before seven, the time they usually ate at night, and maybe she could even take a nap before her husband came home later in the evening.

"I didn't have Art Club today. There was a concert instead." Satsuki changed into her favorite pair of flower-embroidered slippers and followed her mother down the hallway to the kitchen.

"Really? What kind of concert was it? Did you like it?" Yoshiko asked.

Before Satsuki could respond, a slim woman dressed in pinstriped business pants and a matching black jacket stood up from the kitchen table and allowed herself the only smile she had given anyone in weeks. It was Yoshiko's younger sister, Aiko.

"Who cares what kind of concert it was."

"Heeey, Aikobachan. I didn't know you were in town." Satsuki hugged Aiko. They both sat down at the table while Yoshiko brought them each a cup of green tea.

"Hey, *Okaasan*[14]. You should be sitting down, not us."

"*Onechan*[15] has always been like this. She constantly works and never bothers to stop, even when she's about to burst from being pregnant."

Yoshiko set the cups on the table. The steam from the tea saturated their faces in hot mist. "Hmmm… seems you are busier than me these days, Ai-chan. We never see you anymore. Did you finally meet a nice man at work?"

Aiko choked on the tea she had just sipped. "Meet a nice man? Are you serious? I work with a bunch of idiots. My boss is the only one who is halfway interesting, but he's never in the office. Never mind me. It's boring, really, to talk about my work or my life. Sacchan, we're being rude to you. Tell us about your day, please."

---

14. *okaasan*—mother.
15. *onechan*—sister.

Satsuki slurped her tea and stared at her mom, shuffling between the table and the rice cooker, which sat on top of the island shelf built right into the kitchen wall. The kitchen was split into two sections, but that did nothing to help the lack of space in it. The table, chairs, cooking utensils, dinnerware, even stacks of books and a small television were crammed into the compacted area. To the right of the small kitchen was an even smaller *tatami*[16] room. A blubbery heat streamed through the sliding, glass balcony door of the kitchen, soaking both rooms in humidity. Satsuki wrinkled her face up and let out an exaggerated sigh. "Well, my school day was the same as it always is, except at the end, like I was saying, there was a concert. It was the drum group from Hiroshimakanon High School."

"Did you like them?" Aiko asked.

"No. Well, maybe I did. I think they played everything well, but how would I know? I had never heard drums played like that before, so I couldn't know if it was good or not, right?" Satsuki slouched in her chair. That wasn't entirely true. In her mind, a snapshot of the *taiko* drum at the Shinagawa Aquarium appeared.

Aiko nodded. "I know exactly what you mean. I was always bored to death whenever other schools came and tried to show off. Idiots." Satsuki and Yoshiko laughed. Aiko's cell phone vibrated from somewhere inside her jacket. She frantically dug it out and flipped it open. A sigh escaped her pursed lips. *Maybe it was bad news from work*, Satsuki thought, *or maybe the message screen was blank.*

Yoshiko began to pull an assortment of vegetables and meat out of the refrigerator. "So, can you stay for dinner?"

"No, sorry. Something's come up at work."

Satsuki knew Aiko would say she had to leave. Since Satsuki and her family had moved back to Hiroshima, she had only eaten with them a couple of times. Aiko and Yoshiko had been close growing up, but several years ago, when their parents died of heart attacks less than a year apart from each other, Aiko had retreated into the busy offices of an international trading company. She

---

16. *tatami*—a straw floor mat that is found in many Japanese style homes.

practically lived there. Gone were the days of sisterhood bliss. But Yoshiko never pushed her sister to be close again, like they had been growing up. She figured that Aiko would come around when she was ready.

"What are we having for dinner tonight?" Satsuki asked.

"Veggie dumplings, salad, and rice. It's okay if you have to leave, Ai-chan. I'll tell Hideo you stopped by and wanted to say hello."

"I did? You know, your husband could try to be home with you more, but then, who am I to talk? What time is he going to be here, anyway?" Aiko guzzled the last of her tea.

"He's usually home by eleven, but some nights it's later."

"Hmm. Well, then. Goodbye. I'll call you. Goodbye, Sacchan." Aiko hugged her niece and waved at her older sister as she disappeared into the hallway and out the door.

Satsuki tapped her fingers on the table to mimic the sound of her aunt's high heels. Yoshiko motioned for her to help cut up the lettuce for the salad. Satsuki skipped over to her mother. "*Okaasan*, why is Aikobachan single? She's so beautiful. Doesn't she like boys?"

"What do you mean?"

Satsuki poured water over the lettuce and tossed it around in the strainer. "I mean, is she gay?"

"Sacchan!" Yoshiko stopped what she was doing and braced herself against the counter, trying not to explode with laughter. "No, she's not gay! She's too busy to be interested in dating. And she wasn't lucky like I was to meet a wonderful guy like your father."

Satsuki rolled her eyes. "Sure, whatever you say."

In the beginning, things were amazing between Yoshiko and Hideo. They had married right after entering university. She soon became pregnant with Satsuki and decided to become a housewife, happily leaving her interest in graphic design behind. Hideo had always managed to balance their lives with work and doing fun things, like trips to Asa Zoological Park and Miyajima Island.

When Satsuki got older and asked for a brother or sister to play with, Hideo and Yoshiko both decided it would be a great idea to try, even though they were both thirty four years old. Life was not always easy for them. They argued like most married couples do, and lately their relationship was suffering due to Hideo's demanding work schedule. Yoshiko always wanted to talk with her husband when he came home from work, but instead sat, night after night, watching her husband eat dinner in silence. Yoshiko wanted to believe they were still okay, but she did wince a little after she had called her husband "wonderful."

Satsuki splashed water at her mother, ejecting both Hideo and Aiko from Yoshiko's mind completely.

"I think the reason why Auntie is single is because she just doesn't know how to have any fun."

"Really, is that so?" Yoshiko scooped up rice with the *shamoji*[17] and flung it right at her daughter's face.

"Okaaaaaaassaaaann!!!!"

Satsuki went straight to her room after dinner. When she opened the door to her room (which was almost never shut), a plump, milky white cat sprung up on its paws and rubbed itself across Satsuki's feet.

"Chi-chan, what did you do?" Satsuki scooped Chibita up into her arms. The two-year-old feline purred like he had ten smaller cats stuffed inside his bloated cheeks. "Did you shut the door? I was wondering why you didn't come say hello to me. I thought you didn't like me anymore."

Chibita kneaded Satsuki's chin with his paws, then licked her face.

"I know what that means. You're hungry, aren't you?"

Satsuki kissed Chibita on the nose, then laid him down in a pile of dirty clothes beside her bed. She pulled out a bag of cat food from a cubbyhole space between her computer stand and a stack of plastic storage bins filled with her winter clothes. Chibita licked his lips as Satsuki poured heaven into his bowl.

17. *shamoji*—a flat rice spoon used in Japanese cuisine. It is used to stir and to serve rice.

"Delicious, isn't it? I'm sure after waiting this whole time to eat that you would think anything tastes good."

After petting Chibita for a few minutes while he devoured his meal, Satsuki shed her school uniform and threw on a pair of shorts and a camisole. Her room was sweltering. She turned her television on but kept the volume at the lowest possible setting before she couldn't hear anything. There was nothing on, anyway, except a funny talk show on Shin Hiroshima. The featured guests were Megumi Kurihara, better known as Princess Megu, and Saori Kimura, two of Japan's most popular volleyball players. They were spiking balls at the talk show hosts, who were running around a tiny gymnasium in their underwear to avoid getting hit. Satsuki watched with mild interest. It was too hot to laugh.

Of course, it didn't help that Satsuki's walls, balcony sliding door window, and big, Tibetan-style, hand-knotted rug that was sprawled out in the middle of the room, were covered with heat magnets. A plastic desk camouflaged with Disney stickers (Satsuki had forgotten what color the desk was underneath the canopy of cartoon characters) stood in the corner opposite the bed, along with a glutted bookshelf sputtering novels everywhere, and a body mirror that leaned against a wall shelf near the faux-frosted balcony window. Satsuki's television sat on the desk with a stuffed animal audience. Moogles, Hello Kitty, Stitch, a deflated Eeyore, bears, and penguins crowded around the silver screen, using Satsuki's shirts and skirts as blankets. Her collection of special edition *Kamichama Karin Chu* manga formed a dubious pyramid on top of uneven past issues of *Popteen* (mostly unread, as Satsuki couldn't stomach all that *gyaru* bullshit), *MIG*, *Nicola*, and *Shonen Jump* stacked high in front of her balcony doors. Plastered onto the walls were posters of Ai-chan, Nocchi, and Kashiyuka from Perfume, anime characters, and her favorite *Dragonquest* and *Final Fantasy* heroes. Pinned onto these posters were pictures of herself with Chibita as a kitten, pictures of herself as a toddler, elementary school acquaintances (including Rie; keeping her photos reminded Satsuki of their fun adventures), and drawings she did of Tifa Rokkuhato of *Final Fantasy VII*, who, with her long, black

hair and feisty personality, Satsuki considered to be a cousin re-
lated by digital blood.

Anyone who stumbled into Satsuki's bedroom and saw these
things might think it belonged to an awkward fourteen-year-old
boy. The last time Aiko had set foot in there, she had called it "an
otaku's[18] wet dream."

After Satsuki cooled off, she lay down on her bed and decided to watch a downloaded episode of *Kamichama Karin* on her
Nintendo DS. Chibita hopped onto a pillow beside her. Satsuki
rested her head on top of Chibita's smooshy body, as was her ritual
most nights. Chibita didn't seem to mind this at all. With his belly
full, he licked himself complacently, sometimes licking Satsuki's
hair by accident.

"My Shii-chan, always making sure I'm okay," Satsuki said to
herself, referring to him as the pet cat of *Kamichama Karin's* main
character, the orphan teen, Karin Hanazono. "Shii-chan" purred
his approval.

Satsuki picked episode seven of *Kamichama Karin*, where
Karin meets for the first time the "other" half of her friend, Himeka
Kujo (i.e., the original Himeka, who was split into two identical-
looking children that possessed important God data research.
They each unknowingly depended on each other as well. If one
was stronger, the other was weaker).

Satsuki was infatuated with their strange connection and had
watched this episode many times, but could never figure out why it
always made her feel so comforted. Whether it was this or the fact
that she was exhausted, her eyes started to slip out of focus. She
fell asleep with the Nintendo DS clamped between her fingers, not
making it past the title song of the introduction.

Darling, open your eyes...

18. *otaku*—this phrase has been saturated in Japanese pop culture to mean many things. Among
them, a person who is obsessed with manga, computers, J-pop idols, music, but mostly it's
now used to describe anyone who is devoted or obsessed to something in their lives. It has
historically taken on a negative connotation when describing a person.

Who am I?

Seul Bi catalogued this question, along with many others, in her perfectly shaped skull. The ocean water erased its Etch-A-Sketch border across the dotted sand. It swirled around Seul Bi's feet, sending a strange but familiar shiver up and down her entire body. The ocean was rediscovering itself wave after wave, as it did most days and nights here along the Kona coastline in Hawaii.

While Seul Bi gazed at the ocean on this first morning of vacation, it somehow seemed perfectly natural to wonder who she was. There was so much unknown out there, floating in the salty waters and below in the deep-sea caverns that very few people ever visit in the flesh (most get their education from television documentaries). Who *wouldn't* ask themselves about life's big mysteries when gazing upon something that a person could describe as "esoteric" and not be wrong in their description?

Seul Bi felt part of this endless blue in front of her and all of its secrets, because the question about what it held inside was the same kind of question she asked herself on a daily basis.

So, who am I, really?

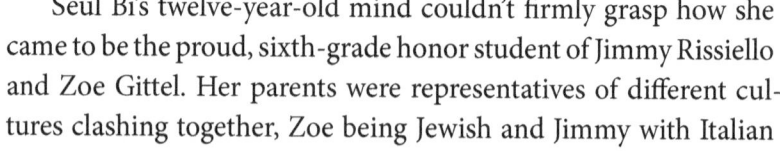

Seul Bi's twelve-year-old mind couldn't firmly grasp how she came to be the proud, sixth-grade honor student of Jimmy Rissiello and Zoe Gittel. Her parents were representatives of different cultures clashing together, Zoe being Jewish and Jimmy with Italian blood circulating in his veins. Her own racial background was neither. Seul Bi was Korean.

"It's kinda weird," Seul Bi murmured, "to think, the last time you and Mom were anywhere near this ocean, it was to go get me from that orphanage. It's just, you know, crazy to think that I came from somewhere across... *this*."

Seul Bi stood at the water's crest with her father. She almost forgot he was there. Almost. Jimmy's words filled the air around them both.

"Yeah, you probably would've swam across to us if we didn't come get ya, so it wasn't like we had a choice in the matter. You enjoy too much being spoiled by us."

Seul Bi wrinkled her brow.

"Dad, you tell me this every time I ask you this, but really, I mean, seriously, how did you guys get so lucky to have me?"

Seul Bi laughed, but her voice was engulfed in her father's simultaneous baritone chuckle. They both kept walking along the capricious Kona shoreline. Both kept placid in the warm Pacific air. Back home in Evanston, Illinois, it was winter, and the air there was serpentine and stealthy, sneaking into every crevice of clothing and biting the skin. Here, only lukewarm ocean spray clung to their bodies.

"Seriously, though, me and your mother waited a long time to get you. We were on the waiting list for... man... it felt like an eternity. Then we get a call, and the next thing you know, we're staring at your cute little face in the Sun-Duckie-or-whateva-you-call-it orphanage in Seoul. Your caretakers told us some monk found you on the steps of a temple, wrapped up in wet blankets because of the drizzle coming down when they found ya, crying like crazy. But yeah... nobody knows anything about your mom and dad, really."

"So I've heard." Seul Bi looked away from Jimmy. Thinking of him as "Dad" right after hearing this story always felt unfamiliar and incorrect.

When she was in third grade, she realized how unfamiliar and unknown her life had actually become. Several classmates at her school in Evanston, the private, whitewashed Pope John XXIII, would glare at Jimmy and Zoe when they went to pick up their adopted Korean child around 3:00 p.m. each day. Classmates would register confusion and resolve to questioning commentary (*Why does she not look like them? What is she doing with two white parents? They probably bought her from a catalogue*). Seul Bi could only stare back with what undoubtedly looked like a pair of crooked eyes to her Caucasian peers.

Yet there she was: small, yellow-brownish skin, with dark brown eyes and slant-shaped eyelids that were covered by oil-blackened hair, her body a mess of joints in awkward angles, her ribs poking out of her Osh Kosh Bigoshes.

She began to worry that she was in the wrong family or that she was taken from her real parents. Jimmy and Zoe explained over a lasagna dinner one night that she was adopted. She was in fourth grade by the time of this revelation, which, at first, felt like a betrayal.

The discussion had actually begun over Seul Bi asking about her name and why it was so different than her peers at school. Her parents explained that she had been found in Seoul and it was lightly raining, so the monks felt the name "Seul Bi Lee" fit perfectly. However, when she came to America, her parents decided to drop the "Lee" surname and give her their last name "Rissiello," but keep her Korean identity intact through her first and middle names, "Seul" and "Bi" (despite having the middle name "Bi," Seul was taught to introduce herself to others and write her name as "Seul Bi." Zoe had felt the combination of those two names was too adorable to change into just "Seul").

They had planned on telling her all of this well before she reached fourth grade, but the subject never seemed to come up in any conversations between Seul Bi and her parents. Until now. It was something that Seul Bi was shocked about at first, then upset because her parents had never mentioned even once that she had been adopted. *How could they do that to me?* Seul Bi had thought to herself many times since that discussion. It was kind of an important fact to know about oneself!

However, a few years later, she skipped proudly through the sixth-grade hallways as the only Asian girl at her school. She had replaced feelings of parental resentment with gratitude. She continuously experienced loving kindness (even though she sometimes thought of herself as a borrowed child) from the entire Rissiello family. Cousins, aunts, uncles, grandparents… they all treated her like she had been in their family since the very second she had been conceived in her Korean mother's womb. They seemed to all accept her unconditionally. And her peers at school eventually stopped treating her as a racial pariah, too.

Today, on this early walk that her dad suggested they attempt before Mom and her entourage woke up (Zoe brought along her sister, Debbie, and her sister's daughter, Beverly, who was the same age as Seul Bi), she felt at home.

"I used to think maybe you and Mom were kidnappers, but you just confirmed my suspicions that you two are just boring Midwesterners who wanted a cute, Asian baby to spice up your lives." Seul Bi playfully leaped a few steps in front of her dad, shoving him in the process.

Jimmy's line of vision seemed distracted by a sudden wave that barreled down into the sand at their feet.

"Well, you know," Jimmy said, grinning like a Cheshire cat, "Korea is just across this ocean, and we can always give you back!" His last three words got lost in Seul Bi's playful screams and laughter, as he picked her up and tossed her into the water.

Soaked and defeated, Seul Bi slowly sat up, didn't say nothing. She looked at her antagonist with a pseudo-pout spread across her face. Jimmy reached his hand out, and when she finally lurched forward to put his massive hand around hers, she found herself, once again, swallowing salty liquid as he pushed her back into an oncoming wave. He then galloped away from her while howling with cartoon-evil laughter.

Seul Bi regained her composure and tugged on her bikini to adjust it from falling off, then started to run after him. She was about to yell at him too, but as soon as her feet sunk back into the warm sand on the beachline, she paused to contemplate the Pacific and its invisible promises. Was her identity somewhere to be found past the distant skyline in her sight? Was her home really with the Rissiello family?

She became enveloped by the possibility of belonging to the ocean instead, perhaps as a water spirit from the deep in human form. Or maybe the magnitude of her present surroundings was simply overwhelming. After all, she had never seen the ocean before this trip, at least not with conscious eyes.

Seul Bi sifted through the sand and picked up a shiny, black stone, along with pocket-sized sea shells. With all the energy she could muster, she skipped the stone into the oncoming tide. The shells spiraled in every direction, sprinkling into the water with a pitter-patter that echoed rain drops. She had a sudden, intense urge to just swim as far as she could into the Pacific and try to locate a current of answers.

Where is home, and who am I?

An amplified adolescent thought, and one more question that, for now, she stored in her endless myelin rolodex. She tugged again on her bikini and pursued her dad with the very opposite and childish purpose of revenge.

Hideo brushed his teeth with his head almost parallel to the sink faucet. It was 6:00 a.m., and even though it was his day off, he was used to waking up this time every morning. There would still be a last-minute-scheduled conference call between him and his South Korean clients at eleven, so waking up before the sun drilled sweat-filled holes in him provided a chance to review his notes for the phone meeting. Hideo also wanted to watch the Carps baseball game in the afternoon, so he hoped to be finished with his work and then have the rest of the day to sit and relax, maybe even talk with Satsuki about how she was doing in school.

Ah, I think I will save that conversation for next week. Or the week after. She just needs to stop playing her Nintendo DS so much and reading manga, and then she'll be fine.

Hideo considered this as he gargled and splashed water on his face. He'd had a difficult teenage existence as the son of a widowed mother and had had no time for games or manga. He had a job by the time he was fourteen and kept it until his entrance into university. It was there he met Yoshiko, got married, and increased his workload by two. He was offered an international sales position at Mazda right after completing school, but it required long stretches of overseas travel, and the instability and long work hours kept him from connecting that much with his wife or daughter.

His hard work was paying off, though; he was close to becoming a *kacho*[19] within the international sales department, as his years of being a *kakaricho*[20] and supervising the lower-level employees were highlighted with countless days and nights spent at Mazda demonstrating what it means to his underlings to be the

---

19. *kacho*—the boss or main supervisor.
20. *kakaricho*—supervisor to junior employees at a corporation.

archetypal "proficient" worker. Despite such dedication to his job, Hideo did love Yoshiko and Satsuki in his own private way.

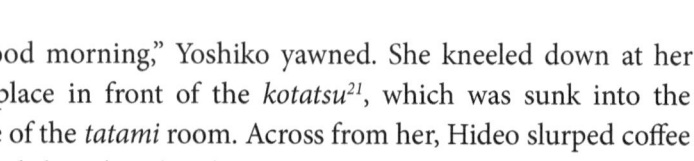

"Good morning," Yoshiko yawned. She kneeled down at her usual place in front of the *kotatsu*[21], which was sunk into the middle of the *tatami* room. Across from her, Hideo slurped coffee and read the *Chugoku Shinbun* from the previous night. He had come home from work and gone straight to sleep, pausing only to sample a plate of leftover dumplings Yoshiko had left on the table for him.

"Morning," Hideo replied in a barely audible voice.

"Still tired?" Yoshiko asked. "Why do you get up so early when you have the day off?" She was used to having the morning time to herself during the week. She had expected the weekends to be no different, either. Satsuki usually stayed in her room all weekend long, but for the past year, she had awakened on Saturdays and Sundays to find Hideo sitting in the *tatami* room. Her daily routine of waking up and cleaning, along with the quiet joy she received from a few hours of being alone and moving at her own pace, was skewed by his presence. She imagined herself talking him into going back to sleep for a few more hours, but all she could do was patch onto her curled lips a faint grin.

Hideo shrugged. "I have a conference call that was scheduled at the last minute yesterday, and then, after that, I want to relax or maybe talk to Satsuki about school."

"I see. Do you want some tea?" Yoshiko didn't wait for his answer. She got up and set the electric tea maker to eighty-one degrees Celsius, filling the top with water and the strainer with fresh leaves.

"Sure."

Yoshiko rubbed her stomach. She felt a good-morning nudge from the child inside.

---

21. *kotatsu*—a low, wooden table covered by a futon and has some sort of heat source underneath it. Often a centerpiece in Japanese living rooms.

"Well hello, little one! I just felt a little kick. Do you want to feel?"

Hideo's eyes widened. "Uh... really?"

"Of course. Here, give me your hand."

Yoshiko stood in front of her husband and lifted her pajama shirt. Hideo flinched. He imagined her belly was a lumpy grocery sack with the baby's hands and legs making indentations in the stomach lining. He put a few clumsy fingers on Yoshiko's warm, spectral flesh and pressed down, lingering long enough to make him realize he couldn't remember the last time they'd had sex. It was sometime after he'd been given the news about the pregnancy, but when was it, exactly? Five months, possibly six months ago?

"Do you feel her?"

"No, I don't think so."

All Hideo could feel was sadness coiled around self-pity. His groin started to ache. He also noticed that his fingertips were becoming unsteady, so he pulled his hand away and bowed his head in a half-hearted apology.

Yoshiko unrolled her shirt back over her stomach and poured two cups of tea.

"Hmm... maybe she fell asleep?" *Probably not, though*, she thought to herself. *That's just her way of saying you should go back to bed.* "Anyway, I have that ultrasound appointment tomorrow afternoon. Are you still coming with me? You can see our daughter. Who knows? Maybe she will wave at you." Yoshiko giggled while blowing on her steamy tea with short, dagger-like breaths.

"Uh... well, you see, I have to leave tomorrow on a business trip." Hideo scratched his arms and turned his head towards the empty television screen. He sipped the boiling tea without thinking and blistered his tongue.

"*Itai*[22]! *Itai*! *Itai*! I think I just burnt my entire mouth!"

Yoshiko didn't ask if he was all right. She slouched down and let out a sigh. Everything in the room slouched and sighed as well.

"Where are you going this time?" she mumbled.

Hideo slapped his tongue against the inside of his cheeks, checking for any sensation. It made a wet, smacking noise, like a

---

22. *itai*—"OUCH!"

mop swishing over a dirty floor. He waited until his mouth cooled down before answering. "South Korea. I'll be there for a week. I was just told about this last night. They need me to oversee a major production deal in Seoul. That reminds me... would you mind driving me to the airport tomorrow?"

Yoshiko didn't raise her head. Her face was gaunt. "What time?"

"In the morning. Will that interfere with your appointment?"

"No. I told you my appointment is in the afternoon."

"Oh, right. You did, didn't you?"

Hideo turned on the television. He knew Yoshiko was hurt, but he didn't know how to deal with it. He was never any good at comforting people. When a co-worker's mother had died, Hideo had patted him on the back, said he was sorry, and then launched into discussing some account inconsistencies in his co-worker's monthly report. Hideo's compassion always tiptoed out of the room when nobody was looking, himself included.

Something soft collided with Yoshiko's backside.

"Good morning, Chi-chan." Yoshiko dragged her fingers through his fur. Chibita circled around her before disappearing underneath the *kotatsu*. Except for Satsuki's bed, it was his favorite resting spot in the apartment. And since he almost never left Satsuki's side when she was home, Yoshiko knew it was a good bet that Satsuki was also awake and on her way down the hallway.

"Goooood morning."

Satsuki appeared, just as Yoshiko expected. She grabbed a cup of tea and a banana and plopped down beside Yoshiko, wiggling her toes in front of Chibita's face. He playfully lunged at them.

"So, what's up? *Otousan*[23], you're up early for it being the weekend and all."

Hideo didn't say anything back to Satsuki. He flipped on a news channel and distracted himself with yet another special update about North Korea wanting to launch a test missile over Hokkaido in the next few days. This was the third time over the past five months North Korea had threatened to disrupt the uneasy peace between their two countries. It was on every channel, and it was

23. *otousan*—father.

all the newscasters seemed to care about anymore. Hideo began to worry about his trip. Yoshiko, however, remained indifferent. She stood up.

"I'm tired. I think I'll go back to bed."

Seul Bi stared ritualistically into the velvet black air of her room, her eyes scorched from remaining open so many hours. Night after night, she became mummified in a tomb of displacement, listening to the Japanese instrumental band Mono on repeat while succumbing to an upright fetal position on her single bed. Ten-year-old memories of the first real time she felt alive, during that vacation in Hawaii, wouldn't vacate her mind. She felt apprehensive, nervous. It was 5:00 a.m. in the frosty morning, and soon she would board the Purple Line train at the Davis stop for another eight hour shift at Rainbow Private Residential Hospital.

If only I had known, Dad, what would happen that morning, I could have stopped you and Mom from going into the water.

Seul Bi forced herself off the bed and into a pair of tabi slippers. Her legs and arms wobbled as they were in a state of entropy from sitting completely motionless all night. She slowly walked to the bathroom.

The twenty-two-year-old lived alone in an apartment on the tenth floor of a high-rise structure that was just three blocks from her Aunt Debbie's house (where she went to live, or rather, exist, during her teenage years) and three train stops away from where her mom and dad were buried in Cavalry Cemetery.

What was left of them.

Seul Bi slipped out of her pajamas and turned the handle of her shower, waiting for the warm, steamy fog to surround everything in sight. However, no amount of fog could hide the messy randomness in her apartment. Her clothes were scattered like confetti everywhere. A flat-screen TV sat lopsided on a broken, wooden stand with dirty plates piled next to it. Her laptop was perched upon a desk next to the bed, and directly across from the television, several rows of drawing tablets were unevenly stacked against the wall.

"Ouch, fuck."

She stepped into the hot water only to jerk back awkwardly. Waiting a few minutes for the temperature adjustment, this time she cautiously tiptoed into the shower. The water was tolerable to her prickly morning skin, even comforting.

Seul Bi closed her eyes and forgot herself for a little while.

CHAPTER 5

Yoshiko swung the Mazda right at the airport terminal sidewalk, rubbing its tires on the aging curb. This wasn't the first time she had misjudged distances in parking attempts. She always joked with Hideo about how ironic it was that she was such a terrible driver, yet he worked for a car company known for their high safety standards.

But Hideo never laughed when she brought it up. On the contrary, he considered her poor driving skills a liability to his reputation. What if she was in an accident and somebody at Mazda read about it in the newspaper? It made Hideo uneasy to let her drive, but what could he do? Yoshiko took care of everything and often needed the car to run errands or shop for groceries. And with Yoshiko being so far along into her pregnancy, she relied on driving their car now more than ever.

Satsuki didn't wake up when Hideo opened the rear door to grab his briefcase and the other two travel bags that were romping around in the trunk the whole forty-minute drive from their apartment to Hiroshima Airport. She was sprawled across the back car seat with her head propped against her *Dragonquest* metal-slime pillow she had brought for the car ride. Her ears were covered with a pair of vibrating Denons connected to her iPod, which had fallen out of her hand and onto the floor. Satsuki was used to this kind of sleeping posture, as she usually assumed it on the bus ride home after cram school, her brain wet and heavy with exhaustion.

Yoshiko rolled down her window.

"Goodbye."

Hideo's eyes seemed to plead with his wife, as if to say to her that he wanted to apologize for not being more available to his family, but instead, he waved his farewell and disappeared into the airport. Yoshiko sped off without looking back.

Traffic had started to swell along Aioi-Dori. Yoshiko drove from the airport in Mihara and straight to Hiroshima City's shopping district. Satsuki attended a branch of the Daiei Cram School there, but finding it amongst so much congestion on the road wasn't going to be easy. It was located in the sub-level basement of a four story office complex that was cloistered among a row of larger housing and business units. Yoshiko's cheeks flushed with a scaly pink color as she stuck her head outside the car door window. She looked for the narrow side alleyway that the school was packed into. She remembered it being somewhere near Chuo-Dori. She couldn't really see much of anything, however, as the cars in front of them were like slugs desiccating in the afternoon summer inferno, blocking everything from view with their heated, bloated, metal frames. She rolled her window up and gulped down what little was left of her bottled water.

"Satsuki, wake up." Yoshiko reached back and tapped her daughter on the head with the empty plastic bottle. Satsuki woke up and tossed her Denons off, then squinted at her mother. Her eyes were taking time to adjust from the nebulous space underneath their eye flaps.

"Uh… where are we? Did we get to the airport yet?" Satsuki yawned.

"Yes, sleepy head. We dropped off *Otousan*, and we're almost at your school. I need help finding it. Do you know where it's at? I've only been there once before."

Yoshiko recalled how she and Hideo had gone to the cram school a few days after moving into their new apartment. She went with Hideo to pay the tuition and discuss Satsuki's enrollment into a general mathematics review course. The Daiei administration office explained that the center where the classes took place was usually reserved for post-junior-high studies, but some local families had begged them to create courses for elementary kids' induction into junior high school's exam-heavy environment. Thus, an intensive series of lectures on science and math were added. Although most of the students who attended on the weekends were preparing for high-school entrance exams, Satsuki was allowed to participate because she had entered Nakahiro Junior High after the school year had begun.

Satsuki peered out the back window. "Ah, it's hard to see from Aioi-Dori," she said. "Can you just let me out at Chuo-Dori? I'll walk the rest of the way. I want to grab something to drink at the Lawson near the school."

"Do you have money?" Yoshiko asked. She pulled out a 500-yen coin from her purse.

"Yeah, but thanks, anyway."

"You're welcome. Are you going to have time, though, to get a drink?"

"I think so. Why?"

"Well, because it's almost time for your class. I think you're going to be late. Sorry I couldn't get you to class sooner. The traffic is terrible on the weekends, you know?"

"Mmm, I guess so." Satsuki flipped her cell phone open and looked at the time. It was almost noon, so she would have to hurry down Chuo-Dori. "*Okaasan*, can I just skip today?"

"NO!" Yoshiko's voice skipped a couple steps on the volume escalator before coming back to a normal tone. "*Otousan* paid a lot of money and had to pull strings to get permission for you to attend this class. We want you to do well in math. Your grades are average, and how will you expect to get into a good high school around here if you can't compete with your classmates?"

Satsuki sighed. "I know, I know. It's just that I thought you didn't want to go alone to your ultrasound appointment. And besides, I really wanted to see my *imouto* in her stomach mansion."

Yoshiko laughed at Satsuki's clever remark. "Well, I would like the company, actually, and I'm sure your *imouto* wouldn't mind if you said hello, but honestly, *Otousan* would be mad at you if he found out. He wouldn't be happy with me, either."

"Who cares what he thinks? He's never home and you're always by yourself. It's not fair," Satsuki murmured. She shoved the Denons and iPod into her oversized handbag.

Yoshiko parked in front of a clothing boutique, careful this time to not shred any tire rubber against the curb. While driving to the airport, she had been quietly fuming at her husband for talking on the phone for several hours the day before. She was especially pissed that he was missing the ultrasound appointment. But how could she be mad at Satsuki for what she said or felt? Yoshiko felt exactly the same.

"I'm gonna drop you off here. Can you jump out?" Yoshiko asked.

Satsuki stumbled out of the car without answering her mother. The overwhelming heat immediately sucked the air out of her lungs.

"Phew! It's hot!" she exclaimed.

Yoshiko leaned away from the open back door. It felt like invisible waves of magma were pouring into the car from the outside. "What time will you be finished with class today?"

"Same time as every oth—oh… wait a minute."

"What is it?"

"I just remembered that I have to look for glitter for my art project. I probably won't make it home until just before dinnertime, actually."

"That's fine," Yoshiko said abruptly. She was starting to get anxious. Her hair was already sticking to her face, and her seat felt like a boilerplate. "Good luck today. I'll see you later."

Satsuki responded with a stilted goodbye wave, then disappeared into the throngs of families and teenagers walking along Chuo-Dori.

CHAPTER 6

FINDING THE SPINE

7:15 a.m. Late as usual.

"Good mornin', Seul Bi."

A tall, black man opened the doorway to Rainbow's common area.

"Morning, Morris, How are you? Sorry I'm late."

"Nah, it's okay."

"So, did anything happen last night?"

"Just Marisa couldn't sleep, so I gave her a p.r.n."

"Whatddy'a give her?"

"Ambien. She didn't come out of her apartment after that."

"Good job, Mo."

Morris looked down at Seul Bi and winked. He was almost two feet taller than her and bulky as a tank. His voice bum-rushed the room, and his arm muscles, which he spent so much time working out at L.A. Fitness every single day, bulged through his dress shirt. It was easy to understand why Morris worked the 11:00 p.m. to 7:00 a.m. night shift during the week.

Seul Bi winked playfully back, then opened the mini-refrigerator in the common area and grabbed a bottled water.

"So, is Mary around?" she asked while sipping her drink quietly.

"Nah, you're the only one here. I would stay, but I gotta go to the gym."

Morris grabbed his tote bag, which was next to the couch and two wicker chairs set up for residential community gatherings. Next to these was a metallic table that, although circular, somehow injured everyone who walked by it with its awkward legs. The running joke was that you could always tell who lives at Rainbow by their bruised kneecaps.

"Mo', you don't need to work out, you already are a toughie." Seul Bi poked Morris's bicep, cooing in mock flirtation. Morris blew air through his lips.

"Pssshh... shit, I need to work out. You know my Lulu always be feeding me. Seriously man, she always be feeding me every chance she gets!"

They both laughed.

Rainbow Residential Hospital was a three-floor private mental health facility created by Dr. Daniel Nathan, an esteemed senior physician and valued professor of medical research at Northwestern University. Dr. Nathan had wanted to create a safe place for adolescents with behavioral disorders, particularly eating disorders like anorexia nervosa and bulimia. Therapy occurred Monday through Friday from 10:00 a.m. to 3:00 p.m. at Rainbow's counseling center in downtown Evanston. The weekends were non-structured so that the residents could decompress from the intense rounds of therapy.

The residential building was nestled right alongside the coast of Lake Michigan. The surrounding neighborhood was filled with rows of nondescript apartment complexes housing mostly college students and upper-class types. Comparably, the cost of living at Rainbow was congruent with Evanston's condominium prices: an estimated $25,000 a month. Thus, wealthy families of the adolescents receiving treatment could also feel safe knowing their children were not exposed to the abnormal types who reside in, say, a state-funded hospital or public adolescent mental health facility. Residents typically stayed for a minimum of three months.

It was at Northwestern University where Seul Bi was asked to join the staff at Rainbow by Dr. Nathan, her academic advisor. He had been impressed with seeing her name on the Dean's List every semester. He'd also liked her introverted nature, so he encouraged Seul Bi in her senior year to join the staff at Rainbow once she had graduated. After Seul Bi had learned from him that not talking about yourself was part of the job description at his facility, she'd accepted his offer without hesitation. She then spent her first year after graduating lost in reveries and quiet routines.

Seul Bi rubbed her eyes and stared at the computer screen in the office. It was 7:52 a.m. Nobody else had shown up for work.

"Mary's later than me today. Hmm," Seul Bi thought out loud to herself. It was rare for Mary, who was a supervisor at Rainbow, to not show up for work at least a half hour before her scheduled shift.

While Seul Bi waited, she thought about something that Ariel, a recent admission to Rainbow, had said earlier that week:

"So, physics promotes the idea of molecules being in two different places. The idea that we exist all together all at once." Ariel poked at the air in an attempt to illustrate a line zigging from point A to point B. Seul Bi stared at the invisible markers.

"Uh huh. Go on."

"So yeah, don't you see? Time only exists if there is a motion between those molecules, but alone they, they... well, you, know. They just are... there." The last word propelled forth with a coughing sound.

"Ariel, I think you should tell your advocate these thoughts." Seul Bi gave her the standard response to something a resident said that was symptomatic of their illness.

Ariel was clinically psychotic and convinced she could build a time machine. Seul Bi wasn't sure if Ariel's words were fiction or real physics concepts, but the idea behind it seemed compelling enough. She even wished that Ariel would build the time machine so she could go back into the past herself.

I would leave footprints again in the sands of Kona. I could've stopped my life from becoming so... ambiguous.

As she thought about Ariel's words and about the past, Seul Bi leaned forward in the chair, cupping her hands underneath the seat cushion. Her forehead pressed against the computer monitor. A small cackle of electricity rang out into the silence. *So routine*, she thought to herself with a sigh.

Today would proceed like any other. Mary and Seul Bi would have a community meeting with the residents at 8:45 a.m., followed by medication distribution. The residents would then proceed to therapy from 10:00 a.m. to 3:00 p.m., spending the evening decompressing from their treatment sessions. The common area was still but soon would bustle with morning activities. Seul Bi stood up to stare at the common area from the door of the office entrance.

"Come on, Mary, get here so we can get this fucking day over with, already," she growled at the door.

And just like that, Mary opened the door with a quiet promise of monotony following her inside.

Satsuki stood in front of the cram school's barred front window, sipping an apricot drink she had just purchased at the nearby Lawson. The bars crisscrossed across the glass, slicing it into many slender rectangular rungs. She thought maybe at one time the place had been somebody's apartment before being converted into a study center. Why else would bars be on the window? *Probably so that us students wouldn't get any ideas about leaving once we're inside*, she thought to herself while peeking inside. Class had begun.

"Great," She said with a sardonic laugh. She really dreaded these weekend sessions, but her parents insisted that she attend. Satsuki ran inside, bowed in apology, and dove into the first empty seat she saw by the door.

The class was divided into four groups of desks. Each one had four to five students sitting at them. Two instructors, both young males who Satsuki guessed were recent university graduates, rattled on about the quadratic formula and X and Y variables while circling the desk clusters. Rows of fluorescent ceiling lights dipped everything in the room with a bright milky glow.

Satsuki scribbled the problems on the board into her notebook. She pulled out a pencil and chewed the top, her mind blanking at the letters and numbers on the paper. She loathed algebra, hating it even more than Hiroshima's muggy summer heat. *It was never this ridiculously hot back in Tokyo*, Satsuki thought to herself. *It was never this boring, either.*

When her cell phone vibrated inside her handbag, Satsuki was relieved to procrastinate from solving the tiresome equations. She quickly dug her cell phone out and silenced it. The instructors didn't seem to notice the noise. Her lips formed weightless words as she read the incoming message:

TAKANARI-KUN: I didn't think you were coming.

Takanari Oda, whose face always seemed to be smothered in grease and pimples, was seated at the table to the right of Satsuki. It was nothing unusual for him to text her during cram school. The only thing peculiar about it was that he would never look at Satsuki while texting her. This always made her think one of two things about him: that he was either really shy (maybe because he was self-conscious of his acne, or the fact that he was always sweating, or that he was labeled as an *otaku* by the rest of his classmates) or really scared he was going to get caught texting during class.

Takanari also attended Nakahiro Junior High with Satsuki. They were in the same homeroom together and participants in Art Club. Both had recently been assigned to work on Art Club's gigantic collage for their school's annual atomic bomb memorial celebration in August.

SATSUKI: Had to take my dad to airport.
TAKANARI-KUN: Did you get the glitter for the paper crane section?
SATSUKI: Not yet. After cram school.

Satsuki needed to buy enough glitter to cover all the paper cranes to be glued onto the collage. She wanted each of them to sparkle against the colorful, interconnected drawings and pictures. Mrs. Takahashi, the teacher that directed Art Club, had praised her for the idea but also warned her that accomplishing this wouldn't be easy.

Satsuki had imagined over one hundred cranes that would form a kind of "living frame" (as Kensuke Oda, another boy in Art Club, liked to call it). She hoped that if the collage was a success, her classmates would finally pay some real attention to her, or that maybe she would meet a cute boy who would constantly appreciate her artistic talent and want to offer his undying love and support. *Aahh, if only I could meet somebody like Kazune Kujyou.* Satsuki mused. *I could be Karin Hanazono, and Kazune would protect me throughout junior high, just like in Kamichama Karin.*

The reality, of course, was the total bitch opposite. Satsuki was ignored by almost everyone in her class. She was referred to as "that girl who transferred from Tokyo," even though she had been born in Hiroshima. Not that fitting in with her classmates would've been any easier if her family had decided to stay in Hiroshima and not relocate to Tokyo. The popular girls, like Izumi Kano, surrounded themselves with an impenetrable bubble of superficiality. They were discovering that wearing gaudy jewelry, false eyelashes, and bleaching their hair blonde to contrast with their abnormal tans would brand them as "sexy" or "hot" by the boys at Nakahiro Junior High. Compared to her own barely-made-up self, Satsuki liked to think of these popular girls as the K.K.K.: The *Koda-Kumi-Kogyarus*[24]-in-training. They ruled the hallways and the hearts of everyone.

Along with them, there were the athletic girls who joined the volleyball and tennis clubs, the geeky *otaku* types, and stragglers who drifted between cliques. Satsuki didn't fit in with these crowds either. She was too frail and skinny to be a sporty girl, having dropped out of Volleyball Club within less than a week of enrolling (Tennis Club within a day and a half). The nerds didn't like her because she was just an average student, and the drifters were too busy trying to fit in permanently with any of the Nakahiro Junior High cliques to recognize her existence at all.

Not even the school bullies gave a shit about her. One morning, right before homeroom began, Satsuki congregated with all the other students in front of the shoe racks near the school's main entrance. It was the daily routine of everyone at Nakahiro Junior High to wait until the last possible moment before putting on their mandatory *taiikukan baki*, or inside shoes. As Satsuki slipped off her favorite pair of loafers and stored them in her assigned cubbyhole, a shrimpy-looking girl standing next to her suddenly dropped to the ground, shrieking in pain. The girl clenched her left shoe with both hands. Satsuki called out to her, asked what happened, but the girl was too busy crying and yanking the shoe off

---

24. *kogyarus*—"high school gal." This refers commonly to a sense of fashion in Japan that teenage girls ascribe to that reflects upon an almost outlandish sense of dress and makeup. These type of girls have been associated with various extremes in Japanese culture, from being fashion leaders in Japan to being teenage prostitutes that get paid to date older men in Japan as well.

her foot to hear anything. The moment it came off, however, the answer was clear to Satsuki and the crowd who had gathered to see what was going on.

She had been stabbed in the foot with paper tacks hidden inside her shoe.

Immediately Mai Matsushita, who was Izumi Kano's closest friend and better known as the ideal "Kuu-chan" to her classmates (thanks to her perfect blonde-and-brown-streaked hair and intricate nail designs), started laughing so hard that her chalky voice became hoarse. It ignited her idolizers to point and cackle as well.

"What did she do? I heard it had something to do with showing up Kuu-chan in class the other day."

"That's what you get for crossing Kuu-chan."

"Serves her right."

"You know how mean Kuu-chan and her friends can be? She's lucky it's only a bloody foot."

The story circulating through the crowd was that Mai couldn't keep up with the girl during P.E. They had been paired up for running laps around the gym. Not even halfway around the second lap, Mai lost her breath and began whining and complaining that she didn't want to do the exercise anymore. Their teacher scolded Mai, telling her that if she lost her "arrogant weight," then she might have a chance against her petite running partner. The real reason why Mai couldn't keep up was because of the Lucky Strikes hidden in her locker. And since she couldn't just as well tell her teacher about this, Mai blamed the girl for the teacher's humiliating comment and promised that torture and pain would be all the girl would remember of junior high.

"Try to run now, bitch," Mai yelled at the girl, who was wringing the blood out of her sock while rocking back and forth on the ground. Satsuki wanted to help, but her knees were like neodymium magnets that locked her legs together in chilly fear.

"Come on, Kuu-chan, let's get out of here," a follower suggested. Somebody else shouted that a teacher was coming.

Mai didn't pay any attention to the warning. She walked over to the girl and walloped the top of her head. The girl crumpled to the floor in agony.

"SEE YOU IN P.E., BITCH!" Mai snarled. Moments later, the teacher showed up and disbursed the crowd, most of whom were laughing so hard they were having a hard time rushing inside to beat the homeroom tardy bell. But Satsuki couldn't move. She was in hypothermic shock.

A cell phone rang. Several seconds passed before Seul Bi realized it was her own. She fished the phone out of her purse. The LCD read: BEV CUZ.

"Hey, what's up?" Seul Bi said. Her cousin Beverly's familiar squeaky voice answered.

"Heeey yourself. What'cha doin?"

"Nothing much… just sitting here, I guess." Seul Bi shivered. She had been walking home from work, and while shortcutting through a park near her place, stopped to sit down on a bench. But as for how long she'd been sitting, well, she couldn't be sure of that.

"Um… okay, where's 'here' exactly?" Beverly asked.

"Oh right, sorry. I guess it would help if I told you where I'm at. Um… I think I'm near some park by my place."

Seul Bi tried to rub out the patchy numbness on her legs. It seemed the cold had found her, found Evanston. The city sky was a pallid gray with trees adopting similar, washed-out tones. Specks of snow freckled the ground near the bench Seul Bi sat stonily upon. It wasn't quite winter yet, but then again, Evanston never really committed to a season.

Beverly sipped something while talking.

"Why are you at a park? It's cold, cold, cold! And also, why don't you get a car, already? Or at least a bike, for Christ's sake! You definitely are a strange one, Bee."

Beverly didn't wait for a reply but continued to chatter on in her typical, aloof manner.

"Yeah, so, anyway, me and Mom were, you know, wondering if you wanted to get something to eat? Say yes, because I really don't want to go out with the Deb, and Mark can't make it. He's got some homework that requires him to be part of some kind of afterschool bullshit assignment."

"Really?" Seul Bi quickly interjected, taking advantage of her cousin pausing for breath. She stood up and tried to shake the warmth back into her legs.

"Yeah." Beverly continued, "and he's doing this bullshit homework assignment with a knob-gobbler skeez from his gender theory class. Whatever, though. I can just picture my face all over the news once I castrate that bitch's vagina from in between those filthy pork-chop legs of hers."

Seul Bi paused for air herself, then gurgled her words with laughter.

"Wait, Bev… knob gobbler? Where did you get that wonderful expression from?"

"It was on a porn site Mark showed me."

"Ahhriighhty then. So, wait, do you even know this girl?"

"Well, no, but that's beside the point, you know? I just don't trust the elitist cunts at Northwestern."

Seul Bi snorted. "Well, what about me then? I went there. Does that mean you don't trust me?"

"Well, I suppose you're okay. Maybe the elitist part still applies though. Ha ha."

Both of them tried to speak simultaneously.

Seul Bi's voice prevailed. "Wait… what? Elitis—"

Beverly interrupted. "Yeah, well, who else would decide to just sit at a park by herself unless she would rather be alone than with her family?"

"What?"

"At least, as your cousin, I thought about inviting you to a nice dinner. After all, you're practically my sister."

Seul Bi's face wrinkled in mock disgust, though it was getting harder to move any muscles in her face, thanks to a slapping, cold, draft wind leaving red marks all over her forehead, cheeks, and chin. She started walking around, hoping that would help loosen up her tendons.

"Ooooh, I see. I see. Well, I deeply thank you for the invite and humbly accept, but let's be honest, you are only wanting me to go to spare you the agony of your mother's incessant tongue, which she uses more than you. And you have single-child issues."

Without raising her voice to its usual crescendo in soprano, Beverly sipped her drink purposely loud and calmly retorted:

"Only an elitist cunt would think that."

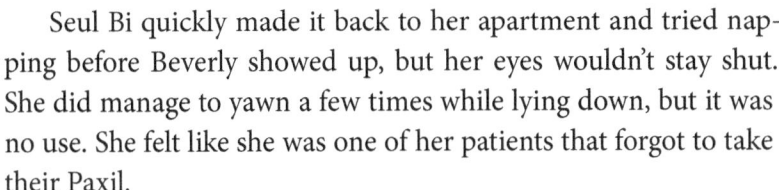

Seul Bi quickly made it back to her apartment and tried napping before Beverly showed up, but her eyes wouldn't stay shut. She did manage to yawn a few times while lying down, but it was no use. She felt like she was one of her patients that forgot to take their Paxil.

She slipped off the bed and went over to the only window in her apartment. The curtains had been left open from earlier. She scanned the street below for any sign of her cousin. She didn't have to wait long. Beverly's spider-black Mazda collided with the sidewalk curb in front of Seul Bi's apartment complex. It was a recycled joy for Seul Bi to watch Beverly's inept driving, her peering down at the black paint trails on the cement before opening the car door. Seul Bi threw her coat and shoes back on and went outside.

"What's up, girl?" Beverly asked Seul Bi, who almost tumbled out of the apartment complex's front doors and onto the sidewalk.

Seul Bi yawned. "Heeey."

"I can see you're tired. What, no sleep again?"

"It's not so much that I don't sleep as it is I constantly dream these… I don't know… moments that feel like they're too real, you know?"

Beverly offered Seul Bi a quizzical gaze before both of them hopped into the Mazda. She then pulled a quick U-turn from the makeshift parking spot.

"Mmmhmm. I get that way, too, sometimes…" Beverly said, her voice trailing off. She jabbed at the volume dial on her stereo, and trip hop squeezed out of the tiny Mazda speakers. It was enough noise to prevent further discussion about any kind of "moments." That's exactly what Beverly wanted. *No heavy thinking right now. I can't think about what the hell you're talking about, my dear cuz. I just need to pick Ma up from home and get dinner over with so I can find out what's up with Mark*, she thought to herself.

Seul Bi was engrossed in a window-linear equation. Every time in the car, almost on cue, when Beverly turned on music, Seul Bi raptured right out of the passenger seat. *I love you, cuz, but damn, you wanna talk about real? You live in La La Land; that's what's for real.* Beverly laughed out loud at her cheezy mental pun. Seul Bi didn't even flinch.

Soon, though, Beverly began to feel a similar displacement. She steadily lost herself in a collage of past moments. It had been strange at first to have Seul Bi live with her, especially since all of their relatives treated her adopted cousin like some kind of bastard residue left over from Uncle Jimmy and Aunt Zoe after they had died. None of them seemed to know how to handle the situation of whom Seul Bi should live with. Gone was their unconditional love. Their Uncle Frank even suggested she be sent back to the orphanage in Seoul. Beverly's mom squashed that ridiculous idea, scooping up Seul Bi before she could be hurt by their family's communal apathy.

Beverly remembered how, right after Seul Bi came to live with her and her mom, she would press firmly against her cousin's body at night while they slept together in the same bed. Seul Bi cried every single night for the first few months, leaking tears everywhere. Beverly remembered the slick sheen of her cousin's skin and how her own body's smoothness created a slippery tension between them. They were like conjoined twins floating in the womb.

Later, when things finally settled down, both girls traveled the high-school hallways together. Each one would sit in class and turn their cell phone on silent while furiously text messaging each other. They talked about their English teacher, Mrs. Mattillo, and her incredibly large head. Or why their friend Kara always smelled like she was on her period. They ate lunch at the same table, drove to school with their friends, and even went out with the same boy, Joey Gestone, during the summer between their sophomore and junior year. Sadly, Joey hadn't caught on until after Beverly and Seul Bi broke up with him—on the same day. Beverly texted him the words: *We're done. Thanks.* Seul Bi told him in person with a quick, "Sorry Joe, this isn't working out. Bye." Both simultaneous red slips were planned, of course.

Beverly and Seul Bi were inseparable until Mark, a transfer student from some small farm town in Pennsylvania, strolled into Beverly's senior physics class one morning. Mark immediately reminded her of her favorite actor, Mark Wahlberg. His eyes seemed to glide around in their sockets like flimsy razorblades. He was slightly tanned, defined (the first time she had seen him, she had definitely seen the makings of a six pack under his T-shirt), and talked with a polite overbite. Beverly couldn't remember the first time she actually spoke to him, but she could always recall the first time they made out, which was after the both of them were assigned to build a mousetrap car together in physics class. It was around that time that Beverly started to spend every single day with Mark. Things went well until they realized their intense, physical attraction created a sordid and inhospitable purgatory for them both—neither one of them talked much to each other. They only kissed, touched, and fucked.

And sure enough, Beverly and Mark routinely broke up and always bickered, but fucked each other back into a calm reprieve that sometimes only lasted until Mark pulled off the condom. The uncertainty between them continued even after high school.

The worst part was that she had traded Seul Bi for Mark. Gone were all the late-night, marathon phone sessions between her and her cousin. Same with hanging out together. Mark had practically moved into Beverly's room right after Seul Bi had moved out. In fact, it was one of the reasons why Seul Bi had decided to live on her own; she didn't want to be around two people so hopelessly addicted to each other. It was unsettling to Seul Bi, who, right after graduating from high school, lost all interest in guys or dating. Her focus became college, her life being defined one syllabus at a time.

It was the same with having friends. For Seul Bi, hanging out with her high-school buddies devolved into occasional phone calls from them, then only texts, then random Facebook wall postings, and finally them pretending to not recognize her whenever they crossed paths. Seul Bi was just as guilty, always exclaiming that she had too much homework to do, or she didn't feel well, her two favorite excuses. By the time she finished college, she had completely shifted her life's focus towards the emotionally draining work at Rainbow, and lately, trying to figure out why, day or night, she was constantly stuck in reverie-mode.

Beverly still tried to reach out to Seul Bi and involve her in things, but it was obvious to her that the sisterly bond she shared with her was gone. Probably for good.

When Beverly pulled in the driveway to her home, her mother was already walking towards the car. A soft, papery snow fell from the sky just as they arrived. Seul Bi waved at her aunt through the frost-bitten car window. She always wore the same Benetton winter coat and the pink cashmere Burberry scarf that Seul Bi bought her as a Christmas gift a few years ago. Her aunt's predictability was comforting in a way.

"What took ya so long?" Debbie said, tucking herself into the back seat of the Mazda. She leaned over and kissed both girls on the cheeks, then shook her hair. "Geez, my hair is turning white from the snow falling, and I already got white hair, girls. Let's get going!"

Finding parking on Main St. was easy. The air was turning sharp and cold as the snow changed into a heavy downpour of sticky, white slush. Debbie, Beverly, and Seul Bi hurried inside the restaurant doors and were immediately blasted with hot air from the heater vents above the entranceway. The place was empty, except for the all-Thai staff. It was almost completely silent too, except for some kind of poppy Asian music playing in the background.

A hostess stepped towards them.

"Hello, welcome to Siam Paragon, would you like a table by the window?"

Seul Bi was sure the answer to that question was obvious but shook her head politely and pointed at a table in the middle of the room, next to a fat, stone pillar decorated with coy fish. Seul Bi enjoyed staring at the pillar every time she ate at Siam. It reminded her of something blissful in her past, but she honestly couldn't think of what it was.

As soon as they were seated, Debbie turned her attention to Seul Bi.

"So, how is work? And how are your drawings coming along?"

"Well, work is you know… work. And as for the drawings, I've sold a few small pieces, but no real commissions just yet."

Beverly clicked her tongue. "Maybe you should try drawing rainbows or flowers or something? Instead of whatever those… images are that you draw."

"Shut up!" Seul Bi snapped back while laughing. "You know that ain't me. I am… 'preoccupied,' I guess would be the word."

I really don't have a choice, my ignorant cousin, Seul Bi thought to herself.

"Nah. 'Single' is a better word," Beverly quickly retorted.

"Shut up!" Seul Bi flicked Beverly's arm. Beverly sneered at her.

Debbie parted them with a wave of her hand. "Stop it, you two! I have to agree with my daughter on this one, though. Why *don't* you get yourself a man?"

Seul Bi grimaced like she was in pain.

"Um… interrogation much? Between work and the drawings, I have no time for a guy, you know? Plus, I'm not sure I want to date anyone after seeing how Beverly and Mark act towards each other."

Beverly's eyebrows made two perfect arches. "Huh? What does that mean?"

"You two together is like watching a bad car accident or something. It's brutal, dude."

"Fuck off, Bee!"

"Hey! Watch the language!" Debbie interjected. All three busted up laughing.

A waitress walked over to them with three sets of chopsticks and tableware and sat them down on the table. She didn't know what was so funny but smiled anyways at them.

"Are you ready to order?"

Debbie spoke first. "I will have the, uh, Kung Pao chicken, and I know my daughter's going to want the chicken teriyaki. Right, Bev?"

"Sounds good."

"Perfect. Seul Bi, what about you?"

"I will have the chicken teriyaki, too."

"And three Cokes, please," Debbie said while handing the menus back to the waitress.

Still smiling, the waitress repeated their order back in a thickly accented voice and then disappeared through the kitchen's curtain door.

Debbie tapped her fingers on the tabletop.

"Seul Bi, why don't you eat Korean food here? You always get Japanese. I mean, they serve all kinds of Asian food, and I figured maybe, you know, you would want—"

"I can barely use chopsticks," Seul Bi interrupted. "Sometimes, I swear, I'm whiter than both of you put together. I mean, I can't speak Korean and don't like Korean food. Actually, I guess that makes me a Twinkie."

"A what?" Debbie frowned with an open mouth.

Beverly yelped. "Ma, she's saying she's yellow on the outside, white on the inside. A Twinkie, you know? Or if you prefer, a banana. Duh."

Debbie's lips moved but failed to produce any words.

"Ma, Bee has yellow skin but isn't Asian like our waitress. You know, with an accent and a job at an Asian restaurant."

"Oh my God," Debbie murmured, shaking her head in half-serious, half-mock shock. Seul Bi and Beverly both looked at each other and did their best impressions of kindergarten kids on a playground, wailing with laughter. Their voices produced a harsh echo in the empty space, causing all the candles lining the walls to flicker with derision at the outburst. When the waitress brought their Cokes shortly afterwards, more laughter ensued. This time the waitress laughed with them, though she still had no idea what was so funny.

Debbie waited for the eventual lull to come in her daughter's and niece's comedy routine. The moment it did, a thought rushed quickly to her lips. "Well, sweetie, I think you should still recognize who you are. I mean, you grew up in America, but your mom and dad would have wanted you to be you. And I think that means being Asian in your identity."

Seul Bi sat expressionless while contemplating her aunt's words.

Which mom would that be, Aunt Deb? The one who was your sister or the one whose uterus I slid out of?

Beverly sipped her Coke loudly. Debbie continued.

"See, sweetie, I think maybe it's us that don't recognize you, not you who doesn't, you know, get yourself. I mean, your drawings, for instance, maybe you should look to them for your... ethnic voice?"

Beverly couldn't grasp her mother's words or demeanor.

"Ma, what are you trying you say here? Stop being so heavy, you kn—" Debbie put a finger to Beverly's wet lips.

"All I'm saying is that if you advertised your artwork over in Korea or Japan, then maybe somebody there might get what you're doing. I mean, it could help you reconnect to who you really are deep down. What'd ya think?"

Seul Bi tried to smile. *What do I think? That you just proved how very little in touch I am with being Asian. I didn't think to put any of my work on Korean or Japanese websites for selling things. I'm not sure I would even know how. Still...*

"Hmm. Thank you for the advice. I mean, I hear what you are trying to say, and I really appreciate it. I'll think about it." Seul Bi shrugged her shoulders and pretended to be nonchalant about her aunt's words. "Anyways, I'm starved. I can't wait to eat."

Upon hearing her cousin mention eating, Beverly felt her stomach growl.

"Hey, Bee, listen to this." She stood up and pressed her flat stomach against the side of Seul Bi's head. Another rumble, this time leviathan in size, vibrated Seul Bi's entire skull.

"There's all the advice and answers you'll ever need, cuz." Debbie, Beverly, and Seul Bi nearly burst into tears from laughing so hard. The staff at Siam Paragon looked at them with vexation and were, for the first time ever since they opened, grateful there were no other customers in the restaurant.

CHAPTER 9

SHE HAS

a

STRONG HEART

"Okay, you know the drill. Just hold still for me."

Dr. Yoshimoto dabbed what looked like a piece of chalk on Yoshiko's parous stomach. An alien noise burst out of the monitors in front of her.

"Mmm... everything sounds healthy. She has a strong heart."

"It sounds so fast," Yoshiko said. "It surprises me every time."

"That's good. It should be fast."

"Really?"

"Yes. The baby is growing and needs more oxygen as it gets ready to come out."

Dr. Yoshimoto handed the Doppler Stethoscope to Nurse Sawa, who stood, cheery-lipped, by the exam room door. She had assisted on all of Yoshiko's visits.

Yoshiko thought it strange that the swooshing sound was her unborn daughter's heartbeat. She had the same exact thought at her last ultrasound appointment, too (had she thought this way during her pregnancy with Satsuki? She couldn't remember). Thank God for Hideo, who had managed to squeeze some time from his busy work schedule to be present at that last appointment. Yoshiko remembered him cupping her hand in his, her lightly tracing her fingers on his warm palm, him telling her that everything was going to be all right. He had made her completely forget how weird the swooshing noise sounded. *Why can't he be here now?* Yoshiko thought to herself. Just thinking about it irritated her.

"Now, let's see how she looks."

Nurse Sawa dimmed the lights while the doctor squeezed some watery gel out of a plastic bottle with a pineapple-ring cap. It reminded Yoshiko of ketchup containers used at picnics. She knew it would feel cold but didn't squirm when he squirted it onto her abdomen. He then sloshed around the ultrasound transducer over the gel, forming a murky image on the computer screen. Yoshiko could make out a jigsaw shape.

"Can you see the face?" Dr. Yoshimoto asked.

"I think so."

"See there," Dr. Yoshimoto said, pointing at the ultrasound monitor. "Her profile looks amazing. There's the forehead, nose, upper lip. I believe she's developing nicely."

Yoshiko was twenty-eight weeks pregnant, and for the second time in her life, she was hearing words like "profile" and "third trimester." It had felt so much easier to hear these things with Satsuki. Maybe that was because the nine months of pregnancy with her hadn't been complicated at all, nor had her body really changed much. And all the weight she had gained vanished in only a few weeks after Satsuki was born.

This time around, however, her ankles swelled, her back constantly ached, and her mood swung between happy, sad, and bitch. She knew this time that it wasn't going to be so easy to escape being pregnant and all the pain and heartache that came with it. Yoshiko's hand drifted towards the empty chair beside the exam table.

"She looks so beautiful," Yoshiko said, her half-deflated voice tapering. It was a toss-up as to which was worse: her unborn daughter's "amazing" profile or the fog of loneliness inside the exam room, which not even bright-eyed Nurse Sawa could penetrate with her optimism. *I should be happy, but I guess my mood swings must be getting the best of me right now,* Yoshiko told herself.

Crows orbited the housing complex, doing figure eights in the sky. *Somebody must have left food on their balcony*, Yoshiko suspected. *Or perhaps the crows are building nests underneath the metal perches where our neighbors keep their satellite dishes.* Whatever the reason for their arrival, it wasn't really that surprising to Yoshiko, considering the kind of scorcher the day had been so far. For the crows, the housing complex equaled shade, rest, and food. Yoshiko thought the same exact thing as she dragged several heavy grocery bags inside the front door to the housing complex.

While most of the crows eventually landed on balconies (a few still flapped around in the air, while some of the other ones took to rooftops and electrical wires, apparently immune to the intense summer heat), three stragglers dive-bombed onto the ground near the complex's front door. They hopped towards Yoshiko, taking turns cawing and fluttering their wings. They seemed really upset about something, but about what Yoshiko had no idea. She couldn't help but laugh at their antics, however. They were so plump and dirty that she pictured them inside her head as a trio of tarred and feathered infants.

The moment Yoshiko stepped inside the apartment, she felt completely drained. Her exhaustion was mostly from being out in the heat all day. After the ultrasound appointment, she had gone shopping to pick up *tonkatsu*[25] for dinner. It was curry night.

While preparing everything, Yoshiko realized that she had forgotten to pick up an onion for the sauce. Good thing she had kept the rice cooker turned on all day. It was still half-full from the night before. She would just add some more rice, along with extra carrots, to the curry mix. Problem solved.

25. *tonkatsu*—breaded, deep-fried pork cutlets.

Between yawns, Seul Bi spotted an ant climbing up her bathroom wall. She was sitting cross-legged on her bed in front of six large drawings. Suddenly her gaze leapt towards the open door to where she had just sat on the toilet for an hour. Her stomach seared with pain. The chicken teriyaki from Siam Paragon earlier in the evening had torn up her insides. She rubbed her abdomen and sighed. *So much for my "Asian" identity, Aunt Debbie*, she thought. *I think I just shat it out.*

The ant had disappeared from view, and while straining to find it, her eyelids felt like cement blocks were hanging from them. But as much as she tried, it was impossible to sleep.

Six drawings. She had, over the past ten years, drawn as many as twenty-five in a week, but this past month, only six. Her routine was simple enough: she would first put the 18x24 Strathmore Premium Recycled sheet of paper on a large, cardboard square and place them both on the ground. Lying next to the paper, sometimes for hours in the silence, she visualized her 6B charcoal pencil stabbing messy black dots into a shape. She would then mechanically rake her pencil over the charcoal resin, molding a filmy structure to each applied line. She often pressed so firmly that an impression was left in the cardboard underneath the paper.

The images were always the same:

Hands.

Arms.

No bodies attached.

Floating aimlessly in a bleached white universe.

One of the drawings was a slender arm hatching from a cracked egg, its hand reaching towards the unseen. Another sketch yielded a menagerie of twisted, gnarled fingers, curling awkwardly across the paper. The other four sketches were disembodied arms and hands, each resonating with a hidden affliction, and almost every one of them watermarked with her tears.

Her mind was convinced that, when she had looked into the water that day ten years ago, this is what she had seen left of her parents.

Yet her memory was beguiling. Seul Bi had scrawled hand portraits across her notebooks throughout elementary school and scribbled numerous appendage-shaped drawings after signing her name on tests back in second and third grade, well before she had lost her parents on that vacation trip to Hawaii.

She could never figure out what her drawings meant. She thought that maybe they represented mistakes in her past, which had somehow been shoved out of her mind and onto paper, but she always ended up dismissing this idea. Instead, she felt more than anything else that these drawings inexplicably meant she wasn't whole anymore. But what did not feeling "whole" anymore mean, exactly? And why did she always feel this way, it seemed, right after she sketched these drawings of orphaned hands and arms?

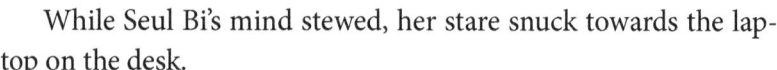

While Seul Bi's mind stewed, her stare snuck towards the laptop on the desk.

"Oh, why the hell not?"

She decided to listen to her aunt's suggestion and put some drawings up online for sale. It was somewhat exciting, though more nerve wracking, to think that somebody besides her might like her artwork. She pictured that same somebody buying one of her drawings and dissecting its hidden meaning with guests at a dinner party. And when they'd figured it out, she could ask them to explain why she can't draw anything else but hands and arms, each one convoluted and coiled up in stupid mystery.

Hmm, now, which drawings do I choose? The six she had laid out on her bed were the most recent images to manifest on paper, so maybe that would be a good place to start. They were also the most fresh among the preserved piles lying around her apartment.

Seul Bi shrugged. "I guess these will do." She slipped off the bed and tiptoed across the icy floor to her computer, tapping the keypad so the screen full of meandering manta rays (her custom-made screensaver) would vanish. The Yahoo homepage appeared, and she began to sift through internet sites online. Hours passed before she finally selected a few fancy looking Korean and Japanese dealer sites with homepages translated into English. She then took pictures of the six drawings, wrote out brief descriptions of each one, priced them, and uploaded everything to the sites. Easy enough.

BRRRIIIINNNG!

Seul Bi felt her chest tighten and then relax as her cell phone rattled around on the computer desk, signifying a text message. Only one person she knew ever sent random texts to her this late at night.

BEV CUZ: U up? I bet u are!

Seul Bi peered at the time on her computer display. It was almost morning, although outside the window looked like the blackened corner of a closet.

SEUL BI: Yeah. Why r u up this early?
BEV CUZ: I just had the best sex of my life!

Seul Bi cringed and turned away from the phone screen.

SEUL BI: Um, good for you?
BEV CUZ: Ha ha. Thanx. I think me and Mark are fine now.
SEUL BI: Sweet dude.

BEV CUZ: Oh yeah, thanx for helping me out
with mom.
SEUL BI: Sure np.
BEV CUZ: Can't sleep?
SEUL BI: What else is new right?
BEV CUZ: Right. Well, u wanna come hang out?
SEUL BI: Now? Or do U mean later?
BEV CUZ: Later! Duh.
SEUL BI: Um sure. Ur welcome for dinner btw.
BEV CUZ: Ha. Well, gotta get dressed and
go home.

The thought of her cousin naked made Seul Bi feel a pang of revulsion.

SEUL BI: Wait dude… you just had sex? How
long ago did you finish? Don't tell me this
very moment!!
BEV CUZ: Gotta go! Lol. TTYL.

"Fucking gross!" Seul Bi screeched. Despite this, she laughed and felt grateful for her cousin's irreverent behavior. Her crass text messages were a welcome distraction from looking at life like a mannequin observing itself in a store window's reflection.

Satsuki returned from cram school shortly after dusk. The summer heat had finally receded, so Yoshiko decided to open up the kitchen balcony windows and give the apartment's air conditioner a break. Both she and Yoshiko sat at the *kotatsu* for dinner, enjoying the occasional breeze that gushed into the *tatami* room, and watched the evening news. They hoped to see a shot of Seoul, as the reporters droned on and on about the possible North Korean missile launch. Satsuki ended up devouring two plates of curry but offered to clean up everything so Yoshiko could soak in the bathtub for an hour. Yoshiko conceded and soon found herself shrouded in steam and foam bubbles.

When Yoshiko finished with her bath, she found Satsuki faceplanted in her art project. It was spread out on top of the *kotatsu*. Drool leaked from Satsuki's lips, and pieces of glitter mottled her cheeks and chin.

"Come on, Sacchan, wake up. Time for bed." Satsuki lifted an eyelid open. Her mother stood over her, grinning.

"Good night," Satsuki groaned. She staggered into her bedroom with a trail of sparkles lifting into the air behind her.

"Good night. Try to get some rest."

"Haaaai."

After Satsuki shut her bedroom door, Yoshiko stepped onto the balcony and brought in the dried laundry. She then shut off the lights, fed Chibita a snack, and went to bed.

Why didn't Hideo call me and let me know he was okay? Yoshiko wondered. She lay in the permanent indent that her husband's body had left in their futon bed. Since Hideo had started to work late nights at Mazda, she had become used to falling asleep alone. It still got pretty lonely sometimes, but always in the morning, her husband would be lying next to her, a triangular set of moles on his back greeting her when she woke.

Tomorrow morning would be the first in months that her husband had spent the night away from home.

The last time Hideo was on a business trip, Yoshiko had a strange dream. She was standing on an incline in the middle of what felt like a building without walls. There was a ceiling above her, but it was covered in smoke. She also couldn't see anything around her, as a group of businessmen and women surrounded her on every side. The men were all dressed in vented black jackets and plain, knee-lined pants. Ties hung under their bleached collars. The women wore long–sleeved, blue blouses with knee-length skirts and pearl necklaces around their necks.

Neither the men nor the women said anything. They stared vacantly towards the incline's summit. Yoshiko thought she could make out an open door up there. She tried to move toward it, but everyone was stuck together in a tight, human tape ball. It reminded her of being on the Chuo Line in Tokyo when hundreds of day workers funneled into the train cars after work.

At some point in the dream, the ground started tilting upwards, and Yoshiko pushed and pulled people out of her way to stay vertical. She forced herself towards the top of the incline, but with every step she took, the sloping surface beneath her feet started to feel more and more slippery. She looked down and noticed that piss was everywhere, cascading in all directions. It took a few seconds before she realized all the businessmen and women had soiled themselves raw. The piss continued to flow from the bottoms of pants and skirts all around her. Despite this, everyone remained perfectly still.

Yoshiko almost reached the top when the incline became completely vertical. Yet nobody fell except her. She tried to hold onto shoes and legs but couldn't quite grasp onto them for more than a few seconds. Her body was the ko[26] in a dirty game of human

---

26. *ko*—The balls used in the Japanese game of Pachinko.

Pachinko, smashing into pins made of flesh that did nothing to stop her acceleration downwards. Faster and faster she fell.

Right before she woke up, the last thing Yoshiko remembered was plummeting into a bottomless moat filled with piss.

CHAPTER 12

PAUSE

for

SUBMISSION

"He… put… tinfoil on his dick and fucked me… in… my… *ass.*"

Marisa slammed her wrists repeatedly against the arms of the metallic chair. Seul Bi sat opposite Marisa in the office, listening to Marisa's confession. Both squirmed around in their seats. The office door suddenly drifted open (the slightest breeze always caused it to open on its own), but no sound crept inside. Seul Bi didn't notice any breath rising from her lungs, either. It took a full minute after Marisa's statement before Seul Bi realized she was holding her own breath, afraid of what Marisa would say next. Marisa, however, picked up on Seul Bi's stunned silence, and immediately her eyes glazed up.

"I'm sorry. I'm so, so sorry." Marisa couldn't hold back any longer and began sobbing uncontrollably.

Seul Bi reached over and placed a shaky hand on Marisa's shoulder. She offered her a tissue with the other hand. It was times like these that Seul Bi wished she worked at McDonald's, flipping burgers. What could she possibly say to this poor girl who was sexually abused in one of the worst ways imaginable? Still, the least she could do was offer Marisa a compassionate shoulder to lean on.

"No, no, no, you don't have to be sorry, sweetie. Listen, you didn't do anything wrong, okay? And you're safe here. I promise."

Nineteen-year-old Marisa Thomason was Rainbow's first ever admission. She had been in treatment centers since the age of twelve. Her diagnosis was post-traumatic stress disorder, which she had received after being raped repeatedly by her father, and anorexia nervosa. She had also attempted suicide three times in her life, each time more dangerously close to succeeding than the last. Her method was to take Bic razors and cut long incisions from wrist to elbow. Marisa's arms always looked like a mahogany mosaic. Seul Bi perpetually worried that Marisa might attempt suicide a fourth time, so she scanned Marisa's arms for any fresh cuts.

None were visible, but that didn't mean there weren't cuts some-place else.

"Sweetie, listen," Seul Bi said in her best professional-calm voice. "I have to ask you something. Did you cut yourself at all?"

"No. I... wanted to really... bad though," Marisa managed to whisper in between sniffling and coughing.

"Are you sure? You can tell me."

"I'm sure, but like I said, I almost did."

Seul Bi felt relieved. She offered Marisa a comforting smile. "Well, I'm really glad that you didn't. I mean that, Marisa. And thank you for telling me about your feelings and also for coming to me before you did anything."

A pregnant tear swayed from Marisa's chin, and Seul Bi quickly caught it with her finger. Unsure of what to say next, she leaned towards Marisa and held her hands. Marisa looked away towards the replica painting near the door. It was a rare giclee print of "The Broken Bridge and the Dream" by Salvador Dali.

"Do you want to hear what he did to me next?" Marisa asked.

Seul Bi paused before answering. "If you're comfortable telling me, sure."

Shit, Seul Bi thought. *I don't think I'm comfortable at all with what you might tell me.* She braced herself, but nothing could've prepared her for what Marisa admitted next:

"Well, since he hurt me from, you know, what he did, I couldn't walk... so he carried me to the bathroom and threw me down in the tub. I didn't see the dirt piled in the corner of the bathroom, though. I mean, he must have got it... from... outside. To this day, I still don't know where it came from. All I remember is him shov-eling dirt on me until I was buried. The worst part was that the dirt was full of... of... of..." Marisa's voice failed. She piled her face into both her hands, breaking Seul Bi's grasp.

"It's okay, sweetie. What was it full of?" Seul Bi asked. Marisa looked up at her with trembling lips. She uttered one word:

"Worms."

8:50-9:40	ENGLISH
9:50-10:40	SCIENCE
10:50-11:40	MATH
11:50-12:40	P.E.
12:40-1:30	LUNCH
1:35-2:25	SOCIAL STUDIES
2:35-3:25	ART

"Sooo boring," Satsuki thrummed. Her subject schedule for the day was depressing. She sat in her homeroom while Mr. Nakata, the science teacher, lectured about Hawaii's seismic activity. It was another humid and hot Wednesday, so hot, in fact, that it reminded Satsuki of sitting inside an *onsen*[27]—with her clothes on.

She wished it was Thursday because, at least then, her science class would be substituted for fifty minutes of music. That wasn't half as boring. Satsuki did her best to stay awake during Mr. Nakata's lecture, but her head bobbed around in a sleepy exorcism. The rest of the class also struggled to keep their eyes open. Only the chattering cicadas outside seemed to care.

Mr. Nakata's subdued intonations continued to mollify the students. It wasn't until he stood in the front of the classroom and pointed to a picture of Hawaii hanging on the chalkboard that anyone seemed interested in his words.

"Who here has been to Hawaii?" Mr. Nakata asked the class. A few students raised their hands. "I see. Well, for the rest of you who haven't been to Hawaii, in the future, you will not have to take a plane or boat to reach it."

Several students sat upright.

27. *onsen*—hot spring that is a popular tourist destination for Japanese and foreigners visiting Japan.

"Ah, I have your attention, I see. That's right, Hawaii is moving four inches every year towards Japan."

The whole classroom filled with cries of "What?" and "That's impossible!" Satsuki paid no attention, however. She scribbled kitties and chocobos all over her textbook cover.

"Anyone want to guess why?" Mr. Nakata paced back and forth. A lone hand in the back of the room slowly climbed into the air. Everyone turned around to see it belonged to Megumi Ayase, one of Nakahiro Junior High's best volleyball players.

"Yes, Ayase-san."

Megumi cleared her throat. "Is it because of Hawaii's volcanoes?"

"Ah, good guess. You are semi-correct. If we look at the Earth, we know it's made of plates, each moving about four inches a year. And the oceanic Pacific Plate is…"

Satsuki spaced out and didn't hear the rest of Mr. Nakata's explanation. She only caught something about "underwater earthquakes" and "brimstone pits," but Hawaii moving closer to Japan didn't capture her interest. She was more concerned about the collage for Art Club than anything her teacher had to say. It needed to be finished soon, but she still had so many things left to do with it.

Later, after getting six out of ten probability problems right on a math quiz and then losing in the first round of the handball challenge in P.E., Satsuki needed a break from her school day. She snuck away during lunch, first stopping to grab her Nintendo DS and Denons out of her backpack, and then headed straight for the bathroom. Everyone at Nakahiro Junior High knew that the only way to find a moment of peace and quiet during their rigorous class schedule was to visit either the nurse's station or the bathroom. Satsuki preferred the latter.

After checking to make sure the bathroom was empty, Satsuki locked herself inside a stall. She nibbled on a piece of tofu as she plugged her headphones into the Nintendo DS. Time for *Kamichama Karin*. She selected episode twenty, where Karin receives a surprise kiss from her future husband and protector, Kazune Kujyou. Satsuki brushed her pinky over the top display screen. *It's not fair. Do I have to be a goddess in order to feel something that special?* she languished. It wasn't that she wanted her own version of Kazune to knock on the stall door and plant his lips on hers. What she really wanted, she realized, was a life where that was even possible.

The bell at 3:25 p.m. did not offer its usual reprieve for Satsuki. She had to wash down the entire chalkboard during the compulsory afterschool cleaning, then drag the Art Club collage out of the supply closet. Humidity coated her skin; she didn't notice that her shirt was wet in several places from splashing soapy water on herself. As Satsuki finished her work and began unfolding the gigantic cardboard collage, she overheard Mai Matsushita and Izumi Kano talking behind her back. "I bet she stinks like an overused toilet," Mai whispered. Izumi Kano responded with spirit-murdering laughter. Satsuki pretended to ignore them. It was better to act like nothing had happened. After all, she didn't want to end up like that poor girl with the paper tacks stuck in her feet. Luckily, Mai and Izumi lost interest in saying or doing anything else to her, so Satsuki waited until they left, along with the other students in the classroom (except the Art Club members), and began folding paper cranes by herself.

The collage's "living frame" was almost finished. Satsuki just needed to sprinkle glitter on each of the birds' wings, glue them to the outer edges of the collage, and then collect a few more pictures to place inside the frame. "One more day, and I can be done with this damn collage," she huffed.

By the time she had reached her fortieth crane (only thirty more required folding), Satsuki felt drained. She packed up her origami paper and waved goodbye. The rest of Art Club didn't seem to notice, except Takanari. When she walked past him, he pointed at his watch with a greasy finger and snorted.

Eww, like I care what you think, butter-face, Satsuki thought to herself. *You're so annoying.* She rolled her eyes at Takanari, then hurried out the classroom door. She couldn't wait to get home and forget about school.

Three minutes to 7:00 p.m., Seul Bi was considering having Siam Paragon deliver food to the residence. *Definitely not hungry for chicken teriyaki*, she thought to herself. Mary raced to complete the shift report and leave for the evening. Seul Bi fixed her gaze on the desk phone.

"You gonna be all right, Miss Worker Bee?" Mary said while adjusting her glasses.

"Yeah, just thinking maybe I should eat something."

"I hear that. I'm about to go home and try to find something to eat. Or maybe I'll stop somewhere. Anyway, you look like maybe you got something else going on, besides just bein' hungry."

Mary knew the admission from Marisa earlier in the evening had shaken everyone. When Seul Bi told Mary about the conversation, Marisa had been placed on 24-hour community room status. This way she could be monitored by staff for any self-injurious behavior or emotional outbursts.

Mary peered out the office door. Marisa was sleeping on the couch, occasionally kneading the cushions with her legs.

"So, Bee, you okay with staying overnight here after what happened today?"

Seul Bi had tried for hours to erase the confession from her thoughts. As soon as Mary had sat down to talk with Marisa, Seul Bi had run outside into a nearby alley and wept. *I don't think I can do this anymore*, she had thought to herself while crouched down on the asphalt. *What the fuck am I doing working here? I can't help these kids. I don't even know how to fix my own problems, which are bullshit problems compared to what these kids are fucking going through. I still have the rest of this evening and all night, too. FUCK!*

Her weekend double-shift had started at 3:00 p.m. and would not be over until 6:00 a.m., when Sarah, another resource staff member, replaced her for the morning rotation. Seul Bi wondered if she wept more for her own insecurity and fears than for Marisa's tragedy.

"Bee?"

Seul Bi had completely zoned out while thinking about her own emotional outburst in the alley. She broke her trance-like stare to grin at Mary. "Yeah, I think I'll be okay. I appreciate you asking me and also for dealing with it. I'm happy you scheduled yourself with me today. I just had a late night last night, that's all."

"Okay, you was looking like you were traveling through space again, honey. I just finished the shift report and sent it to Dr. Nathan. Um, you can use the company card to get yourself something to eat, and I'm sure I don't need to tell you this, but keep an eye on *that one*." Mary whispered the last two words and pointed a finger towards the common area. "Make sure you check on her every half an hour. I know that won't be a problem for you, though, since you never sleep, anyway."

Seul Bi laughed, but hunger pangs mixed with uneasiness about the next eleven hours alone at Rainbow made her lips quiver slightly. "All right, Miss Mary, thank you."

Mary stepped outside, saying goodbye to Ariel, who was sitting in the patio area. Jason, who was Rainbow's only male resident, slouched in a chair next to her.

"Everyone be good, and see you in a few days. Bee, you call me if you need anything, but try not to, 'cause it's been too long of a day."

Seul Bi stood in the threshold and waved at Mary as she exited through the fence door. Just then a gust of snow ushered down towards the ground near the entrance. A thorny cold pricked at Seul Bi's skin.

"Hey Ariel, Jason, aren't you guys cold?" Seul Bi asked.

Ariel held up her cigarette. Jason coughed.

"Cigarettes keep us warm. Maybe you should try one."

"Nah, you know I don't smoke. Come inside soon, it's almost time for your meds."

Seul Bi spun around on one heel to head back inside but paused at the sight of the mezuzah. Its dull grey box nailed just above the lintel guarded Rainbow's threshold. Dr. Nathan always touched the mezuzah whenever he would visit the residence for weekly inspections. When Seul Bi first saw him engage in this ritual, she asked about what was written on the mezuzah. Dr. Nathan told her that it was a reminder to everyone about their sense of belonging to God. Seul Bi had shrugged her shoulders at his answer. This concept was more foreign to Seul Bi than her birthplace.

"That's my problem," Seul Bi admitted. *No faith in anything or anyone.*

"What's your problem?" Marisa's voice arose through her arms, which were scattered across her face.

"Oh, nothing. Sorry." Seul Bi's eyes shifted from the doorway to the couch. She sat next to Marisa. "Sometimes I speak out loud, and it's like, you know, in plays, like, um, what's it called? A soliloquy, I think?"

Marisa strained to lift her head out of an arm barricade. "...Um, right. You talk to yourself. And we're the ones who are crazy? I think you need some of Ariel's meds."

Seul Bi clicked her tongue against the roof of her mouth. "Ha, ha, very funny. Anyway, I see you're awake now, and just in time for your meds, too. Thanks for reminding me."

The cabinet with the meds was in the common area. A small padlock kept residents from stealing anything inside of it. Actually, Seul Bi was aware of the time for dosing but wanted to make Marisa feel productive. She walked over to it and unlocked the door, setting out the medicine tracking form to be signed by everyone who eventually would file into the room for their prescribed meds. Marisa was the first to receive medication.

"Hey. You gonna be all right tonight?" Seul Bi said while grabbing the bin filled with the resident's pill bottles.

Marisa yawned. "Yeah. Thank you for earlier. I know this is all shit I need to tell my therapists, but it's nice to have ya around."

"Oh, sure. You don't have to thank me, sweetie. I understand, or, at least, I mean, I want to understand, you know? I'm just happy that you're here and you're safe."

Marisa scooped her meds from the pill bottles and swallowed them all in their proper dosage amounts. Seul Bi didn't worry about Marisa hoarding or abusing the meds, unlike some of the residents.

Jason, for instance, tried to stockpile his Methadone pills. He had been caught hoarding the pills several times, and each time his excuse was that it helped him doze off and sleep peacefully. It was the opposite with Marisa, however, who relied on her exact med cocktail of 200 mg of Seroquel, 0.5 mg of Xanax, and 100 mg of Imitrex to survive another night.

Ariel and Jason stumbled in from outside, rubbing each other's arms.

"IT IS COLD!" Ariel yelled.

"Fuck, that's right, it's time for meds." Jason darted past Marisa while Ariel sat on the couch. Marisa sat next to her.

"So, what were you guys doing outside?" Marisa felt goose bumps rising under her skin. A quiver of cold still lingered in the air from the door being open.

Ariel's eyes widened. "Oh, you know, just talking about the schematics for a time machine."

Seul Bi offered a disapproving frown. "Really?"

"Nah, not really. I'm just fucking with you. I know how much Dr. Nathan would shit all over the floor if he heard me say that."

Everyone except Seul Bi burst into laughter.

"Yeah, I know what you mean, Ariel," Seul Bi said. "So, do you, um, want your meds?"

Ariel snorted. "There ya go, sedate me into submission. You know I still like ya, though. Besides, I'm so tired all of a sudden, I don't think I got room in my busy night schedule of sleep, sleep, and… wait a minute… *more* sleep to uh, build a time machine. Even if Jason *did* help me."

Jason's laugh was muffled by a mouthful of water. He had sipped as much as his cheeks could hold from the sink faucet underneath the medicine cabinet. Seul Bi observed him gargling with his two 10 mg pills of Methadone before swallowing them. After this, he downed his 600 mg of Seroquel, 15 mg of Mirtazapine, and 400 mg of Lamictal. His throat always felt like it was being scalped when he swallowed all these pills.

More residents trickled into the common area from upstairs. Ariel jumped from the couch and headed right for Seul Bi.

"Oh shit, here comes the rest of the herd. I need my meds now!"

"Right on." Seul Bi already was inking her signature on the med tracking sheet next to Ariel's name. "Okay, you got your Lithium 900 millis, 20 of Abilify, and your Lamictal 150. I think you are good for tonight, Miss Winter."

"Thank you Miss… Rissiello. That is so weird to say considering you hardly have any, um… uh… *Italian* features," Ariel said, suppressing a giggle.

Realizing everyone immediately looked in her direction, Seul Bi's face turned scarlet. "Well, I like spaghetti. Does that count?"

Please don't remind me about being adopted, she thought to herself while everybody laughed.

———

Later that evening, Seul Bi found time to order food from Siam Paragon (This time it was pad thai. It would be a long time before she had the teriyaki chicken again). She dimmed the overhead lights in the common area, then watched from the office doorway as Marisa tossed and turned under the weight of her dreams.

Seul Bi wasn't intimidated by Marisa's restlessness. In fact, as the heatless sun rotated from its duties in the sky, she prepared to have another one of her own tension-filled head trips. *We could be like dream sisters*, she realized, after watching Marisa sleep.

Both were smothered in an envelope of sadness, stuck on repeat visions of their tragic pasts.

One father was still rattling his serpentine coils.

One father was trapped in watery bubbles, spinning blood droplets around and around.

"Sleep, sister. I hope at least one of us gets rest tonight," Seul Bi whispered while retreating into the office. The residents of Rainbow were so silent Seul Bi couldn't even hear their muted conversations through the vents near the computer desk. This wasn't unusual during the overnight shift, however. In the late a.m. hours, the residential building could easily have been mistaken for an abandoned mental asylum. Yet there *was* something strange about the quiet perched in the air over Seul Bi, who couldn't figure out what was so different about tonight than all the other nights she had spent double-shifting.

Seul Bi finished the daily online activity report for the evening, then ran upstairs to make a final inspection of the apartments and also check on the residents. Only Abbey Goldrich, who had just spent her twenty-second birthday at the residence a few days ago, was eating a cake-sized bowl of chocolate ice cream in her kitchen. This was a good sign, given that Abbey had struggled with anorexia the past few years. Her current diagnosis, however, was more focused on her anxiety disorder than anything else.

"How ya feeling, Abbey?" Seul Bi asked, after stepping inside Abbey's apartment. "Any more panic attacks like last week's?"

"Well, today I panicked when I thought somebody ate my ice cream, does that count?"

"Wow. Even this late at night you are derisive as ever. That was actually funny, so, no worries."

"What's 'derisive' mean?"

"Never mind, sweetie. After you finish devouring your ice cream, try to get some sleep, okay? I gotta get back down to the office."

Seul Bi didn't wait for another smart-ass response from Abbey. She headed straight out of the apartment and down to the main entrance hallway.

Though it had only been a little over ten minutes since she had left the common area, she felt like a sentry leaving her guard post unprotected. In fact, the same night of Abbey's panic attack, the doorbell to the common area had rung at 3:00 a.m., but nobody had been visible from the peephole or windows. Abbey, who had been downstairs, sleeping on the couch, was jostled into paranoia. Seul Bi too. Who could have done this? A resident? Somebody pranking people in the neighborhood? In the morning, Seul Bi and Abbey had laughed about their speculations. Abbey was content to just believe that their unexpected, late-night visitor was *obviously* the ghost of a past resident. Yet Seul Bi didn't mention to anyone that she felt something wasn't right about it.

When Seul Bi sat in the office chair, she remembered it was time to send the nightly report to the professional staff. It took only a few minutes to type it up and send it out. Click. Done.

Hmm, what can I do now to kill time tonight? She wondered. Eight more hours to go.

An idea slapped her mind: *My artwork!* She typed in one of the website addresses that listed her drawings for sale. Six charcoal sketches appeared on the monitor screen.

Arms.

Hands.

Fingers.

Flesh puzzles.

Hovering in digital cyberspace.

Seul Bi flinched at the images. The black and gray tones were blurry, forcing her eyelids to become tiny slits. Ah! She almost forgot—she had dimmed the office lights down to a low, iridescent glow. *Not that it really matters,* she thought. It wouldn't take too long before she would be someplace far away that was overflowing with sunlight.

B I R T H   O R I G I N

BIRTH ORIGIN: Can you meet me in front of
Pacela by the Mistubishi large screen?
SATSUKI: When?
BIRTH ORIGIN: In 30 minutes
SATSUKI: I might be late.
BIRTH ORIGIN: It's ok. See you soon.

Satsuki guzzled down a Coolish while reading her mother's messages. She had walked only two blocks from Nakahiro Junior High, which meant that she would need to either catch a bus or taxi to Pacela. She decided to find the nearest bus stop and check its sign post's QR code for arrival times. She pointed her cell phone at the fuzzy inkblot square and a schedule appeared on her cell phone's LCD screen, blinking good news: A bus was about to arrive.

I wonder if this bus will have air conditioning or if it will be broken like the last bus I took. Or worse—what if it's crowded? she fretted. Her body felt waterlogged after being stuck in the air-condition-less school all day. Two minutes later, however, Satsuki was relieved; the bus felt like a thermos filled with ice cubes. She considered riding it past the Pacela stop in Motomachi and not getting off until she was shivering cold, but being late would probably piss her mom off. And besides, there were too many old people stinking up the seats around her.

She spotted her mother standing in front of the large Mitsubishi television screen outside Pacela. Her mother was wearing a white maternity dress and had her favorite purple scarf wrapped around her neck. One of the things that Satsuki could always count on with her mother was that she wore that scarf, no matter how hot it was outside. At least Yoshiko stuck out among the crowd of on-lookers with their heads tilted upwards at the screen. A highlight video of an old sumo tournament was nearing completion, with the final and most important match about to take place.

"Hi," Satsuki called out.

Yoshiko spun around to see her daughter waving.

"Hey. You made it in record time, I think."

"Really?"

"Uh huh. So, did you take the bus?"

"Yep."

The crowd near them started to chatter and point at the wres-tlers onscreen. Yoshiko's eyes swung like pendulums between look-ing at Satsuki and what was going on above them.

"Are you actually watching sumo?" Satsuki asked.

"Yes. Asashoryu and Hakuho are fighting for the title, but I'm sure Asashoryu will win. He's the best *yokuzuna*[28] ever."

Yoshiko's voice leaped an octave as she said this. Satsuki's mouth immediately fell open, her tongue stuck to the back of her throat. She was slack-jawed partly from surprise, but more from disbelief than anything else.

"Oh my God, seriously, *Okaasan*? I can't believe you just said that."

"What? Are you surprised I know about this?"

"Hahahaha. Very. By the way, I think this match already hap-pened, and they're replaying it. And also, just so you know, nobody likes Asashoryu anymore."

"Really? I see... well, I don't really watch that much to know who is important or well-liked in sumo and who isn't."

"Wait, you're really serious about watching sumo?" Satsuki was flummoxed.

"Well, sometimes I watch it when you are at school. You see, me and *Otousan* used to watch it together. I really wasn't interested at first, but the more I watched, the more I appreciated *Otousan*'s passion for the sport. And watching it now really reminds me of

---

28. *yokuzuna*—a champion sumo wrestler.

when we first met and how he used to talk so much about what he wanted to do with his life. He wanted to be a deep-sea explorer. But I guess, when we had you, he felt he should work for Mazda to support us, as apparently, there was no money in deep-sea exploration back then. I dunno about now, if that's true or not. Anyway, he dropped that whole idea of being a deep-sea explorer and became obsessed with sumo instead. For many years, we watched sumo. You really didn't know this?"

Satsuki almost lost her balance laughing. "Oh God, that was sappy, but kinda cute, I guess. I have never once seen you guys watch anything together, except the morning news. A deep-sea explorer? We haven't been to the ocean to swim since, since... I can't even remember the last time."

"Hahahaha, I know. To be honest, I don't particularly like swimming, and *Otousan* is always so busy with work that it's impossible to take a family trip anywhere."

It figures. What else is new? Satsuki thought to herself. "Yeah, he's really busy, isn't he? So you really, honestly, like sumo?" she said.

"What do you mean?" Yoshiko asked.

"Well, I think you like watching sumo because it reminds you that you're not the only one with a weight problem."

"Sacchan!" Yoshiko feigned anger at the remark. The weight gain from her pregnancy hadn't been all that much, actually. It was the same as when she'd had Satsuki: just a small baby bump and some extra padding on her ass. Most people didn't notice she was close to giving birth. She changed the subject. "Anyway, are you hungry?"

"Yes, a little, but I bet you're really hungry," Satsuki teased. She couldn't help herself.

"You're horrible, Sacchan!"

"I know. Wait until my *imouto* arrives. We will be quite the terrible duo."

Satsuki smirked and twisted around on one foot, lifting her other foot off the ground in a salchow jump. *That's right. TERRIBLE. She can be my Mai, and I will be her Izumi, but we won't paint our nails flashy colors or wear stupid hair extensions and wooden platform shoes that clip clop like horses when we walk down the hall like they do! I mean, who wants to take all that time in the morning to make themselves up, anyway? Not me, and for sure not my sis. I barely even like wearing what little make up I do have on. My imouto will feel the same, I'm sure. We'll refuse to be Barbie sluts.*

A pair of unborn feet kicked the inside of Yoshiko's stomach. "I think your *imouto* agrees. She just did a flying kick in my stomach."

"Really? Really, really, really?!"

"She did, I swear! She's must be super excited to meet you or really hungry. Probably both." Satsuki smiled so much that her cheekbones began to ache. She rubbed her mother's stomach.

"So then, what shall we eat?" Yoshiko asked.

Satsuki didn't need to think about her answer: "Spaghetti. I have a huge craving for meatballs and pasta."

"Fine by me," Yoshiko said. "I won't be the only one who looks like Asashoryo."

Yoshiko couldn't decide what she wanted, so Satsuki ordered the same thing for both of them. It was at least an hour before they finished gorging themselves on her choice, the penne rigate with meatballs. During dinner, Satsuki complained to Yoshiko about school and the art project she was in charge of getting completed before summer break. She also griped about how her school exams made it difficult to get anything done. All she really wanted to do was just watch *Kamichama Karin* and play *Dragonquest* on her Nintendo DS. Yoshiko merely encouraged her to "do her best." She didn't really have any personal connection to her daughter's adolescent experiences. Her memories of junior high had been evicted from her brain a long time ago; in their place lived Hideo and Satsuki and nothing else. Except maybe being pregnant, but feeling short of breath, having abdominal pains, and the extra fat on her otherwise skinny, sharp body was something she actively tried to forget.

After their meal, Yoshiko felt tired, but she wanted to spend time with Satsuki and shop for baby clothes. Satsuki suggested they skip the drab stores located inside Pacela and instead walk a lap through the much "cooler" outdoor Hondori mall. Yoshiko agreed, even though she knew her feet would feel like cinder blocks by the time they walked the couple of streets to reach the shopping mecca. She didn't want to go home yet. It reminded her of Hideo. *He hasn't called me, and it's already the middle of the week*, Yoshiko thought to herself. *I'm sure he's really busy with his business deals, but I know the real reason is because he's engaged in an extramarital affair with soju*[29] *and karaoke.*

Besides, Satsuki's face was shimmering. She had let her shifty teenage wall down, and Yoshiko figured what better chance to take advantage of this than right now? Sure, they had always been close to each other, but between her pregnancy and Satsuki entering Nakahiro Junior High, both of them were now living in different worlds. And Hideo? He might as well have been living in a different universe.

---

29. *soju*—Korean vodka.

Zoe hoisted her suitcase onto the bed. She had already unpacked everything in it, except the first chapter of her dissertation. It was on multiple intelligences, something she knew very little about.

Zoe didn't really know why she had decided to pursue a doctoral degree. She had made the decision just a month before taking the trip to Hawaii. She had come full circle at Northwestern University; having received her undergraduate degree in education there and also her master's degree, she had been hired to teach introductory psychology courses there as well. Now she would be a student again? It was hard for her to believe she would continue to bleed purple this much longer. Oh, *Whatsoever Things Are True*!

But grading tests and giving lectures had become sooooooo routine after fifteen years. Her life had been buried under a pile of exams. And for these last few years, she had begun to experience a pulsating restlessness as well. It was the same kind of feeling she had felt right before venturing into Evanston's Korean consulate office and demanding a baby from their bewildered receptionist.

She remembered how the constant tremors of needing a child after failing to conceive one nearly drove her insane. Try and try and try, and never a baby showed up. No matter what they did, Jimmy and Zoe remained a barren couple. Doctors, therapy, fertility charts, vitamins, everlasting fuck fests... nothing worked. And for Zoe, the pressure had felt like rusty clamps digging into her skull and tightening more and more each year. Three years to be exact, but four if you count the year before Jimmy and Zoe had gotten married.

The adoption process was, surprisingly, easy. Zoe had never considered herself or Jimmy suitable parents to raise anything. When they moved in together for the first time, they adopted a cat, but it ran away after a month of living with them. And neither one were good at dealing with problems. What if their child ended up on drugs, or pregnant at fifteen, or worse, a regular at Cook County Jail? If these things ever happened, Zoe couldn't imagine herself being understanding or sympathetic. Jimmy wouldn't be, either. She'd pictured him running in the opposite direction from authoritative rearing. It wasn't his style at all.

So, when the adoption counselor interviewed them both and wouldn't stop referring to them as the "perfect prospective parents," something lifted off them both. Correction; the curse of inadequacy, spawned from their impotent attempts at getting pregnant and failure to keep even a cat in their house, was proven to be nothing more than a long con.

Seul Bi had been a good kid growing up and was turning into the kind of young woman that Zoe admired: prodigy smart, wide-eyed about the world, a daddy's girl. Sure, the cracks in Seul Bi's kid façade were starting to show, and the questions were pouring out of those cracks all glug-like. Questions that Zoe didn't have a clue how to answer, but this really didn't bother her. She knew everything would turn out just fine.

And besides, she had Jimmy.

He had a titanium spine when it came to Zoe. Since that first moment of meeting each other, way back in tenth-grade study hall, she had envied his easygoing charm. It was like he could tell that her whole JAP persona was as fake as the stereotype itself. Her whiny, spoiled, dressed-to-the-gills-in-designer-clothes image was all a façade designed to please her rich, Jewish friends. Not only did Jimmy see through her, but he encouraged her to figure out her real identity and never gave in to her selfish whims. Zoe was impressed that, no matter how hard she tried, she couldn't ensnare Jimmy with bickering or defensive posturing, either. Instead, he laughed at Zoe's complaints and calamities, preferring to ruin any chance at them fighting by joking and never taking things too seriously. Somehow he even won over her parents, who initially complained that, since he was Italian and Catholic, maybe she could date him for a while. But marry him? Fuggedaboutit!

Yet marry they did. And as Zoe stood there in their bedroom at the Ala Kona beachfront rental unit, fingering the front cover of her unfinished dissertation, the only "thank you" on the acknowledgements page inside of it was for her husband. It read: "To Jimmy, your colossal smile persuades me to retain my grip on things."

"Hey Zoe, what'cha up to?" Debbie glided into the room. She quickly noticed the messy bed. "Did ya get any sleep? Looks like you didn't."

Debbie further surveyed the room, doing her best to not burst into a knee-bending laughter fit. The bed sheets were shaped into a teepee on the mattress. The see-thru thong Zoe had worn last night hung from a bedpost. The white comforter did nothing to hide the "wet spot." There was no denying it: Jimmy and Zoe had indeed behaved like pygmy chimps last night, and for that matter, every other night, since arriving on the Big Island.

"Ha, well, you know my husband. He is, um, never a dull moment, I guess." Zoe's face was slightly more crimson than her sunburned arms and legs. "Where is Jimmy, anyway?"

"Oh, he's outside wandering around with the kids, I think," Debbie said. She instinctively moved past her sister-in-law to make the bed, but decided it was probably a bad idea. She didn't want to touch anything that might have her brother's bodily fluids on it! Instead, she side-stepped towards the bedroom window.

"You know, Deb, I would think he wouldn't want to be around kids so much after teaching them every day, but maybe since the girls are older than his third graders, he doesn't mind so much, you know?"

"Nah, he's like a kid himself. I think he feels more comfortable with the girls because he acts like he's twelve all the time. I don't think he's been inside all morning." Debbie strained to look out the window, but the sun blasted her face with light.

"Guess it's gonna be hot again today. No surprise there."

"It felt hot all night, actually," Zoe said, not realizing her double entendre.

Debbie smiled broadly at Zoe.

"I'll bet."

After Debbie left to go find Jimmy and the girls, Zoe dashed into the bathroom next to Seul Bi's room and locked the door. She was determined to hoard every possible minute under the shower faucet's water drool. Zoe had already taken a shower right before the sun had come up, but this time it wasn't to scrub the stain of sex off her body. Zoe did her best thinking in the shower.

Seconds after shutting the door (which was really nothing more than a glorified shoji screen, or at least Zoe thought), Zoe noticed something peculiar about the toilet. A rock and several seashells caked in sand dotted the porcelain seat.

"That's cute," Zoe said. *Gifts from my ingenious husband and daughter, perhaps?*

While a morning breeze meandered into the bathroom through an open window, she bent over the toilet for a closer view. Her disheveled hair immediately knocked the coal-colored rock and a couple of the shells into the bowl. A reverse water fountain sprayed Zoe's entire face.

"GOD DAMN IT!"

Zoe, the human Pogo Stick, jumped right into a towel rack. She was about to laugh at her clumsiness when she heard a "pssst" coming from outside the window. Her curiosity pushed her to see who was there. As she flitted towards the front of the window, a small, green creature hurtled right onto the front of her shirt.

"EEEEEK!! HOLY SHIT!!" Zoe screeched and fell backwards into the shower, knocking the thing to the ground in the commotion. *What the hell was that?* she wondered, as she watched it scurry up the wall and out the window as quickly as it flew in. It looked like a lizard. Zoe was out of breath and confused. *BUT if it was a lizard, how did it fly into the window?*

"Don't worry, it doesn't bite!"

Zoe then heard exaggerated laughter, that of a man and a young girl.

"JIMMMMY!!! SEUL BIIIIIIIIII!!"

Sometime later, Zoe and Jimmy decided to take everyone out to dinner. Again.

Every evening on the island had been spent driving up and down Ali'i Drive in search of a new restaurant. Debbie and Zoe joked about how these car rides were like playing games of Frogger. Tan bodies squeezed between cars on the road, and bicycles trickled through the double-line gaps. Life was everywhere.

"Seul Bi, sweetie, can you hear it?" Zoe pointed towards the western skyline. The ocean tide slurped against the rocks by the beachfront. Palm trees, which were huddled for miles along the coast in shady clusters, swooshed in perfect unison with the waves. Seul Bi pressed her face against the car window to look at them.

As she leaned back on the rental car's leather backseat, her skin felt sticky against the padding. It was uncomfortable, but what could she do? Debbie sat between her and Beverly in the backseat, her mom and dad in the front.

"Yeah, Mom, sure. That just reminds me, it's hot. Can you turn up the air conditioner? I don't think it's working."

"What do you want me to do? It's already on the arctic temperature setting," Zoe pleaded. Both Seul Bi and Beverly moaned. Zoe flapped her hands towards Jimmy, who cleared his throat and changed the subject.

"So, guys, uh, where are we going? Do you want to hit up Honu's or maybe that one place, what's it called?"

Beverly took a deep breath, then spat out an answer. "Humahikiwhatchamacallitshack?"

Everyone laughed. Debbie and Zoe tried repeating the tongue twister but couldn't manage to even get past the first three syllables.

"I think that's named after the official state fish or something," Jimmy said. "Anyway, I say we go to Honu's. They have hamburgers with pineapple toppings that I've been meaning to try."

"Yeah, but you can get hamburgers anywhere, even with pineapples," Debbie chimed in. "We should go back to that one place with the blackened sashimi and garlic shrimp. It was amazing."

"Yeah, Mom!" Beverly squealed excitedly. "I want to go there. That place had mai tais."

Earlier in the week, Debbie allowed Beverly a few sips of her mai tai, and since then, Beverly had asked for one every single time they went out to eat.

Debbie pinched her daughter's arm. "NO! You have a few more years before you can decide to become a professional alcoholic, okay?"

"Ouch, that hurt, Ma! Uncle Jimmy!!" Beverly whined.

Jimmy glanced at his niece in the rearview mirror. "Don't worry, Bev, Honu's is only a few more minutes away. At least that is what it says on the map, anyway. Oh, and before I forget, Zoe, your sister told me that you finally pulled out your dissertation? You still doing it on the multiple intelligences or some other thingy?"

"It's *just* on multiple intelligences, Jimmy." Zoe sighed. "And yes, even though I barely studied multiple intelligences during my undergraduate years, I didn't decide to change it or anything since coming here. Although after this morning I did briefly consider changing my proposed thesis to how some people are gifted at repetitious stupidity." Zoe glared at both Jimmy and Seul Bi.

"Hmm, I have no idea what you are talking about, honey," Jimmy said. He and Seul Bi winked at each other.

"You know what I'm talking about! That crazy lizard didn't just fly into the bathroom window on its own." Zoe quickly slipped her pinky up Seul Bi's nose, then punched her husband in his meaty arm.

"That's so disgusting! Why do you always do that?" Seul Bi screwed her face up in protest.

"Honey, you want me to wreck? You shouldn't hit me while I'm driving. I could take us right into the water."

"That wouldn't feel half bad, actually," Beverly chimed in. "Do it, Uncle Jimmy!"

"Are we theeeerre yet?" Seul Bi's nose twitched. She could still feel her mother's finger inside her nostril. "I'm hungry."

"Me too," Beverly added.

"Both of you shush or else!" Zoe threatened light-heartedly.

"OR ELSE WHAT?!" Seul Bi and Beverly simultaneously shouted back.

"Or else you guys won't be petting the manta rays tomorrow."

Debbie and Jimmy looked at the girls and shook their heads side to side in unison, chanting "Uh oh" and "Now you girls are in trouble!" An argument broke out as to whether or not the manta rays would come anywhere near their rental home, which was a few feet from the ocean shoreline. There did seem to be an honest chance that they might, given the fact that they had seen the rubbery creatures gliding through the waters almost every day, mostly in the morning under the dawn's pink sky. As a way of saying goodbye to Hawaii, Seul Bi had suggested to pet the manta rays. Her parents had praised her for the meaningful idea.

"HEY GUESS WHAT?" Jimmy yelled over everyone, "WE. ARE. FINALLY. HERE!"

Everyone's attention shifted to a wooden sign with the word "Honu's" on it. Hawaiian natives dressed in hula skirts and colorful leis buzzed around tables that overflowed with obvious tourists. The outdoor patio creeped right up to both the parking lot's edge and the ocean's lip, puncturing the air with the smell of cooked Kalua pig and salty Pacific water. Bright orange birds played hopscotch on the tops of the tiki torches near the bar. The whole scene was a postcard in motion.

"Hey, Aunt Zoe, maybe this place has manta rays," Beverly said while they all slid out of the car.

Zoe pretended to gasp. "Do you mean to pet or… to eat?"

Beverly looked at Seul Bi but didn't say a word. She didn't have to. It was obvious that her Aunt was terrible at making jokes.

⸻

Night had sunk in. Honu's noisy customers were placated by the soft strumming of a ukulele and people ingesting way too much alcohol. The remains of dinner littered tables everywhere, while smoke from the Luau's greasy imus floated overhead, creating a hazy texture to everyone's visage. Seul Bi spotted her aunt Debbie, at the bar, ordering another mai tai (Honu's was offering a two-for-one special on their girly drinks for the evening). It was her sixth. Beverly had snuck enough sips from her mother's drinks that she now slouched in her bamboo chair, fast asleep.

Seul Bi sat beside her cousin but paid her no attention. She was too busy observing how there were so many darkened faces with slanted eyelids surrounding her. Natives, she thought, or maybe

Asian tourists? Korean? Japanese? She couldn't tell the difference. Her ears caught some garbled vowel-sounds coming from their mouths. *I need subtitles,* she thought while sighing and propping her head up on the table with her hands. *They look like me, but are they me?*

Seul Bi had joked about being the spicy solution for a boring, Midwestern home, but seeing all these dark-skinned Asians made her question the validity of her adoption. Perhaps it was because she didn't stand out in Hawaii like she did back in Evanston. Or maybe it was because they were geographically close to Korea. Whatever the reason, Seul Bi suddenly felt detached from her adopted family.

Jimmy tossed a straw at Seul Bi. "Hey, you okay? You look lost in thought."

"Yeah, are you tired or something?" Zoe asked, backing up her husband.

Seul Bi wanted to say to them how she felt but decided to keep her feelings private. She didn't want to hurt their feelings.

"I'm fine. Maybe a little tired. Why don't you two go dance?"

"Great idea, sweetie," Jimmy said. "You're always full of great ideas."

"I know."

Zoe took Jimmy's hand and sprung up from the table. "How about we leave after this dance? We should probably go soon, anyway, or else Aunt Debbie might die of alcohol poisoning." Aunt Debbie was, of course, oblivious to their comments. She sat at the bar, nursing a mai tai and flirting with the bartender. Seul Bi could hear her aunt insisting the bartender take sips of her fruity drink.

"Have fun," Seul Bi mumbled. She continued to focus on the faces of every Asian person either working or partying at Honu's. *They all look so happy, so content to be themselves,* she thought. *Why can't I be satisfied with the way things are?* Puberty blues, she guessed. If it was the fact that she was becoming a teenager, it didn't make her feel any sort of relief for knowing this. All she could do was sit there at the table and mentally ask herself over and over again, *Why the heck am I here?*

Jimmy and Zoe found a spot to dance next to another couple who were busy stepping on each other's toes. More people followed their cue. The music felt like it was getting louder as everyone tried to shimmy and scamper to a ukulele song.

"So, are you having a good time here in Hawaii?" Jimmy asked. He placed his hands on his wife's hips. She purred her approval.

"Yeah, yeah. I love it. I mean, it's so… amazing to be here and not stuck in a snow drift someplace in Evanston, you know? I just wonder if Seul Bi is okay. I mean, look at her. Doesn't she seem out of it to you?" Zoe glanced over at their daughter, who was slumped over the table and staring at everyone. She looked both restless and lost.

"Nah, I think it's just, you know, something to do with her being here in Hawaii and seeing all these Asians with their families and stuff."

"Oh, really?"

"Yeah. She's starting to get to that age where she isn't a kid anymore and needs to figure out who she is." Jimmy kissed his wife and spun her around. She yelped.

"Whoa. Mister Fancy Pants! Ha ha. Are you sure, though, she isn't still a kid? I mean, I seem to recall meeting her flying lizard friend this morning. Or was that all *your* doing?"

Zoe pressed her face onto Jimmy's chin and stared up at him, her eyebrows mashed. Whenever she did this, the nine-inch gap between the top of her head and the top of his head seemed to disappear completely. Zoe felt him shrug his broad shoulders and watched his lips quickly turn upwards.

"Well, missus, I think you should just make sure you're nice to the little green guys here. I mean, you probably stepped on the flying lizard's little sister and he came after you for some revenge. Plus I know how you get annoyed sometimes at little things."

"Wait, what does that mean?" Zoe tensed up.

Jimmy pulled her rigid body close to his and stroked her hair. "Nah, it's nothing. I just mean you seem to be uptight all the time. I just want you to relax and enjoy our vacation here. That's all I meant."

"Well, it's hard. I mean, I got the paper to work on and my classes back home. I just got a lot on my mind, you know?"

Jimmy offered Zoe a kiss on her forehead. She closed her eyes.

"Look, all that stuff needs to be far away from you right now. Why don't you focus instead on the fact that we're doing pretty good right now?"

Zoe slinked closer to her husband. They were now pressed together in a firm embrace.

"Yeah. We've had… what is it now? Fifteen good years of marriage? Plus the years I knew you before getting married?"

"Mmmhmm," Jimmy uttered.

Zoe continued. "It's just that I don't want to be one of those wives who get divorced and bitter after spending that much time with their husband."

"What? Baby, why are you talking about that? We—"

Zoe interrupted. "No, I know, I know. It's just that, lately, I've been feeling so damn anxious all the time. It probably has nothing to do with you. I dunno. Maybe I'm just getting old and senile?"

"You mean like menopause?"

"What? Yeah, that's it, honey. Menopause. Your answer for everything that's wrong with me these days." Zoe loved how Jimmy always used humor to deflect anything serious, although it could be frustrating sometimes for her more serious approach to life. However, tonight, that was what she needed—a reminder that everything was proceeding in a normal pattern.

"Listen," Jimmy began to say while tracing a soft line with his fingers up the crease in Zoe's back. "Even though you have all this pressure constantly weighing down on you, I think you're perfect. I knew what I was getting into when I married you. Your neurotic behavior is a major turn-on for me."

Zoe rolled her eyes at Jimmy. "I don't think it takes much to turn you on, judging from how we've spent every night here."

Jimmy raised his eyebrows. "Yeah? Well, I can't help it. We haven't spent much time together like that lately."

No time, actually. Jimmy and Zoe's schedules were opposite each other. He would be getting home from teaching his third graders while she was heading out for night classes at Northwestern University. They only had time to say hello and goodbye to each other. By the time she returned home, Jimmy would be asleep in front of the television, his belly full from takeout. Zoe worried about the distance between them, but lately, what had become more important to her was getting the dissertation completed. Being in Hawaii felt almost like an inconvenience, except dancing with her husband and making love to him every night reminded her why she was married to her easygoing husband in the first place.

Zoe concentrated her eyes on sand that clung to her sandals. "I know what you're saying, Jimmy."

Jimmy danced with Zoe, neither one saying anything else, until Zoe noticed that a small drop of water landed on her feet. *Wait... am I crying?* she thought to herself. *What the hell? Maybe I am going through menopause!* She squeezed her eyelids shut, but no tears came out. Was it Jimmy? She opened her eyes and looked at her husband, who was gazing up at the stars.

"Uh, I think it's going to rain," Jimmy said.

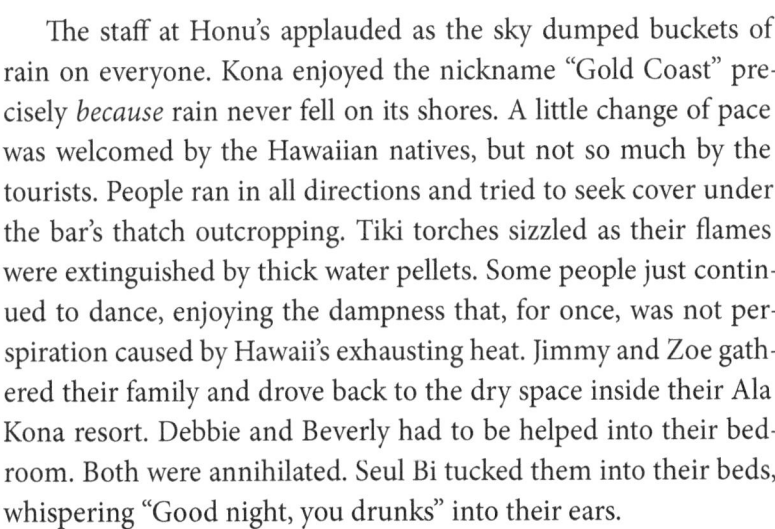

The staff at Honu's applauded as the sky dumped buckets of rain on everyone. Kona enjoyed the nickname "Gold Coast" precisely *because* rain never fell on its shores. A little change of pace was welcomed by the Hawaiian natives, but not so much by the tourists. People ran in all directions and tried to seek cover under the bar's thatch outcropping. Tiki torches sizzled as their flames were extinguished by thick water pellets. Some people just continued to dance, enjoying the dampness that, for once, was not perspiration caused by Hawaii's exhausting heat. Jimmy and Zoe gathered their family and drove back to the dry space inside their Ala Kona resort. Debbie and Beverly had to be helped into their bedroom. Both were annihilated. Seul Bi tucked them into their beds, whispering "Good night, you drunks" into their ears.

"Like mother, like daughter," Zoe added. They fell asleep within seconds.

After kissing both her parents good night, Seul Bi also went to her bedroom, but not to sleep. She opened up a sliding glass door that allowed her access to the shared terrace next to her parents' room and sat down. Within minutes, her parents were moaning. Seul Bi tried not to think about what they were doing. Thankfully, thunderclaps drowned out most of their sex noises.

The rain was also falling in furious waves that sprayed Seul Bi's feet. Because of this, she pulled her legs up to her chest and pressed her back against the resort's cobblestone wall. It made her wince in pain. She then tried scooting away from the edge of the terrace, which was guarded by spiral aluminum poles. She thought of twisty licorice as she looked at them. When she finally found a halfway decent spot against the wall, she peered through the spaces between the poles and focused on the ocean that twitched underneath a restless heaven above.

I am yours.

I am yours.

I am yours.

"You're my real mother," Seul Bi whispered into the wind that lifted her hair up off her shoulders. Each strand formed hypnotic curls that hovered beside her face. Seul Bi empathized with her mother's anxious waves. She, too, was stirring inside. Being in Hawaii with her "parents" conjured some deep insecurity which had now reached its apex. Sure, Jimmy and Zoe loved her and supported everything she did, but they could never provide an answer to that nagging question always in the back of her mind:

Who am I?

Seeing all the Asian families at Honu's had reminded her that she had been abandoned at birth. The thought was something Seul Bi fought from entering her brain, but it couldn't be helped. Tears slipped from her eyes.

She assumed an upright fetal position against the wall, watching the rain as it covered everything with slimy, humid moisture. She listened to the thunderous bass drops in the sky that sounded like muted arguments between demigods in the dark clouds. She imagined that this was what it felt like to be in the unfamiliar comfort of her Korean mother's womb.

I don't know who I am at all.

She rocked back and forth while envying the black rocks nestled against the beach. Would the water below nurture her, too, in its embrace?

Her tears fell faster now.

Shards of lightning scribbled on the clouds.

I guess I am yours in the end...

"It looks busy."

Yoshiko was surprised. Hondori was clogged with tourists, teenagers, and old-timers that normally would be found here on the weekends. People gushed in and out of the many restaurants and shops stacked underneath Hondori's buttressed, semi-circular rooftop. A few musicians strummed jazz chords while being cloaked in the elephantine shadows of Hiroshima Carps red baseball banners flapping on poles above them. Fortune tellers, peddlers, teens hidden behind rococo fashions, and artists were camped out between the storefronts. Every time they went to Hondori, Yoshiko joked about how it was turning more and more into the Haight-Ashbury of Japan.

For Satsuki, the crowds, and especially the neon lights that were like glowing bibs on every building, always reminded her of Akihabara. She had been surprised with a trip to Tokyo's Electric City by her mother one autumn day after she had just turned nine. She felt like she was instantly transported into a videogame. Under a pastel sky, there were girls wearing superhero ribbons in their hair and passing out tissue packets like they were health boosters, impassable blocks of computers and cameras, and blips and bleeps blasting out of every stickered window and open arcade door. It was here that Yoshiko bought Satsuki her Nintendo DS. It was here that Satsuki's imagination jumped out of her brain and started to live on its own.

Although Akihabara had downloaded into her mind, it was quickly uninstalled a few years later when Satsuki prepared to relinquish the title of *hitorikko*[30]. She thought about this while looking for things to buy her unborn sister in Hondori's scattering of clothing stores. Both she and her mother were looking forward

30. *hitorikko*—the only child in a family.

to having another female in the house, but Satsuki was more excited by the fact that the girl wouldn't need to be operated by A or B buttons.

"Do you think this looks okay?" Satsuki held up a purple, woolen beanie. It was so big that Yoshiko could have worn it to match her scarf.

"Sacchan, how big do you think her head is going to be when she's born?" Yoshiko and Satsuki both hit a harmonic squeal with their laughter. In store after store, they sifted through bins of clothing, laughing and talking loudly, until finally settling on a pair of knit stockings and three Lilo and Stitch one-piece pajamas.

When they were done, Satsuki held Yoshiko's hand and tugged her in the street towards a husky man who was sitting on a blanket full of paintings. She had spotted him right before entering the last clothing store. The man was round with beans for eyes and definitely had a sweating problem. Satsuki almost changed her mind about talking to him when she saw perspiration trickle down from his nose to his chin, but something lured her to his strange display. Yoshiko looked at her daughter with a "Why are we here?" gaze stuck on her face.

Satsuki read out loud the sign taped to the blanket: "Hello, my name is Kuma. Please sign my guest book. I have a message for you! Only 1,000 yen!" Next to the blanket, calligraphy drawings the size of index cards were sprawled in every direction. There were black ink portraits of birds and flowers and trees, but the drawings were predominantly of hiragana and katakana characters. Some had kanji characters as well. They seemed to be the names of various people, but who exactly? *Those who paid for Kuma's service?* Satsuki guessed.

"Do you want a... message, Sacchan?" Yoshiko's tone was skeptical, but she nonetheless whipped out her purse wallet and took out a wrinkled 1,000-yen bill.

Satsuki didn't hear her mother, though. Her attention was focused on Kuma now. He had suddenly been approached by a group of teenage girls still in their school uniforms. They seemed interested but started laughing and buzzing to each other about which one should get a message. Kuma swallowed back a sigh of disappointment and forced a polite smile instead. *What a bunch of idiots*, Satsuki thought to herself. *I wonder if he ever gets mad when he deals with such dumb members of our species?* She squinted at them in disgust, but they were lost in gregarious indecision and didn't seem to notice her, or anyone else for that matter. When the tiniest girl in the group pulled out a camera and snapped a picture of Kuma, they all squawked in synchronization, "Purikura!" and then hopped away towards the nearest photo sticker booth.

"Well? Do you want to try this or not?" Yoshiko said in a pseudo-impatient pitch. She waved her hand in front of Satsuki's scowling face.

"Yes. Sorry. I was about to throw my cell phone at those girls."

Yoshiko clicked her tongue. "Be nice."

Satsuki rolled her eyes at her mother (who didn't pay any attention), then crouched down beside Kuma. She suddenly became aware that she, too, was dressed in her school uniform. "Excuse me. I would like to receive a message."

"Ah, yes, that's great," Kuma answered in a pillow-soft voice that belied his fatty frame. He sounded relieved to be dealing with an actual paying customer. "Please sign the guestbook."

Satsuki inked her signature into the daily visitor log. She noticed that there was only one other name scribbled in it for the day's earnings. *It's in the middle of the week, so that's why*, she thought to herself. *Or maybe he tells people things they don't wanna hear.*

Kuma handed Satsuki a mat to sit on. Yoshiko took the opportunity to rest her feet and sat beside her daughter on the mat. After wiping a thin film of sweat off his forehead, Kuma half-nodded, half-bowed, and then began to paint.

Penetration. It seemed like Kuma was tossing around whatever he could find inside Satsuki to help guide his brush. He painted and stopped and painted and stopped, each pause holding her in a peculiar stare. His eyes were like permanent glue bonding fast to her skin. Yet at the same time, they were all surface, like he wasn't looking at anything, because what was inside of him had disappeared and overflowed with her.

The painting only took Kuma five minutes to finish, but Satsuki felt like it took forever. She could barely push any air out of her lungs. She was caught in that mysterious vacuum within Kuma's eyes.

"Here," Kuma said. He slid the finished work over to Satsuki, who smiled at him in thanks (although her gratitude was more for releasing her of his strange stare than anything else). She picked up the picture and held it to the side so that her mother could also see what was on it:

It was Satsuki's name written in hiragana, with lines falling off the surface edge. Satsuki's first thought was that the character on the card-sized canvas was not her name but perhaps a code word for some locked level on one of her Nintendo DS games. She dismissed the silly idea almost as soon as it popped into her head, but then again, what was this supposed to mean, exactly? It could be anything.

She also wondered why her curiosity drew her to Kuma in the first place. There were plenty of people like him all over Hondori. Why him, and why now? Not knowing the reason was an itch under her skull. She couldn't figure out what her drawing meant and was about to ask for an explanation when Yoshiko suddenly stood up. Kuma climbed to his feet as well.

"This is beautiful!" Yoshiko exclaimed. "You did a great job! How much was this? 1,000 yen?"

Kuma folded his hands in front of him. "Thank you. And yes, it's 1,000 yen."

"Here you go. Thank you." Yoshiko paid him, then began to wobble away. "Come on, Sacchan."

"Wait. I'm not ready to go," Satsuki pleaded.

Yoshiko looked up at the roof. Turtle-shaped clouds were beginning to blot out what little light was left in the day. "It's getting late, and I want to take you somewhere before we go home. We need to get going if we want to reach the place before it gets too dark out."

"Where are we going?" Satsuki asked.

"It's a surprise."

Satsuki loved surprises. Just hearing the word "surprise" from her mother was enough to break Kuma's spell. She got up to leave, but after giving a quick head bow to Kuma, she signaled for her mother to wait. There was still one thing that bothered her about the painting she held in her hands. She took a step towards Kuma.

"Have we… met before?"

Kuma's left eyebrow arched up in sync with the left corner of his mouth. It was like a string tied the two together. "Ahh, that's the question, isn't it?"

Satsuki shuddered. "What… do you mean?"

"Look at the lines that are before and after your name on the drawing. Do you see them?"

"Yeah, I see them, but I don't understand what they're supposed to represent."

"Your message is simple, actually. I think you and me and your mother and the girls who were here before you, we are all the same. And you have the power to influence what's around you."

"I have the power to influence people? How?"

"Maybe you didn't realize this about yourself, but you have a strong imagination which binds you to everyone else in the world."

Satsuki contemplated his words. "So, what you mean is that—"

Kuma interrupted. "We are all connected."

"Sacchan, let's go." Yoshiko started to walk away, parting people in her path.

Satsuki didn't fully understand what she was hearing, but she knew it was something that she wouldn't forget anytime soon. For now, her mother's voice was all she could hear. She tucked the painting inside her backpack and hurried down the street towards her mother.

We are all connected.

I N S I D E

the ——

G R A Y   T I M E   M A C H I N E

"Um, *Helllllloooooo*? Do you know where you're at right now?"

Seul Bi looked back at the sliding glass door on the terrace, expecting her mother or father to appear, but instead, a skinny girl with black curls for hair stood in the doorway of the office. It was Ariel, who bounced up and down on one foot, innocently smirking. Seul Bi immediately realized that she had spaced out big time. She glanced at her watch; it had been well over two hours since she had begun staring at her drawings on the computer screen.

The air wasn't warm or wet but very cold. Seul Bi touched her face. She'd expected it to be moist from crying and the rain, but it was dry like her mouth. *Back to reality*, she thought to herself.

"Ah, Ariel, sorry. I was um…"

"You went someplace just now, didn't you? Someplace back in *time*, maybe?" Ariel said this while continuing to smirk. It was obvious that she wanted to ensnare Seul Bi in a conversation about her favorite subject.

"What? No… I mean, I don't know…" Seul Bi could hear a familiar, rhythmic thumping outside the office window. She massaged her eyes and glanced at the window, then back at Ariel to make sure her mind wasn't playing tricks on her. *Am I really back in Evanston?* She wondered.

"So, what can I do for you, Ariel?"

"Nothing. I just wanted to tell you that it was raining outside, and if you have to shut any windows or anything, you should probably do it now before we get flooded. It's coming down pretty hard. I couldn't sleep, so I went outside for another smoke, and the next thing I know, it started pouring like a motherfucker!"

"Oh, thanks. That was nice of you. Do you want me to give you a p.r.n. for sleep?"

"No, it's cool. Do you want some of my meds?"

"Why would I want your meds?" Seul Bi crossed her arms and stood up from the chair. Her legs felt sore from sitting so long in one place.

"Well, you seem like you're not... *here*," Ariel whispered the last word and chuckled.

Seul Bi appreciated her attempt at humor, even if it was a little inappropriate.

"No, miss, I'm fine, thanks. Anything else?"

"Nope. Talk to you later." Ariel walked backwards into the blackness of the common area.

"Good night. Try to get some sleep for me." Seul Bi sat back down again.

"You sure you don't want any of my meds?"

"Good night, Ariel."

"Right. Later."

Long after silence returned to the building (with only the occasional noise hiccup from creaky pipes within the walls), Seul Bi remembered what Ariel had said and tiptoed to the door in the common area. She was careful not to wake up Marisa, who was swaddled in her blankets and snoring loudly. There weren't any open windows in the common area or the main foyer area, and all three doors leading into the residential treatment center were, to her best knowledge, locked up for the evening. But she was curious to see just how bad it was raining outside. Earlier in the week, there had been snow flurries, and yesterday felt like a full-blown snowstorm. Now rain? Then again, Evanston was unpredictable like that.

She opened the door, almost in slow motion.

A soggy cold fought to get inside, but Seul Bi's small frame stood in its way. She trembled at its touch. The slanted rain surged towards the open door. Seul Bi went to turn around and find warmth again inside when she noticed something peculiar. The mezuzah that hung on the side of the threshold's frame was darkened by some grimy substance. If it weren't for a sliver of dull grey poking out from underneath the muck, she would have guessed the mezuzah was replaced by a tiny black hole.

"What the fuck?"

Seul Bi reached her pointer finger out to touch what was once the mezuzah. She poked at the darkness, and as she did so, her fingertip became spotted with wet flecks of black. She wasn't sure, but she felt like it was the rain which stained her skin. She rubbed her pointer finger with her thumb and noticed it was sooty, like ash.

An image of her receiving the sacrament for Lent at Pope John XXIII flashed in her mind. "Remember, Seul Bi, that you are dust, and unto dust you shall return," Father D'Angelo would utter as he made the sign of the cross with an oily paste on her forehead. One time the ash felt so heavy on her forehead that her whole body became off-balanced by the weight. She remembered spending that whole Wednesday in a vertigo slush.

Seul Bi looked up at the murky night air and felt that same loss of equilibrium rush forth to claim her balance. She almost fell forward onto the patio stones, which now resembled charcoal. A part of her wanted to go back inside, but instead, she opened her mouth to taste the rain. She wanted to convince as many of her senses as possible that this was no dream. Heavy droplets immediately hit the back of her throat. At first, it felt like normal rain, but a few seconds later, her gag reflex kicked in, and she nearly vomited up her pad thai dinner from earlier. Her mouth was coated in Thick. Filthy. Ash.

Evanston was turning into the belly of a barbecue grill.

For several miserable minutes, Seul Bi hemorrhaged soot-tasting phlegm while trying to scrape the black off her cheek's insides. She couldn't believe this was happening. What was causing the strange downpour? A factory explosion, perhaps? Or a malfunctioning factory blast furnace erupting into the night? But there weren't any factories that she knew of anywhere close to the residence. Maybe it was from a nearby house or apartment complex that had caught fire? She didn't hear any fire truck horns or ambulance sirens. Actually, she didn't hear anything at all outside, except her own grunts in between coughing and trying to spit out the taste of ash from her mouth.

As she stood outside in the quiet, wondering about the ash storm, a flurry of high-pitched squeals and cries erupted from inside the common area, jostling her back inside the residence. It was Marisa, who had awakened from some kind of bad dream, or worse, a possible night terror episode. Seul Bi knew she had to calm her down quickly and quietly. A few more minutes of Marisa's shrieking, and there would be a mutiny to repress from awakened, irascible residents.

"HE'S HERE!"

"Hey, little sister, it's okay. There's nobody here. Listen to me. You're all right, okay? Just calm down now." Seul Bi sat next to the frightened girl, and for the second time in the past twenty-four hours, held her hands.

"Another bad dream, honey?"

Marisa nodded.

"Can you try to lie back down for me?"

"He was here. I saw him."

"Who? Your father?"

"Yeah." Marisa pressed the pillow against her face to stop crying. "He was trying to… to… touch me," she stammered.

Seul Bi grasped Marisa's hands tight and scanned the room. A light panel flickered above their heads, causing awkward shadows to dance on the ceiling. Anybody who didn't work at Rainbow night after night would probably think a large group of blurry men were breaking in, but Seul Bi was used to the misleading shadows. There was no need to worry about them.

Outside, however, was a different matter. She knew she couldn't explain the ash storm to herself or anyone else. And as she sat next to Marisa, a feeling of dread began to peck at her insides.

"Nobody is in here, Marisa. It was just a dream. And even if it wasn't, I'm not gonna let anyone hurt you, you hear me? You're safe now." Seul Bi tried her best to sound convincing despite her own doubts. Marisa's body sank back into the couch, and she relaxed her grip on Seul Bi's hands.

"Will you sit here with me, just in case?"

"Sure, hon."

Marisa yawned. "Please don't leave."

"I'm not going anywhere. I'll sit right here with you. Try to rest, okay?"

"Okay."

Hours passed. Seul Bi looked out the window and noticed there was no sign of change outside. Streaks of ash crept down the glass, making everything around the window appear old and dusty. She had expected that, come morning, there would be black mounds to shovel. Not sleet or snow, but burned remains. Of what, though, she didn't know.

Marisa was lying still with her eyes wide open. She was stolid, almost snakelike in her appearance, trading eyelids for brille and vigilance. Seul Bi felt apprehensive while sitting in the chair beside Marisa. She was afraid of waking the poor girl from her quasi-catatonic sleep. *Thank God nobody else woke up,* Seul Bi thought. It would be morning soon…

RING! RING!!

The doorbell to the common area entrance rang. Seul Bi stood up but almost buckled under her sleep-paralyzed legs. Her watch said 7:00 a.m.

"Wow, I must have been really tired," she said to herself while yawning several times. She shook both her legs to regain feeling in them and reached for the lock.

It was resource staff member Sarah. She was an hour late for her shift.

"WHEW! IT IS COLD OUTSIDE! DID YOU SEE HOW…"

"Shhh! Marisa's here." Seul Bi waved a hand towards the couch, but not before Sarah stomped her furry boots on the doormat.

"Sorry. Here I am all late and shit, talking loud and stomping. Did anything happen last night?"

"Marisa had a night terror, but other than that, it was a quiet evening, I guess."

Sarah went over to the coffee machine on the counter and clicked the "ON" button. Some strands of red hair leaped out from underneath the furry ushanka that covered her head.

"Did you get a chance to see all the snow outside?" Sarah asked.

Seul Bi's whole body went numb. She had noticed the snow from Sarah's boots but thought it was just from the alleyway behind the residence. For some reason, sloshy heaps of snow could always be found there, even when there was none falling from the sky, and Sarah always walked through the alley for work.

"Wait, it snowed?"

"Yeah. We got maybe two or three inches."

Seul Bi ran to the door and flung it wide open. Both the patio and the backyard were concealed under a white tarp. The mezuzah seemed to sparkle from the ground's reflection.

"Sarah, did you notice anything weird about the weather, or was there anything on the news about a fire or something near here?"

"No. Why?" Sarah said. The coffee maker gurgled.

"I dunno. It's just that, well, maybe I thought I saw something last night, but I guess not. I must have been *really* tired."

"Yeah, you must have. You want some coffee to wake you up?"

Seul Bi didn't want coffee. She wanted answers. Sarah cupped the coffee pot to warm her hands while Seul Bi put her coat on and stepped outside. Seul Bi yawned again.

"No thanks. I'm going home now. Have a good shift."

"Oh, um, okay. Well then, take it easy. And get some sleep."

As Seul Bi walked to the Davis Purple Line stop, she began to feel sorry, but like all the times she received the ash cross and listened to Psalm 51 being recited during the Lenten ceremony, she didn't know why or what for. There was definitely something wrong, though. Her mouth still tasted like an ashtray, and she was pretty sure there was a strong smell of rotting decay hanging in the air this peculiar morning.

CHAPTER 19

THE AGE
of ....
VIABILITY

The whole city seemed to be pancaked together with streets and trees, bikes and people, soil and water—all of them ignoring their beginnings and endings. It was like a slide show without any pauses between the slides, and Yoshiko and Satsuki were walking between the frames. They hadn't gone far from Hondori, but it was now a speck lost in the background scenery. Their new destination: a slim sidewalk next to the Motoyasu River, near Otemachi Park.

"I need to sit down and rest my feet for a minute." Yoshiko found the first bench she could on the pathway and plopped down on it, heaving a few breaths of relief while kneading her thighs. The weather forecast had predicted an 80 percent chance of rain around nightfall, but except for a string of fat clouds, the arrival of dusk didn't bring any cumulonimbus monsters with it. Twin lights that hung from posts along the sidewalk had doused everything with such brightness that the sky had become an azure color, the kind that shows up on a clear sunny day. *So much for the weatherman's predictions*, Yoshiko thought to herself. She had brought a folding umbrella just in case, but now wished she had left it at home. She was already carrying enough around with her.

Satsuki took a seat at the far end of the bench, concentrating on all the twin lights. They were every few meters apart and looked like car headlights racing down a busy street above their heads. She already had so much on her mind, with the collage deadline coming up soon and Kuma's words, which didn't make any sense, and now some kind of "surprise" her mother had promised her. Her head felt heavy from all the mind weight.

"So, do you know why I wanted to come here with you?" Yoshiko kept rubbing her skin, hoping to brush the soreness from her body.

"No clue," Satsuki flatly responded.

"I haven't been here in a while, but around seven months ago, me and *Otousan* came here on a date. I'm pretty sure it was the night your *imouto* was conceived."

Satsuki stopped staring up at the lights and swiveled her entire body towards Yoshiko in surprise.

"Really? That's... seriously?" Even though she had to squint in order to make out her mother (staring at the twin lights had stamped her retinas with residual light circles the size of moons), she could tell that Yoshiko was all glimmery-like.

"You're surprised by this? Believe me, I was, too. There was no reason for our date. It wasn't like there was some festival or either one of our birthdays to celebrate. Our wedding anniversary wasn't for a few more months, either. Even the weather wasn't particularly nice. I remember being cold and wrapped up like a homeless person.

"Anyway, your father told me that he knew I was stressed out and that my face was starting to look like our neighbor, Sato-san. Pretty soon, he said, I was going to want a pet duck, so he wanted to make sure I would still want him and not end up like Sato-san and her webbed-footed friend!"

Both Satsuki and Yoshiko laughed at the thought of Sato-san and her silly duck.

"So, wait," Satsuki said, "was that the day you and Otousan told me you were going to see a movie?"

"Uh huh. We had pizza, and then I *thought* we were going to see a movie, but *Otousan* took me here, and instead, he talked to me about his father."

Satsuki didn't say anything. Her grandfather had passed away when she was very young, and it was hard to weep over yellowed photos of him, or for that matter, whenever her parents mentioned him at all.

Yoshiko continued. "I wasn't really sure why *Otousan* wanted to tell me about his father, but he just came out with it, and it turned out to be a good thing, as I felt much closer to *Otousan* afterwards."

"Why, what did he tell you about *Ojiisan*[31]?" Satsuki asked.

31. *ojiisan*—grandpa.

A coughing fit stopped Yoshiko from answering right away. She cleared her throat before Satsuki could ask if anything was wrong.

"Well, *Ojiisan* survived the bombing of Hiroshima, which I already knew, but what Otousan told me that completely took me by surprise was that *Ojiisan* also survived the bombing of Nagasaki."

Satsuki was speechless. Her mouth and eyes widened so much that her face looked like a triangle of dinner plates. She had already known that her grandfather was a *hibakusha*[32], but she had no idea he was a *nijū hibakusha*[33]!

"I know, pretty incredible, right?" Yoshiko said with a chuckle. "I asked if *Otousan* knew about this for a long time, but he said that *Ojiisan* made him promise not to tell anyone. He didn't want anyone to make a big deal out of it. Can you believe that? He was so humble and didn't think he was special at all. *Otousan* figured because it had been some time since *Ojiisan* passed away, he could finally tell me. His heart was burdened by keeping the secret, I guess, though I'm not sure if 'burden' is really the right word. I think what he really wanted was to share about what an amazing man *Ojiisan* was. I know they were very close."

"So, how did he survive?" Satsuki asked.

"Ah, right. *Ojiisan* worked on oil tankers, and at that time, Japan was struggling to keep their ships afloat. I guess it had something to do with submarines and the threat of those ships sinking being so great. So, he and a couple of colleagues were working in a shipyard but were suddenly ordered to Nagasaki for another assignment that was similar to the one they were doing in Hiroshima. This assignment was more urgent and needed to be finished in just a couple of weeks. What they ended up doing, *Otousan* didn't tell me. I don't think he even knew.

"Anyway, the morning that they were supposed to leave for Nagasaki, that was when the bomb dropped on Hiroshima. *Ojiisan* survived because he had forgotten his travelling documents in his locker at the shipyard. The authorities insisted that anyone going

---

32. *hibakusha*—survivors from the bombings of either Hiroshima or Nagasaki or both.
33. *nijū hibakusha*—a person who survived both bombings of Hiroshima and Nagasaki. These individuals are very rare.

back and forth in Japan carry papers at all times. He walked back from the bus station for almost twenty minutes, and that's when he saw the American B-29 bomber in the sky. A few moments later, a bright light filled the sky, and *Ojiisan* was thrown high into the air and into a ditch that was luckily filled with water. His colleagues at the bus station died instantly.

"*Ojiisan* lay there for a long time, only seeing darkness around him. When he got up, he walked around until he found a nearby dugout bomb shelter. The people inside told him that he had been badly burned. *Ojiisan* had severe burns on his arms, and half his hair had been singed completely off his head."

Satsuki wrinkled her eyebrows into a frown. "That's crazy," she said, grimacing.

"Yeah, but the most amazing part is what happened next," Yoshiko said, pausing for a moment before continuing. "*Ojiisan* stayed in Hiroshima for a few more days, going to a makeshift hospital that had thousands of people lying around with severe burns. He told *Otousan* that seeing these people, many of whom didn't even have faces and looked like they were skinned alive, made him feel ashamed for taking the doctor's time up. He received treatment for his wounds and was told that his right eardrum was almost blown out, but he would live.

"So, after that Monday, he spent time helping the wounded at the hospital but still felt he should continue with his orders and travel to Nagasaki. On Thursday morning, he took one of the few still-working trains left to Nagasaki and reported to his director who wanted him and his colleagues to get started working on some top-secret project. The director was actually mad at *Ojiisan* for saying that a bomb had wiped out the whole city. He couldn't believe it, but just as he was giving *Ojiisan* a verbal tongue lashing, there was another bright flash of light. *Ojiisan* knew what was coming next, so he ducked immediately for cover, and as the building crumpled around him and on top of his director, killing him and everyone else in the building, *Ojiisan* survived because he had taken refuge under a steel desk. He dug his way out of the wreckage, and to make a long story short, went back to Hiroshima and straight to the hospital that had treated his wounds just a few days before this happened."

Yoshiko gripped her back and stood up. She motioned for Satsuki to follow. It was time to head back home. A biker pedaled around them on the sidewalk in the direction they headed. Satsuki shook her head in silent reverence. Yoshiko took her daughter's hand. Satsuki gripped it and squeezed out her awe into Yoshiko's palm and fingers.

"Sacchan, I wanted to share this story with you because it seems like school has been stressing you out. And I know you're upset that *Otousan* is away on his trip, but he's like *Ojiisan*, who had a strong sense of responsibility. I think that this strong sense of responsibility passed on to *Otousan* and now to you. I think it's sort of funny that *Ojiisan* had *Otousan* at such a late age, and then—*ITAI!*"

Yoshiko bent over. Pain zapped her spine.

"Are you okay?" Satsuki asked.

"Yeah, I think so. I must have been sitting so long that my body is protesting the idea of walking around." Yoshiko's voice quivered with nervousness. The pain had resided immediately, but it had felt unlike anything she had ever experienced before. Or had she? She trolled her memories for when she had carried Satsuki in her belly. Nothing came to mind.

"I'll be fine. Look, the Motoyasu Bridge is just up ahead, and we can catch a bus home."

They walked a few more steps. Yoshiko was about to tell Satsuki how *Ojiisan* suffered from radiation sickness and the constant fear of death, and this was why he had chosen to have Hideo much later in life, but her ears suddenly felt like they were being clubbed. She let go of Satsuki's hand and jammed as many fingers as possible into both ear canals. Satsuki asked her mother what was wrong, but Yoshiko didn't hear her daughter's question. A burning sensation shot from the left side of her head to the right, overwhelming her capacity to respond. The volume of the entire world was quickly becoming unbearable. Yoshiko twirled around, searching for the source of the volume swell. There was a noisy crowd of teenage boys smoking cigarettes on a stone outcropping next to the

Motoyasu Bridge. One of the boys was skipping rocks across the water, and another one rode a silver sports bike in circles around the group. Where the sidewalk merged with the Motoyasu Bridge was also polluted with the sounds of traffic and a bird emulating a crosswalk signal on constant repeat.

"*Okaasan*, you're bleeding!"

Yoshiko couldn't hear what Satsuki was trying to tell her, but she did notice the absolute terror in her daughter's face.

"What's wrong?" she asked while unplugging her ears.

Satsuki pointed at the ground below her. "You're… bleeding!"

Yoshiko looked down and saw that the bottom of her white maternity dress, which hung a little lower than her knees, had a red bib. Beneath it, there was an oval-shaped puddle of blood. *Did I forget to wear a sanitary napkin today?* Yoshiko thought. *Wait a minute, why would I wear a napkin? I'm not spotting, and I haven't had my period since, since, I don't remember when!* She was running out of justifications to help her deny what was happening to her. Her underwear suddenly felt very wet and heavy.

"Oh my God…" Yoshiko lurched forward, somehow managing to stay on her feet, but not for long. She pressed her hands between her legs to try and plug the leak. Another blast of pain whipped down her back and straight to her crotch in response. She lost her balance.

She lost control.

By the time Yoshiko hit the ground, Satsuki was already fumbling around with her cell phone and trying to dial 119. When she reached a dispatch operator, she yelled into her cell phone that her mother was bleeding badly and they should come quickly to the Motoyasu Bridge. But the dispatch operator was more interested in telling Satsuki to calm down. This made Satsuki furious. "JUST FUCKING GET HERE NOW!" she screamed. The sound of her own voice charged everything with static fear. Satsuki fell down and began sobbing next to her mother.

"I think the baby is coming," Yoshiko managed to utter in between panting breaths. She didn't notice that her underwear had been torn into confetti shreds. Her hands had instinctually pulled the cotton apart. She was trying to do something, *anything*, to stop her uterus muscles from going into spasms and cramping. But nothing worked; her vagina had become a kettle pot filled with copper-smelling broth.

"What can I do? Just tell me what to do," Satsuki asked in a panic. She picked Yoshiko's head up and put it in her lap.

Blades of grass decorated Yoshiko's cheeks and forehead. Tears filled her eyes. Spit foamed in the corners of her lips. "I, I, I… don't know. I just … it hurts. You shouldn't swear at peo… ple."

Yoshiko tried to smile, but her mouth wouldn't stop clamoring for air. Her whole body was stuck on autopilot, trying to bring her in for a safe landing. *If the baby is born now, can she live?* she wondered. *I'm only around 28 weeks, so maybe this is just a bad case of Braxton Hicks contractions. Damn it! I can't remember if the lungs are developed enough now for her to live on her own. What did Dr. Yoshimoto call it? Was it the age of via, via, via…*

"Somebody help! Please!" Satsuki's screams interrupted Yoshiko's thoughts.

She stared hard at her daughter, who was frantically waving at the group of boys and anyone else who would pay attention. Yoshiko's face wilted. The boy on the bike pedaled over, followed by two more of his pals, and a young couple who were walking hand-in-hand down the sidewalk trail hurried towards where they were in the ring of scarlet grass.

"Please… Sacchan… I'm embarrassed. I don't want… to bother… anyone."

Yoshiko wanted to sit up and show everyone she was okay, but her body was fastened to some invisible board that was super-glued to the earth. Suddenly what felt like an iron scourge lashed at her insides and caused her body to spasm with color-draining agony. Her voice became unhinged. Screams vomited from her mouth. Yet before her interior was shredded by an invisible lictor, she remembered what Dr. Yoshimoto had told her:

Viability.

Another pain spike ripped her further apart. Yoshiko dug her nails into the ground. Clumps of grass came flying up from underneath her shaky hands.

"NO! NO! NO! PLEASE, NOT MY BABY!!!! NOOOOOO!!!!"

Her legs had spread open involuntarily, and her vagina emitted a horrible sucking sound, like the sound of a backed-up septic tank being pumped out into a hose. She mustered enough strength to lift her head and peer down at her blood-splattered legs. What she witnessed was something that she would never forget for the rest of her life: a twisted rope of licorice-colored flesh shot out of her vagina and into the air. It bent into a ninety-degree arc, then hurtled straight to the ground with a large, splashing noise.

The boy on the bike lost his balance and fell over. His friends and the couple stopped running, their mouths open wide. They, along with Satsuki, were paralyzed in muted shock.

Yoshiko had given birth to an arm.

Later, while riding in the ambulance, Satsuki dipped a white cloth in water and held it on her mother's forehead, but her tears were already doing the job. Yoshiko had passed out seconds after she had expelled the arm. She was also in hypovolemic shock from blood loss. The paramedics told Satsuki that her mother was having a miscarriage, and under their breath, she could hear them tell each other that it was the worst miscarriage they had ever seen. Satsuki was rattled by their confession. Somebody else in the front of the ambulance asked her where her father was or if there were any other relatives they could call. Satsuki's tongue couldn't do anything but tremble. She prayed to Buddha in her mind, even though she had never once tried to ask Him for anything. She prayed that He would save her mother and her little sister.

Yoshiko opened her eyes and found herself in the dream with all the businessmen and women standing on an incline. She could see the ceiling, still covered in puffy smoke, and the outline of a door about thirty businesspeople in front of her. She was wearing her white maternity dress but nothing else. No shoes, no underwear, no purple scarf. A putrid smell lingered in the air.

She started to squeeze between all the people in their vented black jackets and long–sleeved, blue blouses, struggling for what seemed like hours to reach the top of the incline. At some point, the ground, as she knew it would, became a steep, vertical tilt. She fell to her knees, scraping against the surface of the incline. It felt oddly familiar. Yoshiko noticed that the ground was actually a series of unevenly woven *tatami* mats. She hooked her hands into their edges, trying to slink her way up.

A strong odor approached from all sides, mixing with the stench of decay already present. She expected it to be from the piss (like in the other dream), but this smell was more metallic than acrid. She didn't need to guess what it was. A blood river had begun flowing down the incline, threatening to carry her away in its powerful undercurrent. She managed to grab onto the ankles and arms all around her and pull herself up to the doorway. There was a room inside it. She planted her hands on either side of the doorway and lunged forward.

It took a few minutes before Yoshiko caught her breath and stood up. Thankfully, the ground inside the room wasn't vertical. She turned around to face the door, but a lumpy cloud of smoke filled the threshold, forcing her to turn back around and move deeper into the room. It was pitch black and endless in every direction, except in the direction she faced.

Standing in front of her was a solid panelled baby crib on four long, wooden legs. It was glazed in the room's blackness. The front and back boards didn't reach much higher than Yoshiko's stomach, but the frame's width and overall size was spacious enough that it could contain comfortable bedding. Perfect for a newborn.

Yoshiko walked towards the crib like she was in a funeral procession, unsure if she wanted to see what was inside of it or not. The mere sight of it made her want to cry. *Go back, go back,* she tried to convince herself, but it was useless. Something pushed her forward.

Drip, Drip, Drip, DRip, DRip, DRip, DRip, DRip, DRIp, DRIp, DRIp, DRIp, DRIP, DRIP, DRIP...

With every step that Yoshiko took forward, the dripping sound grew louder. It wasn't until she reached the front of the crib that she noticed dark red liquid leaking out of every crack in the crib's sideboards.

Drip, Drip, Drip, DRip, DRip, DRip, DRip, DRip, DRIp, DRIp, DRIp, DRIP, DRIP, DRIP, drip...

The crib was full of blood, draining through the cracks and onto the ground (and subsequently out the doorway to the room), yet at the same time, remaining completely full. The blood swished around like somebody was stirring it with a ladle, but nobody was there.

Yoshiko leaned cautiously over the crib, trembling from nausea and sadness. "No, no, no, no," she whimpered. This was the reward for climbing to the top of the incline? It didn't make sense! She knew that this was a dream and that dreams rarely, if ever, conform to the rules of logic, but seeing the crib made her want to scream and burst into tears from a very real feeling of complete and utter disappointment—the kind that melds with your consciousness and becomes a part of you.

Deep down inside, Yoshiko knew why she felt this way all of a sudden, but didn't want to accept the reason. Didn't want to admit it, either. She focused instead on the sobs escaping her lips, with only a single question sloshing around her brain: *I've become hollow, haven't I? Hollow, afraid, empty... incomplete.* As the dark red liquid continued to pour out of the cracks in the sideboards, clear liquid sorrow bloomed from her pores.

DRIPDRIPDRIPDRIPDRIPDRIP... DRIP... DRIP... DRIP... DRIP... DRIP. DRIP. DRIP.

Suddenly, bubbles floated to the surface of the crib's swirling blood pond. Yoshiko's tear-slicked eyes opened wider than she thought was possible. "Nooooo," her lips wordlessly mouthed. *Please don't be in there. Please. Please. I can't face you.*

She managed to shake her feet out of their fear entropy and step away from the crib, but by then, it was too late. A shrill whistling noise sounded off above her head. As Yoshiko lifted her blinkless gaze upwards, an overgrown fetus burst out of the ceiling's murk and rocketed into the crib. It shot straight to the bottom of the blood pond, banging against the crib's floor with a loud THUD, but just as quickly, it sprung back up to the surface, twisting and jerking in every direction.

The impact drenched Yoshiko in bowlfuls of blood. Her vision turned crimson. She wanted to scream, but the only sound that slipped from her mouth was a long, scratchy moan. Dryness had lacerated her scorched vocal cords. Her throat filled with bile. She tried turning around to run, but the feeling of paralysis had returned. It pooled in her empty stomach and gradually spread throughout her entire body. She couldn't cry or vomit or move a muscle. The only choice she had was to squint at the fetus through the blood dripping into her eyes.

That's when she noticed: she wasn't the only one in a muted, semi-blind state. The fetus's mouth and eyes were sealed shut with placental slime.

Was that all they had in common?

It began coming back to Yoshiko in perfect, high-definition clarity: the clumps of grass she dug her fingernails into, her underwear that felt like a hundred-pound dumbbell made of blood-soaked cotton, the absolute fright steam-rolled on Satsuki's face, the boy falling off his bike, the licorice-colored rope of flesh between her legs. But before Yoshiko could decipher what she was seeing in this dream and if it played any role in what had already happened, the ground shook with earthquake force, knocking her completely off balance. She reflexively reached for the crib wall, but missed it, plunging elbow-deep into the gore.

The crib's screws threatened to pop right out of their holes from the room's violent contractions. Yoshiko's arms felt like they were about to pop right out of their sockets along with them. Both she and the crib vibrated in sync with the floor, the walls, the world. It seemed, at any moment, that the dream itself would split in half and drop her into the stasis of darkness—tired, sore, and distant.

Blood spilled over all four sides of the crib, spattering red everywhere. Yoshiko repeatedly slipped on the wet ground but managed somehow to keep her balance, only to dunk her entire upper body into the crib during every tremor. Each time this happened, streams of blood wriggled like tapeworms into her nose and mouth. Perhaps even worse than this, the fetus darted around like a pinball in the erupting blood and ricocheted off her face, arms, breasts. Every hair on her body stood on end when its slick, rubbery flesh touched her own skin. She tried slapping it away, and that's when she saw something that made her wish she'd been stabbed in both eyes:

One of the fetus's arms was missing, and in its place was a rotting stump.

The echoes in the tunnel were not from distant murmurs. They were voices from the television. Seul Bi was in the middle of a deep slumber and an even deeper dream, wandering around a moss-speckled cavern, complete with mazes and mildew wrapping itself around her feet with every step. It wasn't until a capricious wind bounced into her, nipping at her neck and anywhere else that flesh was exposed, that her eyelids fluttered open.

An advertisement about a new kind of diet program was on, and that meant it was late. Probably very late. The show had played after midnight every single evening that Seul Bi had been awake during the past month.

"Not this shit again," Seul Bi whined into her pillow. She rolled out of bed and went to the kitchen.

The nightshade that mixed with the soft glow of the television screen was disorienting. She wasn't sure about the exact time she had lost consciousness, but it had been sometime before noon. Her mind hadn't immediately let her sleep after getting back from work yesterday morning. She had sat on her bed with a stoic expression on her face, contemplating her night at Rainbow. *Maybe it was better to forget about what had happened.* That was the last thing she remembered thinking before passing out.

"Hmm... what should I eat?" Seul Bi decided on chicken ramen noodles after inspecting some leftover spaghetti made by her Aunt Debbie. She shoved a glass under her sink's faucet and guzzled an entire glass of water. She did it again, then walked over to the frosted window beside her bed. Immediately she began to shiver.

"Fucking cold! Christ!"

She looked down and realized that she was only wearing a thin, spaghetti-strap tee and her favorite polka-dot, boy-short underwear. They barely covered anything on her slender body. She jerked back from the cold seeping through a slit in the window frame, then grabbed the comforter from the bed and wrapped herself in it.

Chicago is out there, hiding in the snow, she thought. The Windy City threatened to pounce on Evanston with its rimy claws. Growing up in Evanston, she had never wanted to visit Chicago. Evanston was filled with people who would say "good morning" to you if you passed them on the sidewalk after working an all-night shift. If your eyes made contact, people would even smile in your direction. Chicagoans, however, never reciprocated any kind of neighborly etiquette. Their eyes were either tracing the cracks in the street or staring straight ahead.

Ironically, Seul Bi had at age twelve perfected the museum sculpture mien of Chicagoans. On her very best days, a very slight upwards turn of her lips would flicker across her face when somebody passed her on the street. She could easily pass herself off as somebody who had lived in Chicago her whole life.

However, only a handful of times in the past ten years did she try exploring the city by herself, but even then, she would only venture as far as Rogers Park. Whenever Beverly joked with her about this, Seul Bi always told her that it was because she didn't need to go anywhere else to find great food except the multi-ethnic neighborhoods of Rogers Park, but that was a complete lie. The rest of the city was too intimidating for Seul Bi. It was menacing, and somehow waiting even, to drag her away into a skyscraper dungeon as its prisoner.

"Ahh, hot, hot, hot!!"

Seul Bi slurped the ramen in between taking sips of water. The stupid diet infomercial continued chirping on in the background. She couldn't take it anymore. She turned off the television and waited for her laptop's monitor screen to flash the familiar Windows logo. Once the internet clicked on, she logged on to her Hotmail account and found she had one unread message. It was from somebody with an unusual email address, one she had never seen in her inbox before: Narumiruna444@yahoo.co.jp.

Seul Bi's eyebrows arched. The message was sent only a few minutes before she had awakened. *That's strange. Who would be sending me something so late?* She thought. The subject line was blank. *Probably spam.* She swallowed more ramen noodles and opened the message anyway:

```
Dear Miss Seul Bi,
I saw your pictures online and was very
moved by them. I am interested in buying your
pictures. I would like all of them if they
are still available. Is $600 ($100 for each
picture) acceptable to you? I am sorry if the
amount is too low. Please let me know if you
would accept my offer when you have the time.
Thank you -Narumi
msn messenger: Naru444
```

"Holy shit!" Seul Bi yelled. She grabbed her phone to text her cousin about what she had just read. A minute passed before Beverly's response came back:

```
Can't talk right now. Busy.
```

Seul Bi didn't even have to guess what she was busy doing. *I just wonder how Mark feels about her taking the time to text me back while they're fucking,* she thought. *Whatever.*

Seul Bi read Narumi's message over and over again. She imagined herself back in sixth grade and finishing her tests several minutes before anyone else in her class. This had happened regularly, and in every single instance, she would be careful to lay her pencil down without her peers knowing and then scan the room to see if anyone else was close to being done. It had been her habit to wait for somebody else to take their test up front for the teacher to grade before turning in her own work. She didn't want to draw too much attention to herself in class. At home was a different matter. She was a giddy mess on those days, shrieking to her parents about being first to finish and then basking in their praise for a job well done. She felt the same way now as she did back then.

And even though Seul Bi's parents weren't around anymore, and her debauched cousin was distracted, as usual, with her boyfriend, she wanted to share her happiness with somebody. Anybody. She decided to sign into her MSN instant messenger account and check to see if this Narumi was online. Before she could even invite Narumi to be her friend, her IM screen started to flash bright orange. A request to be added to Narumi's friend list filled the screen, followed by a chat box popping into view.

```
Naru444: Hello? Is this Miss Seul Bi?
```

Seul Bi's hands flicked away from the keyboard. It was like an electrical spark had zapped her fingertips. *What the hell... was she, like, waiting for me, or something, to sign on?* she thought. The sign-in dot next to this Narumi's name was bright green, indicating she was definitely online. Seul Bi inched back to her keyboard and began typing.

```
LSBwillsetUfree: Hi how are you? This is
Seul Bi. Are you the person who wants to
buy my drawings?
Naru444: YES!!!!
LSBwillsetUfree: Where are you from?
Naru444: I am from Japan. I found your site
online and really enjoy your pictures.
LSBwillsetUfree: Japan? Really? That's so
crazy! Thank you so much!
Naru444: Please forgive my low offer of
money. It is all I have at the moment.
```

Seul Bi pushed her hair out of her face. It had crept in between her and the laptop monitor. She couldn't care less about the money and was still acclimating to the idea of being recognized by somebody who existed on an entirely different continent.

```
LSBwillsetUfree: No, it really is more
than enough. I have a PayPal account you can
send the money to if that is easiest for you.
```

```
Naru444: That is fine! I will send tomorrow.
I am sorry but I am really busy at this
moment. Could I message you again
tomorrow night?
LSBwillsetUfree: Sure. Same time?
Naru444: Yes. I want to ask you something
before I send the money. Is that acceptable
to you Miss Seul Bi?
LSBwillsetUfree: Sure. Just call me Seul Bi.
Naru444: OK. I will ask you my question when
we speak tomorrow. Good night.
LSBwillsetUfree: Same to you.
```

Seul Bi was intrigued by the question this mysterious individual wanted to ask. She clicked the "Yes" option to Narumi's friend request and then tried to eat more noodles, but her hunger was dissolved in jittery anticipation. She tossed them in the garbage can by her computer desk, then turned off the laptop and assumed the fetal position on the bed.

I'm not tired, but I need to rest, damnit! I wish I could just fast forward to tomorrow night. What does she want to ask me? And why did she message me but then leave so quickly like that? Ahh. Maybe this is a joke being played on me. Or maybe I'm still sleeping, or just, just, fuck. I dunno. My life has become a Jean Cocteau movie. I should have paid more attention in art cinema class. Then I would know what I'm saying. Meh. I must be tired after all. Time for act one, act two, act three... finit?

Seul Bi felt like this was just the beginning of something, but of what, she didn't know.

Aiko sifted her fingers through Satsuki's hair. The two of them were half asleep and squished together on two chairs that were leg locked beside Yoshiko's hospital bed. It was hours after the ambulance had docked in Hiroshima Municipal Hospital and hospital staff carted Yoshiko off to surgery. Doctor Yoshimoto and a team of surgeons had not been able to save the baby; they had watched in helpless horror as it had been pushed out of Yoshiko's uterus in pieces. They did, however, save Yoshiko after almost losing her due to so much blood loss. An intensive treatment of I.V. fluids and pain medicine had stabilized her, restored her to consciousness, but she still needed to be monitored for at least a few days. Aiko watched her older sister's eyes flip-flop underneath their lids. *She must be having one hell of a dream*, Aiko thought to herself.

Aiko covered herself and Satsuki with an extra linen blanket from the hospital room's closet. Her frilly blouse and business jacket didn't do much to stop the cold breeze gushing out of the air vents. She had been in a late teleconference meeting with her boss, who had been, as usual, out of the office. After excusing herself politely, she jumped into a cab and arrived thirty minutes after Yoshiko had been rushed into surgery.

She had found Satsuki lying down on a bench in a hallway adjacent to the surgical unit. It didn't take long for her niece to curl up on her lap. The only thing she felt could be done at the moment was try to calm the poor girl down, who was hyperventilating from shock and swept up in a crying cyclone. But when she asked about what had happened to Yoshiko, the only response she got was her jacket and blouse drenched in tears, snot, and saliva. *It's amazing how much comes out of us when we hurt*, Aiko considered while wincing from holding back her own tears. *But I can't cry right now. I have to be strong for Sacchan and remain calm for both*

Sacchan and Neechan's sake. I can't let the fireball of rage inside of me consume my actions or my thoughts.

Aiko had a reason to be pissed off. Hideo had waited an hour to return her call after she had left a message urging him to come home immediately. When he called back, she explained to him what had happened, but he told her that he couldn't fly back from South Korea for another two days. He then asked if she could look after Yoshiko and Satsuki until he came home. She hung up without saying a word.

Yoshiko was a buffer between Hideo and Aiko, who had disliked each other ever since the first time they shook hands in front of the Hiroshima Carps' baseball stadium. She had been dating Hideo for almost a year, and had decided it was time for her sister to meet the man she was falling in love with. They all decided it would be best to meet at a Carps baseball game.

There was something off about the way Hideo had acted towards Aiko. Maybe he was trying too hard? Or perhaps it was his gratuitous groping of Yoshiko, like he needed to let everyone around them know what a great couple they were. Aiko couldn't figure it out.

His attempt at small talk also irked her. He would ask her a question and then get distracted by Yoshiko and the game. And no matter how many times he apologized for the interruptions, she only grew more acerbic towards him. Finally, by the seventh inning, Aiko dragged her sister into a bathroom to complain.

"What do you see in him? He is immature and annoying, and I know that I'm younger than you and don't know anything about boys, but seriously, what do you see in this guy?" Aiko protested.

Yoshiko wagged her right pointer finger in the air. "You're right, you don't know anything about guys. The last guy you dated was also the guy who broke your heart, so how can you like any guy you meet? Hideo is always there for me and doesn't let my phone calls go to voicemail, unlike some people I know. And he buys me gifts and treats me like a queen. I have dated a couple of men in my past, and he is the most qualified to love me. I wanted you to give me your honest opinion, but now I realize that's not possible, is it?"

What could she say to that? Aiko had been hurt by her last boyfriend, even though they had only gone out for three months. But it had been her longest relationship, and she had believed that things had been going really well between them, until one night, after an argument, her boyfriend said he "wasn't happy anymore in the relationship." Aiko was so shocked that she barely could ask why.

It was about her long work hours and her prudish behavior in the bedroom, he complained. When she asked what the hell he was talking about, he simply shrugged and told her that this shouldn't come as a surprise. "You didn't even notice the fact that, half the time, when I texted you at work, I was saying nice things to you and trying to make you feel good, but you never once texted me back anything in return," he said. "And you give really, really shitty blowjobs."

His words were like a machete hack to her heart. They broke up the Friday before Golden Week started, so she turned her cell phone off, bought four six-packs of Asahi beer, and lay in bed for five days straight. She spent most of her vacation drinking and watching rented soapy teen dramas. The rest of the time she spent relentlessly questioning herself about ignoring his messages and what she did wrong during oral sex. It had been her first time performing fellatio on any man, but she had researched online what to do and even watched porn (something she had never done before) to learn how the experts do it. Thanks to these preparations, she eventually felt confident that her oral skills were sufficient enough to make him cum.

And cum he did! She constantly blew him at the beginning of their relationship, never failing once to make him climax. Yet towards the end of their relationship, he would ask her to stop, despite not ejaculating. He always insisted that it wasn't her fault and told her that she had the best blowjob skills of any woman he had ever dated. She believed him each time, never questioning whether or not he had liked it. But his change in behavior didn't make sense to her. And she didn't know which was worse, the fact that he had lied to her about her blowjob skills, or that she couldn't figure out what made him lose interest in their relationship.

Ignoring his text messages. Giving "really, really shitty blow-jobs." Were these accusations or statements of fact? Whatever they were, Aiko was shocked into apathy and denial because of them. And so, after that Golden Week, she decided on two things: to dedicate herself to work first and foremost, and to making sure no man would ever take a surprise dump on her heart again.

Or her sister's heart.

I knew it. I fucking knew it. You are a shitty bastard after all. Aiko's mind repeated these phrases over and over again. It was all she could do to keep from yelling at full-lung volume. She checked her watch: 2:00 a.m. They had been at the hospital for hours, and the moon was spreading its milky light in wet streaks across everything in the room. Aiko pulled the blanket that covered her and Satsuki up around her neck and chin. For some reason, she felt naked in the glowing surroundings. Maybe it was because Yoshiko was always the responsible older sister, the more approachable half of their sisterly duo. She was the good daughter, too—never forgetting to send a card or visit their parents on every birthday and anniversary right up to their deaths. Aiko had consistent amnesia about these things, but she couldn't help being enabled by Yoshiko's sense of duty to everyone she cared about.

And now the one person she cared about more than her parents or me, even enough to be impregnated by, isn't here when she NEEDS him the most, Aiko mentally complained to herself. She reached over to stroke her sister's tangled and matted hair. All the shade left in the room seemed to be gathered around her older sister's body. Aiko dangled her hand over Yoshiko, unable to penetrate the darkness like it was penetrating her.

"I'm sorry I got your blouse all wet."

Aiko jumped. Satsuki's voice was wire thin, but in the sound-sucking vacuum of the bleak hospital room, her words sounded like shrieks blasting out of a megaphone.

"What? It's no problem. Why did you wake up?"

Satsuki sat up with a gaping yawn. "How can I really sleep with everything that's happened, you know? I mean, I'm tired, but... I dunno. I guess I can't even think right now."

"I know what you mean," Aiko said. She felt a yawn from deep inside her chest. For a split second, she wondered why people seem to automatically yawn when somebody else around them does. "Well, don't worry, okay? Everything is going to be all right. Your mom lost a lot of blood, but she's getting really good medicine and could be out of here as early as tomorrow."

"Is *Otousan* here?" Satsuki asked, ignoring Aiko's reassurances.

"No, he's not."

"Oh." Satsuki's face seemed to droop straight down to the linoleum floor.

Aiko sighed. "Well, I mean, he will be here. I'm not sure about tonight, but he'll be here soon enough. Don't worry, sweetie." Aiko hated to lie, but telling Satsuki the truth that Hideo wouldn't be around for at least another two days would probably crush her. She hoped that Hideo would somehow *try* to make it back sooner, but her faith in him had lasted just seven innings of a baseball game and had never returned. She had, at best, tolerated Hideo for the sake of her sister.

Not so anymore. *You fucking bastard,* Aiko thought to herself, gritting her teeth. *You cock-sucking piece of shit. I hope she leaves you. I really, really do.*

"Thanks for being here," Satsuki said, pressing her slippery and shaky arms lightly around Aiko's neck.

"What? Oh, you're welcome." At first, Aiko embraced her niece, thankful for being released from the hate cage where her thoughts were tearing Hideo to shreds. Satsuki's gratitude was just what she needed to calm down. But then a blistering heat surrounded her niece, and seconds later, the hospital room felt like a closet with windows for walls on the hottest day of summer.

"Hey, do you have a fever? You feel really hot," Aiko said, pressing her hands against Satsuki's face. A burning sensation shot through her fingertips.

"I do?" Satsuki dragged her fingers across her forehead. "I didn't realize—"

"Let me get you some water," Aiko interrupted. When she stood up, Aiko didn't take more than two steps before her legs gave out from under her. She nearly fell flat on her face. Numbness from sitting in the chair all night spiked the nerve endings in her lower body. She quickly steadied herself but waited until some feeling returned to her legs before attempting to walk again. If this had been any other time, Aiko might have laughed at herself, but because Satsuki didn't notice her clumsiness, didn't even snicker, she thought it best to pretend like nothing happened.

"I know water won't take a fever away, but at least you can *feel* cooler, you know? Besides, I was going to get myself a drink, anyway. I need to wake up."

"Thanks," Satsuki dragged. She watched her aunt hobble out of the room.

When Aiko was out of view, Satsuki's eyes sharpened into razorblade slits, and her lips curled into a tightly-wound, steel trap. She recalled what happened earlier; every detail and drop of blood came rushing back to the front of her mind. Her first inclination was to cry, but she had done enough of that already. No, instead she needed somebody to blame for what had happened, for the death of her little sister. Her best friend. Her equalizer. Her savior from the bottom-of-the-ocean loneliness that she felt.

Her gaze wandered over to where her mother was piled underneath blankets like a wrecked car in a junkyard. She made up her mind to blame the world and everyone in it for what had happened. Any sort of need for human interaction began to drain out of her and was replaced with a giant bag of scalpels. People would just be bags of bones and organs, and she would cut them all up and toss them in the trash. Yes! Yes! Yes! This was the only way to make it right, the only way to avenge her *imouto's* death.

As Satsuki curled up on the chair, a shrill, whistling noise panned back and forth in her ears. It absorbed the distant chatter of nurses at the medical station down the hall, the I.V. bag shooting medicine into the tubes buried in Yoshiko's right forearm, the occasional creaking from the ventilation shafts. What the hell was causing this noise in her ears? Was she imagining it? Was this a way to distract herself from the fact that her mother was lying in the hospital bed with stitches between her legs? She didn't think so, but then again, she couldn't be sure—it had become so loud in her ears that she couldn't hear her own thoughts.

Her brain felt like it was being euthanized. There seemed to be no point in resisting. She stood up, walked around the room, tried covering her ears, even tried stepping briefly into the hospital hallway to look for her aunt (Where did she go, anyway? There was a water fountain a few feet away from Yoshiko's hospital room). Other than the volume being jacked up to eleven on her skull's amplifier, nothing changed.

Still, this did not particularly upset or scare Satsuki; the more she concentrated on the noise, the more she heard a familiar melody buried inside it.

It's dissolving. It's vanishing. It's unraveling. It's passing away, without a trace...

It was like waiting in line for hours to get movie tickets and not knowing if the movie would be sold out by the time she reached the box office window. Seul Bi knew this would be a day that clawed at her insides with apprehension. Still, she tried to stay busy, heading out to her favorite coffee shop for a chai latte and afterwards to the Evanston Barnes & Noble, which was filled with reliable distractions: Flamenco-style music playing over invisible speakers at a volume level just slightly above comfortable, a new display shelf being put together by employees, people scurrying around the two-story bookstore trying to find a magazine or book to read. People being sucked into paper word-vacuums.

There wasn't a seat of any kind available on either level of the store. Seul Bi paused at the front entrance to consider the easiest way to the magazine racks. More than likely, she would have to stand and read the magazines, but that never bothered her. She was used to, and even liked, the bookstore being this busy.

Seul Bi zigzagged between the new release tables and readers both sitting and standing until she reached the familiar sight of magazines on rows of endcap displays. The magazine section was not that big, but its aisles were nearly full.

She made her way towards the arts and entertainment section. Two young women, both wearing black aprons and matching black khakis, stood there huddled together while flipping through the same *Cosmopolitan* magazine. They talked about cutting hair. *They're probably from the cosmetology academy a few buildings down from here*, Seul Bi guessed. She ignored their pesky chatter and eventually spotted a brand new issue of *Hi-Fructose*. She scooted past the two women and grabbed the magazine off the rack.

Seul Bi devoured every article and picture in the magazine. Her interest peaked with a feature on the Japanese wood painter Audrey Kawasaki. The artist's erotic depictions of adolescent girls tucked away in Art Nouveau landscapes flung Seul Bi into a trance. She imagined her hand drawings being the subject of feature articles. She pictured herself as the shy but magnetic center of attention in Chicago's art community. But did she really want these things? It seemed like her mind was pulling her in a different direction.

A few hours after leaving the bookstore, Seul Bi sat on her apartment floor and sketched the Kona skyline of her memories. She drew palm trees that swooshed from an invisible breeze and an ocean whose coastline was someplace outside the Strathmore paper's edge. She also drew several bridges that hovered just above the waves. Her mind needed to release its creative energy. Well, that, and it served as a reliable distraction from another night in Evanston, which would surely bring with it an icy coma and more waiting around for what Narumi was going to ask.

Seul Bi paused from drawing to text Beverly. *A conversation with her would be a definite time eater*, she thought, but there was no response from her cousin.

A draft wind from the window coiled itself around everything in the apartment, causing rows of tiny bumps like rivets on a steamship to form all over Seul Bi's skin. In the summertime, Seul Bi would lightly caress with her fingertips the parts of her back she could reach and also her arms and ribs to make goose bumps swell up, but their appearance now felt like winter's leprosy. She decided to abandon her sketch and jump into the blankets on her bed for warmth. A few minutes later, she closed her eyes and saw several bridges that hung over ocean water. She skipped down one of them, falling asleep as she crossed over to a sun-drenched plateau.

The familiar bleep from her laptop's tiny speakers signaled it was time. Seul Bi peered at the clock on her desk. She had fallen asleep for little more than an hour. There was no doubt that Narumi was the person making her computer chirp. Who else would it be?

Yawning, Seul Bi tippy-toe-stretched and jogged in place for a few seconds before looking at her chat screen's contents.

```
Naru444: Hello Miss Seul Bi? Are you there?
LSBwillsetUfree: Narumi? Konnichiwa.
Naru444: Konnichiwa. You speak Japanese?
Genki desu ka?
LSBwillsetUfree: No, not at all. I only know
a little bit from watching Japanese movies
and anime. What is "Genki desu ka"?
Naru 444: "Genki desu ka" means how are you?
LSBwillsetUfree: Oh, right. Thanks for ex-
plaining! I'm fine. How are you?
Naru444: I'm great. Were you sleeping?
LSBwillsetUfree: No. Well, yes, but… it's ok.
I was waiting for your message.
```

Seul Bi had checked her laptop earlier in the day and realized that it would be the middle of the day in Japan when they were supposed to speak with each other. She yawned again and looked towards her window. Outside was a milk splatter.

```
LSBwillsetUfree: How is the weather where
you live?
Naru444: I have not gone outside today. I
have not been outside for a few days…
LSBwillsetUfree: Why?
Naru444: I have not been feeling well.
```

Seul Bi wondered how she could have been so busy the other night when she hadn't left her home and was sick. Maybe this is what she had meant by saying she was busy, though; Seul Bi didn't want to talk to anyone either whenever she was under the weather.

```
LSBwillsetUfree: I hope you feel better.
Naru444: Arigato gozaimasu. That means "thank
you." Would you like to learn more Japanese?
LSBwillsetUfree: I would love to. I
sort of feel like I speak a different
language already.
```

Naru444: Really? why?

LSBwillsetUfree: well, I was adopted. Plus
I'm always quiet and give off a "foreigner"
vibe to everyone I meet. No offense to you
of course.

Naru444: No offense taken. You say you were
adopted? What is your nationality?

LSBwillsetUfree: Korean. My parents went to
Korea to adopt me. My dad was Italian and my
mother was Jewish, so people looked at me
funny when they saw me with them, back when I
was a kid.

Naru444: That is very interesting. I did not
guess you were Korean.

LSBwillsetUfree: well, except for where I was
born, I don't identify myself really with
being Korean. I really am not sure what to
identify myself as anymore...

Naru444: well, what about your parents? Do
you feel you are Italian or Jewish like them?

LSBwillsetUfree: I don't identify myself with
either of them. My parents died when I was a
kid so I didn't get to know them very well.

Naru444: I am so sorry. I did not mean to
bring up such a painful memory.

LSBwillsetUfree: It's ok. It was a long
time ago.

For Seul Bi, saying "it was a long time ago" was a convenient way to stop questions about what happened to her parents, but it was not really accurate at all. She had replayed the morning they died in her head so many times it might as well have been happening now! Thankfully, most people didn't ask any more questions once they got her pre-programmed answer. And even if they were still curious, she deflected questions by asking questions. This was easy enough to do; everyone she knew practically got high off talking about themselves. So she resorted to one basic formula that kept everyone away from digging into her past: ask questions, wait for the response, repeat. It was simple.

Her role as counselor at Rainbow was perfect for this reason. She never needed to explain how she felt about her past or her identity. She could focus on the patients and their tragedies and sorrows. And there were plenty of these things to go around at Rainbow. She was always busy, handling emotional outbursts or cutting episodes or suicide attempts. Not sharing anything personal was a way to avoid getting too close to patients who, if given the chance, would use any sort of self-confession to manipulate her to get what they want. But she had been careful to confide in neither the patients nor the staff at Rainbow, and she managed to keep those around her far away from ever knowing too much about her life.

Yet something about Narumi made Seul Bi want to answer all her questions. She was shocked she could feel this way after being guarded for so long. Narumi seemed so interested in both her and her artwork. Maybe it was time to open up to somebody, and who better than somebody who lives in a distant country and could vanish with a single mouse click?

Seul Bi did have one question for Narumi though:

LSBwillsetUfree: So yesterday you said there
was a question you wanted to ask me. What
was it?

A long pause followed. Seul Bi checked to make sure the internet was still working. The network icon still gleamed brightly on the laptop's taskbar—no problem there. She was about to ask Narumi if she was still there when the dialogue box lit up with a response:

Naru444: I am sorry. I did not mean to keep
you waiting. I was not sure if I should
ask you the question anymore. You have been
through loss in your life and I can sense you
are sad.

LSBwillsetUfree: No, it's totally ok. Like I
said, it was a long time ago, and you seem so
nice and interested in me! It actually feels…
good in a way. Plus, you ARE buying my
drawings and I don't want you to change your
mind lol.
Naru444: Arigato. Ok, I wanted to know… what
inspired your drawings?

Seul Bi began to type one of her standardized responses but
hesitated. Beverly and Aunt Debbie always asked this kind of question, and she always answered them with "I don't know," or "I guess
it just sort of came to me." Better to be ambiguous, she thought.
She didn't want to tell them the reasons. Would they really want to
know why she was obsessed with sketching hands and arms? Yet
Seul Bi suspected that Narumi was going to ask her something like
this. She hadn't fretted about it, though. In fact, it was the opposite: she'd anticipated the inquiry with all the fervor of a hospital
patient about to receive a new kidney. Or heart.

Seul Bi continued typing.

LSBwillsetUfree: I have never told anybody
this, but it's what I saw the day my parents
died.

CHAPTER 23

A DOOR.

A CAT.

LAST CHANCE.

On the afternoon that Yoshiko left the hospital, the rain finally came. It leaked out of the air like water from an old hotel shower faucet. The resulting syrupy drizzle stuck to Satsuki, Aiko, and Yoshiko the second they exited the hospital's main entrance doors. There was no doubt in their minds that the day would follow the summer script of pouring humid molasses all over Hiroshima City. They were right, too—neither the rain nor the heat let up until close to midnight that evening.

Yoshiko had spent one night in the hospital and miraculously recovered by the next morning. Well, physically, at least. The blood loss had not been enough to cause any permanent damage, but the psychological pain inflicted was anybody's guess.

Yoshiko meekly nodded and didn't say a single word when she crawled into her bed back home. Right before lying down, she hugged Aiko but shook her head side to side when asked if she needed a glass of water or hot tea.

Aiko could sense that Yoshiko didn't want to speak about what had happened. She stood for a moment in her sister's bedroom, then went out to the kitchen and flicked on the electric tea maker. Its grumbling gears couldn't be heard over the thunderclaps outside. It seemed like an entire crowd from a Hiroshima Carps baseball game was standing inside the apartment and cheering. Aiko couldn't hear anything but the storm.

Right after coming home, Satsuki went to her room and shut herself inside. Chibita had been waiting for her by the bedroom door, purring with anticipation of being fed. Satsuki scooped up the hungry cat and tossed him lightly onto the bed.

"Are you hungry, Chi-chan? Sorry we didn't come home last night. Were you worried about us?"

Satsuki filled Chibita's dish with food before peeling off her wet clothes and slipping into her favorite pair of shorts and a camisole. A cold breeze from outside barreled its way past the balcony door and rippled right through her. Despite the groggy heat, she dug a hoodie out of her winter clothes storage bin and tossed it on as well. No sooner did she lie down on her bed when her cell phone vibrated. She checked the message:

TAKANARI-KUN: Where are you? We have to finish the mural!

Satsuki checked the time: 2:20 p.m. If she were in school, her social studies class would just be ending, and she would have to pick up where she had left off with the "living frame." There were only thirty cranes left that needed to be folded and doused in glitter. Takanari was probably sweating more than usual over it. Seeing his message sent reverberations of indignation up and down her spine.

How can I finish the living frame now? Nothing matters anymore, especially what you think or want me to do, Takanari-kun.

Satsuki shut her cell phone off and then threw it across the room. It bounced against the wall before landing on her plastic desk covered in Disney stickers. Chibita's ears perked up, but he was too busy chomping away at his long-overdue meal to care. *The poor thing must've been really hungry*, Satsuki thought to herself. She stood in the middle of the room, staring at him. Her eyes burned like overheated griddles from tiredness. She was tired of everything, for that matter.

Fuck the living frame. Fuck it all to hell, she thought to herself.

Another breeze came through the crack and stabbed at her bare legs. She went to shut the balcony door all the way but instead stepped out onto the slender ledge. She was immediately hit in the face with stretched-out raindrops but didn't flinch or run back inside. Her room was stuffy from two days of packed-in heat; the air actually felt cooler outside than inside her room. Definitely less combustible, too.

Satsuki leaned over the edge of the balcony's slippery wall and let the rain cool her angry head. It was no longer drizzling but coming down wave after wave like an ocean turned sideways, falling from the sky.

For a moment, the sound of water banging against everything it touched made her forget where she was. Staircases, balconies, tall buildings, and the pointy rooftops of houses below her all became triangles, squares, rectangles, and arrows pointing up. Geometry without definition. Their dilapidation scars and foggy windows were enhanced in the blur of wind and rain.

She knew it wouldn't last long, though. She wondered if it were possible to bang her life's memories out of her head by smacking her face against the wet stone she was leaning against. Or maybe she could stop creating memories altogether. Perhaps she could live hidden among the Chugoku mountains. The thought appealed to her, but looking down at the busy street three stories below, it seemed that jumping from the roof of her housing complex that was five more floors up would be much easier than living a cold and sequestered life somewhere in between nature's rocky, lumpy breasts. It would also be nothing to head upstairs, bounce off the housing complex ledge like it was a diving board, and plunge head-first into the rain. It would be like diving into the deep end of the Osawa Community swimming pool back in Mitaka, when she was younger. Except this time, the tragic memory of her sister would be like an anvil tied around her head, sky-rocketing her down towards the pavement and not the bottom of the Osawa pool from her past.

As thunder continued trumpeting in the sky and a parade of umbrellas formed on the sidewalks, Satsuki somehow heard Chibita's familiar purr to the right of where she stood. He had finished his dinner and planted himself in front of the closet door at the end of the balcony (near her bedroom entrance). He purred again, but also wagged his tail in apparent agitation.

"What's wrong, hmm? Oh… I know. You know what I'm thinking, don't you? If I jump, who will feed you and take care of you, right? Not *Okaasan*. She can't even take care of herself right now.

And *Otousan* is never home, anyway. So, I guess that just leaves me, huh?"

She didn't have to look inside her room to know Chibita had eaten every last morsel of food in his bowl. She slowly walked over to him and knelt down in front of his face. He rubbed his head across her leg and extended his neck to press more of his weight against Satsuki's body. It was his way of letting her know that he completely agreed with everything she had just said.

"Aww... Chi-chan."

You are the only thing keeping me in this world right now. Thank you for needing me. I mean, nobody else really needs me, except maybe Okaasan. It would be really sad if Okaasan lost both her daughters, don't you think?

Chibita licked Satsuki's palms, but his usual way of letting his coarse tongue slink against her in long strokes was replaced with abbreviated, poking motions. He paced back and forth, his tail mimicking the movements of both his tongue and legs, then turned away from her and faced the door.

"Chi-chan, what's wrong? Do you want me to open the door for you? There's nothing in there, remember?"

Satsuki swung the door open and remembered the first time she had seen it when they moved in. She had promised herself to stay away from it as long as her family lived there. Something about it gave her the creeps.

She couldn't really figure out why, though. The inside was nothing more than a grimy closet space to store laundry poles and racks. The floor space could fit one, maybe two people, but it was cramped and covered in the kind of filmy dirt you could write your name in. There were also two cement slabs that comprised the closet's back wall and were separated by what appeared to be a crooked line of grout. Satsuki wondered if they were both actually doors to a hidden apartment. If that were the case, nobody had come out of the doors for a really long time! Each one had collected overgrown bushes of cobwebs in their corners, and strands of dust yarn hung from the ceiling. They swayed back and forth from a muggy wind that began slithering around Satsuki and Chibita. The space within the closet was like a solitary confinement cell that held filth and silence as its prisoners. And although Satsuki didn't know it yet, this would soon veraciously describe her own internal heartspace.

"AACHOO!"

Satsuki sneezed, breaking the tractor beam of bewilderment that had frozen her in place in front of the open door. Chibita flinched at her outburst but continued to remain fixated on the balcony closet, refusing to step inside it, his hair raised. He let out a sharp hiss. She wasn't sure why Chibita wanted her to see the great big nothing that was inside, but he was obviously disturbed by it.

He hissed again, this time with an accompanying growl.

Ahh, he's probably just being prissy, not wanting to get his paws dirty, Satsuki thought to herself. *No, wait... that's not it. Something bad happened here, didn't it? Okaasan said the people who lived here before had just gotten married and had no children but were expecting. They moved away after only a few months of living here, though. Okaasan mentioned that one of them had family who lived in Kure, so it would be easier to raise their... their... baby... there when... it... was... born...*

Satsuki knew she had fucked up thinking about this, as her mind immediately teemed with unwanted recollections: Her mother writhing around in the grass and spurting blood everywhere. Her mother's white legs and white maternity dress camouflaged in red. The placenta slowly deflating like a popped meat-balloon while sinking in the amniotic river gushing out of the broken cervical canal. Everyone around them paralyzed with an awful fear. The purple scarf hanging like an umbilical cord off the ambulance stretcher. No sooner did Satsuki think about these things did they blend into a single, paroxysmal emotion:

Indignation.

She wanted to destroy everything and everyone, including herself, and if Chibita hadn't distracted her, she would have done it, too. Those around her had let her down, and now her "baby" sister was dead. Big fucking mistake.

Her hatred was like an electrical surge. It caused the lanugo-like hair on her arms and legs to stand straight up. She snapped her eyes shut and rubbed her temples. She wasn't afraid of letting this rage take over but was frightened of what might happen to those around her once it did.

Chibita hissed again, this time while looking directly at her. *Maybe you can sense what's inside of me now, but there's nothing you can do to save me from this. Nothing. Nothing. Nothing. Noth—*

A knock on Satsuki's bedroom door interrupted her thoughts. She ran inside her room and swung open the door before there was another knock. With such anger funneling through her entire being, she imagined how surprising she would look to whoever was knocking, but it was she who ended up being surprised. In the doorway was her father, whose cheerless face showed neither comfort nor elation at seeing his daughter for the first time in several days.

"Hello," Hideo said.

CHAPTER 24

RAPTURE
of
THE DEEP

Ever since the first morning in Hawaii, Jimmy awoke before anyone else and marinated in the Kona morning tide. The Hawaiian moku was a cozy vestibule for the faithfully relaxed tourists that migrated to its beaches every year. Today, though, was different. It seemed to Jimmy that there wasn't anybody in Kona but him, his family, and the thousands of small crabs that sidestepped on the beaches with sluggish indifference. There was no human traffic on any roads for miles.

Maybe it has something to do with the weather, Jimmy thought. The fading purple air, leftover from the previous night's thunderstorm, rolled over the mildew-calm ocean.

As Jimmy lay down right where the beach met the ocean and let the water ripple over his body, he imagined that all the tourists were in hiding. They probably wouldn't come out of their beachfront rentals for hours until later on in the day, when the sun covered the island with its glaring dome of light.

But for Jimmy, this was preferred. He vastly enjoyed the reprieve of people cluttering the beaches and speeding down the streets. It was especially relaxing since there were no tourists with surfboards anywhere in the water. He could only take so many wipeouts by the hordes of amateur surfers before it became less amusing and more an annoyance to his morning water-basking routine.

He was not only grateful for the lack of people distractions, but he also felt hyper-sensitive to everything around him. He was able to completely soak into his surroundings without worrying about wading into human riffraff. And thanks to the lack of people polluting the beach this morning, he quickly spotted several curious globs that bobbled in the ocean. It took only seconds to register what the "globs" actually were.

"Hello? Is anyone up?"

Jimmy scampered into the Ala Kala resort home and headed straight for the kitchen. As water droplets beaded between his toes, he scoured the counters, pushing aside potato chip bags and salsa-stained paper plates until three sets of snorkeling masks were visible. They were bundled with three neon yellow spare air canisters (a local diving instructor had told them this would be perfect for shallow diving, since nobody except Jimmy wanted to learn how to dive the proper way. According to the instructor, the spare air canisters were "Thirteen inches, two pounds, and good for thirty breaths."). Jimmy grabbed them, then went upstairs and jumped onto Seul Bi's bed, letting his entire body weight pancake his daughter.

"Come on. Get up," Jimmy said.

A stern "I'm up!" bellowed from somewhere underneath him.

Seul Bi sat up in slow motion, yawning and rubbing her eyes raw. She didn't remember coming into her room from the terrace.

"Why? It's so early."

"It's those manta rays. They're hanging out close to the beach. Hurry up downstairs. You'll see."

Seul Bi was instantly alert. "Really? Give me a few seconds, and I'll be down."

Jimmy ran out of Seul Bi's room and into the adjacent room where his wife lay on the bed. He proceeded to kiss her bare shoulders and neck, the only flesh visible in the temper tantrum of blankets on the bed.

"Hey, honey, get up."

He decided to be more taciturn in waking Zoe. His body had been on her most of the night.

Zoe grumbled.

"Baby, come on," Jimmy said, "me and Seul Bi are going down to the ocean. I'm pretty sure I just saw some manta rays that were swimming really close to the beach. Here's a mask and a spare air canister. We should get down to the beach before they leave, so get up, okay?" Jimmy kissed her stringy hair and tickled her ear.

Zoe yanked her face from the pillow. She wasn't sure if she had just dreamt Jimmy talking about manta rays, but a snorkel mask and spare air canister lying on the bed beside her proved it was real.

Jimmy and Seul Bi raced each other to the beach, diving gear in either hand, and were careful to not step on the jagged seashells and other debris poking out of the sand. The previous night's storm winds had seemingly dragged mountains of junk out of the ocean and onto the beach. They avoided the mess, for the most part, and simultaneously jumped into the soapy, warm water.

"Where are they, Dad?" Seul Bi asked.

"I think maybe thirty feet in," Jimmy replied. "I'm pretty sure I saw them feeding at the surface."

Both of them treaded deeper into the water. The palm trees just north of the resort home began to sway from powerful squalls. They bent towards the coast's cliff at angles which threatened to snap each tree into two. It seemed as though they objected to Seul Bi and Jimmy swimming in the water. They waved their branchy fingers with more rustling disapproval when Zoe appeared at the beach's threshold.

"Hey guys, wait for me." She yawned several times before hopping into the water. She then butterfly stroked right into Seul Bi's back. Both giggled before Jimmy kissed them and motioned for them to follow his lead.

"Is Bev or Aunt D. up?" Seul Bi asked.

Zoe shook her head. "Uh… no, I don't think so. Did you *see* how much those two drunks had last night?"

"I know! Like mother, like daughter, right?" Jimmy said while laughing. He accidentally lapped water into his mouth but spit it out before the salt could dry his tongue. "Come on, we're getting close."

After a few minutes of swimming, each of them felt something hot rising from underneath their feet and to the surface. It was like a Pacific spa jet stream set on high.

"Dad, the water got really warm," Seul Bi said.

Jimmy smiled. "I know. I just peed."

"Eww, that's disgusting!" Seul Bi yelled. Zoe splashed water at him. Jimmy laughed at them both.

"Just kidding. I'm not sure why it's warm, but anyway, this is where I saw them. Let me go under the water for a second and check around, okay?"

"Sure, Jacques Cousteau, go right ahead," Zoe squawked. She was out of breath from the swim and was impressed that neither Seul Bi nor Jimmy were fatigued. She wished for a life jacket that would hold her up. She poked her feet downwards to see if she could touch the ocean floor. She couldn't feel or see anything in the murky fabric beneath her.

Jimmy didn't need to dive more than ten feet down when he saw the manta rays. At first, they appeared to be nothing more than bony skeletons covered in black-spotted blankets, each performing graceful summersaults in the water. He had counted four of them, but he wondered if maybe more lurked beyond his vision. One of them noticed Jimmy and began to break off from his friends, looping around them until it was within touching distance.

Jimmy reached out his hand and almost accidentally put his fingers into the gaping mouth of the ray, which was open. It darted above his head, revealing a snow-colored stomach. Jimmy held out his hand again and watched his fingers sink into the jelly mass. The ray had stopped swimming and seemed to actually enjoy Jimmy's fingers rubbing against it.

Jimmy also remained transfixed and didn't want to stop touching this magnificent creature. He inspected it more closely. It was shaped like a banana peel with two flapping wings, which he guessed were at least ten feet across in diameter. The mouth funneled what looked like ocean dandruff deep into its bowels. Plankton? Several bright yellow fish also trailed alongside its tail. They buzzed around like bees in their colony, fearless of their host. The manta ray reminded Jimmy of an alien spaceship, drifting in a liquid constellation, with speckled stars on the move.

Fucking amazing, Jimmy marvelled. He raced back to the surface to tell Zoe and Seul Bi about what he had just done.

"Guys, holy shit!" Jimmy exclaimed. "I mean, crap. Sorry. I just petted a manta ray!" It was amazing!"

"Whoa! Really?" Zoe and Seul Bi both said at the same time. Seul Bi swam over to Jimmy. "I want to see! I want to see!" She began adjusting her snorkel mask in place on her face.

"Yeah, really," Jimmy said. "There's one not that far down. I also saw three more down there. It's strange because I had read that they are usually attracted to light on the ocean floor which brings the plankton or whatever. Why they are this close to the surface, I have no idea, but it's awesome for us! Anyway, you guys gotta come down and see them. And save your spare air if you can."

"Aye aye, Captain," Zoe said while saluting Jimmy. "Ready, Bee?"

Seul Bi and her both took deep breaths and dove straight down. Jimmy stuck his snorkel mask in the water and watched their descent before joining them. He noticed that the manta ray he had petted was still hovering in place. The other three rays were ascending towards their friend, eager to greet Zoe and Seul Bi. These were not shy as the Kona tour guidebook he had read suggested. They were like Caspers, friendly ghosts of the Pacific.

Zoe, Seul Bi, and Jimmy each took turns touching the manta rays. None of them wanted to surface for air, so all three began to sip from their spare air tanks. The rays weren't in any hurry to leave, either. They seemed to enjoy all the attention, especially from Seul Bi, who repeatedly tickled their massive underbellies.

Zoe exchanged underwater smiles with her daughter, as she, too, was enthralled by what she could only think of as a cosmic petting zoo. There was no other way to imagine it in her mind; time was as useless here as it was in space, and the blue-black darkness surrounding them was mostly brightened by these starry creatures—and little else. Only a few rays of sunlight managed to poke at them from above. Everything felt dim, distant, quiet. Peaceful, even.

At this point, Jimmy's paternal instincts kicked in. *There has to be a caveat to something this perfect*, he reasoned while inspecting the area around them. The ocean floor was, he guessed, fifteen to twenty feet below them. He also noticed that it was covered with shiny, black rocks. They were near a volcanic basin, but that wasn't uncommon for the Hawaiian coast. What was disconcerting to

Jimmy, however, was that the opaqueness of the black rocks concealed a nearby rocky cliff. The only reason he had recognized it was because schools of fish caked in rainbow makeup darted underneath its shade. What other surprises were there? Not knowing the answer to this question unnerved Jimmy. It was time to move his family more toward the coast.

As Jimmy motioned for Zoe and Seul Bi to follow him towards the beach, he saw a simmering glow below the cliff's natural rock awning. *Maybe that is what the manta rays were attracted to*, he thought to himself. He debated for a few seconds whether or not to explore the light. He wanted to be cautious...

What was below that cliff became too much of an irresistible temptation. He swam to the surface, inhaled as much air as his lungs would hold, and plunged downward. Zoe and Seul Bi looked at him but decided not to follow, much to his relief. They were entranced by the rays, which were still just as curious about Zoe and Seul Bi, nudging at their arms and legs.

Jimmy caught a current that propelled him straight beneath the cliff. His ears popped from the sudden change in depth. He shook it off, quickly reaching the uneven and mushy ocean bottom. Right away, he slipped and sunk into what felt like leg-swallowing quicksand. He eventually had to hold onto the cliff's rocky vertebrae and thrust himself around to the other side, all the while holding the tank of spare air close to his mouth. The water grew warmer with each step.

After reaching the other side, the source of the glow was immediately apparent: a single shaft of light breaking through a crack in the ocean floor. Bubbles squeezed out of the crack with jet-spray speed. As Jimmy swam closer to the light, he looked back and realized he couldn't see Zoe or Seul Bi anymore. The cliff wall was blocking his view.

This didn't worry him as much as his rapidly diminishing air supply. When he checked the spare air tank's pressure gauge, it indicated that he was almost halfway through his thirty breaths. *Already? Damn! I'm going to run out of air soon*, he thought to himself.

If I could just take a closer look...

Zoe wondered if anyone had ever been boiled alive in the Pacific. The water around her and Seul Bi felt like it was on fire. She looked up at the glassy ceiling of water. The sun had been tackled by the clouds. There was no warmth anywhere to be found up there. No, she suspected the heat was coming from someplace in the depths. *Or something.*

All of a sudden, something bellowed below them. A cracking noise, which at first was just a faint shudder, but gradually the volume increased to a swell, filled the ocean room. Zoe and Seul Bi both looked at each other. Both registered fear in one another's eyes. The manta rays stopped their curious circles around them. They flapped their heavy wings and swam towards the beachfront. *Maybe they're trying to tell us we should go back?* Seul Bi thought to herself. She swore that they were opening their mouths not to shovel water into their slimy filters but to offer a wordless warning against whatever was about to happen. Even the schools of fish that swam near Seul Bi and Zoe darted in all directions, changing their routes with one singular movement of synchronization. It was like looking at several flags being forced to wave in unnatural directions by typhoon winds, threatening at any moment to rip them into shreds. The water was now empty, except for Zoe and Seul Bi and gallons of fear.

The water had become painfully still.

That was until a few seconds later, when the ground erupted with tremors that felt like they could tilt the Earth's axis. Sand and soot popped out of invisible tubes like confetti. Plants floated away with their astonished roots twisting in the currents, and huge chunks of the cliff's wall blasted apart in every direction. Only a shiny beam of light from beyond the collapsing ledge escaped the destruction.

Perhaps in a stroke of luck, Zoe and Seul Bi were propelled up to the surface by the force of the tremors. When they had filled their lungs with enough air, they screamed. Their bodies shook from panic and the rocking waters around them.

"Mom, what happened?! Oh my God!"

"I dunno! I dunno! Did you see your father?"

Seul Bi started to sob. She shook her head in an unfortunate direction.

"Oh my God… he's still down there, then!" Zoe put her face close to the lapping water so she could attempt to make out anything below. It was a moving mountain of blackness. Salty water stung the inside of her nostrils.

She knew what must be done.

"Okay, listen to me, Seul Bi. I dunno what's going on, but I think your father may have got hurt in what just happened. He could be trapped under something. Maybe the cliff. So I'm gonna go try and find him and help him if he needs it."

"No, Mom! Don't go!"

"Listen to me. Where is your can of spare air?"

"My what?"

"SPARE AIR! WHERE IS IT?"

"I'm sorry. I think I lost it."

Zoe frowned. Going after her husband would be extremely difficult and dangerous without her daughter's tank of spare air as a reserve. She knew there was a very real possibility of drowning with only her tank as her sole source of air. It was already half-empty. Zoe swam over to Seul Bi and hugged her.

"Okay, Seul Bi, here's what I need you to do, and don't argue with me. Swim as hard as you can to the beach and get Aunt Debbie."

"But Mom, I'm scared, and I…"

"SEUL BI! Listen, there is no time! I love you. Now SWIM!"

Zoe didn't wait for Seul Bi to respond. She swam straight for where she had last seen Jimmy. In just minutes, her ears popped with enough force she imagined that both sides of her head now leaked grey matter from holes in her Eustachian tubes. Yet she resisted the urge to swim back to the surface or squirm at the pain, swimming straight into the intangible mess that swooshed the rocks and plants around in menacing gestures. She wondered if this is what a Cessna plane felt like, bumping around in dark storm clouds.

The things you think of before you die.

Seul Bi tried to move her arms and legs and swim for the shore, but she was in a state of entropy. Or maybe it was shock. Or maybe she thought about helping her mother. *But that means I have to swim down there... no way. No way. Mom will bring Dad back. She has to. She will.* Bright birds circled above Seul Bi and cawed at her indecision. She looked at them, so safe in their sky nests and out of the lecherous water. She couldn't take their noisy beaks. She put her mask on and dove under a beckoning wave that was just about to splash down on her head.

When Zoe's feet finally touched the shifting ocean floor, her head was throbbing. She couldn't see anything on either side of her. She reached her hands out and walked no more than two feet when a light crept through the foggy muck, fastening to her body like a swimsuit made of leeches. It wasn't light from above. The sun would never send its rays to live under such a dangerous, suffocating tarp. She ran in slow motion towards the brightness. *Please let him be over there*, she thought. Already she was close to ten, maybe twelve breaths left in her spare air tank.

Seul Bi swam faster than her arms could part the invisible path to her parents. The water seemed to catch on fire around her. Ahead she could see a sliver of white that appeared out of place.

Zoe's fingers traced their way around a jagged slope. Her feet stuck to the ground with every step. The fleshy mounds of her heels sizzled on the black rocks. She was cooking on a lava skillet. Zoe had no choice but to dash forward until she reached the light. It was almost ethereal, climbing out of a huge crack that revealed an uneasy mantle. Everything refused to stop moving, including rocks that spilled from above, where the protruding ledge once gave shade to the abundant sea life. What used to be the cliff was now just a pile of granite that was sliding into a growing, glowing trench. The light shaft illuminated everything the trench sucked towards itself, including two arms that were sticking out of the granite pile.

Oh my God, Jimmy! Zoe started to cry but quickly regained her composure. She didn't want to let go of the chance that Jimmy could still be alive. She imagined herself carrying him to the surface, giving him breath, forcing him to wake up. This time, Zoe would be the strong one in the relationship. She went to work, digging and punching and clawing the scorched rocks around the arms.

But Zoe didn't want to look at those arms. She could sense there was something wrong with both of them. The flesh was wrinkled and bunched up near the elbows and wrists, like rolled-up skin sleeves. Out of the corner of her mask, she noticed white bone splinters where the fingers should be. They twitched in sync to Zoe's spazzy pawing at the scorched rocks. She tried her best to put the grisly scene out of her head. She kept working, knowing that, in a few seconds, she would have to go back up for air. Yet with every rock she removed, another took its place.

Seul Bi splashed through the beam of light that was her only compass to finding her parents. She swam downwards until her mother came into view, kneeling in front of a staggering pile of rocks stacked high like a burial mound coated in black enamel. She also thought she saw two arms sticking out of the mound, reaching for her mother's feet. But as she darted further down to help her mother, the ground ruptured once more, and the resulting blast wave skewered the light in all directions, propelling her right back towards the surface.

Zoe lost her balance as the earth quaked all around her. Rocks slammed against her body as more of the granite plot fell into the widening chasm of light. Blisters that had formed on the backs of her ankles burst like party poppers filled with serum confetti. Her skin was badly cut and bleeding, and she wasn't sure how breath still found its way to her lungs (she had used up her last breath of spare air a few seconds ago and was using the empty tank to dig through the rocks). She wanted to give up. Unfortunately, the ocean was not done with her yet. She struggled to her knees, accidentally grabbing the boiled arms for support. Both of them instantly ripped from their sockets.

Blood spurted out in slow-motion arcs from the torn arm veins. Zoe released her grip and tried to push the mangled limbs away, but they hovered as motionless as the manta rays she had petted only minutes before. She fell back down on her knees and heaved up bile, which she spit out before pressing her body against the rocks for support. As she attempted to stand up again, she noticed a swollen, chewed-up face of a man staring at her from within the rock cascade. Both eyelids were gummed over their eye sockets. A nostril leaked brain tissue, and his cheeks looked like the bottom of a badly burned pan. Two rows of milky white teeth were untouched in the lipless mouth.

Jimmy!!!! Zoe's body was shutting down from lack of oxygen. She knew this was it. Jimmy was dead. She saw no life in that face, and she didn't have enough strength left to pull him out of the death pile. Certainly not to carry him to the surface. And it was becoming impossible to stand any more. Her entire body began to wobble and seize. Finally, her legs completely gave out. The ground continued to quake, offering nothing in the way of a comfortable, makeshift grave for her to lie down in.

At least I'm going to die next to my husband, Zoe thought. Her face turned to look up one last time towards the distorted image of sky among the tornado of dirt and rocks and blood and appendages that now twisted above her. It was then she noticed the purple bikini of her daughter. *Seul Bi...*

Beetles of terror crawled with lightning speed from Seul Bi's toes to the top of her skull. She had seen the ocean floor groan and her mother fall. She watched as her mother's body jerked with convulsions, the two arms listlessly bobbing up and down beside her. And when her mother appeared to offer a goodbye with a final glance, letting go of the empty spare air canister as she did so, Seul Bi attempted to *will* herself into swimming straight down to the ocean floor. She had no idea how to save her parents, but she had to try and do *something*; they had saved her twelve years ago from a life without parental love. How would she live with herself if she let the Pacific claim their lives? They didn't deserve to die. Not yet. Not like this.

Yet determined as she was to stop tragedy from happening, she suddenly saw something that could never be erased from memory, something inexplicable and so terrifying that all she could do was point an impotent finger at her mother's legs.

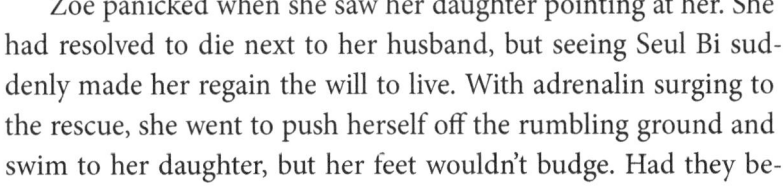

Zoe panicked when she saw her daughter pointing at her. She had resolved to die next to her husband, but seeing Seul Bi suddenly made her regain the will to live. With adrenalin surging to the rescue, she went to push herself off the rumbling ground and swim to her daughter, but her feet wouldn't budge. Had they become ensnared in the rock pile, or possibly seaweed? When she looked down at her feet, what she saw made her wish it was mountains of granite or kelp that had rendered her immobile:

Two hands were clasped around her ankles.

Zoe almost shrieked but stopped herself, as that would have meant giving up her last few remaining breaths. Instead, she bent down to pry the hands off of her ankles and was shocked to find that the hands belonged to Jimmy! His face was bruised, and both his eyes and nose were wrapped in seaweed, but the lips she recognized in an instant. She had kissed them so many times during their fifteen years of marriage. She wanted to kiss them now, to tell him that everything would be okay, but her suffocating mind singularly occupied itself with a terrible, illogical question:

If that isn't Jimmy underneath those rocks, then who—or what—is?

Zoe looked over at the body she'd spent so much time digging out. The chewed-up face stared back at her with those milky white teeth. Zoe swore the "thing" was smiling at her, but she was blacking out and couldn't think straight. Her lungs were collapsing with water. A tremor began to rip the world apart. She needed to save Seul Bi, come back down for Jimmy, but there was no more time. No more time…

An explosion from the belly of the lighted chasm produced destructive ripples of force. Sand mountains crumbled, the reef evaporated, and the ray of light was extinguished, draping the ocean floor in shadows. The last Seul Bi saw of her mother and father was their lifeless bodies slipping over the edge into the abysmal unknown.

The force of the explosion also rocketed Seul Bi into the world above. She tasted air, but the ascension was too fast. She passed out while hearing herself yell for help. When she woke up, it was only moments later, but this time it was her Aunt Debbie whose voice flooded her ears. Seul Bi had landed on the beach in front of the resort home.

Debbie stood over her, yelling, "What happened?" over and over again.

Seul Bi was too paralyzed from shock to answer her aunt. All she could do was sit up and stare at the ocean. Somewhere in the distance, sirens began to wail. Tide water splashed onto Seul Bi's body, which was scratched up from landing on sharp rocks in the sand. Salt stuck inside every bloody cut as well, but she didn't flinch from the pin-pricking pain. The capricious Kona beach had become a disappearing echo, and in its place was a reservoir of death.

"Seul Bi, what happened? Where's your mom and dad? Huh? Seul Bi? Seul Bi? I will be right bac—"

Debbie didn't finish her sentence, but her mouth remained open in disbelief.

Two wrinkled pieces of flesh that resembled arms and hands had washed up beside them.

Seul Bi gazed at the limbs with comatose eyes, then continued to stare out at the Pacific.

My parents are dead, and I'm an orphan again.

She remembered those arms bobbing around next to her mother. They were orphans, too.

CHAPTER 25

NINE SETS

of ··

THREE BEATS

When Hideo had received the call in his hotel room from Hiroshima Municipal Hospital, he had just gotten finished with a round of paperwork in preparation for a sales meeting the following day. It was with the various Mazda franchise owners operating in Seoul. He had been there for only a few days, but it had already seemed that things were going well with his overseeing a production deal that included development of a rigorous advertisement campaign in the fall. The idea was to capitalize on a recently passed law in South Korea that lowered the expensive tariffs on all import cars. Mazda appeared ready to jump out from behind car distributors Hyundai and Kia and finally create a level playing field for Japan in South Korea.

Hideo's job was to do market analysis and assist in calculating these consumer needs. There were five others on his team who did various other tasks, but he felt the burden of a successful outcome to this trip lay on his shoulders. He did *not* want to mess this up. He couldn't mess this up. So, when the hospital nurse told him in an unusually imperative tone that he must come back to Japan right away (although the nurse wouldn't specify why, revealing only that Yoshiko had been admitted to the hospital), Hideo was too worried about his performance as a Mazda employee and forgot his matrimonial duty to his wife.

It's probably not that serious, he rationalized. *She could be giving birth, and if it's anything like the last time, then she'll be in labor for at least a day or two like she was with Satsuki. I could probably make it back right as the baby is being born. That would be great. No waiting around for hours in a smelly hospital. Ha! When she sees me, she'll probably have the baby right then and there.*

Hideo tried several times to reach both Yoshiko and Satsuki, but when neither one answered his calls, he began wondering if maybe something really was wrong. He decided to stay busy and review for the upcoming sales meeting the next day. *One of them will call me if they need me,* he assured himself.

When Aiko left a message urging him to get home immediately, Hideo was taking a shower and didn't hear the hotel's front desk calling to inform him about it. He knew right away this would not go over well with Yoshiko's hot-headed sister. She had resigned herself to talking with him only when absolutely necessary, and if he ignored her calls or didn't respond to them, an argument was guaranteed to ensue.

He called her back and was surprised—she barely said a word to him. Aiko's explanation of what had happened was like a sharp pinch to his soul: *Yoshiko had a miscarriage. She almost died from blood loss.* What?

He felt terrible for Yoshiko, but what could he do? If he left now, that would cripple Mazda's ambitious stake in South Korea's central car market. He had to meet with the team, go over their strategy with presentations, and lay the groundwork for their potential lucrative deal. He knew that his boss would understand and even sympathize, but leaving would brand him as unreliable. Indeed, the world of a salary man was sometimes cutthroat, and Hideo's neck would be dangerously exposed.

He also didn't have the emotional capacity to think about what had happened. He got things done in his position at Mazda precisely because of his inability to let emotions interfere with work. Additionally, setting up the platform for increased sales of imported cars in Seoul would certainly mean a promotion, and he had been determined to reach this goal. He wanted to tell Aiko how close he was to getting everything in place there in Seoul, but he decided to ask her if she could take care of Yoshiko and Satsuki for at least two days, which was the earliest he could possibly return home and still accomplish his objective. He knew that she wouldn't understand, and he could feel her polar stare right through the phone. She hung up before he could say anything else.

As Hideo stood there, knocking on Satsuki's door, the hallway seemed to shrink with every second he remained in it. Something about the suppressed conversation with Aiko made him catch the first available flight back to Hiroshima. He had been attacked all night by questions with invisible strings attached to them that had tugged his tired body all over the hotel bed. What would he do if Yoshiko died of complications from the miscarriage? If he lost his wife, how could he keep his job and raise Satsuki by himself? Hideo knew that the right thing to do was fly back home and be present for his family.

He had opened the front door with the usual *tadaima* greeting, but nobody had heard him come in. The television in the *tatami* room was unusually loud, which probably meant that Aiko was watching it. Whenever she came over, she liked to watch television at a deafening volume (she explained to Hideo once that it helped her remember what it was like to attend rock concerts before getting her boring job in international sales, where the only thing loud in her life were the jet engines on her business flights and her irate boss when stocks were down). He had been relieved, actually, that she hadn't heard him enter the apartment.

He went first to check on Yoshiko, who was in their bedroom on the futon bed, embalmed in blankets. Her breathing undulated between slow and comatose. Hideo didn't want to disturb her slumber, so he next decided to speak with the one person in the apartment that always, it seemed, offered him sanctuary after a difficult day at work (or an argument with Yoshiko).

Yet when Satsuki opened her door, she scowled at him, and he recoiled with surprise. There was no solace or comfort to be found in his daughter's eyes. He was simultaneously greeted with a vacant stare by Aiko, who had run out of the *tatami* room and into the hallway the moment he had said hello to Satsuki. Hideo began to wonder if he should have just stayed in Seoul after all.

"May I come in?"

Satsuki didn't respond, didn't move, didn't blink or shake her head. She was like a vertical corpse.

Hideo didn't wait for an approval. He knew it wasn't coming. He cautiously stepped into her room. The air inside was full of balm and mugginess, making breathing difficult. He spotted the culprit responsible for the inhospitable climate. Surprisingly it wasn't his daughter, but the open balcony door. He glided past Satsuki and slid it shut.

"I tried to call you. I wanted to tell you that there was no way I could get back here last night," Hideo lied. He didn't want to explain that his first instinct had been to stay in Seoul and continue working. Satsuki was indifferent to his explanation; she turned her back to him. He leaned against her desk and crossed his arms, coughing up some phlegm to help with forming his next words.

"I'm sorry. I think it will be a long time before *Okaasan* will recover fully, so maybe you can help out around the apar—"

"Help? HELP??!" Satsuki barked. "HA HA HA!!!!! SO where were YOU when we needed help? Hmm? WHERE?!"

Hideo kneaded his temples. He'd had about all he could take from everyone. Especially his daughter. "That's enough! I'm here now. Do you want me to leave and go back to Seoul? There are still problems with North Korea going on, and I feel lucky that nothing hap—"

"Do whatever you want." Satsuki shrugged her shoulders and sat on her bed, staring out the glass balcony window as she did so. The sky, along with everything else around her, grew dimmer. Her mind conjured up an image of the Hiroshimakanon High School Kumidaiko group with their strident drums.

Figures you just change the subject, she thought to herself. *You can't deal with problems. You always run out. That's why you took a job so far away. It wasn't to support me or Okaasan. It was so you can have an excuse not to be responsible. Fuck you. You're nothing to me anymore.*

Nothing.

There's no reason for me or you to talk anymore.

Enemy.

Enemy.

Enemy. Nine sets of three beats. Speed them up. Advance towards the enemy.

Hideo had heard enough. Sleep deprivation made his patience dissolve quicker than normal. He massaged his neck. Aiko was still lingering in the hallway, he suspected, so maybe it would be best to leave Satsuki alone. He would need all the energy he had left for his sister-in-law.

As he walked past Satsuki, Chibita jumped onto the bed next to her. He lay down on her lap and purred while licking his front paws. Hideo looked at Chibita and was reminded of something he had bought at the airport, on the way back from South Korea.

"So anyway, I'm going to talk with Aiko-chan and then order some food. Sushi, maybe? And before I forget, I, um, got you something." Hideo grabbed his briefcase from outside the door and opened it on her Tibetan rug. What he pulled out he didn't show Satsuki at first. Instead, he slowly and carefully unwrapped it before setting it down on the desk. The big mystery turned out to be a snow globe with an encrusted porcelain stand attached to it. The word "Chicago" was inscribed on the front of the stand, and inside its glass orb, jittery, white flakes bounced around between plastic human figurines underneath a skyline of toy skyscrapers. When he motioned for Satsuki to come over and look at it, she didn't budge.

"I got you this snow globe. I bought it from an American who was sitting next to me at the airport in Seoul. He spoke perfect Japanese. He told me that he had bought this for his girlfriend at an airport in Chicago, but his girlfriend hates Chicago and didn't want it. Had a bad experience there, I guess, the last time she was in America and went there. She's half-Korean, half-Japanese, you see, living in Seoul. So anyway, I told him about you and how you might like a souvenir from America, and out of the blue, he offered to sell the snow globe to me, so then I paid…"

Hideo stopped talking. It was obvious that Satsuki couldn't care less. He sighed and tapped his fingernails on the snow globe's glass dome. When he went to leave, he almost tripped over a plastic bag on the ground beside the door. He hadn't noticed it when he walked in, but as he bent over to see what his feet had bumped into, a pair of knit stockings and three neatly folded pairs of Lilo and Stitch one-piece baby pajamas tumbled out of the bag.

He averted his eyes, gasping for a breath that threatened to make him come undone if he didn't suck air into his chest immediately.

He didn't try to put the clothes back into the bag. He hopped over them and out into the hallway, shutting the door. He had thought that getting out of Satsuki's room would somehow make things better, but Aiko was waiting for him right outside the door. Her arms were crossed, and her cheeks were fire-engine red.

This must be what Vietnam veterans experienced when they fought one war just to come home and fight another with their own countrymen, Hideo thought to himself. He had recently watched a Vietnam documentary on Hiroshima TV late one night, and afterwards, couldn't evict the graphic images of warfare out of his mind for days.

"Ah, why couldn't I have come home in a body bag instead," he muttered to himself.

"What did you say?" Aiko asked. Hideo hadn't realized he spoke loud enough for her to hear his scurrilous words.

"Ah, nothing. How is Yoshiko? She was sleeping when I went into the room to say hi."

"She's fine, I guess."

"Has she been sleeping long?" Hideo asked.

"When she got here, she went straight to the bedroom and fell asleep, but you wouldn't know that, would you?" Aiko's words were dunked in acid. She wanted to scream at Hideo and had been rehearsing what she was going to say while standing in the hallway, but her sister would probably wake up from the commotion. Still, she vowed that he wouldn't get off so easily.

Hideo ignored her question and went into the kitchen and sat down. She followed close behind him. "Don't worry, I won't tell your daughter that you lied about coming back here early." Aiko went to the refrigerator and pulled out a bottled water. She slammed the door with a swing of her hips against the handle.

"Stay out of it," Hideo growled. He, too, wanted to yell at Aiko. Who the hell did she think she was? Still the annoying, younger sister who didn't get enough attention as a child, he supposed.

Aiko sipped her water. "Don't worry, I will. But don't bother lying to your wife. I already told her about our conversation."

"I think it's time you leave. Thank you for helping Yoshiko and Satsuki, but I am here now, so…"

"No. I'm staying."

"Fine. Suit yourself."

Hideo left the kitchen in a hurry. He went into the *tatami* room and sat down at the *kotatsu*, focusing as best he could on the television screen and nothing else. Aiko was really starting to piss him off, but he didn't want to argue with her. Instead, he imagined crawling into the futon bed next to Yoshiko and passing out for a week straight. A loud bang from the kitchen tore through his brief reverie, however. It didn't take a genius to know who was responsible for the interruption.

Damn her!

Aiko must have dropped a cup or plate into the sink, he thought. *She probably did it on purpose.* Hideo tried to ignore her and flipped through the channels until he spotted a news bulletin regarding the North Korean missile crisis. Apparently, America and the rest of the United Nations had intervened to establish diplomatic talks and suspend any type of hostile military actions indefinitely. Hideo was curious if he had received any messages from his teammates back in Seoul about this. The potential outlash from a missile launch had been averted, which meant a much better chance of success at his team's sales objective. He reached into his pocket for his cell phone but froze when Aiko took a seat beside him at the *kotatsu*. She slammed her bottled water down on the table top.

"So, it seems like North Korea has settled for another round of meaningless peace talks," Hideo said, hoping to change the atmosphere between them into something a little less charged. "I was starting to get worri—"

Aiko interrupted. "Same old Hideo, always changing the subject," she sneered. "Tell me, do you love my sister?"

"What?"

"You heard me. Do you LOVE MY SISTER?"

Hideo couldn't believe it. Where did she get off asking such a question? Forget changing the subject then, it was time to give her a piece of his mind! "STAY OUT OF THIS!" He shouted at her. "You don't have any right to say anything to me. You are never here.

You don't provide for my family, and I don't care that you're her sister, because you're never…"

"I'm never what? AROUND? Is that what you were going to say? YOU have a lot of room to talk! You're the one who is never around when his family needs him. You're nothing but a ghost in this…"

"Stop being so damn melodramatic!"

"I'M NOT BEING MELODRAMATIC! You're an asshole!!!! I told my sister when she met you that it would be a mistake to marry you, and guess what? You have done nothing but prove me right! You have become a vapor trail."

"What are you talking about? Vapor trail? Seriously, where do you come up with thi—"

Aiko stood up and backed away from Hideo. "It's true! You started out being so nice and supportive. You seemed like such a great guy to everyone, but then you had Sacchan, and the next thing you know, you come home late from work, you stop taking trips for vacations, and I get phone calls from Yoshiko every night telling me how you two don't even talk that much anymore! And you're obviously not there for Sacchan, either. So, what happened, huh? Knowing you were going to have another child scared you too much? Is that it? Or do you love your job more than Yoshiko? You are a selfish asshole, and after not being there for my sister when she needed you the most, you proved it! I can't believe you, and I will never, ever forgive you for—"

Hideo jumped up. "SHUT UP! WHY DON'T YOU LEAVE ALREADY?!"

"NO! I'm not going anywhere until—"

"Enough."

A soft, female voice suddenly cleaved through the middle of Hideo and Aiko's quarrel. Neither one had noticed Yoshiko, who was hunched over and holding her stomach, limp into the *tatami* room. Yoshiko turned off the television and leaned against the wall next to it. She cleared her throat. Hideo and Aiko were too thunderstruck with surprise to say or do anything.

"Aiko," Yoshiko said at last, "thank you so much for helping me, but my husband wants you to leave, so I think it's best you go." Yoshiko was about to tell her sister that she would be knocked out from all the pain medication very soon, but instead, she ended up coughing several times in a row.

"Are you all right?" Hideo asked. Before Yoshiko could respond, Aiko dug herself out of the paralyzing resin in the room.

"Look, I think you just need to lie back down and get some rest. And I'm gonna stay, all right? In case you need anything. You're still recovering, so I think it's—"

"NO!" Yoshiko interrupted. "Didn't you hear what I just said? I don't want you to stay. My husband just got home from his trip, and I'm sure he's tired. And right now, I just want to sleep in peace. So, please leave, okay?"

Aiko's first inclination was to argue with Yoshiko. How could she take Hideo's side after what he did? She was the one who had spent the past night and day worrying about her and Satsuki! She was also the one who had kept a bedside vigil the entire time at the hospital! Not Hideo! After all these years, Aiko thought for sure the bastard had finally given her the vindication. That and a chance to finally be closer to Yoshiko by being there for her in Hideo's emotional absence.

After hearing her sister's request, however, Aiko realized that she was making things worse by getting upset at Hideo. This was a battle she could never win. she knew absolutely nothing about the bonds of marriage. And the last thing Yoshiko needed right now was somebody fighting over her *or* her husband's shortcomings.

While her eyes swam in tears, Aiko found herself thinking there was only one thing she could do to help: leave without making a fuss, despite feeling betrayed. Ashamed, too. But if this is what Yoshiko really wanted, then it couldn't be helped. So, without saying another word, she shook her head, grabbed her coat, and ran out of the apartment.

Neither Yoshiko nor Hideo tried to stop her. In fact, they both remained in the same exact spots they were in before she left. What felt like several minutes passed before Yoshiko ended the stare down between them and dragged herself back to the bedroom. She continued to cough. Hideo followed her.

"Can I get you anything? Water? Tea?" Hideo asked.

"No," Yoshiko responded curtly.

"Thank you for talking some sense into her. She was starting to really get on my nerves. I think she never knows when to shut up." Hideo laughed apprehensively.

"I didn't tell her to leave to make things easier for you," Yoshiko shot right back. "I'm going back to bed now. I'm not sure when I can feel good enough to take care of things around here, so can you stay home and help out?"

"Yeah… sure. I talked already to my boss, and he said I could take off as much time as I needed."

Yoshiko snorted. She knew before the week is over, he would be back at his precious job. She spread out on the futon bed and pulled the covers up to her chin. Her coughing had seemed to subside the moment she had lain back down, which was a small relief, but nonetheless one that Yoshiko was grateful for.

"Can you close the door, please?" she said.

"Sure."

Hideo closed the door and left his wife alone, despite wanting to tell her how sorry he was for what had happened. He knew it would be a long time before that door would be open again.

A curtain of black pixels swathed the monitor screen.

> Naru444: Miss Seul Bi, are you still there?
> LSBwillsetUfree: Yeah….sorry about that.
> Naru444: Is everything ok?
> LSBwillsetUfree: I think so. It's hard to talk about what happened to me when I was a kid.
> Naru444: I am so sorry for your loss.
> LSBwillsetUfree: Thank you.
> Naru444: You're welcome. May I say one more thing to you?
> LSBwillsetUfree: Of course.
> Naru444: My hope for you is that you will learn to live with what happened to you that day. If you do not do this, what is inside of you will tear you limb from limb. Losing somebody you love, especially your parents, can be dangerous if it is not dealt with properly. Again, I am deeply sorry for your loss.

Seul Bi slipped into auto pilot the moment somebody said they were sorry about her parents' deaths. She had heard those words often in her life, but the words never penetrated or made a difference, not even from this peculiar new friend. In fact, she was often disappointed in herself for expecting her lonely life to be repaired by condolences.

Why DO I have to feel better?

The thought slammed against the inside of her forehead. Anytime somebody was sorry that she was twice orphaned, there wasn't any release from the post-traumatic pressure valve. All she seemed to have, day in and day out, were unanswered questions, an empty apartment with no answers, and ants crawling on her walls that, like most people in her life, seemed to not care at all about any of her shit.

Seul Bi sighed and began to type something but changed her mind. *How can this lady really know what I'm feeling?*

    LSBwillsetUfree: I feel better now that I've
    told you about that day.

Seul Bi lied, of course. It was the polite thing to do. After all, Narumi was paying her for the drawings, not for friendship or truth. The story was to make the sale happen, and Seul Bi was surprised at how fast she repressed the actual memory by lying.

    Naru444: That is good to hear.
    LSBwillsetUfree: Well, I appreciate your in-
    terest in me and I hope that we can speak
    again soon.
    Naru444: Me too. I am not sure when we can
    speak next though. I am very busy.
    LSBwillsetUfree: No problem then. I guess
    whenever you are online again and I am on-
    line, just hit me up.
    Naru444: Absolutely I will! Thank you
    so much! I will send your payment in a
    few minutes.
    LSBwillsetUfree: NO, THANK YOU! I can't be-
    lieve you are actually buying something
    I made.
    Naru444: They are…special to me.
    LSBwillsetUfree: They are?
    Naru444: Yes.
    LSBwillsetUfree: HOW?

A long pause followed. Nothing.

LSBwillsetUfree: How are they special to you?

More digital silence.

LSBwillsetUfree: Narumi, are you still there?
what did you mean?
Naru444: THE ARMS AND HANDS CRAWL ALL OVER ME
AT NIGHT.

Seul Bi gasped for air, much like she did underneath the water ten years ago. What the fuck? Her fingers floundered on top of the keypad as she tried to type.

LSBwillsetUfree: Hello?

Seul Bi waited with nervous anticipation for an answer. Seconds after she posted her question, a message shot across the dialogue box:

Sorry! This user is not online.

Narumi had signed off.

How could Narumi have seen the same thing? There were plenty of nights where Seul Bi had mistaken her comforter for a soggy arm or leg, only to jolt upright in bed and discover it was just her tears that made the bushy blanket wet with memories. Had Narumi *experienced* something similar? What exactly had happened in this mysterious Japanese woman's past? And who was she exactly? Was she even from Japan? Perhaps the most unsettling question Seul Bi mulled over was if this person actually knew her but was pretending not to. The questions were exploding like firecrackers in her paper skull. If only she knew more about Narumi...

Hold on a second. Seul Bi stood up, then typed something fast on her laptop. While standing on what seemed to be spinning toothpicks for legs, she rocked back and forth and waited for a screen to pop up which would tell her where to start looking for answers. It was PayPal's homepage. After accessing her account, she scrolled down her records and located a gift payment of $600.00. The sender's name was "Anonymous." She ignored this for now and clicked the "details" button under the transaction history, but nothing else about the sender was revealed. There was no actual home address to send the drawings or even a name to locate the address with, either. And the optional message box did not include any friendly greeting or specific instructions to follow.

Seul Bi wished there had been a clue here about who Narumi actually was, but instead, she could only guess the real identity of her benefactor. She began to shiver, both from fear of not know-ing anything about Narumi and also from the cold that had leaked through her windows. The whole situation made her crave the warmth of her bed, so she switched the laptop to sleep mode (this way she could save the cryptic IM chat session for later scrutiny) and burrowed under the placental bed sheets. She must have been exhausted and didn't realize it; within minutes of lying down, her eyelids sealed shut. She didn't resist falling asleep but thought to herself before losing consciousness about how much she missed her parents and wished they were there to watch over her as she slept.

There was another door shut that day.

After Hideo left her room, Satsuki immediately sank down to the floor beside her sister's clothes and stuffed them back into the plastic shopping bag. Watching her father spill them had spun her on a merry-go-round of emotions. She felt apathy, anger, sadness, and most of all, alone.

Alone and festering with a hatred for the world which not only had betrayed her but had stolen the one person who could've made things even in her life. It was just her and Chibita now, who was lying on the bed in a purring slumber; an odd juxtaposition to her own unrest.

There would be no more tears to offer. Not to anyone. Not even to her unborn sister.

No more.

It was during a class trip to the Hiroshima Peace Memorial Museum where Satsuki had first heard about Yuko Yamaguchi's "The Angry Jizo." One of the chaperone teachers had told them about a smiling Jizo statue that had stood on a street corner in Hiroshima, before the atomic bomb was dropped onto the city. On the day after the bombing, Jizo's body was buried in sand and debris, but a young girl spotted him and came crying for water. When he saw her tears, his smiling face metamorphosed into the face of Deva, an Indian god of rage. Jizo tried to help the poor girl by offering his own tears to drink, but she died. Immediately the Jizo's head turned to sand. His stone body lay headless for days and days until an old man put a round stone with three holes in it on top of the torso.

A few days after the trip, Satsuki had looked up a picture of The Angry Jizo online. The circular image she had found, with two hollow carvings in the stone's face for eyes and a small, tightly shut mouth for a third hole, had completely terrified her. That sense of helplessness the Jizo must have felt… it's smile lost forever to anger and sadness… *failing to save the poor girl…* the story had given Satsuki an awful premonition that one day she would feel that way about her own life. It took months after the trip before she could completely shake that feeling off and force The Angry Jizo's story out of her mind.

Yet here she was now, ironically, *exactly* like The Angry Jizo. Her heart pumped only rocks through its chambers, and each stone beat against the inside of her heart's walls like hundreds of tiny war drums.

She had become chiseled rage.

Well, if I've become like Jizo-sama, Satsuki thought, *then I should give my imouto some clothes while she plays on the river-bed in limbo.* She hooked her arm under the shopping bag's handles and dashed out onto the balcony, running directly for the outdoor closet. She smacked at the door handle until the door opened. Its hinges moaned and squeaked. She wasn't worried that her parents or Aiko would hear her and ask her what she was doing. They were too busy acting out their little soap opera in the *tatami* room. Chibita didn't stir either. She tossed the clothes inside and pushed the door shut.

By the time Aiko had left, Satsuki had locked both her balcony and bedroom doors, shut the curtains, and turned off all the lights. Then she sat on her bed like a Buddhist monk in the lotus position. The darkness in her room made her drowsy, but not enough to fall asleep. Her mind drifted to thoughts of the river Sanzu in the afterlife. She saw herself floating down it while yelling out for her unborn sister, who she knew was somewhere on the riverbank. Everyone else in her life had been pulled under in a downstream current, and the possibility of returning to normal shores had all but vanished.

Where she ended up, there was no more Nakahiro Junior High or stupid girls like Izumi Kano or making collages for Art Club. No more greasy-faced boys like Takanari or shopping trips with her mom to the Hondori mall. Satsuki had drifted far, far away from the world.

PART TWO

Thrush along the center.
Difficult distances kept her from crossing
The underbelly of illusion.
She sidestepped stones and twirling trees
Careful only to the eyes of fire.

CHAPTER 28

Seul Bi stood motionless at the end of a snow-soaked sidewalk and hugged herself as best she could to keep warm. All around her, rows of Italianate houses enclosed by fences were shadowy and dark, showing no signs of life. It was not hard to imagine why everything was quiet. It was 6:00 p.m., and the cold had already made travelling anywhere difficult.

She was on her way back home from Northwestern University. She had been asked by Dr. Nathan to participate in a biofeedback test. All of the workers and residents of Rainbow had been given the same test in the past several days, but Seul Bi hadn't scheduled a visit until the very last possible day of testing. She had other things on her mind. Weeks had come and gone since her chat with Narumi, and still, not a single message from the lady who claimed to have arms and hands crawl on her at night.

Seul Bi turned towards the houses and watched her foggy breath rise up into a starless sky. She could only imagine who lived behind the cornice bracketing and arched windows. Probably college students or small families. Maybe they were having supper at this hour or watching television while talking on the phone, or getting ready to go out and catch a movie at Century Theater.

Thinking about this made her eyes watery. She knew that nobody would be waiting to eat dinner with her or laugh at her occasional wry sarcasm back at the apartment. Just more loneliness. She blinked back tears and continued walking.

What could possibly change things now? She had always felt a kind of slim comfort from attempting to connect with anyone. It wasn't for lack of trying, however. Her latest efforts included going to the Evanston Barnes & Noble and asking the staff questions that she already knew the answers to:

"Excuse me, do you know where I can find the latest book from Miri Yu?"

"Um, did you read this book about manta rays?"

"What would you suggest for somebody who is into understanding the brain and theta waves?"

This last question was inspired by the biofeedback study that Dr. Nathan had conducted on his patients and staff. In fact, during Seul Bi's own interview, she had been told that her theta wave activity was similar to a thirteen-year-old child. But strange enough, this made sense to Seul Bi, as the recent, unexplainable events in her life could likely be products of an overactive adolescent imagination.

After several times, she swore the Barnes & Noble employees finally figured out what she was up to, but it was obvious that they weren't upset (or just didn't care) about her harmless ploy. They probably pitied her more than anything else, but most of the time they just looked at her with a strange curiosity, the way a cat might stare down a spot on the wall, unsure if it was predator or prey.

Guy or girl, Seul Bi always imagined they were thinking the same thing about her: *Well, you aren't like everyone else who comes in here asking about stupid vampire books or mommy porn. So, that means you aren't stupid, at least. But you don't wear glasses, and didn't you know? Glasses score you geek points in Barnes & Noble. But then again, you are Asian, so even without the glasses, you still got the whole cute-Asian-girl-in-a-bookstore vibe going on. Yeah, sure, I'll help ya out. No problem.*

The payoff for Seul Bi, what she savored the most and could always count on, was the employees' awkward stares, their fumbling around on a store computer as they looked for where the book she'd requested was hiding in the store, then following them around the maze of bookshelves, the triumphant discovery yells, and finally, the grateful exchange of "Thank you so much for your help" with "You're welcome, anytime." Then came her favorite question asked by her new faux friends, followed by her usual, unspoken response.

"Is that all you need, miss?"

I need more than you could possibly ever give me.

Seul Bi's patients were also helping to quench her loneliness. One of the most important lessons she had been taught in her undergraduate ethics course was to never participate in personal exchanges. It would only lead to boundary issues. But she never had a problem with maintaining a professional distance at Rainbow. She only empathized with the residents, never once identifying them as "friends." Instead, they gave her emotional nutrition another way.

Whenever a resident complained of a headache or of feeling nauseous, Seul Bi would normally offer them a p.r.n. and instruct them to lie down for a while, but lately, she would also take their blood pressure with an aneroid monitor. She would strap the archaic Velcro cuff around their arm and feel their wrist for a pulse while pumping the rubber bulb to squeeze off circulation. Besides making sure that residents weren't experiencing hypertension or hypotension, it was also an opportunity for her to experience an innocent, physical connection through the tactile exchange. She was shamefully aware of how creepy, or even downright pathetic, her actions were, but some days the need to not feel alone was too overwhelming for her to bear.

Then again, so what if she took phony trips to Barnes & Noble or stole pleasure from being a little touchy-feely with patients? She spent so much time at work that she couldn't really go to bars or *do* whatever it was that "normal" people *do* to meet each other. To create connections. If she were to end up meeting somebody, she knew that never in a million years would it work out between them. She was no good at opening up; her mind was too distracted with the past. And lately she was preoccupied with finding answers to who Narumi really was, or whether it had really rained ash or not that night at Rainbow. This meant that she was more often than not left yearning to be touched emotionally or physically by someone, anyone, or anything.

Except the cold.

As she reached her street, the temperature seemed to plunge straight into the ninth level of an icy hell. It ignited her senses. She could hear an ambulance siren wailing somewhere in a distant Chicago neighborhood. It was like a baby crying in the back of a cathedral. The shrieks mixed with the whipping sound of the wind made Seul Bi break into a wild sprint the moment she saw her apartment building. Once inside, she nearly tripped three times scampering up the stairs to her floor.

She stopped to catch her breath in front of her apartment door, and it became immediately obvious that somebody was cooking hamburgers in one of the apartments beside hers. The smell stunk up the entire hallway, and for some reason reminded her of the South Boulevard stop on the Purple Line in Evanston. The train station there usually smelled like a girls' locker room, full of 99-cent soaps and cheap deodorant. She quickly unlocked the door and ran inside her apartment.

Immediately the hallway's foul stench was replaced by the smell of three-day-old leftovers, mostly from Siam Paragon. She paid no attention to it, and headed straight for the bathroom to take a hot shower.

She must have left her television on from earlier. An evening weather news bulletin flashed across the TV screen, offering an optimistic forecast of summer temperatures within the next few days. Seul Bi laughed at the prediction while struggling to slip out of her shirt, unzip her pants, and avoid getting ice on her already wet socks, all at once. She had to work in the morning (the first of four days straight), and who knew how cold Evanston would be at 7:00 a.m.?

Chibita slit open pockets of air between the bed and the knot-infested black beard of hair that swung from it. *Everything's blurry and different upside down*, Satsuki mused, as she lay half off the bed with her head suspended like a yo-yo against the side of it. Blood dripped into her cranium and rushed towards her facial orifices, threatening to pour out of them if she didn't sit up soon. Her room also filled up with roaming, phantom spots from her vision decreasing. They hovered around with almost no books or toys or furniture to prevent their retinal collisions. Well, there was a box of tissues and several plates of untouched food on the floor. There was also a notebook facedown next to a stack of empty Junsui Anzui bottles. When Satsuki finally did sit up, she realized that her bedroom had become blurry and different much earlier than today.

Most of Satsuki's things had been stuffed inside boxes and shoved into her bedroom closet. The desk had long ago been stripped of its Disney stickers, which were wadded up and stuck on the ends of cat hairs strewn across the floor. Most of her stuffed animals and dirty shirts and skirts that were once stacked in front of the television had vanished from sight. They had been replaced with dust blobs. The television had been unplugged and the cord tied into a pretzel knot. Shoved between the few remaining Moogles, bears, and penguins on the desk was the snow globe that her father had given her almost eight months ago, on the day Satsuki decided to barricade herself inside her bedroom and never come out.

Once Satsuki had said goodbye to society, her life had become a matter of simple routines. She slept more than she was awake.

She ate four times a week (a year ago, she was 148 cm and weighed a healthy 45.3 kg, but had since dropped to 40.8kg). She took baths at night while her parents slept. She snuck out in the evenings to shop at the Lawson nearby her family's apartment. Here she could purchase her favorite drinks and snacks. Sometimes she would take a short walk around her neighborhood. Mostly though, it was routines, routines, routines: Lying on her bed while playing videogames on her Nintendo DS. Endlessly watching *Kamichama Karin* episodes. Listening to her iPod. Singing her favorite Perfume songs. Cuddling with Chibita.

At first, Hideo and Yoshiko had been indifferent to Satsuki. Both of them had been too busy dealing with the emotional fall-out of the baby's death. Hideo had returned to his desk at Mazda after just two days of sitting at home watching television, and Yoshiko couldn't muster any words or feelings in response to Hideo's attempts at a quick reconciliation. She had become human Novocaine, numb to everyone. And the cramps in her cervix had lasted a month, so she had confined herself to a pattern of sleeping for twelve hours a day and spending almost an equal amount of time in the bathroom on the toilet, hunched over in pain.

Aiko was too proud to visit and had waited a month and a half before calling to check up on Yoshiko. The only other person besides Hideo or Aiko that Yoshiko had spoken with in those first few months was Satsuki's principal, Mr. Kobayashi, who, upon seeing the news from that day and at the request of Satsuki's teachers, had called to extend the school's condolences. He also had politely inquired about Satsuki returning to Nakahiro Junior High. Yoshiko had apologized for the inconvenience and informed him that she would discuss the matter with her daughter. But Yoshiko hadn't *really* been sorry. She hadn't been anything. She had decided to let Hideo handle Satsuki.

When Yoshiko started making dinner again, she did manage to set a plate of food outside Satsuki's balcony door every night. *No need to try and force Satsuki out of the room to talk,* she told herself.

She couldn't even look at Satsuki; doing so would surely remind her of her other daughter, who was, much like herself, dead and in pieces.

As for Hideo, every time he tried opening the door or demanding that she come out, Satsuki yelled at him to leave her alone.

"Why don't you just go back to South Korea?!"

"Maybe you can fly farther away this time!"

"That's what you're good at! Just get out of here, and leave me the hell alone!!!!!"

It didn't take much verbal gut punching from Satsuki before he stopped even saying good morning or goodbye to her.

One day in September, Yoshiko felt that she might be ready to see Satsuki again. She offered to help Hideo convince Satsuki to stop her self-imposed societal withdrawal. He was too shocked at his wife's offer to say no, so together, they stood side by side in front of Satsuki's bedroom door and pleaded for her to come out and just talk with them. The door shook violently in protest. "Earthquake!" was their initial reaction, but then they both guessed that it was more likely Satsuki kicking the door on the other side with both of her feet (Although, the way the door practically careened off its hinges, they would have thought maybe two enormous sledgehammers were banging against it). They retreated into their bedroom to discuss what their next move should be, but neither one could decide on anything except to give up and avoid going anywhere near their daughter's bedroom for the rest of the day.

Hideo and Yoshiko's botched attempt to draw Satsuki out of her room hadn't been a total loss. Both slept a little more peaceful that night, even allowing their bodies to brush up against each other in bed. And it had been the first time in a long time that either one had had a real conversation with each other. But the very next day, Yoshiko went right back to ignoring Hideo.

Chi-chan,

Can you see Hawaii from here?

My Chi-chan, always looking at the crows when they try to eat my food. They are as big as dogs! How can they be so fat in winter? I think the only thing that makes me happy these days is watching you hit the balcony door with your paws. Like a snowball hitting the glass, you and your furry, white fist. So, so funny! Those fat crows just smirk at you with their sickle-sharp beaks. But I know if the door were open, you would kill them all. I know how you feel. If I opened my door, I would kill them all, too.

Don't worry Chi-chan, one day you will have your revenge. Until then, we will just have to deal with those thieves. You know what, though? I think maybe Okaasan feeds them more than me.

I wonder if Hawaii has crows? Wait, that's a silly question. I'm sure they have them. I know they have cats, and that means you wouldn't be alone there, would you, Chi-chan? Maybe you can make a friend? Hmmm? We've been inside for so long, maybe Hawaii has finally floated close enough for me and you to walk there. I'm sure the cats there will like you.

Oh, that reminds me... I know you like it when I call you "Shii-chan," because every time we watch Kamichama, you perk up at the sight of your female counterpart. She's pretty, isn't she? I bet you like her more because you understand her, don't you? You know what she knows. I used to think you liked watching her because you are a boy cat and she is a pretty girl cat, but now I get it. She protects Karin, and you protect me and act like my shield. You help me keep control.

I think I made the right choice. Life is more quiet now, except when I listen to my iPod, of course. I hope you're not tired of hearing me sing Perfume's song, "Edge," over and over again. You probably figured out by now that it's my favorite song of theirs, even from since before this all started.

Wow. When this all started... seems so far away, almost like it never happened. Like I'm seeing a new world with the sharpest part of me...

Maybe I was always this way and didn't realize it. But now... I see things more clearly. I've bounced back.

How can I describe it to you? It's like that one time when I tried to watch Kamichama with Okaasan. Do you remember that? It was the episode when Karin yells her silly battle cry: I am God! Well... that battle cry is not so silly anymore to me. And even though Okaasan didn't understand what Karin meant by yelling that, I did. I mean, I do now. Now it makes total sense to me.

While Okaasan and Otousan continue their pathetic attempts to save our "family," I decide when I want to watch my anime, when I eat, or if I want to take a bath at 3 in the morning or not at all. I can play Dragonquest on my Nintendo DS, or listen to Perfume whenever I feel like it. Nobody can tell me what to do anymore. NOBODY.

I read online that there is even a name for people like me who decide to lock themselves inside their rooms and stop associating with everyone: hikkikomori. I don't like this title. That's not what I am. Those people all sound like big losers who are afraid to face the world. Well, I think maybe it's the other way around—that the world and everyone in it is afraid of me. At least they should be. They should be.

Chi-chan, I'm like Karin Hanazono now, aren't I?

I AM GOD!!!!

"So, where we eatin' for lunch?"

Sarah flipped through a phone book. Seul Bi sat at the computer, typing away while her co-worker searched for a restaurant that could deliver food to them. This was their routine.

"Go ahead and order whatever you want for yourself. I'm not really that hungry," Seul Bi answered haggardly. The truth was that she was so hungry she could eat a pile of food, but she was behind on the daily report. She decided to work through lunch and get everything updated so she wouldn't get stuck doing it minutes before her shift ended.

"You're such a busy worker bee. I'll save you something out of whatever I order, okay?"

"Thanks, Sarah. I appreciate it."

"Well, I appreciate you doing that fucking dreadful and pointless report every time we work together. You know how much I hate that fucking thing."

"It's not my favorite either. By the way, could you check on Marisa and... um..."

"Abbey? Sure, and while I do that, I think I'm gonna figure out what it is that I want to eat."

"Thanks much." Seul Bi shrugged. She wasn't sure why Abbey's name had slipped her mind.

A few seconds after Sarah disappeared inside the stairwell leading up to the apartments, there was a tapping noise just outside of the office door. Seul Bi didn't turn to see who it was. She kept proofreading the daily report.

"Did you forget something, Sarah?" She asked as she finished reading her last typed paragraph. When she turned around, a surprising face was staring at her from just outside the doorway.

"Sorry, it's Marisa. Are you busy?"

"Yeah, but it's no biggie. What's up?"

"Nothing much."

"I thought you were Sarah. She was just on her way to check up on you. Did you see her?"

"Uh-uh. I must have just missed her."

Seul Bi pointed towards the metallic chair where, the last time both of them were in the office, Marisa had confessed about her traumatic childhood rape. Marisa slinked over to the chair and sat down in slow motion. She was carrying a large, brown bag. Something inside of it clanked around as she tried to set the awkward thing on her lap.

"So, what's in the bag?" Seul Bi inquired. "Wait, don't tell me. It's a big box of tissues because you're about to tell me something really emotionally devastating?"

Marisa grimaced in mock disgust. "Miss Rissiello, you are really bad at making jokes, you know that?"

"Yeah, I know. My attempts at humor suck. But seriously, though, you didn't go to your therapy sessions today, and I was wondering if, um, maybe, you know, something is wrong or bothering you, perhaps?"

"Nah, nothin's really wrong with me right now. I just wanted to stay back to tell you something, but you've been really busy all day."

"What did you want to tell me?"

"I got you something." Marisa poked at the front of the bag.

"You did? What is it?" Seul Bi leaned towards Marisa.

Marisa pulled out of the bag a narrow, wood-framed lamp. It was octagonal shaped, with tan paper walls. A cord snuck out one of the sides. The wooden beams dividing the walls had calligraphy etchings. Maybe Japanese? Seul Bi couldn't tell. She reached for the lamp and ran her fingers over its edges, shaking her head in disbelief that this lamp now belonged to her.

"Oh my God! Marisa, it's beautiful. This is for me? But you know I can't accept gifts."

"It's okay. I talked to Dr. Nathan, and he gave me permission."

"Really?" Seul Bi said skeptically. Dr. Nathan was very strict about exchanges of gifts between the resource staff and the residents. She supposed that Marisa might be lying, but it would be easy enough to find out if she was or not. One phone call to Dr. Nathan would confirm it.

Marisa's head bobbed up and down enthusiastically. "Yeah, I know. It surprised me, too. You know I had—"

Seul Bi cut her off. "I can't believe it! This is so amazing. Sorry to interrupt ya, but… really, wow. I mean, I'm blown away. Why did you decide to do this for me?"

"Well, you really helped me out the other night… er wait… wasn't it a few weeks ago? You know what night I'm talking about, right?"

"Yeah, of course." *How could I forget?* Seul Bi thought to herself. "Go on."

"Right. So… when I told you about everything with my dad… it just somehow made things easier for me. I mean, I'm still going through shit, and I'm probably never going to get better, but you made me feel safe. That's hard for me, you know? Anyway, there's an actual story behind this lamp and what it represents, but first, let me show you something."

Marisa sprung up and turned down the lights in the office. She plugged the lamp's cord into an electrical socket, and its paper walls suddenly danced with brightness. Before Seul Bi could object to any of this (being in a darkened office room with a resident felt more unethical to her than receiving a present), greenish-yellow spots materialized into the shadowy air. They looked like glowing polka dots on an ethereal dress.

"Oh my God, Marisa, it's beautiful. Are these…"

"Lightning bugs?" Marisa pretended to cradle their fluorescent bodies in her hands. "Yep. I figured you would like this."

"Oh, what does this mean here?" Seul Bi asked while rubbing the calligraphy etchings.

"Right," Marisa began, "the story. Well, the reason why I got this for you was because, apparently, fireflies are pretty symbolic in Japanese culture, and I know you're Korean and not Japanese, but I figured you would still like it, anyway, because it's Asian, and also because… well, because of the meaning of the words written on it. I did some research, and they're supposed to say 'hitodama.' This means something like human souls, or souls of the fallen? Anyway, the folklore I was reading and what made me want this for you was that lightning bugs are supposedly the souls of the newly dead who sort of… hang out here in this world before their souls are ready to leave for the next one.

Seul Bi wrinkled her brow in puzzlement. "And this story made you think of me?"

"Well, I guess this reminds me of you because you seem so sad sometimes. I mean, I can tell that you get really sad because I've gone through so much, and it's obvious to me that you must have been through a lot as well. I always wonder about what you might have lost that makes you so sad. The weird part is that you are always so supportive and nice to me. But I can sense that, inside you, there is something still… hanging around, I guess."

What could she say? Seul Bi couldn't force out any words. She wanted to cry, to unravel and confess to Marisa about the losses in her past, but that wouldn't be appropriate. She had never once crossed that ethical line of confiding in a patient. That would only breed the kind of countertransference-type situation that therapists and residential workers like her lose their jobs over.

But still… how could she ignore what she was feeling? In all honesty, she couldn't remember when the last time was that anyone gave her a gift (at least one that didn't have the title "Christmas" or "birthday" attached to it). And not only that, Marisa's high-powered perception had uncovered the weakest point in her that kept her vulnerable, no matter how hard she tried to hide it. It was the longing for resolution to her own past trauma, for the chance to be somebody's daughter again, for the drifting that defined every hour and minute of her days to end, all these things that could be summed up perfectly by Marisa's description of her. *Something still hanging around.*

Oh Marisa, Seul Bi thought to herself, *that Something isn't just hanging around inside of me, but controlling my every move and my every feeling.* As difficult as it was, Seul Bi knew that if she thought any more about it, she would risk losing not just her job but herself as well. So she sat up in her chair as far as her back would let her and donned her best counselor face, ignoring the razor pangs of grief slicing her stomach walls.

"Marisa, I don't get gifts very often, but this is beyond a gift. It's just… it's just wow, you know? Thank you. It really does mean a lot."

Seul Bi stood up and flipped on the lights, then unplugged the lamp. Marisa mouthed the words "you're welcome" to her.

Time to change the subject, Seul Bi thought. "So, Miss Marisa, I'm guessing you don't have anything to do today?"

"Nah. I'm just going to head back to my room and maybe lie down or watch TV. I really wanted to give this to you, so I stayed back from my counseling. Your shift would've ended before my counseling sessions would have, so…"

"Aww. Really, you didn't have to do that."

"No worries." Marisa smiled at Seul Bi reassuringly, then excused herself out of the room. It was rare to hear any sort of cheer in Marisa's voice. Seul Bi even thought for a second that Marisa could've almost passed for a healthy, normal teenager who was never abused or raped as a child. *Almost.*

No sooner had Marisa left than Sarah appeared in the doorway. Her gaze immediately landed on the lamp.

"Wow, that's gorgeous-looking. What is that?"

"It's a Japanese lamp. Marisa got it for me."

Sarah froze. "Marisa?"

"Yeah, I know. She said that Dr. Nathan gave her permission."

"Really? Do you believe her?"

"Yeah. I mean, she seemed very sincere. She said I looked sad, and this reminded her of me."

Sarah relaxed after Seul Bi said this. She went over and plugged the lamp in for a quick demonstration. The lightning bugs hopped all over the room walls.

"So, you said Marisa bought this and thought of you?"

"Mm hm."

Seul Bi didn't offer any more explanation than this. Sarah just nodded her head, didn't ask why. She was used to Seul Bi backing away from these types of conversations involving self-disclosure. If Seul Bi really was sad, Sarah knew she would never know the reason why.

Seul Bi resumed typing up the daily report, trying her best to not dig back into her feelings she had had when Marisa gave her the lamp. It would've been easy enough, she supposed, to confide in Sarah. There was a very easygoing camaraderie between them at work. The problem was that Sarah had never asked Seul Bi to do something outside of Rainbow. This sent a signal to Seul Bi that either Sarah was not interested in her as a person, despite always showing a professional courtesy towards her, or that she was too busy in her personal life to have time for another friend. Or she could just be fucked up, which was always a possibility with those who choose the counseling field as a career choice.

"Oh, you know what? I just thought of a question I wanted to ask you. Do you know where Morris has been?" Seul Bi asked. "I haven't seen him lately."

Sarah shrugged her shoulders and sat down in the chair beside Seul Bi. "I think he took some vacation time. Why, what's up?"

"I haven't seen him for a few days now, that's all. We usually talk in the morning. He's so funny, don't you think?"

"Yeah, he cracks me up." Sarah looked at her watch. "I hope the food comes soon."

"Where'd ya end up ordering?"

"Where do you think? I ordered from Siam Paragon. It's the only guarantee of food being delivered without any problems."

"So true! By the way, how's your thesis coming along?"

Sarah sneezed into her arm crease. "It's taking fucking forever. I have so much research left to do."

"Bless you." Seul Bi gave Sarah a tissue. "Here ya go." Sarah blew her nose in it.

"Thanks. I think I might be getting a cold."

"Hmm, I hope not."

"You and me both."

"So, your thesis, what's it about again?"

"Oh, um, it's uh, on multiple intelligences. I'm proposing that there could be a ninth intelligence added to the eight core ones. It would be existential intelligence. I'm not the first to do that, though."

"Oh, really?"

"Yeah. I just am following up on what others have thought about for a long time. So, I'm kinda in the process right now of looking for more proof of existential intelligence."

"I see," Seul Bi said. Wasn't multiple intelligences the topic of her mother's dissertation as well? She couldn't remember exactly. She continued to work on finishing up the report. When she reached the last line of the email, she sent the message to every employee at Rainbow and then reclined back in her chair and sighed.

Sarah chuckled. "Seul Bi, do you have any idea what I'm talking about?"

"Ah, is it that obvious?" Seul Bi laughed, but she couldn't hide the fact that her mind was elsewhere. She was too busy shifting away from the feelings brought on by Marisa's gift, which were amplified by the recollection of what had happened after returning from Hawaii. She had received her mother's personal items in a filing box. Inside it had been clothes, makeup, and the dissertation. She had attempted to read the first few pages of her mother's work, but had broken down in tears and couldn't finish it. She never touched the dissertation again after that day.

Sarah didn't pay any attention or take offense to Seul Bi being lost in the clouds. Since there was nothing else to really talk about between them, she decided to explain in more detail her thesis.

"So, basically, there's like, eight intelligences; there's musical, verbal, logical and mathematical, kinesthetic, spatial, interpersonal, intrapersonal, and naturalistic. But I think there should be another type of measurable intelligence that deals with the spirit or metaphysical.

"I did some research and found out that some parts of the brain, when stimulated, seem to suggest a kind of awareness to what we cannot see with our own two eyes. You know, like people who go into religious seizures, that sort of thing. That part of the brain is recorded as having massive activity when something like that happens, especially when it comes to mapping theta waves. It seems to indicate some powerful force, like an *a-ha* moment that we all kinda get from time to time. Dr. Nathan refers to it as the seven-megahertz spike. It's like when your mind just… pans out and into someplace that isn't here. You know what I mean?"

Seul Bi's eyes flipped on their hi-beams. "Wow, you know what? I actually *do*, for a change, know what you're saying. Dr. Nathan's test on me the other day showed that I had some kind of extra stimulation in my theta waves. What a coincidence you are talking about that now."

"Yeah, strange isn't it? So wait, what did Dr. Nathan say, exactly?"

"Uh, I dunno, something about me having the brain activity of a young teenager. I have an overactive imagination, apparently."

"Oh, I see. Well, that supports exactly what I'm saying, then, right?"

"Yeah, it would seem so."

Seul Bi stared down at Marisa's gift. Sarah had set it on the floor beside the desk. The lightning bugs seemed to be crawling across the tan lamp sheets. Something about their shapes were pulsating and twisting around as though they were prying their legs from the sticky glue that held them prisoners. Then again, maybe it was just her imagination.

The doorbell rang. It was probably the delivery guy for Siam Paragon. Since Rainbow was just five streets away from the restaurant, any food order from them arrived exceptionally fast. Seul Bi heard Sarah open the door and first sneeze and then squeal with excitement at her lunch arriving so quickly.

She didn't get up to join Sarah in the common area, however. She continued to stare at the lamp and imagined herself as a lightning bug, waiting for eternal closure.

D R U N K

with ....

S P I R I T S

He knew it was there. He could feel it playing hide-and-go-seek underneath his fingernails.

Dirt. The kind that accumulates from a past that included rolling around in compost filled with bad choices. And it couldn't be picked out or washed away. Of course, he tried to remove it, one drink at a time, at various *izakayas*[34]. He slouched on stools every night after work and tried to disinfect himself with glasses of imported *soju*. He never spoke with anyone during these purification rituals, either. Instead, his head slung low like a wire-framed picture on a loose nail in the wall, threatening to smack against the bar top and crash into unconsciousness at any moment.

"Another one, sir?" asked the bartender in his Jamaican-colored hat.

Hideo waved him off. He sat this night in a cozy *izakaya* two blocks south of Jonan-Dori. The bartender moved away from Hideo to fetch drinks for a noisy, young couple at the end of the bar. Hideo turned towards the two lovebirds and snorted under his breath. Watching them flirt with each other reminded him of his very first naïve advances towards Yoshiko, back when his heart was vying with his fear for that first kiss with her. Back when they laughed all the time at everything, most of all at themselves.

Back before it all went to shit.

Hideo tossed three crumpled-up, 1,000-yen bills onto the bar and slinked out without drawing any attention. He shivered in the cold February air. "No more *soju* for me, Bob Marley," he muttered to himself. It didn't matter if he guzzled down another glass of his favorite drink. The dirt would still be there in the morning.

....

34. *izakayas*—Japanese bar.

During the drive home, Hideo's buzz was like wearing smudged glasses that made everything blurry. A beast with barley flesh and alcohol blood growled and thrashed around in his stomach. He didn't feel well at all, but going home and staring at Yoshiko's back while she slept would make him feel even worse. The past year had been a laundry cycle: Work. Izakaya. The car ride home. Nausea. Loathing. Dreamless sleep. Repeat. Repeat. Repeat. Repeat.

He managed to reach his neighborhood without throwing up or hitting anyone. He found a rare empty parking space in front of his housing complex and decided to park there. *I guess this is my lucky night*, he thought to himself. Since his normal parking spot was a reserved lot inside a parking garage three streets away, He could sleep in an extra ten minutes. *Ah, but is that really something to be excited about?*

He turned off the engine and looked up at his apartment's kitchen door, which led out to the balcony shared with Satsuki's bedroom. Uneasy shadows were spread across everything in sight. He blinked and turned away, unable to focus with his blurred vision. He was developing a headache, anyway, from the reminder of what awaited him inside the apartment's lonely walls. *Siberia,* he thought to himself. *That's the only thing up there waiting for me.*

His fingernails rototilled the car steering wheel for almost ten full minutes. He couldn't stop brooding over his daughter's self-imposed exile from society and especially his marriage that had become worthy of a thousand divorces. A walk around the block sounded good right about then.

He stumbled out of the car. After a few dizzying steps, he lurched towards the rusty bike rack beside his housing complex and leaned against it just long enough to avoid a face plant into the ground. The world was spinning faster than normal on its axis, and the stars above were huddled together in a cloudy ditch beside the full moon in the sky. As a result, the entire neighborhood had become opaque and scribbled out of view with blackness, except for one spot to the left of Hideo. It was a hidden grove behind a tall ring of trees, but he knew exactly what was there waiting for him. He clumsily walked past the trees, whose branches bowed and whispered their welcome as he did, and there, on a sandy platform, was the neighborhood *jinjya*[35], wearing a white sweater of starry illumination.

Yoshiko had been thrilled about the *jinjya* residing next to their home. She told Hideo over and over about how this was a good omen for peace, but he wondered how much of that sort of logic was true. He was never really religious, or more accurately, never had a need for religion in his everyday life. Yet he didn't ignore the importance of people's belief systems, either. He treaded somewhere between the secular and the devout, much like the city of Hiroshima itself, with its sprawling, modern buildings juxtaposed to ancient temples and shrines built centuries ago. Perhaps *kami*[36] could be felt in all things, but for Hideo, his ability to connect with the spirit world was captured by the mousetrap of humanity—confusion. He wasn't sure about what was right or wrong and had so many questions about doctrines of faith that it seemed easier to just remain indifferent towards all of it. He had felt this way ever since entering adolescence.

Besides, the Japan he lived in moved too fast for things like meditation or rituals. He was a businessman, working five to six days a week or more, and on the verge of losing his family to trauma-induced hate. Where was the *kami* in that?

As Hideo passed through the dust-painted *torii*[37] gate, he considered returning to his car and driving until sunrise. The calm emanating from this place was so unfamiliar that it frightened him. The *honden*[38] looked like an ancient abandoned house. The pathway leading up to its threshold had shadows stretched across it like tripwires. Unfortunately, an unlit, stone lantern adjacent to the entrance offered no guidance behind its cracked glass. Twin statues of lion dogs, who were supposed to be protectors of the *jinjya*, drooped on their pedestals beside the stone lantern and

---

35. *jinjya*—a Shinto shrine whose main purpose is to house one or more Shinto spirits.
36. *kami*—in the Shinto faith, these are commonly known as divine spirits.
37. *torii*—traditional Japanese gate found in front of a Shinto shrine or within one. It symbolically marks the transition from the profane to the sacred. A gate between this world and the spiritual world.
38. *honden*—the most sacred building inside a Shinto shrine. This is what the enshrined kami inhabits.

showed no suspicion in their lazy eyes. Even the house-sized *honden's* gabled rooftop was softened by a pearly tint.

Nothing moved or breathed here except Hideo, and his instincts told him that there might be danger in the still surroundings. *Driving drunk would be safer than this*, he thought to himself. As he turned around to leave, a rustling noise on the right side of the *honden* made his blood congeal. *I'm not alone*, he thought, *but who else could be out at this time of night?* A stray cat (he had seen so many lingering around the housing complexes in this area), or perhaps a teenage couple defiling this sacred spot with their make-out session? Suddenly he had the awful feeling that if he took another step, something terrible would happen. He closed his eyes and ironically did what so many others do when they visited a *jinjya*—he prayed for safety.

Fortunately, his prayer was answered. A gust of wind delivered a parcel of clarity to Hideo, who opened his eyes just in time to discover the rustling noise was not a cat or teens hiding in the background, but several wooden plaques slapping against a plywood wall. "Ahh, of course. It's just the *emas*," he said to himself. The knot in his stomach was untied. He decided to have a look at them.

Even though it was in a dark spot next to the *honden*, he counted over twenty-four *emas* that hung from hooks stuck in the wall. Each of them carried written prayers and wishes of various kinds: one was a student's desire to pass an upcoming exam, another the hope for a better marriage (which Hideo had also yearned for this past year), and several more had decorations of animals and small children hoping to be blessed.

Hideo reached his hand out and dragged his fingers across a row of *emas*, contemplating the possibility that their inscriptions would be received by the *kami* residing at this *jinjya*. He reflected on his attempts at curing the deepening sickness that plagued his family, but rationalizing things, ignoring what had happened, and late night drinking binges failed to spark recovery. Not that he had expected his actions to do any good. *I should write down my own wishes*, Hideo thought, *but there aren't enough empty spaces to fit them all.*

It wouldn't matter, anyway. Hideo had completely Xeroxed his father's unapologetic existential paradigm. In fact, his father had completely foregone religiosity after surviving the bombings of Hiroshima and Nagasaki. Right before his death (when Hideo was just eight years old), he had told Hideo that it was just pure luck he didn't die on those two perilous days in Japan's history, and that he wished he had been disintegrated. Living was a lifeless affair. Nightmares had leeched onto his brain every night for many years after the bombings. He had suffered tremendous migraines, and after witnessing so much carnage and destruction, it had made him question the importance of his existence. It was no surprise that he ended up wearing starched collars, carrying a briefcase, and aimlessly working for a machine export company the rest of his life. There was no reason for prayers or spiritual reverence in that kind of workplace—only respect for grinding it out at the job.

Hideo knew this kind of desperation all too well. He trudged home quickly after thinking about his father, but not before the wintry night air turned his whole body into a numbsicle.

It wasn't much warmer inside the apartment. While lying under the covers and facing Yoshiko's glacier-white backside, he couldn't warm his blood back to normal body temperature. The alcohol was done boiling his insides.

Yoshiko hadn't woken up or faced him since he had undressed and slipped under the covers, but that wasn't unusual for her. He had rarely seen her face for more than a few minutes in the past eight months, and he questioned whether or not the person sleeping beside him now was his wife or a doppelganger. Whatever she was, the absence of warmth or a relationship left him palpitating for hours.

That is, until an unexpected inspiration lassoed him right out of bed.

The chance to correct things with his family was right in front of him. *That's it!* Hideo thought excitedly to himself. *I didn't go to the jinjya so that my prayers could be answered. They're worthless, anyway. No, I went to the jinjya because Yoshiko's prayers haven't been answered. And it's my job to make sure they are! Ah, why didn't I realize this before? I drive by the jinjya everyday on my way to work!*

What Yoshiko really wants is to not deal with everything by herself, but how can I get her to accept my help? She won't talk to me unless it's to tell me she forgot to pick up something at the grocery store. Or to ask me to not turn the television up so loud at night when I come home. Then again, why else would I have gotten that parking space so close to our home on this night, of all nights? I was supposed to visit the jinjya, and I was definitely supposed to see the emas hanging up there. She needs to know that I really mean business when it comes to helping her get through this whole thing. First, I gotta get her talking to me, then take her out on some dates, and then we can visit the jinjya together. Who knows? Maybe I can get Satsuki to go along, too. It's about time she came out of her room.

Hideo felt heat rush back to his body. Feeling content with his plan, he laid back down onto the bed, and for some reason, couldn't help but think about the fact that every glass of *soju* he drank tonight must have had a *kami* swimming in it. They all got washed down his esophagus and into his stomach and now were uniting together to help him form a plan to save his family. "Drunken spirits," Hideo whispered. He started to laugh but quickly placed a hand over his mouth, then fell asleep feeling phosphorescent for the first time in many months.

"So, can you come over tonight?"

Seul Bi had finished work and was about to finish up grocery shopping at Jewel Osco when Beverly called. While checking out, she looked at the digital clock beside the row of cash registers. She wondered if the cashiers preferred to know how much longer they had until the end of their shifts or if a manager put the clock there as a form of work torture. The time read 5:34 p.m.

"Uh, sure. Is Aunt Deb. cooking anything, or should I pick up something at the store?"

"Wait a second." The phone rattled around and made a clicking noise as Beverly fumbled around for something.

"Uh, no, I don't think you have to get anything. Mom's making us chicken cacciatore."

"Us? Does that mean just you and your mom or…"

"Or what?" Beverly interrupted. "Mark is going to be eating with us, too, so don't start pouting. You're not gonna be a third wheel."

Seul Bi rolled her eyes. "Yeaaaaah, sure. Whatever, though. It's fine."

"Really?"

"Yeah, I mean I'm not doing anything tonight, and to be honest, it would be nice to have some company. I haven't seen you guys in a while, and lately things have been… well, I dunno. They just have been…"

"Fucked up? Ridiculous? Retarded? All of the above?"

"Ha ha. My life's like a Mad Lib. Fill it in with your choice of expletives."

"I was always good at Mad Libs, except for some reason when they always asked for a thing, I would write 'cock' every single time. What do you think that means, Miss Psychology Person?"

Seul Bi grinned. "That you have penis envy?"

"Really? I mean, I love Mark's cock, but—"

"Enough already, modest mouse! Jesus! Anyway, I'll be over in a few minutes."

"Do you want to be picked up?"

"Nah, I'll walk. It's not so bad out today. Thanks for the offer, though."

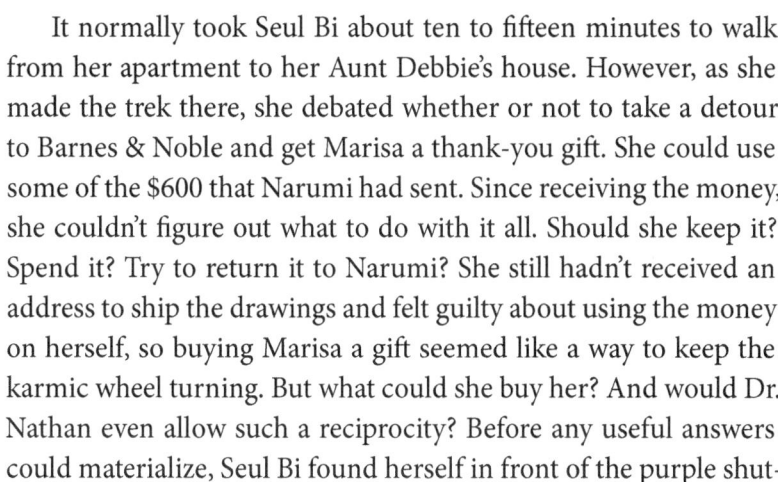

It normally took Seul Bi about ten to fifteen minutes to walk from her apartment to her Aunt Debbie's house. However, as she made the trek there, she debated whether or not to take a detour to Barnes & Noble and get Marisa a thank-you gift. She could use some of the $600 that Narumi had sent. Since receiving the money, she couldn't figure out what to do with it all. Should she keep it? Spend it? Try to return it to Narumi? She still hadn't received an address to ship the drawings and felt guilty about using the money on herself, so buying Marisa a gift seemed like a way to keep the karmic wheel turning. But what could she buy her? And would Dr. Nathan even allow such a reciprocity? Before any useful answers could materialize, Seul Bi found herself in front of the purple shutterboards on her Aunt Debbie's front porch. Decision made.

The night drudged on in routine fashion. Debbie made her mysterious chicken cacciatore (nobody could ever figure out the special ingredients that gave the meat its inescapable saccharine taste). Beverly and Mark bickered like an ornery, married couple stuck in a nursing home, and everyone hung out in the living room, watching television until midnight. Nobody moved much until Debbie stood up and yawned.

"Well, Mark, girls, I'm going to bed."

"Good night, Ma," Beverly said. Mark echoed his girlfriend's words.

Seul Bi, who was sprawled out on the floor beside the Ektorp sofa (Seul Bi had made her Aunt Debbie buy the sofa from Ikea the summer after her parents had died. It was her favorite piece of furniture in the house. Much to her chagrin, it was also where Beverly had been nestled against Mark all night), stood up to hug her aunt.

"Thanks for dinner. The chicken cacciatore was so frickin' amazing!"

"Anytime, hon'. You know you are always welcome to eat with us. Speaking of which, are you staying over tonight?"

"Um, I don't think so. I'm probably gonna go soon. I have to work tomorrow pretty early."

"Ah, well, it was nice having you over. Good night." Debbie hugged her one more time.

"Good night, Aunt Deb."

After Aunt Debbie left the living room, Mark sat up and lit a cigarette. He blew a puff of smoke towards Seul Bi. "So, what's up with you? You've been quiet all night. Mad we're on your couch?"

Seul Bi jerked her head back, waving the smoke away from her face. "It's a sofa, not a couch, and no, that's not it."

"Soooorrry. Sofa, couch, whatever," Mark said. A trickle of laughter slipped his lips. "So, what is it, then?"

Seul Bi managed a limp smile. "Ah, nothing, I guess. I have so much on my mind. I was just thinking about everything that has happened to me in the past month." She put her hands underneath her butt. She didn't want Mark or Beverly to see her palms sweating. Something inside of her was uneasy and making her nervous, though she couldn't be sure what it was, exactly.

Beverly snatched the cigarette from Mark's lips. "What else is new with you, though? I mean, you are one of the most, like, introspective people I know. But sometimes you remind me of a little, plastic astronaut on a toy moon."

"Introverted, not introspective," Mark said.

"What? You know what I mean, you dick!" Beverly pinched Mark's arm. He screwed his face up in a feigned expression of pain.

"Play nice, you two," Seul Bi said, wagging her finger at them both. "So, you think I'm lost in space, huh?"

"Plastic astronaut on a toy moon, eh? That was pretty poetic of you, by the way," Mark added before Beverly could answer Seul Bi's question.

Beverly ignored Mark. "No, it's not that. All I'm saying is that sometimes I don't know if you're, like, mentally speaking, here or… somewhere else, you know? And I think that you've kinda, sorta been this way for a long time now."

"Hmm." Seul Bi plopped down next to the sofa and scratched the back of her head. "I think I've just been caught up in so much stuff lately, and…" She paused. Should she tell Beverly about the ash storm, or Narumi, or about the increasingly frequent flashbacks to the day her parents died? All these things made her feel like she was chewing on a clay brick. They filled her with dread.

However, Seul Bi appreciated her cousin's concern. It provided just the shred of confidence she needed to talk about herself. "The things is, I've been thinking a lot lately about what happened to my mom and dad."

Beverly leaned towards Seul Bi. "Wait, your real mom and dad, or—"

"No, no, your aunt and uncle. I never think about my real mom and dad. I mean, what's the point? They obviously didn't want me, you know? So, it has nothing to do with them. What I can't stop thinking about is that maybe something or somebody in my life has been trying to speak to me, but I'm just not sure what it is or even who it could be, or even what they're trying to tell me. But I feel it. And this all started in Hawaii, right after my parents died.

"It's the strangest feeling, too—this feeling like somebody is talking to me, or the other feeling I have all the time, which is that I'm living somebody else's life. Maybe it's because it's so surreal that my parents are gone, and they died the way they did, you know? Anyway, I guess that's why I'm so preoccupied lately. I'm sorry."

Beverly pretended to shake Seul Bi. "Don't be a shit, cuz! You don't have to apologize for something like that. I get it, I think. I mean, I dunno, it's not like I don't think about that day, either."

It was true. Beverly did think every now and then about the mysterious deaths of her Aunt Zoe and Uncle Jimmy. She mostly remembered how she'd slept through that entire morning. She also sometimes wondered what would've happened if she had gone into the water with her cousin. Would she have done something to try and save her aunt and uncle? Or would she have died right alongside them on the ocean floor?

But Beverly didn't want to think about any of those things now. Nor did she want to ruin the rest of the night by getting all serious and heavy-hearted with Seul Bi. It was time for a distraction.

"You wanna know what I think, cuz? I think you just need to forget about all of that for now and laugh. How about we watch something funny?"

Mark raised his hands in the air with excitement. "Oh, I know what we could watch!!!"

"What?" Both Seul Bi and Beverly asked at the same time.

"*Trading Places!*"

"Mark! You're so stupid sometimes! That movie is, like, ancient, and I doubt we even have it." Beverly wiggled out from under Mark and went to the kitchen.

"It's okay, I thought it was funny." Seul Bi patted Mark on his leg. "Let's just throw whatever in."

When Beverly returned from the kitchen, she turned the living room lights off and popped in some random comedy, jumping on top of Mark with a lascivious giggle. Seul Bi lay down on the living room floor by the television and tried to ignore their makeout noises. About forty-something minutes later, she decided it was time to leave.

Walking home wasn't going to be fun. The winter witching hours would no doubt bring with them a freezing temperature. But at least she had a good excuse if her cousin asked why she was leaving so quickly. She pulled her coat on, stood up, and crept to the front door, but not a word came from Beverly's or Mark's lips. Their tongues were too busy slipping in and out of each other's mouths. She grimaced at them. Their slurping noises made her feel anxious, and to make things worse, she started to feel nauseous. She let herself out the front door and began walking as fast as she could back to her apartment.

Not a single car drove down the snow-glazed streets. A few streetlights flickered, but only the sound of a faint, night wind, which seemed lost in the labyrinth of trees lining the residential sidewalks, could be heard. The midnight air provided some relief to Seul Bi, but now her eyes were stinging.

As Seul Bi dug into her eyes with her gloves, she had a crazy thought: *Maybe I should go to Japan and find Narumi. Then I can ask her what's going on. Maybe she would know. We could compare notes.* The only problem was that she hadn't heard from Narumi in weeks and had no idea what her actual address was in Japan. Or if she was even real. *Is Narumi a figment of my imagination? No, that can't be it. There's $600 dollars from her that's sitting in my bank account. Still... why the fuck would I think we're connected at all?*

Seul Bi continued walking with a steady stride, trying to cover her eyes from the cold. She double-timed it to her apartment complex, and once inside, trudged up the steps, then stood for a moment in front of her door and leaned her head on the worn, wooden trim. She couldn't help thinking that either the cold was messing with her head or that she really did have the over-active imagination of an adolescent. *Or maybe I'm just getting an early start on being a lonely, crazy woman. Or maybe I'm just really tired and need some sl—*

Seul Bi grabbed her stomach. Suddenly her body was becoming smaller and smaller, and everything inside had to be squeezed out immediately.

"Shit!"

She chomped on air as her throat became blocked and borrowed. She managed to swing the door open and make it to the toilet right before a stream of chicken chunks and onion-infested bile cascaded from her mouth and all over the porcelain rim.

"Fuck! Please, no more!"

She continued to gag until her ribs felt like they were cracking. She wondered how it was possible to throw up her entire dinner so violently. In her entire life, she had only thrown up a handful of times. It wasn't something she could ever get used to, unlike, say, some of the anorexic and bulimic girls who she counseled who threw up every single day. Then again, she doubted those girls ever really got "used" to all the ritualistic purging brought on by their irrational fear of gaining weight. It seemed like a necessary evil to them—something that must be done in order to feel normal, even if it killed them in the process.

When she finished throwing up, she struggled to her feet and tried looking at herself in the mirror, but all she could do was cough up a noodle stuck in the back of her throat.

"Fuuuuuuck this."

She splashed some water onto her face, then wiggled out of her vomit-stained shirt and pants and jammed a toothbrush into her mouth. There was an oily, dark color in her studio apartment, but turning on the overhead lights didn't seem like a good idea. Her eyes still stung from the outside air, so she unpacked Marisa's lamp and set it on the computer stand. At the flip of a switch, insects made of a reticent light buzzed around the room without a sound. She was relieved. Their soft glow felt comforting, warm, safe.

Her assuagement lasted for only a brief couple of seconds. When she stepped into the bathroom to finish brushing her teeth, she had an alarming thought:

Why was my front door unlocked?

Seul Bi heard heavy footsteps right behind her. Before she could turn around, she went hurtling into the corner of the computer stand. She crash-landed onto the floor next to her bed, her face smacking off the ground with a loud THUMP!

Everything immediately went black. The lightning bugs vanished. There was no more safety to be found in their glow. Seul Bi felt no pain from the fall, however. Her veins sucked adrenalin into her limbs so fast that she stood right back up to face who or what had assailed her. A tall, masculine shadow was all she could make out, as her eyes couldn't focus quick enough to see the intruder lunging for her once more.

Seul Bi hollered as loud as she could. "HELP ME!!!! SOME-BODY HEL—"

Her words disintegrated. From inside the lingering darkness of the apartment, a hand submerged her entire face in its grip. A crown of fingers dug into the flesh on her forehead. Seul Bi tasted a greasy palm and almost threw up again. She shook her head in disapproval but was forced to wear the claw bridle and not complain. Only her muted shrieks escaped. It was odd, but she couldn't hear anything at all, even when she was next slammed into the bathroom mirror.

As she crumbled onto the floor, a shard thunderstorm rained down on her half-naked body. Giant glass droplets shredded and sliced her all over. She felt her life pouring out onto her bra and underwear, which were quickly becoming stained period crimson from all the blood. Even her brownish skin turned orange from all the red. With chunks of the mirror falling everywhere and a glass girdle circling the entire bathroom floor, she felt like a paper ballerina in a wind tunnel full of razors.

"Some... body... help...!"

Seul Bi tried to pull herself up but slipped on the blood that was oozing out of her. She lay back down again, pulling pieces of glass out of her face. Her cheeks made a popping sound like they were being deflated.

She wasn't sure if her assailant was still in the apartment. She sucked down a huge breath and tried to pull herself up once more, but this time she noticed something strange by the shower curtain. There was a large pile of dirt... and it was moving.

"WhA... tHE... FuCK?"

These three words came out of Seul Bi's mouth in an uneven chorus of tenor consonants and soprano vowels. She felt woozy, tired. She wasn't sure if the pile of dirt was real or if she was losing her mind. She figured that it was probably her brain screwing up from the blood loss.

However, when the bassy moan of a man's voice suddenly filled the bathroom, there was no doubt that Seul Bi was part of a hellish choir recital and not performing a solo. Her assailant had returned and was standing in the bathroom doorway, blocking any hope from getting inside the bathroom. Seul Bi stared at him and gasped.

He was holding a shovel.

"No... please. No... WHAT IS TH...?"

Seul Bi was answered with a swift blow to her ribs. It lifted her into the air and into the shower, knocking the moldy curtain down around her feet. Despite having the wind knocked out of her, she started to scream over and over.

"OH MY GOD!!!! SOMEBODY PLEASE FUCKING HELP ME!!!!"

She hoped somebody heard her desperate screams, but she knew that everyone minded their own business in her apartment complex. It was like a big-city rule, or something. She heard strange sounds all the time, and like all the other residents in the building, ignored them. Now she wished she hadn't.

Seul Bi's assailant walked over to her, dragging the shovel behind him. He then reached for the curtain, and as he bent over, Seul Bi was apprehended with a terrible sight. He looked like charred meat on crumpled tinfoil. His arms and legs were scaly from what had to be at least fourth degree burns, and patches of eschar floating in seeping piles of pus dripped everywhere. His clothes were covered in brown dust, and bits of bone stuck out of holes in the fabric. The man's deformed and blackened face hid any sign of a nose, ears, or hair. Just two eyes stuck in gooey tissue and a toothless mouth covered in blister sores gave any impression of a human at all.

Seul Bi recoiled, kicking the air between her and the man. It seemed to work. He backed out of view, but only far enough to swing his shovel.

"NO!!!!"

Seul Bi knew what was coming next. He began heaving dirt onto her head, some of which landed directly in her mouth, making it hard to breathe. She jerked her head from side to side, dribbling thick grime from the corners of her mouth at first, then spitting out every granule of dirt that touched her tongue as fast as she possibly could. She miraculously avoided swallowing or even tasting any kind of foulness, but her ribs exploded in pain with every breath expelled.

This is it, she thought. The bathroom started to disappear. She felt exhausted beyond words. She wished that her life could rewind back to Kona, back to before the day that changed everything. *What is here for me, anyway?*

There was a faint, tapping noise from inside the apartment. Suddenly a trace of energy zapped Seul Bi back to the present. She hoped it was a neighbor who had had enough of the screaming and banging for one night. *Maybe it's the police*, she hoped. But even if it was, could they really stop this thing in time before it killed her... or worse? She didn't want to take a chance and find out. It was up to her to find a way out of this soil slammer, get the attention of whoever was making that tapping sound, and make a run for the street.

She let out a giant scream. "PLEASE, SOMEBODY FUCKING HELP ME!!!!"

The man paused and swiveled his head towards the bathroom door. The tapping noise was getting louder. This was her chance. With a wincing breath, Seul Bi braced herself against the shower walls and pushed as hard as she could. Her body jerked forward, but she was unable to stand up. The dirt squeezed her legs, climbing up her thighs and stomach. It was then that she realized why the muck was moving when she stared at it earlier:

Worms.

They twisted and arched in every direction, their maggot-like shapes contorting with an unnatural snarl. They wrapped themselves around her torso like seaweed on a boat rotor. Overgrown worms, slimy worms, worms with little pricklies on their skin... they all clamored for her flesh. Seul Bi could feel them burrowing first into her underwear, then her bra. Soon the worms would fill her mouth, and ears, too. So much for her great escape.

The man looked back at her and began to scoop more worm-infested dirt into the shower. Seul Bi resisted one last time, pushing her hands in the way, but her arms were too heavy to keep up. She shouted until her throat burst. She swung her head back and forth. She cried. And while her tears created a muddy bib, chunks of the man's crispy skin fell into her lap. The worms swarmed over the meat. It vanished in seconds.

More of her body slipped beneath the dirt until, finally, she closed her eyes. She couldn't hear the scrapes against the bathroom floor anymore. She was buried completely in the worm necropolis, but she didn't care anymore.

CHAPTER 33

WHAT ONE PERSON CAN ACCOMPLISH

Yoshiko flicked the light cord hanging from the bedroom ceiling. She imagined it was a rope that somebody threw down to her while she sank deeper into an abysmal well's quicksand floor. She could hear Hideo in the bathroom, brushing his teeth and preparing for work. She listened intently for his footsteps getting closer to the bedroom doorway, but he continued to brush and gargle so loudly that she knew it was safe to keep her eyes open. When she was first discharged from the hospital, Hideo would check on her and ask if she needed anything, but he had long since stopped being so patriarchal. She had ignored his benign attempts and had only sometimes responded to questions from him. Hideo hadn't been persistent, so it had become easy to stop talking altogether.

On one occasion, Yoshiko took sleeping pills late one night and forgot to put the blister pack back in the bathroom's medicine cabinet. She had left it on the edge of the table beside their futon bed and fell into a deep sleep.

When Hideo awoke the following morning, he saw the blister pack, and after she didn't acknowledge his breakfast-time greeting with even so much as a toe-twitch, he feared the worst. Minutes disguised as hours ticked by, and all Hideo could do was sit on the bed and whimper. It had crossed his mind that Yoshiko might commit suicide, but he never thought she would actually go through with ending her life. He reached out to roll her over (she had been lying face-down on the futon bed, with all the rigor-mortis panache of a murder victim) but reflexively snapped his hand back when Yoshiko lifted her head a little.

She had been awake the whole time, debating whether or not to continue letting him believe she was dead, but the threat of his fingers caressing her skin convinced her to end the ruse.

Hideo pretended like nothing happened. He feebly shrugged his shoulders in response to her irritated stare, visible between the messy clumps of bed hair covering her face.

It was touching, in a way, to Yoshiko, but Hideo's concern that morning had not been enough to reset their relationship to a tangible expression of matrimony.

Further down, Yoshiko sank into empty space, surrounded by slime-flavored well walls.

"Do you remember that Pachinko place with the funny, English saying?"

Yoshiko didn't hear Hideo come into the room; otherwise she would have closed her eyes and pretended to sleep. She pushed herself up and yawned, frowning at her disheveled appearance in the mirror that leaned against the wall. Thankfully, Hideo went and stood in front of the mirror to straighten his tie, hiding her reflection.

"What are you talking about?" Yoshiko said in a groggy voice.

"You know, that Pachinko place we saw when we went out for our first-year wedding anniversary. Do you remember it? Oh, by the way, did you sleep well?" Hideo tried to sound spry, but he wasn't quite prepared to talk with Yoshiko just yet. His head throbbed, and his eyes burned with vinegary exhaustion from getting only a few hours of sleep.

"Yeah, I got enough sleep. So, it was Pachinko that kept you away last night, was it?"

"No, not at all. I'm not talking about last night."

"That explains a lot."

"I had a late business meeting," Hideo lied. He didn't want to tell her that he spent his night at a bar and then at the *jinjya* beside their housing complex.

Yoshiko snorted. Her husband wasn't good at lying. "Sure. So, why are you bringing up the Pachinko place to me? Did you go there?"

"No, I didn't go there." Hideo laughed. "After I woke up this morning, I thought about when we went out to eat for our anniversary. It was unusually warm for December, so we decided to take advantage of it. We walked up and down Hondori, enjoying the nice weather, and then you heard old, American music coming from one of the side streets next to Hondori. When we looked to see what was going on, we saw those three girls and their partners twisting away to rockabilly. Do you remember them? The girls had those crazy pompadour hairstyles. And their partners were dressed in daddy-o-style shirts and tight Levis. I remember you said I would look good in an outfit like the ones they were wearing."

Yoshiko couldn't help but think back fondly on the memory. "Yeah, I remember that this happened, but what does this have to do with—"

"Wait a second," Hideo interrupted. "So then, right after we watched them dance for a while, we decided to walk around some more, and that's when you spotted the Pachinko place I'm talking about. It was called 'Mammoth Pachinko Parlor.' The front of it looked like our housing complex, except for all the neon lights, of course. And it had that huge wall inscription above its doors with the English phrase, 'You are the game. Fight or flight,' written on it. When we saw this, we pretended to battle each other right in the middle of the street, and you kept saying that stupid English phrase to me over and over again. I couldn't stop laughing, and neither could you."

"I remember now. What a strange thing to bring up now though…" Yoshiko pretended to be unaffected by Hideo's anecdote, but a feeling of euphoria snuck back into her when she remembered that night. It was one of her favorite memories.

"Well, anyway," Hideo said, "I'm going to be late for work if I don't leave now. Have a good day." He ran to the front door and hurried his feet into a pair of Regal straight-tip shoes. "*Ittekimasu*[39]*!*" He yelled, and without waiting for his wife's response, he stepped outside the door and waited.

---

39. *ittekimasu*—"I'm leaving."

Yoshiko heard Hideo say goodbye and was about to get changed into a pair of jeans when her feet banged against Hideo's briefcase. It was leaning against the closet door.

"Hideo, wait!" She ran out the apartment front door and almost straight into Hideo's arms.

"Oh, where's my mind? I was so wrapped up in my story I must have forgotten to pick up my briefcase." Hideo laughed and took the briefcase from Yoshiko with an exaggerated bow.

"Oh, stop it!" Yoshiko didn't return the bow. She surprised herself and Hideo by emitting a tiny laugh instead.

"Thank you. I think they would have fired me if I forgot this."

"No, don't be silly. You work so much, I think they would miss you, for sure."

"Yeah, you're probably right. So... I forgot something else besides the briefcase."

"Eh? What?"

"I forgot to ask you, would you have dinner with me tonight? I was thinking of the J Cafe."

Yoshiko was shocked. Where was this all coming from? First the story about their wedding anniversary and now a dinner proposal? "I... I don't know," she said.

Hideo smiled. "It will be fun, I promise. I know you haven't been out in a long time, but maybe you can try to have some fun. Also, I know you haven't eaten at this place before, and neither have I, but I looked it up online, and it sounds very elegant." He clenched his briefcase with anticipation. He looked like an earnest student waiting to see his final exam score for the school year.

"Can I think about it?" Yoshiko asked.

"Sure, just let me know when I come home. *Ittekimasu.*"

Hideo was thrilled. He had succeeded in leaving the briefcase and had even made her laugh. He started to think that his plan might actually work.

"*Hai, itterasshai*[40]," Yoshiko answered, a curious twitch lingering in her words. She waved to him as he disappeared around the corner and down the steps. Just as he left her sight, the bitter

---

40. *itterasshai*—literally it means "go and come back," but it can be translated as "have a safe trip."

morning frost found her. She jumped back inside the apartment and closed the door but didn't step up from the *genkan*. Why did she agree to think about dinner? She wanted to rewind time and strike their conversation from the record. She stood there and repeatedly asked herself what made her want to eat someplace with her husband, especially after spending so many long months of living like a single mother. It was supposed to be a bento box for dinner, followed by a simmering bath, maybe some web surfing, and lights out by 10:00 p.m. Just another night spent in the pitch-black well. Only now... now Hideo had slid the cover off the well, and suddenly she found herself not breathing the same stale air anymore. She wasn't sure if she was going to go or not, but one thing she knew for certain: her body wasn't shaking from having stood out in the winter cold.

Even if Yoshiko refused his invitation to dinner, Hideo was excited to see a remnant of what used to be his cheerful wife. Her laughter at the briefcase stunt was just the catalyst necessary to continue with his inspired plan. He finished work ten minutes early and drove at warp speed until he reached Hirose Kitamachi. There wasn't a significant amount of traffic to deal with on the ride home, or maybe he didn't notice any because he was too busy daydreaming while humming the chorus from some American techno song he had heard at the *izakaya* the previous evening. It had refused to leave his mind all day during his many business meetings and phone conferences at Mazda. Hideo thought that the lyrics sounded hopeful, despite not knowing English that well. He understood the chorus enough to glean its message: that it's never too late for change. How perfect.

There was that tapping noise again.

For a long time, Seul Bi didn't hear or see anything. She didn't want to. She was caught up in a dream that felt peaceful, safe. No sign of the burned man anywhere. But that damn tapping noise was so annoying! She couldn't ignore it any longer.

Her rescue had come, or had it? She jiggled her eyeballs underneath their eyelids, causing them to break the crusty seal of sleep that made everything dark. When she opened her eyes, blurry shower walls surrounded her. The shower curtain was tangled between her legs. She grabbed at the water handle directly above her head and hoisted herself to a full sitting position, activating dormant pain sensors in the process.

"Ouch. Ouch. Holy fucking Christ," she half-whispered and half-screeched.

Bad idea. Her insides had been booby-trapped with stingers. She swung her hand in a jerky mime-like motion towards her ribs. They hurt the most, and her skin around them had turned into a hardened and purpled mess. She didn't want to cry or yell out for help; the burned man could still be lurking somewhere outside of her sightlines. Besides, her throat was so parched that all she could do was groan. When she did so, a vile odor escaped her mouth. Her breath was like a shit-filled cat litter box. The stench made her tear ducts explode.

She pressed a hand hard against her lips, and with the other hand, pushed slippery knots of hair off her forehead. *Was the water turned on when I was unconscious? It can't be the heater…* she always left her apartment at a cozy seventy-five degrees, no matter how bitter cold it was outside. But the bathroom, at least, felt like an oven that had been left on all night.

She wished she could just go back to sleep, but something was out of place. She looked around and realized what it was—*no worms*. No dirt, either. Just broken glass and bloodstains covering the bathroom's tile floor.

Where were the worms? Had they wiggled down into the drain underneath her? Could they have eaten all the dirt? How long had she been unconscious? Apprehension numbed her from head to toe. She crawled to the sink and propped herself up, making sure her limbs had not atrophied to the point at which they were just putty stumps attached to her torso. After a few minutes of challenging gravity, she leaned her head against the wooden frame of what used to be the bathroom mirror. Chunks of glass spun around in a water pool that had collected in the sink. She picked out a particularly sharp shard to examine her face with, but only glanced at it long enough to notice a stitch-hungry gash on her left cheek and a rainbow of bruises on her forehead.

Despite feeling and looking completely fucked up, there were more important things on her mind, like finding out who the burned man was and if he was still inside her apartment. She gripped the glass against her palm, pointing the sharpest edge away from herself, and crept out of the bathroom.

BAD KARAOKE

at

HOME

"*Tadaima*," Hideo said. Before he even realized it, he was standing in front of his apartment and swinging the door open.

This was it. Had his plan worked? He heard Yoshiko say something in a muffled voice from somewhere inside the apartment. He stepped out of the *genkan* and walked down the hallway. Pressure clamped down around his neck, so he loosened his tie, then began playing out scenarios in his head of what would happen next. She would reject his invitation outright. Or act like she didn't care. Maybe she would tell him it was too early for a reconciliation. Most likely, she would just ignore him. That seemed to be her preferred modus operandi these days. However, he couldn't have been more surprised at what he saw when he laid his eyes on Yoshiko sitting in the *tatami* room, beaming.

"I said *okaeri*, but I don't think you heard me. So, what do you think? Am I dressed okay for dinner?"

Yoshiko was draped in a velvet, black, Les Bijou one-piece dress with diamond-shaped Tuche stockings underneath it. Her alabaster skin noticeably hung loosely on her bones in the dress, but her malnourished appearance accentuated her frail, yet strong, physique. She also had painted her face with a light foundation, choosing to forego lipstick or eye shadow, and had applied just enough makeup to blot out the bags underneath her eyes and the grayish hue surrounding her face. Her hair was long and naturally straight, but for this occasion, she decided to curl the ends so they would bounce as she walked.

"Wow! You look amazing. I can't believe it's you." Hideo was stunned. He set his briefcase down and was about to hug her, but still couldn't bring himself to initiate first contact. It had been a similar feeling when he had asked her to dinner. His affection muscles were slowly coming out of their paralyzed state.

"You can't believe it's me? Me neither. I wanted to surprise you, though. You certainly surprised me with your question this morning." Yoshiko stood up and did a whirl around.

"You look fantastic. Can you hold on while I go get dressed?" Hideo said.

"Of course."

"I'll uh, be just a second." Hideo tried to turn around and head for the bedroom, but he couldn't move. He was punch-drunk from his wife's gorgeous makeover.

"So, are you going?" Yoshiko asked.

"Right, right. Sorry."

Yoshiko laughed and went into the kitchen, brushing against Hideo as she passed him in the *tatami* room's entrance way. The hairs on his arms and neck cackled with static lust. It was the catalyst that he needed to get dressed and get their dinner plan in motion. Within minutes, he presented himself to Yoshiko, dressed in a Paul Stewart zip-neck sweater and matching mushroom-cotton cashmere trousers (this was Yoshiko's favorite outfit. She had bought it for him at Sogo's for his 30th birthday). He was ready to leave just as quickly as he had come home.

"Ah, hold on just a moment," Yoshiko said. She paused from slipping into her coat and knocked on Satsuki's door. "Sacchan, Otousan and I are going out to dinner. Do you want us to bring you home anything?"

She prepared for Satsuki to hit the door with her feet or yell at her, but there was no discernible movement on the other side. Nothing except a muzzle of silence. Yoshiko glanced at Hideo, but his interest in convincing Satsuki to leave her room had evaporated into the velvet fabric of Yoshiko's Les Bijou dress. He would deal with his daughter later. The pained expression on his face right now implored Yoshiko to hurry up.

Yoshiko sensed her husband's impatience and didn't hesitate any further. "Sacchan, we're leaving now," she said. "*Ittekimasu!*"

Sometime after they left, the whole apartment echoed with discordant humming that slithered out from underneath Satsuki's door. She distilled the melody from an American techno song.

The same song her father had been humming earlier that day.

Pathetic.

Chi-chan, why do they think anything will change if they go out to dinner together? It won't bring their dead child back to life. I can't stand to hear their laughing or cheery conversation, like they haven't spent the past year ignoring each other. Why don't they just divorce and get it over with? Whatever. I don't really care.

I overheard this girl talking in class one day about her older sister's obsession with some famous author here in Japan and her books. I think her name was Banana something. Anyway, I picked up one of her books but couldn't understand it too well, except for one tiny part. I read it over and over and over again, and do you know what it said? Something about how living is kind of like a process of forgetting. I think I agree, but I'm not sure. I mean, I want to forget everything and start over, but I can't. I just want to stop being angry, but this feels like my only way to get through every day.

Fight.

Forget.

Fight and forget.

Do you understand this, Chi-chan? Fight and forget. Wake up, eat, drink, play videogames, listen to my iPod, write to you, and try to sleep. I wish I could close my eyes at night. Speaking of you, Chi-chan, sorry I haven't written in a while. I could just tell you all of this I guess. I mean, it's not like you are going to ever read any of this. It might be better to talk to you directly, actually. I hate the idea of writing in a journal or diary or whatever. It's so cheesy and predictable. Like... hey, look at me, I'm so sad and mad, why don't I write down all my complaints in some stupid diary? Nobody wants to read that kind of shit. I guess maybe you would be interested though, because... well, just because. You're stuck in this mess with me, too.

So what do you think, Chi-chan? Will Otousan and Okaasan come home from their date tonight and everything will be all better and back to normal? You don't care, do you? I don't either. It won't change a thing. It really won't.

CHAPTER 36

BEATS.

BLIPS.

BEEPS.

Seul Bi expected at any moment to be attacked, so she braced her shell-shocked bones with every step, but there was nobody to be found. Her front door was latched and locked. The bed sheets were exactly the same heap of cotton dreadlocks from the last time she snuggled in between them. The manta rays meandered across her laptop in their designated screen saving swim patterns. Marisa's tattered lamp hung limp off the computer stand. Her eyes couldn't decipher any clues as to what had happened, but was there anything to be noticed? Something misplaced? A set of ashy toes sticking out from behind a curtain?

Wait. The curtain. She dashed over to the window and shoved the bulky shades aside. Heat immediately blasted her face. When she stepped back into the balmy draft inside her apartment, she realized no snow pasted itself on the windows or even the trees outside or the sidewalk below.

Have I been sleeping that long? She wondered. Her jaw slackened as she saw the sun cooking an Evanston that was wrapped in a cellophane sky.

An icicle had lodged itself somehow between the window screen and its side panel. It was tapping against the window glass. Seul Bi didn't take long to figure out that this had been the promising sound of her rescue from the burned man. It must have been yanked from its crystal socket by the wind. She jabbed at the glass in front of the icicle. The vibrations shook the icicle right off the ledge. She then dug through a pile of clothes near the window for something clean. Her ribcage snickered its painful objection to the search, so she settled for the first wrinkled T-shirt and pair of jeans she found.

She splashed water on her face from the kitchen sink (*better to stay away from the bathroom*, she thought. *Too much glass and blood*) and grabbed some ice cubes for her bruised forehead and ribs. Her body felt too heavy for her legs, so she shifted her weight back and forth on her scuffled feet while rubbing the ice cubes on her face and side. It was painful but relieving at the same time, like a shiatsu massage done with morphine-filled hypodermics.

She didn't know how long she had been unconscious, but she was pretty sure that she had missed coming in for her morning work shift. She searched her apartment for her cell phone until she found it under a fold in the bed sheets. It was dead. She unspooled the charger wire wrapped around her bed frame and waited anxiously for it to charge a few seconds. When she turned it on, her phone squawked with blips and bleeps.

THE PROBLEM

with

OUR HIKKIKOMORI DAUGHTER

Yoshiko was surprised (for the second time today) at the enchanting atmosphere of J Cafe. She had expected the restaurant to be more of a family-style setting with a big, open-spaced dining hall and lots of booths and self-serving pop machines. Instead, there was a narrow hallway flanked on one side by several elevated, *zashiki*[41]-style rooms, each with a circular table, and *zabuton*[42] cushions to sit on. Yoshiko noticed by the piles of shoes at the base of every mini-step ladder in front of the rooms, they were all full to capacity. The opposite side was decorated with a thin dining bar that strutted out from between windows, the wall, and a running-water stream filled with goldfish. There was an almost completely occupied single row of U-shaped box chairs in front of the dining bar that made everyone sitting in them look like they were wearing wooden aprons on their backs. Despite this, a traditional decorum was achieved through the dim lighting, bamboo and dark-stained wood, and scroll-wrapped menus. Yoshiko was thrilled. Who would have guessed this was behind the miniature door that seemed out of place on the restaurant's unassuming façade? She had mistaken it for an entrance to a storage unit.

"I'm happy we came here," Yoshiko blurted out the moment they sat down at the dining bar.

"Really? Me too. I feel like we just travelled back in time to nineteenth-century Japan," Hideo said. The servers' uniforms were traditional, working-class robes and sandals. An enormous piece of parchment adorned with calligraphy and painted flowers hung right beside where they were seated.

---

41. *zashiki*—a traditional Japanese room for sitting. Often seen in contemporary Japanese restaurants trying not to be contemporary.
42. *zabuton*—Japanese cushion that is generally used for sitting on the floor.

"It does have an old-Japan flavor, doesn't it?" Yoshiko agreed. "Ah, anyway, it's been so long since I've been anywhere other than the grocery store. Oh, that reminds me, I need to pick up some cat litter on our way back home."

"Cat litter? You mean we still have a cat?" Hideo laughed.

"Yes, I can hear Chi-chan meowing when I leave dinner on the balcony for Satsuki. I also hear Chi-chan scratch at the window when the crows steal Satsuki's food."

"Oh, really? I had no idea. Do you know if our daughter is still in there, too?"

Yoshiko hesitated. Her fingers wandered across the dining bar to the shallow stream that was filled with goldfish. Several swam up to the surface to inspect for possible food that Yoshiko might give them, and when she poked one with bright-orange scales, it didn't dive back down into the water's safety, but let her massage its gills. *It's probably used to human touch*, Yoshiko thought. *I wish I had its confidence and luster.*

"I think she is there physically, but not really there in her mind, you know?" Yoshiko answered. She continued to concentrate on the goldfish. Several more of them began to crowd around her fingers, which dipped in and out of the water like flesh buoys.

"I'm not sure if she wants to come back, either," Yoshiko added.

Hideo's eyebrows sunk down to his cheekbones. "Maybe you're right, but she needs to come back and be a normal teenage girl again. Do normal teenage things. And actually, I was thinking that there might be somebody who can help us reach her."

"Who?"

"Well, I was reading online about programs like New Start that try to help people who lock themselves in their rooms like our daughter has done. Some of them reportedly don't come out for years. One boy I read about locked himself in his room after being bullied and stayed in there for ten years. Ten years! He only went out at night to buy food and drinks. Can you believe that? Anyway, one of the programs offers a kind of rental sister who comes to the home and attempts to convince the recluse to come out and rejoin society. It's really—"

Yoshiko interrupted. "Wait, don't you think that the only thing hiring a rental sister or whatever they are called does is makes us not responsible anymore for our daughter? This is our problem and nobody else's."

"Yeah, I understand, but—"

"No, I don't think you do. I'm already ashamed of talking to Satsuki's principal and trying to make up lies about why she doesn't go to school anymore. I don't expect you to understand because you don't take the phone calls from the school. You are always too busy with work." Yoshiko sighed. "The fewer people know about it, the better. Satsuki will come out when she's ready."

Hideo knew she was right. Their daughter would reject any type of counseling. She was stubborn like her mother and still severely traumatized as well. It was time to talk about something else.

"So, have you talked with your sister lately?"

Yoshiko was glad he changed the subject. Talking about their issues in a crowded place like this one seemed out of place to her. Everyone else around them was smiling and laughing and wading through shallow ponds of small talk. "It's been a few weeks since she last called. Still the same, always working, and not a guy in sight for her."

Hideo laughed, and the genuine mirth in his voice chopped up Yoshiko's tension. She laughed, too.

"I swear, she's never going to find anyone who can keep up with her," Yoshiko said. "Maybe she should try to have an affair with her boss. He's the only guy in her life that gets her to do anything."

"You're completely right about that," Hideo said. Yoshiko flicked water at him, and by the time their server approached them to take their orders, both were consumed in a playfulness that was, for them, a *new start.*

CHAPTER 38

Twenty-two text messages, ten voicemails, and twenty-three missed calls.

"What the fuck?" Seul Bi exclaimed. She checked the date below the time on her phone's menu screen. A day and a half had gone by since she had blacked out.

"Holy fucking shit."

Seul Bi gasped and shook her head. She had never in her life been passed out for that long. Once, while studying for a final in high school, she accidentally took two Tylenol Nighttime PM pills for a headache. Even then she had only overslept by two hours the next morning. But a day and a half? She didn't want to think about it. She reluctantly listened to her voicemails as well:

"Hey, Seul Bi, it's Mary. Just wondering where you're at. It's 8:30 a.m. Give me a call if you aren't coming in, okay? Buhhh bye!"

"Seul Bi, it's Mary again. Where are you? Did you sleep in? It's 9:20. Are you okay? It's not like you to miss work. Give us a call so we know what is going on. I hope everything's okay. All right. Bye, now."

"Cuz, cooch, cuzmaster, pick up pick up pickuuuuup! Okay. Just checking to see if you, um, got home last night. Wondering whatcha doing tonight, 'cause me and Mark are thinking about going down to the lake and throwing snowballs at each other. He could use your help, 'cause you know I rule like that. Anyway, call me."

"Hey, it's your cousin again. Where are you? Call me."

There was static for the next four voicemails. It sounded like somebody tried to speak through a broken megaphone. Seul Bi couldn't make them out, and after a few seconds of each call, she pressed delete. She was about to delete all of them, but instead decided to play the final two messages:

"Seul Bi, this is Dr. Nathan. Something has happened. I think it would be best if you call the residence as soon as you get this message. Thank you."

"Seul Bi, you all right? It's Bev. Your work called here asking where you were at and why you didn't show up for work the other day. They said for you to call them as soon as possible. What's going on? You okay? Call me when you get this so I know everything's chill."

Seul Bi sat down on the edge of her bed. This didn't sound good. She played the messages again, turning the master volume on the cell phone to five (the loudest), but still couldn't make out the staticky messages.

She checked the text messages next. They were synchronized with both the voicemails and missed calls. All from Beverly or the staff at Rainbow. She did notice a few "unknown callers," but there was no way to tell who might have been trying to reach her. As she scrolled through them all trying to find clues about the past two days, the phone started to hiss with her cousin's familiar ring tone.

"Hello?"

"Holy shit! Finally! Where the fuck you been?" Beverly's voice roared. Seul Bi flinched, almost tossing the phone onto the floor. She had forgotten to turn down the volume before she answered the call.

"Something happened."

"Yeah, I sort of figured. So what happened, then? Oh, your work called looking for you, by the way."

"I know, I just heard your message." Seul Bi rubbed her side.

Beverly sneezed. "God bless me! Yeah, they were looking for you. Said it was really important. Soooo… tell me!"

I haven't talked to them yet. I was, I mean, I'm not sure how to even say this. I, I, I…"

"What? Spit it out already!"

But Seul Bi couldn't. She wanted to say that she was attacked by an ashtray mistaken for a human and buried in worm-filled dirt. That her blood was the mortar, the thing's shovel the pestle. That dirt became mud and consciousness became optional. Maybe it was shock, or an act of repression to preserve herself, but she responded to the question by changing the subject.

"Um… yeah. So what's up with you? What've you been up to the past few days, then?"

"Hey, wait a minute, not so fast there buddy! I know you like to do this sort of thing whenever anyone asks you to spill the beans about whatever the fuck it is you think about in that mystery-machine head of yours, but you ain't gonna pull that shit on me. Not this time!"

Seul Bi laughed, and for a moment, she felt a sliver of normal.

"Aw, it's kinda hard to explain, and I would rather do it in person, you know? I mean, I feel like I was sleeping a really long time and had all these crazy dreams, and then I woke up, and SOME of the dream stuff is true, but some of it isn't, and I don't know whether or not I'm still dreaming. Or maybe it's one of those… those… those you know, those déjà vu thingies? I mean…"

"Hold on. Mark's calling." Beverly clicked over. *Leave it up to good, old Bev to be ADHD and not really listen*, Seul Bi thought to herself. *At least that hasn't changed since–*

"Sorry about that. Mark's on his way over."

"Sure. No problem."

"So," Beverly paused. It sounded like she was taking a long drag from a cigarette. "I'm an asshole. Here I am probably not paying the greatest of attention."

"Uh huh."

"Anyway, I was just about to tell you that, judging from your work calling, I know whatever happened can't be good. But I tell you what. I told Mark to stop by your place and grab you, and then when you get here, I promise to shut the fuck up and listen to you. Okay?"

Seul Bi bit her lip. "Yeah, sure. How long's he gonna be?"

"I dunno, fifteen or twenty minutes, maybe? He's at school, so it just depends on the traffic, you know? The sun is out today, and there's probably a ton of people driving around and taking advantage of the warm day we're having."

"All right. See you soon, then." Seul Bi wiped her face. The temperature seemed to rise with Beverly mentioning the sun's guest appearance.

"Hey," Beverly exhaled into the phone, "are you sure you're okay? I mean, really?"

"Yeah. See you soon." Seul Bi hung up as fast as she could. She was far from okay. The floor was sagging, threatening to drop her into a lacquer-black abyss. Everything around her felt out of place. Herself included. She was reminded of the countless times she had counseled the Rainbow residents who suffered from abuse trauma. Without any exception, each one had told her that, after being hurt by either a stranger or somebody they loved, their sense of safety and security in the world had been destroyed, never to return.

Seul Bi wanted to escape. To disappear. To forget what had happened. Hell, she wanted to forget the past ten years of her life. But if she were to disappear, only an idea of her would be all that remained. She would be forgotten, except as a peculiar footnote in the Rissiello family tree. This thought evaporated her sense of security and safety in the world more than anything else. Somebody almost killed her, but did her life really matter? If she called the police and made a report, would they believe a single word she told them?

Would anyone really, truly care if she had died?

Reality marches on, whether you want it to or not, however. Seul Bi knew that she should probably call work and see what had happened, but she really didn't want to. She was certain that it wasn't going to be good news. The only other time Dr. Nathan had personally called her had been to inform her that twenty-two-year-old Timothy Gabbell, a former resident, had died in a car accident. He had just put his life back together after spending most of his teenage years battling a drug addiction. Seul Bi had been very close to Timothy during his stay at Rainbow. Getting that phone call from Dr. Nathan and being told Timothy was killed was so gut-wrenching that she didn't come to work for several days. Just thinking about losing another patient filled her with a sickening uneasiness, but she decided to do the "responsible" thing and dial work anyway. A familiar voice picked up.

"Hello, Rainbow Residence, this is Mary speaking."

"Hey Mary, it's Seul Bi. What's going on?"

"Heeeeeeey. What happened to you? We were getting worried here."

"Yeah, I was really, really sick. I was throwing up quite a bit, and I didn't leave, or I should say, actually, I couldn't leave the bathroom." *Well, that's half true*, Seul Bi thought to herself.

"Oh, are you okay, sweetie? I hope you ain't coming down with anything. It must be the change in weather. How long you been sick? Since yesterday?"

"Um… yeah, I think so. I mean, I'm not sure, really. I sort of have been zonked out, or something. I'm so sorry I didn't call or let you guys know what happened to me."

"You know we don't mind. You're never absent from work, so we were just worried, that's all. Like I said, the weather might have had something to do with it, but it only got nice just this morning. I woke up and was like, *what the heck happened? Is it summertime?* So anyway, you sure you're all right? You don't sound good."

"No, no, I'm okay, I guess. I mean, I still feel sorta, kinda sick, you know?" Seul Bi examined herself.

"I hear that."

Seul Bi stepped into the bathroom, careful to not step on any glass. The rest of her apartment was being skewed with poles of sunlight, but the bathroom was filled with black, lukewarm air. She changed her mind and drifted back into the apartment's center space.

"Yeah, the weather is something else right now. I can't believe it. Anyway, did I miss much, Miss Mary?"

"Oh my. You haven't heard, have you? Let me put Dr. Nathan on the phone. Can you hold on just a second?"

"What happened? Can you just tell me?" Seul Bi's back muscles tightened.

"I would, but it's just something Dr. Nathan wants to tell you personally. He's actually here today, so you called at the right time. I'll talk to you later."

"Sure. Buh-bye."

Mary transferred the call. Dr. Nathan picked up and was whispering about something that Seul Bi deduced wasn't directed at her.

"Uh, Dr. Nathan?" She asked.

"Seul Bi? Yes, hello. It's so nice to see you've returned to the world." Dr. Nathan's voice reeked with an ostensible cheeriness. She knew it wouldn't last long.

"Hi, Dr. Nathan. I'm sorry about missing work and not calling. I was really sick."

"What's wrong?"

"I'm not sure. To be honest, I'm not sure I'm even in this world anymore, so you might want to hold that comment about me being back in it." Seul Bi attempted to laugh. Dr. Nathan didn't reciprocate.

"Hmm. I see. I can take a look at ya, if you want?"

"No, I'll be okay. I'm a survivor. You know me, hehe."

"Okay. Let me know if you change your mind."

"I will, thanks. So, what's up?"

"Well, something has happened. Two nights ago, there was a visitor to the Rainbow Residence. It was after you had finished your shift that day, I believe."

"Go on."

"Well, it seems that Marisa's dad tried to make contact with her."

"What? You're kidding, right?"

"Afraid not. He tried to come into the residence, but Morris stopped him. Unfortunately, Marisa still caught a glimpse of him, and just the sight of her father… well…"

Seul Bi swallowed a giant ball of saliva. "Oh, no…"

Dr. Nathan continued. His voice sounded scratchy. "Marisa attempted suicide last night."

"Oh my God," Seul Bi whispered.

"I'm sorry. I know you two were close. Sarah told me you had received Marisa's gift right before this happened."

"Yeah, I did. Wait… Dr. Nathan, why are you talking like she's dead? You said she attempted to kill herself right, so, does that mean she's, like… I mean… well, what *does* that mean? How did she try to kill herself?"

"Well, after her dad left, Marisa lied to Morris and said she would be okay. Then she went into the kitchen, took out a cheese grater, rubbed it on her arms until there was no skin left, and then stabbed both her wrists with some sort of kitchen knife. She bled so much that—"

"That what?" Seul Bi interrupted. Anxiety was sinking in fast with every word Dr. Nathan spoke.

"Well, she lost too much blood. It's really a miracle she survived. I mean, after she stabbed herself, she proceeded to lock herself in the bathroom. That's where she stayed until the morning. And none of us even knew she was missing until Marisa didn't show up for her morning meds. You know as well as I do that Marisa is the most punctual resident we have when it comes to meds.

"Anyway, when we found out she was missing and had locked herself inside the bathroom, we couldn't get to her for at least another half hour, maybe forty-five minutes. Morris finally knocked the door down. Thank God he was back from his vacation. But I have to be honest with you, because of all that time spent in the bathroom without medical treatment for her wounds, she doesn't have a good chance of making it."

"Oh my God! Seriously?" Seul Bi gasped.

Dr. Nathan sighed into the phone. "Yes, I'm afraid right now she's in a coma."

"What? Can I go see her? I mean, is she allowed visitors?"

"Well, she's in NorthShore's ICU right now, and it looks like she's going to be there for a while. I think if you went and saw her, it wouldn't do much good at this point. Besides, it might be best for you right now to focus on how you're feeling. Does that make sense to you?"

"Yeah, I hear you, but I just don't know what to think right now. I feel like I'm losing my mind and that I knew, somehow, something terrible like this would happen. Maybe that was it, you know? My mind is so active, and I feel like… like… like… fuck! I just dunno. I just really dunno…"

Seul Bi darted around the room. Anything to keep from crying, but it wasn't working. It reminded her of how she felt listening to Mono for the first time, and how she promised herself that she wouldn't be like everyone else and get all sobby if she ever saw them play live. Sometime after declaring her naïve immunity to Mono's brand of inspired sadness, she got the chance to see them play live at the Double Door in Chicago. At the end of their set, they ended up playing "Yearning," one of her all-time favorite songs by them, and she couldn't hold back any longer. Tears flooded her cheeks, unable to be stopped by anything or anyone. And by the time the song was over, almost sixteen minutes later, her face and soul were both a wet mess.

"Seul Bi, are you still there?" Dr. Nathan asked.

She didn't answer. She couldn't hold back any longer. The tears fell, steady and fast. She covered her mouth and nose so Dr. Nathan couldn't hear her sniffling or whimpering. She wanted to hang up and do something, *anything*, that would make herself feel better. She remained silent on the phone, debating with herself that, if she could just help Marisa get better, then everything would be all right again. Wouldn't it?

But how could she make Marisa better? If she were to ever awake from the coma, she might decide to use a bigger knife and next time finish the job. She was fucked for life, no matter how many years she spends in "therapy." Seul Bi didn't want to believe that Marisa might fulfill her death wish. Yet things like "hope" or "recovery" felt more like sadistic thoughts than any sort of realistic prognosis.

Dr. Nathan coughed into the phone, bringing Seul Bi back from her skeptical, agonizing thoughts. "Listen to me, Seul Bi," he began, "it's not your fault or ours. You have to realize that Marisa has been through terrible sexual and physical abuse, and even seeing her father was enough to cause this tragic action on her part. And I believe that, even if we had stopped her this time, she would have still found a way to do it.

"Anyway, I'm offering you and all the resource staff members a chance to discuss this today, as a team. Can you stop by, say around eight tonight? I know it's late and also last-minute, but I want to make sure you and everyone else are going to be all right."

"Thank you for saying that, but I think, right now, I just need to be alone," Seul Bi countered. Her voice sounded like a hollow echo on the phone. Dr. Nathan started to say something, but she hung up the phone. She didn't want to listen to him anymore.

It's not enough! She thought to herself. His offer to talk about what had happened wasn't going to change anything.

It's not enough!!!!

IT'S NOT ENOUGH!!!!!!!!!!!!!!!!!!!!!!!!!!

The floor gave in.

"So, what do you want for dinner?" Yoshiko asked while brushing a piece of lint off Hideo's suit. The lint's curly shape reminded her of the "@" button on their home computer. Hideo continued to perform his pre-work ritual of thoroughly inspecting his business jacket and tie for stains or dirt or nonconformity.

"Curry would be nice," he replied without hesitation.

"Curry? I knew you would say that."

"Really? What gave it away? The fact that I've been eating curry cup noodles for months now? Or the fact that I could eat your curry for the rest of my life and nothing else and be completely content?"

"Actually, I know you want my curry because you can't cook anything without burning it or messing it up somehow. And I know if you could cook, that's the first thing you would make for yourself."

Hideo grinned. Her theorem was absolutely correct.

"So... you are going to make curry tonight then?" he asked.

Yoshiko burst out laughing.

"Yes, curry it is. Don't worry! Oh, and I'll do my best not to burn it, okay?"

Hideo flashed her an agitated look, but inside, he was grateful for her sarcasm. Yoshiko was starting to remind him of Yoshiko.

Chi-chan,

They went out to go buy food for dinner. I can just picture them walking in that same old grocery store and pushing that same stupid buggy around together. They always go for the buggy with that annoying "Fresta" label on the side when they can just grab any old buggy.

They probably were so busy making out like teenagers that they forgot to get your favorite kind of cat litter. I bet they got you that weird Lion junk with the stones that turn green. I know how much you hate that kind, Chi-chan. Okaasan was probably acting like a Barbie, all dressed up and covered in greasy make-up. I peeked out the window, and I saw them walking down the street. It made me shiver uncontrollably, worse even than on the first day of our unusually cold winter this past year. I don't understand them at all.

It was strange to walk into their bedroom after they left. Their seeds of chaos are cultivated there. I think maybe it's too dangerous for me to be inside their bedroom. What if our imouto's things are in one of Okaasan's white boxes, where she stores the family photos and old winter and summer clothes? Or in the corner of the room beside Okaasan's jewelry stand, or underneath the desk with Okaasan's mirror on top of it? Her memory is there. It wants to ambush me. I can feel it.

But you know what I did? I'm not sure why, but even though the danger was real inside their bedroom, after they left, I ended up lying down on their bed for over an hour. I kept thinking, what would I do if Okaasan and Otousan came home and found me lying there... I would probably start screaming and crying. At the same time, something inside me needed to go back to the place where our imouto was made. I don't know why, but when I lay there, I felt like a cat with no ears and four broken legs at the bottom of a dirty well. I couldn't hear anything anymore. I couldn't move anymore. I was just pretending to be hurt, but I couldn't stop pretending, you know? Chi-chan, could you feel me purring when you finally came into the room and jumped on the bed with me? Just like when I scratch under your chin and rub your vibrating neck?

Do you think our imouto felt it, too?

"WHYYYYYYYYYY???????!!!!!!!!" Seul Bi screamed. She donkey-stomped a half-open dresser drawer, then snatched Marisa's lamp, and with a fastball windup, sent it rocketing across the room. THDGDGSUUUDDDGDGS!! Wood and wire splattered everywhere. She paced around the room, looking for her next victims. That's when she spotted Narumi's unsent drawings neatly stacked on top of each other.

Die.

Halfway in the short distance from her to the drawings, she became a four-legged beast, hunched over and scurrying on her hands and feet to stalk her prey. She pounced and struck and bit and tore pencil tendons from paper thighs. The drawings vanished. She consumed them and their meanings in a hurried paroxysm of disgust and regret. Life was unfair. It was so fucking unfair and horrible.

She chewed on wet flesh. Slivers of paper hung from her trembling lips. A 6b charcoal cloud gathered over her head while she punched and clawed at the spot where the six pictures once were. The walls and windows were buckling under the weight of her implosion. "GOD, GOD, WHY, WHY WHY WHY WHY WHY WHY WHY!!!!!! WHY WASN'T IT ME?? I WISH IT WAS ME. I WISH IT WAS... ME. ME. WHY, I, I, I, CAN'T DO THIS ANYMORE!!! OH GOD..."

Everything was wrong. All fucking wrong. Nothing, not even a moment of her life, had made any sense. Seul Bi's thoughts poured out onto the floor and into the air.

Like random. Scattered. Ashes.

"God iwishiwasherepleaseisthere anywayimissthemsomuchsomuch so FUCKING much God maybe...imean, whyyouknow? didyoutakethem and notmewhy didn'tigod own the crack in the ocean floor why

didyouhavetotake theonly peopleinmylife whocared about me?"

She was a slab of hard hate and apathy. Anger beat her eardrums. Her drawings did not twist or arc for anyone anymore. They were flatlines.

"ImissyousomuchDaddy,Mommy,imissyouimissyousomucha ndicantwaittoseeyouagain."

Staccato breaths. Seul Bi gripped her face tight with both hands and rubbed so hard she half expected to see her eyes and nose floating in the teary snot pool that spilled into her palms. So many times in the past, when she spoke with a patient about some kind of tragedy or trauma, her own past abrasions implanted themselves into the discussions. She cried for Marisa and for herself, and she wished for her parents to be alive again and for Marisa's father to be strapped face-down on a metal sheet and rolled onto the beltway of a steel-melting oven.

Burn, you fucker.

Fucking burn until you're nothing but a pile of grease and ashes.

Transference completed.

The sound of crows squabbling in mid-air replaced the frost-barbed wind that whipped across Hiroshima. Spring had finally arrived. Soon, the arrival of Golden Week and the Hiroshima Flower Festival would have women exchanging their parkas for *yukatas*[43] and leather boots for wooden *getas*[44] to celebrate in the streets with their husbands and children. It was Yoshiko's favorite time of the year.

She had hoped for her change to continue as well. Following the miscarriage, her cervix cramped and bled daily. The pain felt like her entire uterus had been ripped out and while still attached by a fleshy string, raked across a spiky fence. The thick blood flow that accompanied the cramps was like having a second period, but thankfully it only lasted for minutes, not days.

Unfortunately, it seemed the nightmares were never going to disappear. One particular dream plagued her brain almost nightly. The neighbor next door was an elderly widow who lived alone and didn't seem to ever have any visitors. *Her relatives surely must either be deceased or living far away*, Yoshiko had deduced, but in her dream, she heard the sounds of a child playing and laughing coming from the widow's apartment. The muffled giggles reverberated through the apartment's walls. The child sounded very, very young.

Yoshiko couldn't help but wonder every time… was it her baby? For some reason, she would always try to find out if it was by pressing her ears hard against the walls like suction cups so she could hear better, but the dream would suddenly end with a shrill cry and two ashy imprints of smaller hands inside the nervous outlines of her own. Yoshiko always woke up from this dream

43. *yukata*—a summer style kimono worn by both men and women in Japan.
44. *geta*—a traditional Japanese wooden shoe.

bloated and muculent, like the alcohol-soaked gauze used to wash the recently deceased.

Hideo knew how things were. It wasn't going to be easy convincing his wife on the final part of his plan, but so far, everything was going according to schedule. He understood that Yoshiko would need to be dragged out of her emotional muck on a daily basis. It wouldn't be as simple as replacing the past with cheerful, new memories. His strategy employed diversion from the issue altogether. They had treaded cautiously back into a normal routine, which included pre-work morning conversations and going out for occasional dinners. He would sometimes find excuses to come home from work early. Yoshiko cooked more often as well, and during their dinners, she would even pretend to like his acolyte demonstrations of humor (passing off the one-liners he had read in a business journal as his own, complimenting her cooking while reminding her of his horrible baking skills, and worst of all, breaking out in discordant song whenever she proceeded to wash dishes). Indeed, they each played their roles as husband and wife like they were doing it for the first time ever in their lives.

But Hideo feared Yoshiko's backslide into depression could happen at any time. He had to deliver his plan's *coup de grâce*, and deliver it soon. He had waited for Golden Week to finally initiate his plan. Just thinking about it wrapped his spine in sweat, but strangely enough, the tension wasn't unpleasant at all. In fact, he felt like he was perspiring from the steamy aftermath of a twenty-minute-long, hot shower. The sensation was one of comfort, not distress.

"So, is this the surprise you wanted to show me?" Yoshiko asked Hideo.

Both had just stepped inside Hatchidori's front door, which had been propped open with a brick to usher in the cool, springtime air and release some of the greasy cooking fumes out. Hideo's nose wrinkled at the dichotomous scent. The evening rush of customers was in full swing.

"Ah, the surprise is for later. We've been here so many times, I can hardly think it would be a surprise to take you here," Hideo replied. He had wanted to ease slowly into the final phase of his plan by taking her to someplace nearby and familiar. Hatchidori was only a block away from their housing complex and perfect for this very reason.

"Yes, you're absolutely right," Yoshiko said, her words earmarked with playful sarcasm.

"Let's just get *okonomiyaki* to go" Hideo suggested. "It's already crowded in here, and I know a spot that we can sit down outside and eat."

"Sounds good."

It wasn't unusual that Hatchidori was overflowing with people wanting to devour its signature meal. The husband and wife who owned the restaurant were experts at piling on layers of batter and cabbage and soba noodles to form a sloppy pancake topped with a flattened egg and drenched in *okonomiyaki* sauce. Sometimes they were cooked in the drool of the customers who couldn't help but let their mouth juices slip out while they waited for their meal.

Thankfully, the wife, who was busy flipping over two mounds of cabbage at once, spotted Hideo and Yoshiko the moment they walked inside.

"Hi, how are you?!" she managed to yell out over the clusters of conversations around the L-shaped bar and stove.

"Wow, you seem really busy today, but that's normal for you, right?!" Yoshiko yelled back. The woman didn't respond right away. She rolled her eyes and snorted.

"The usual?!"

Hideo raised two fingers. "Yes, two please!" he said.

"*HAI!*"

The woman swiftly added their batch of noodles with the others that were already steaming up the place. It was nice to get such special treatment from her. After all, they had both been coming there since moving into the neighborhood. Who doesn't like to see a familiar face while at work?

"I wonder where her husband is at today?" Hideo asked Yoshiko.

"Hmm. Maybe he's sick or has the day off," she replied.

"Sick? With the weather changing, I can understand that, but has the day off? No way! He practically lives here with his wife. I swear they haven't hired anyone to help them since we started coming here." Hideo laughed. He did notice a younger girl walking around behind the L-shaped bar. She disappeared into a back room after whispering something in the woman's ear, offering no help with cooking the rows of *okonomiyaki*.

"I don't know how she does it," Yoshiko said, as if to read her husband's thoughts.

"I don't know how she does it, either," Hideo agreed, his words cloaked in empathy. Having to do everything yourself is something that, for the past year, had been a daily occurrence for him. Watching Yoshiko everyday lie in bed with her phantom eyes open but empty, always staring at the wall or pretending to be asleep while he got ready for work every morning, and having to walk past Satsuki's closed door in order to reach the front door, had corrupted his belief in his "family." He had been alone for months now.

Hideo flinched and turned away from the woman cooking his food, focusing on a white teardrop plate that rested a few feet in front of him on the bar's edge. He didn't want to think about the past anymore.

"So, I really can't wait anymore. I want to know what my surprise is!"

Yoshiko's playful pouting made Hideo almost choke up the last of his *okonomiyaki* dinner with a loud laugh. They hadn't waited to sit down and eat, but instead shoveled heaps of cabbage and soba noodles into their mouths right after they left Hatchidori. Trying to coordinate eating while walking and laughing was nearly impossible for Hideo, but he loved when Yoshiko acted like a five-year-old girl waiting for her daddy to come home with a gift in his hand! In the past, she only did this when she felt comfortable… or genuinely happy.

"Well, we're almost at the place I wanted to take you," Hideo managed to say between exaggerated gasps of air. "I want to give you the surprise when we arrive. Can you wait just a few more minutes, or are you going to explode?"

"Explode."

"Really? Well, I guess I could show you now, but before I do, can we stop by the *jinjya* up ahead?"

"Ehhh? Really? Why?" Yoshiko whined again in a childish voice.

"You'll see," Hideo replied. He was smiling when he spoke, but his lips quivered nervously, causing Yoshiko to replace her puerile demeanor with an expression that was equal parts curiosity and concern.

They continued walking in the direction of the *jinjya* without saying a word. A small space nudged its way between them. Yoshiko hadn't been to the *jinjya*, or any shrine or temple for that matter, since losing her baby. Just the thought of walking past the tall ring of trees and onto the sandy walkway where the *honden* stood made her cringe. Her heart began palpitating wildly.

"What's wrong?" Hideo asked. Yoshiko hadn't realized it, but she was trembling.

"Noth… nothing," she replied.

"Nothing? You look scared."

"I do? I guess it's because I haven't been to this place in a long time, you know?"

"Ah, well. Look, there's nothing to worry about." Hideo pointed to an old lady who had just passed through the *jinjya's torii* gate and was on her way out to the narrow street. She had a look of serenity on her face and was carrying a lumpy bag of groceries in her arms.

"See, that lady over there is doing the same thing as us," he said reassuringly. "She's just stopping by after getting some food to eat, and from the looks of it, I think she must be happy about something."

Yoshiko still didn't feel comforted, but she curled her lips upwards, anyway, in feigned agreement.

"Yeah, I guess so."

They instinctively walked over to the *temizuya*[45] to wash their hands and faces.

"All right, then. There's something I want to show you." Hideo gripped Yoshiko's hand firmly and walked through the *torii* gate

He was too excited to pay any attention to the stone lantern with a cracked glass frame, or the twin lazy, lion-dog statues, or even the several rows of lit candles that were visible just past the threshold of the *honden's* open doors.

He nearly ran with Yoshiko straight to the wall of *emas*. There they were greeted with a continuous, clanky chatter, as the *emas* bumped into each other with every slight breeze that hopped between their rows.

"So, there's a reason why I brought you to this place," Hideo said.

"Yeah, all right, so what is it, already? I hate buildups," Yoshiko complained. Her eyes darted between her husband and the *emas*, which were covered in writing and decorations. She began to read random ones in her mind.

"Right. Okay, well then," Hideo sucked in a nervous breath. "I know this year has been difficult for the both of us. We've tried really hard to get past what happened last summer, and I'm sorry you were left to deal with so many of your feelings by yourself. I'm... I'm not so good at feelings or showing them, and this is really hard for me.

"Not that long ago, I had come home from the bar, and something told me to visit this place. I'm not sure why I did. To be honest, I—"

"Wait," Yoshiko interrupted. "Sorry to interrupt you, but when you say 'something,' what do you mean by that?"

"I dunno. Honestly, I wanted to take a walk around our block before coming inside."

"Well, why didn't you want to go home? Was it because of me? or was it that you didn't drink enough to fall asleep like every other night?"

---

45. *temizuya*—usually located near the entrance of shrines, this is a purification font to allow shrine visitors a chance to rinse hands and mouth in symbolic purification.

Yoshiko's questions pierced Hideo. She hadn't meant to spit them out with such acrimony, but even going out for *okonomiyaki* and treading upon holy ground couldn't prevent her from resenting Hideo's habitual, late-night trysts with alcohol. She wasn't worried that he might get so drunk he would run off with some pretty, young girl to a love hotel. Since they had been married, he hadn't so much as looked at another female in a way that would provoke a jealous twitch in her heart. No, it was the fact that his drunken outings had encouraged him to not do anything at all. Until now, it seemed.

Hideo wanted to recoil and strike back with a few choice words of his own, but instead of getting angry at her callousness, he reached into the front pocket of his pants and pulled out a flat, wooden board. A rope was attached to it.

"I'm sorry. I didn't mean to make things hard for you," he said.

"What's that?" Yoshiko couldn't tell what Hideo was holding. He was cupping it with both hands.

"Please, let me finish what I'm trying to say," Hideo said in a gentle but slightly beleaguered tone. Yoshiko stopped herself from asking again what was in his hands. She realized this wasn't the right time for questions.

"Like I was saying," he continued, "I'm aware of how hard it must have been for you this past year, with losing the baby and all. I honestly didn't know how to feel about coming back from that business trip in South Korea and seeing you… not pregnant anymore."

Yoshiko winced. Hideo paused long enough to offer a sympathetic smile.

"But I couldn't really think about it too much, you know? I was so busy with work that I felt like fall and winter both slipped past me, and I didn't even notice it! There were so many times I had wanted to talk to you, but when I would wake up and look at your body, this awful helplessness swept over me, like I was standing on the beach and a tsunami wave was coming right at me which there was no escaping from. It was easier to drink and forget everything instead. I guess I became an average, overworked, drunken, salary man. Talk about a cliché!

"Anyway, I'm not sure exactly what happened that night I came here or why I even decided to stop in this place. Maybe it was the full moon that night. I don't really know for sure, but something definitely followed me home from here.

"What I mean is, when I lay down in bed, a thought hit me: I didn't go to this place for myself, I came here for you! I'm supposed to help you with something. And as soon as I figured this out, I had another thought which seemed to make sense: I'm supposed to help your heart say something it has been trying to say for almost a year but hasn't been able to. What, though? I wondered. Well, maybe what you need to say is this."

Hideo placed the wooden board in Yoshiko's hands and flipped it over. On the other side, a painting of a red-bibbed baby with bloated cheeks pointed to an inked inscription that covered the entire surface. It was written in hiragana and kanji, using the Tokyo dialect that Hideo and Yoshiko had become used to using after having lived there for so many years:

元気に産んであげられなくてごめんね。
we are sorry for the miscarriage

あの日の事は絶対に忘れません。
we will never forget the day

これからもずっと覚えているからね。
we will remember you forever

As Yoshiko read the words, she became a human teardrop that hung from the edge of the world. Her emotions cycled: She felt surprised at Hideo's thoughtfulness, angered at the words inscribed on what she now realized was her personal *ema*, and finally, achy from sadness, the kind that was so deep it changed her body mass from solid to liquid.

She slowly brought her wet eyes up to look at Hideo. She opened her mouth and tried to speak but suddenly felt nauseous. She almost vomited up the *okonomiyaki* in her stomach.

"Yoshi-chan, are you all right?"

It had been a long time since he had used "chan," and hearing this endearing honorific gave Yoshiko just enough energy to shake her head up and down. Hideo reached out and touched her hands, but she couldn't feel him. Numbness had coated her skin. She stood there, trembling and twitching.

"You look like you're about to—"

Before Hideo could finish his sentence, Yoshiko's entire body went limp. She would've fallen straight to the sandy ground, but Hideo caught her and hoisted her body up. She wrapped her arms around his frame and wept. It was time. She had kept so much inside for so long, and just as Hideo presumed, she couldn't absolve herself of losing the baby. She couldn't understand why such a horrible thing had happened to her, to Hideo as well, or why Satsuki had locked herself in a room and refused to speak to either one of them.

How ironic... I can't speak now, either, she thought to herself. Almost an entire year of sadness was pouring out of her eyes.

"It's going to be all right," Hideo reassured her. "I promise you things are going to be better from now on."

Yoshiko sniffled and hiccupped, causing both of them to chuckle. "I... I'm sorry. I don't mean to cry so much..."

"It's fine. I completely understand," Hideo said. He stroked Yoshiko's hair. A few soggy strands clung to his hand. "Listen," he added, "we'll get through this together. We still have each other and Satsuki, but now I think it's time we let our unborn daughter finally rest. Go ahead and hang the *ema* on the board."

"Really?" Yoshiko rubbed her eyes. She held the *ema* up to her face. The baby painted on the wood seemed vibrant, happy. She wondered if this could have been what her unborn daughter would have looked like had she lived. More tears slipped down her face. It would be so much easier if she could switch places with her dead child. Would placing the *ema* on the board make her life any better? She wasn't even sure what the word "life" meant anymore. There was her physical self, which existed solely for carrying out the necessary functions of breathing, eating, drinking, pissing, shitting, and sleeping. Yet her consciousness, that part which constituted the "I" in who she was, had completely unraveled. Her memories and feelings associated with things from her past had slipped away. What remained was dull, empty closet space that threatened to collapse at any moment. How could Hideo or anyone else possibly understand this sensation?

While she thought about these things, the *ema* seemed to pulsate in her grip with every second she held it. Since Hideo was trying his best to make things right, she had to at least try to explain her internal bedlam. Yoshiko's throat suddenly felt parched. She swallowed her saliva and tried to speak again.

"I… I'm not sure if you will understand what I'm about to… to say. After I came home from the hospital, I kept having this feeling that I'm not… connected to myself anymore. It was like I woke up every day next to myself, observing my body suck air in and out of its lungs, or watching my teeth chew food, or laying down beside myself in bed as I tried to shut out you and everything else. It wasn't safe for me to go back inside my body, because there was something that I couldn't forgive that waited for me there. Have you ever walked past a dog tied up to a chain and thought at any moment, it could break loose from the chain and pounce on you? Well, inside of my body was something that I truly feared would tear me limb from limb.

"It hasn't been that long since I have begun to return back to who I am. I know this may sound weird to you, but it's like I've been spilled everywhere and now have to clean myself up. So, I want to tell you thank you for trying to help me do that. Thank you for—"

"Shhh," Hideo interrupted. He kissed her softly on the lips. Startled, Yoshiko hesitated to kiss him back, but then she closed her eyes and allowed his lips to linger on her own for a while. The wetness of his mouth caused a heavy sensation to creep up her legs and into her pelvis. Her nausea vanished, too.

Suddenly, the memory of peanut shells littering the ground at Asa Zoological Park flashed through Yoshiko's mind. There she was, with Hideo and Satsuki, all of them trying to avoid crunching the shells underneath their feet as they stopped to look at every single animal. Why had she thought about this, at now of all times? She kept her eyelids shut and continued to embrace her husband. He wrapped his arms around her craggy hips and pulled her closer. When he did, more memories followed: Red banners flapping around at a Carps game, her sister, Aiko, wearing the same pinstriped business pants every time they met for dinner, riding bicycles with Satsuki in Musashino City (that is, when she could persuade Satsuki to not ride bikes with her friend Rie for an evening), the first time she had felt Hideo's flattened, naked body pressed against her own flesh.

"I've missed that," Hideo said. He pecked at her forehead with his lips. She had been consumed in memories and hadn't even noticed they had stopped kissing.

"Me too," she offered weakly in response, her voice barely above a whisper. The look on her face kayaked between distraction and bewilderment.

"What's the matter?" Hideo said, tensing up.

"Nothing. Nothing at all, I promise. You just made me remember stuff that I had forgotten about for a long time. It was a nice feeling, that's all."

"Really? Are you sure?"

"Yes, I'm sure. Thank you so much."

"Well, all right, then. Good to know." Hideo was curious as to what she'd remembered, but decided not to pry. He felt both relief and exhaustion that his plan to win back his wife seemed to finally be coming to fruition. Kissing had felt just like when they were dating, he thought, and it seemed to him that their lives were coming full circle.

"Hang up the *ema*, and let's go home," Hideo said.

"*Hai*," Yoshiko responded earnestly. She found an empty space on the board in the bottom row, placed the *ema* on a peg, and then let go.

Before they left, Yoshiko and Hideo solemnly stood in front of the *honden* and offered a prayer of thanks. Candlelight tangoed around both of them as they each bowed twice, then clapped twice, and prayed. Yoshiko was grateful that Hideo had given her a cork to stop her life from flowing out. Her feet could finally touch the ground again.

Hideo also took the opportunity to clear his mind. He hoped for new memories to be made with his wife. In the meantime, he wanted to try and stash all the thoughts of their unborn child deep in the back of his mind. Even though he hadn't much use for religion, he yearned that his prayer for restoring peace in his marriage would be heard.

When they were finished, both bowed once more, neither one saying a word. A car horn wailed somewhere in the distance, filling the air with its shrill complaint. It was getting dark outside. Pretty soon, the chill left over from winter would saturate everything in a refrigerator frost. Hideo could practically see Yoshiko's skin swell up with goose bumps at the thought of this, so he reached an arm around her shoulders, and together, they walked briskly towards the street.

A single orphan wind shimmied down through the treetops and followed them.

An ant sprinted across the floor near Seul Bi, interrupting the fiery images of retribution. It moved in random circles in between Seul Bi and the paper-fleck-sketch wasteland at her fingertips. Seul Bi lowered her face right next to the insect to focus on its jet black abdomen. Was she hoping for the air passing through the spiracles on its exoskeleton to offer her winds of change? A change from the soft coils stacking themselves around her lungs to a piston-pumping, fuel-burning engine? A change of heart? Seul Bi sniffled. She closed her eyes for only a moment, but when she opened them again, the ant had disappeared. She knew she could only change herself.

That's it, no more. No more feeling sorry for myself or thinking my life was a waste. I'm gonna do something. I'm gonna fix this mess, and maybe all this shit that just happened to me was really a wakeup call or something—maybe a chance for me to feel grateful it's not me in the hospital after an attempted suicide. That's it. I'm going to get answers. I am going to help myself and stop living in the past and start livi—

"BLEEEEEPPP!!!"

Interrupted. Again. The laptop gyrated around on the computer desk like a cell phone set on mega-vibrate. Blurb balloons started to chirp and dance in place of the manta rays, shoving Seul Bi back into the reality spotlight. She ran over to the desk and quickly spotted the blinking, orange, IM chat icon in the screen's left corner.

Somebody was trying to send her a message.

Seul Bi opened the chat box. She couldn't have expected the three words that popped up would be the world's final caveat:

Naru444: listen without distraction

Seul Bi squinted in disbelief at the computer monitor. *Narumi?* It had been almost a month since they last spoke. Narumi had ignored her numerous chat requests and didn't seem to have any other profiles registered anywhere else online, either. Seul Bi had searched Google, Yahoo, and Bing just to be sure. Nothing. Not even a Facebook or Mixi page. She had been concerned at first that something might have happened to Narumi, but as the weeks went by, all she wanted to do was get an address to deliver the drawings. Not that this mattered anymore, as they had just become scrambled pixels on a dirty-floor mural. She figured that Narumi must have had a compelling reason for disappearing, but what was her reason for reappearing?

Suddenly it occurred to her that maybe Narumi was still online. She checked the time next to the message, just to be sure it wasn't sent hours or even days ago (her computer always seemed to deliver unopened chat messages later than they were actually sent). Her doubt vanished—it definitely had been sent only minutes ago, at the same time the computer sprang to life.

Her fingers scrambled across the keyboard.

LSBwillsetUfree: NARUMI!!!! NARUMI!!! ARE
YOU THERE?
Naru444: LISTEN WITHOUT DISTRACTION!!!
LSBwillsetUfree: WHAT ARE YOU TALKING ABOUT?
WHERE HAVE YOU BEEN?
Naru444: LISTEN WITHOUT
DISTRACTION!!!!!!!!!!!!!!!!!!!!!!!!!!!!!!

She wants me to listen to her? Seul Bi thought. *Why won't she listen to me?* An exasperated breath escaped her lips.

LSBwillsetUfree: WAIT CAN YOU PLEASE JUST
ANSWER ME? I HAVE BEEN WORRIED ABOUT YOU!
ALSO, SOME REALLY BAD THINGS HAVE BEEN
HAPPENING!

Naru444: # LISTEN

WITHOUT

DISTRACTION

! ! ! ! ! ! ! ! ! !

! ! ! ! ! ! ! ! ! !

! ! ! ! ! ! ! ! ! !

! ! ! ! ! ! ! ! ! !

! ! ! ! ! ! ! ! ! !

! ! ! ! ! ! ! ! ! !

! ! ! ! ! ! ! ! ! !

! ! ! ! ! ! ! ! ! !

LSBwillsetUfree: HELLO? IS THIS NARUMI?

Naru444:

L T S
L W I T S
W I T S
D R I S
D R A
T R A
T IIIII

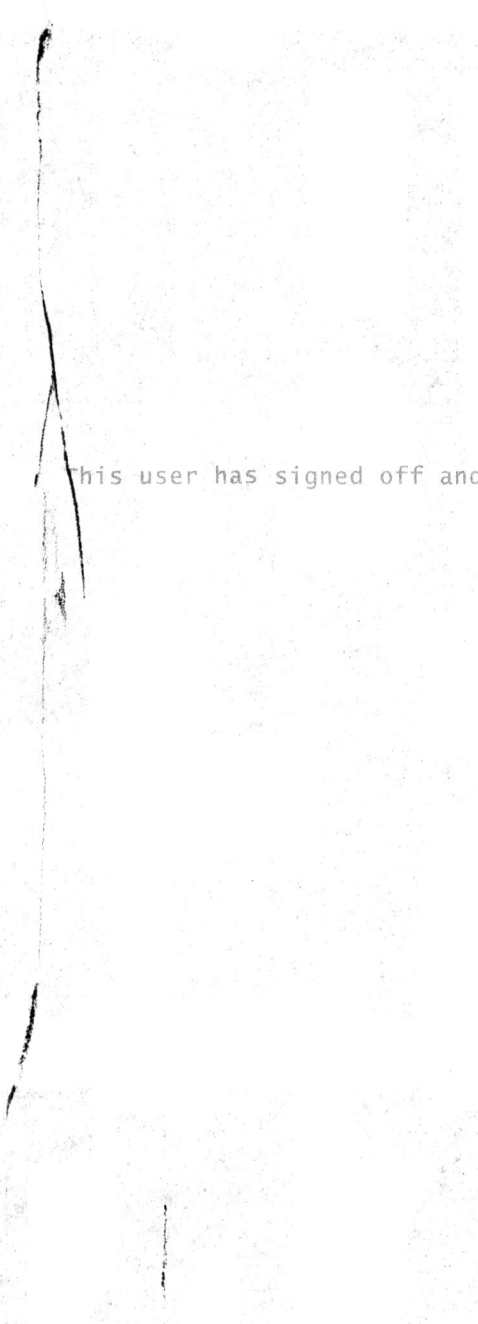

is not available online.

"NO!!!"

Seul Bi shook the laptop, hoping Narumi would fall out of a USB port or send another chat message from wherever she was hiding in the universe.

"NO, NO, NO, NO! GET BACK ONLINE!!"

The laptop blipped, as its green "on" light dimmed in preparation for shut-down mode. *Fuck, I must have accidentally pressed the power button*, Seul Bi thought. She slammed the laptop back down onto the desk.

Listen without distraction... what does she mean by this? Why did she send this to me? Who the fuck is she? Why does this all feel connected somehow? Listen without distraction, listen without distraction, listen without distraction... to her? If not to her, then to whom? Or what?

Seul Bi remembered Mark was on his way to pick her up. Hurriedly, she dug out her North Face jacket, slipped into it while trying to wipe some of the past two days off her face, then grabbed her cell phone and went downstairs to wait outside the front door.

She leaned against the apartment complex's worn brick skin for a few seconds, but quickly started walking down the sidewalk in the direction of Beverly's street. A plan formed in her head along the way. She would spend some time with her cousin and Aunt Debbie and tell them what happened. She would explain to them everything, and then look for answers.

CHAPTER 43

Chi-chan,

They're doing it.

I can't believe this. Okaasan and Otousan came home from their date, and now they are screwing! The walls in this place are worse than paper thin. Did they forget they are right across the hall? Chi-chan, can't you hear them too? You just stare at me and out the window. You don't care, do you? **DO YOU?** *I thought you were supposed to protect me. I wish you could put your paws over my ears and block out their sex noises. It's so horrible and filthy. It makes me sick! I can practically smell them having sex.* **I can't believe them!!!!!**

Why now, of all times? Why today? Something must have happened on their date. Maybe Okaasan forgave Otousan for not being a real husband or a good father. From the sounds of Okaasan's moans, I think she has definitely accepted his apology. How pathetic. If they couldn't control themselves, why not go to a love hotel? I mean, really, why couldn't they just go to one of those places like everyone else and screw their brains out? Why do they insist on doing it here when they know I can hear them… why? Why? Why? Why? Why? Why? WHYYYYYY?

Otousan is grunting now. I want to die. I can't stand it anymore! He sounds like A PIG! He sounds LIKE A PIG! HE SOUNDS LIKE A PIGGGGGGGGG!!

"HEEEEEEEEE SOOOOOOOOOOUUUUNNNNDDDDSSS LIIIIIIIIIIIIIIKKKKKKEEE AAA FUCKING PIIIIIIIIIIIIIIIGG GGG!!!"

Satsuki didn't take time to consider that her words had come out at a frightening high pitch. Her voice lashed out at the uneven calm contained inside her bedroom. Peace buckled under her fury and her agony. It was like she had just been branded by a scalding, orange-hot pincer. "Fight and forget" was seared into her brain tissue. She shut her eyes so hard that her head jerked back from the force. She then smashed her hand down on the desk, causing dust blobs to fly in every direction. Chibita, who had already jolted to his feet the instant Satsuki unleashed her jet-decibel-level diatribe, scrambled for cover. He wedged himself in the cubbyhole, where his food dish sat empty.

Across the hall, Hideo and Yoshiko didn't hear Satsuki's eruption. They continued to slap their bodies hard against each other while laughing and listening to the Beatles on repeat. No doubt Hideo put on his favorite Beatles songs to drown out their ecstasy. But it wasn't enough. The volume continued to keep getting louder, dirtier, louder, dirtier, LOUDER, DIRTIER…

"AHHHHHH!! DIE!!! DIE!!! DIE!!! WHY DON'T YOU BOTH JUST DIE???!!!!!!"

Once again, Satsuki's voiced roared across her room and trampled everything in sight. She flung her journal at her body mirror, which tried to brace itself a little too late for the collision. Cracks immediately appeared like tributaries branching out from a silver river. The journal bounced off the mirror and landed in a pile of empty bento boxes. She then crawled onto her bed and clawed at the posters and photos taped on the wall. Every one of them was shredded into paper pebbles within seconds.

The pictures of Chibita and her childhood best friend, Rie, weren't shown any mercy, either. *Where have you been hiding, Rie? Huh? **YOU BITCH!** You forgot about me, didn't you?* Satsuki shoved the picture of Rie in her mouth and chewed on it until it completely dissolved in her saliva.

When she was finished, the wall could have been mistaken for the side of a dilapidated, abandoned building. Except for pockmarks where Satsuki's fingernails had dug chunks out of the wall, nothing but the taped corners of pictures and posters remained.

It wasn't enough. A massive wave of depolarization caused one neuronal pile up after another on Satsuki's synaptic Autobahn. She hurtled off the bed and stampeded towards the helpless television on her desk.

Fight and NEVER forget.

She gripped the corners of the television and braced herself to smash its front screen against her face, hoping to make a big enough hole for ripping out the electronic viscera with her teeth, but then something else rolled downstage into view:

The snow globe.

It had been her father's paper crane attempt at reconciliation, but to Satsuki, the glass ball resembled the lonely planet she lived on. It was a forgotten Earth buried at sea, a place far away, only recognizable by its porcelain distance marker that was inscribed with a single word:

"Chicago."

She reached for the snow globe and scooped it up in both hands. She half-expected the water inside to boil from her touch, as she wore her anger like fire mittens. Yet the plastic figurines didn't melt or move but only stared helplessly at the voyeur in their sky.

Look at all those stupid people covered in piles of fake frost, she thought. *They probably all have families, brothers, lovers... sisters. They look so happy. So, so, so happy. But I could end them all in a second. That's all it would take. One second to smash them out of existence. Then they would have what I have:*

"Nothing," she said in a wobbly voice. She let a few tears escape, but they felt more like droplets of lava that burned as they slid down her face. Something Pandora-like had been festering for way too long. She had forced herself into becoming a pariah to keep this... entity of annihilation in bondage, but containment was no longer possible. She could feel it punching and kicking at her bones and organs. It wanted out. It wanted out NOW!

I. AM. GOD.

Satsuki heard the sound of glass ripping apart before even realizing she had hurled the snow globe across the room. It smashed against her bedroom door, sending pulverized shards of figurines and skyscrapers in every direction. The collision seemed to knock the entire housing complex thirty centimeters in the wrong direction. Everything tilted and bent right in front of her. Chibita hissed at the sound of the glass exploding, but what could he do except burrow deeper into the cubbyhole? Water had splattered onto the walls and the floor, mutating into an octopus-shaped stain from which liquid tentacles slapped around the room, looking for something to squeeze into submission. Chibita had moved out of their path just in time, but Satsuki wasn't so lucky. Time was moving way too slow for her. The water tentacles swiped her legs out from under her, and she toppled to the ground. Or maybe she fell out of sheer exhaustion from expelling such monstrous energy from her body. She couldn't be sure, but one thing was certain: the moment her body hit the floor, her over-cranked heart started beating at twenty-four frames per second again. She had landed on a crescent-shaped sliver of glass, which instantly sawed into the skin stretched around her shin.

"*Itai! Itai! Itaitaitaitai!!!*"

Satsuki boomeranged back up to her feet, but her dexterous reflex response couldn't keep her from losing balance and crashing into the back of the desk. The television slid right off its desktop perch and almost bludgeoned the top of her skull, hitting the ground with a tumultuous THUD beside her feet. She spider-crawled out of the way just in time, but she couldn't escape the pain that was hammering her wounded leg. The bloated patch of flesh around the embedded glass shard had transformed into a red-tongued, purple hydra. Its heads mercilessly devoured shin and muscle.

Satsuki's eyes expanded into water filled balloons, while whimpers snuck out of her mouth in between cement-block-heavy breaths. Whatever "it" was that wanted out of her didn't leave empty-handed. It took her numbness and immortality, leaving her feeling vulnerable once again.

Was love all they needed?

Suddenly, the volume turned way up in the room. Lennon and McCartney's deafening voices pillaged Satsuki's eardrums. It was like she had crawled inside their guitar amps as well. The walls shook with song. Actually, her sense of hearing, which had been muffled from her tantrum, had just come galloping back. Her head began to pound from sound overload. She could hear with perfect clarity her parents pancaked together behind their closed bedroom door, their strained breaths competing for the same airspace. Somehow they were still oblivious. She heard her own heart thumps as well, and Chibita's meows of concern, and perhaps worst of all, the blood dripping down her leg.

Was love all they needed?

Satsuki smacked her hands against her ears, but it was useless. Sound wiggled through the cracks between her fingers, infecting her head with a migraine-level headache. But the pain it caused was nothing compared to the burning sensation crawling up her thighs. She rocked back and forth on the ground between the desk and the fallen television. A few agonizing minutes passed, and time threatened to slow down once again, but then a revelation was born. She realized what must be done.

"Chibi… Chan," She said, digging her words out of the sand-box in her mouth. "Come… here."

Chibita hesitated. He slinked past his food dish and crouched low outside the cubbyhole. He sniffed the air, searching for the familiar scent of safety.

"Chi-chan, it's okay. Please come here. I won't hurt you."

Satsuki didn't wait for Chibita to respond. Without any hesitation, she snatched the glass shard from the hole in her shin, gritting her teeth from the pain. Blood poured down her leg, mixing with the water puddle that had once been liquid air inside the snow globe. Tears soon followed as she shook even harder than before.

"Chi-chan, I had to leeeeettt iiiiittttt….. oooout. I had tooooo…. I hope they can fooorrggiiiveee mmmeeee. I'm soooo sorry. I trieeed to keeepp it insiidee… but I just couldn't do it anyyymmmoooore."

The jagged piece of glass dropped from her hand. Crying was never something she could control, but thankfully, it rarely ever happened.

Chibita sprinted over to Satsuki and rubbed his vibrating diaphragm against her hip. His usual reflex response when there was trouble.

Was love all they needed?

It didn't work. Satsuki pushed Chibita away from her and continued sobbing. He splashed backwards into the bloody snow-globe water surrounding them both. A look of shock on his face couldn't be helped. He sat down within a safe distance from Satsuki and licked the red-stained snow flecks from his paws.

Satsuki hadn't meant to push Chibita away. Her intention was to hold him and try to focus on what was still left in her life. Focus on the living, not the deceased, not the rejection, and definitely not the fucking hole in the middle of her existence. But she couldn't. The magma had poured out, and the world as she knew it was about to vanish completely. *Is love truly all you need?* she asked herself. Another tired echo in her head.

"It's not enough," she whispered. "It's not enough. It's not enough. It's not enough."

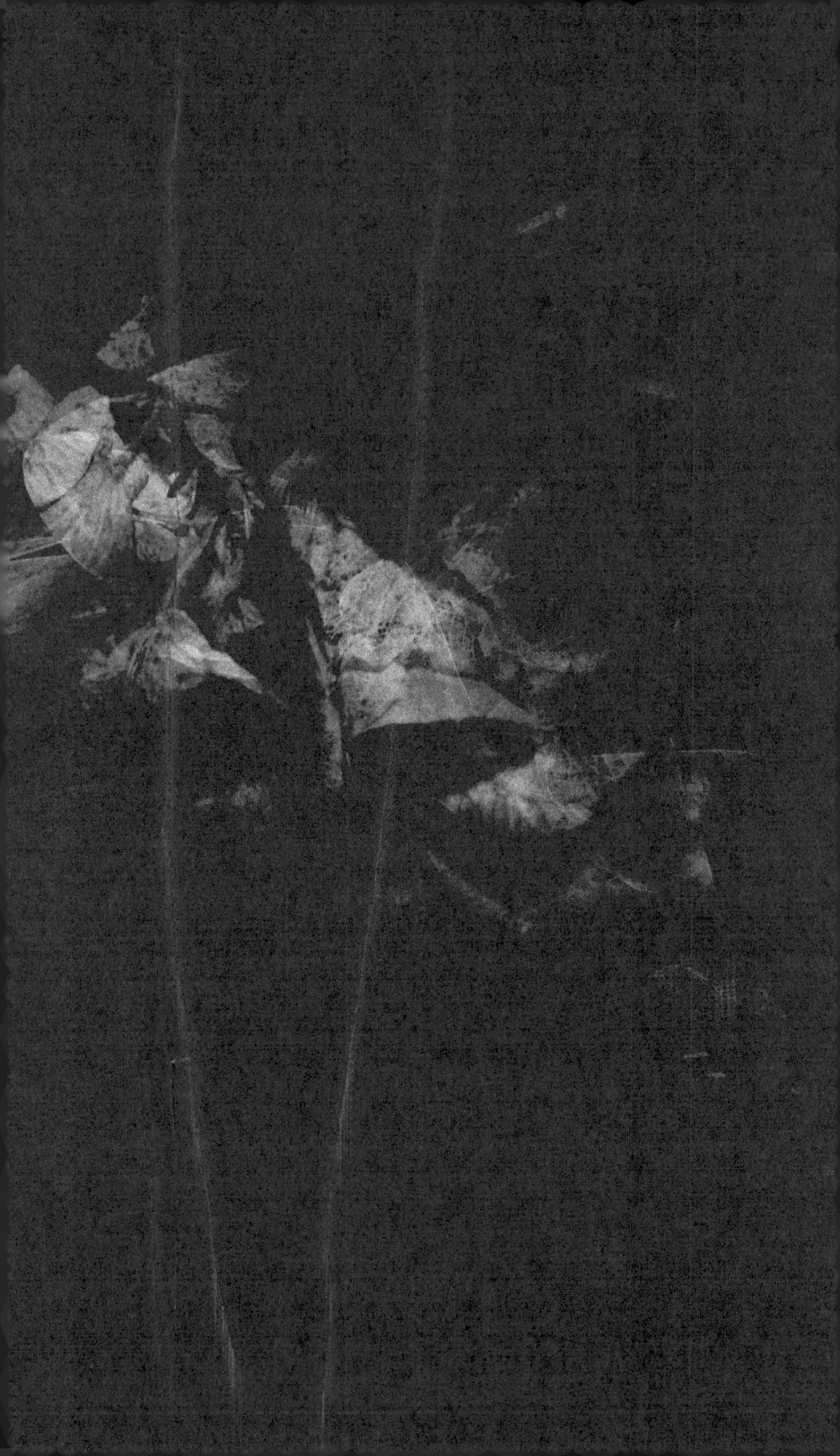

PART THREE

We are all escape artists.

Although Seul Bi had only walked a few feet outside, her clothes quickly dampened in the uncanny heat. She took her jacket off and was about to text Mark to hurry up when she noticed a warbled, shrill whistle from high above. It sounded to her like a million car horns honking at once. It also continued to rise in loudness. Something was hurtling fast out of the sky and towards Chicago.

"What the fuck is that?" Seul Bi asked herself, bewildered.

She scanned the cloudless, blue space above the Chicago downtown area, where she could make out the shapes of skyscrapers stretching out from above treetops and smaller buildings. She searched for a low-flying plane that might be looking to land at either the O'Hare or Midway Airports, but there was no aircraft anywhere in sight.

Seul Bi didn't realize it at first, but she was not the only one who had heard the ominous sound. People were leaning out of their windows and stepping outside their apartment complexes, chattering to each other and into their cell phones their growing concerns. A couple holding hands walked past her and argued loudly about whether or not another terrorist attack similar to 9/11 was about to happen. Seul Bi shuddered at the thought but subsequently felt comforted knowing this wasn't all just happening in her head.

Her phone started to vibrate. She hurriedly flipped it open and saw Mark's name brightly lit up on the LCD.

"Hello, Mark?"

"Yeah, how many other friends do you have nam—"

"Shut up and listen. Something's going on. Where are you at right now?"

"What's going on?"

"You can't hear that loud noise that's coming from somewhere up in the sky?"

"What? No, I don't hear anything. I'm listening to my iPod right now, rocking out, you know?"

Seul Bi couldn't make out any music. Frustration lines streaked across her forehead.

"Whatever, never mind," she said. "Where are you?"

"Right in front of you, about two blocks up. See me?"

Seul Bi stepped to the sidewalk's edge and looked down the road for Mark's Plymouth Neon. He was a block and a half away.

"Yeah, I see ya!" she yelled. The stentorian whistle had rapidly reached a crescendo, making it impossible for her to use a normal speaking voice. She waved at him.

"Hey, what are all those people doing looking up at—"

Before Mark could finish asking the question, his lips were ripped off his face, along with his nose, eyes, and ears. His car levitated off the ground and barrel-rolled into the second story balcony of a town house wedged between two towering apartment buildings. Most of Mark had remained in his car up in the balcony, but his upper torso and part of his head plummeted down onto the street, where people were one by one being vaporized or caught on fire. Those who didn't die immediately but kept staring at the sky had their eyes burned right out of their sockets from an enormous flash of heat that was hotter than a thousand summer suns. The heat was so intense that the couple in front of Seul Bi exploded into thousands of pieces of cooked flesh. Their blood shot so straight and high up in the air that somebody could have mistaken it for dirty, red water spouting from a broken fire hydrant.

The streets split open. Houses and apartment complexes flipped upside down and disintegrated into irregular shapes of all sizes. Smoke tornadoes sprung up everywhere. Department stores imploded, mashing its shoppers into organs, bones, tufts of hair, ripped out tongues, arms, hands, feet, hearts, and pleas for help that could only be heard by the severed ears melting on the broken escalators. And everyone who was still barely alive knew deep down inside their spilled guts that this was just the beginning.

In an instant, the entire world went white, as a nuclear bomb exploded over Chicago. It was the answer to the last question Mark would ever ask. It was what Narumi had warned Seul Bi about just moments ago: *listen without distraction.* Seul Bi definitely heard the thunderous and awful "POP" but didn't see the double pulse of light that signaled detonation. She had shifted her gaze towards Mark at the very last second, which was the only thing that saved her life. That, and accidentally dropping her jacket onto the ground while simultaneously trying to wave at Mark and juggle the cell phone from between her shoulder and ear and back to her hand. Now both the jacket and the cell phone were swept right out of her hands by super-heated blast winds torpedoing through the ignited atmosphere. A scream escaped Seul Bi's lips, but it too, vanished into the hellfire oblivion centimeters above her prostrate body.

Downtown Chicago, with over forty thousand people and some of America's largest skyscrapers in its perimeter, had been decimated. A fireball over one million degrees Fahrenheit in its center floated like a fat balloon just above what used to be the Willis Tower. All that remained were black and gray columns of smoke that toppled over each other, forming a thick, mushroom-shaped cloud of debris. Gnarled Corten steel beams from the Richard Daley Center twisted around pieces of the Aon Skyscraper's Mt. Airy white façade, which now had all the luster of ninety-year-old dentures.

Blast waves gutted the John Hancock Observatory, causing all eleven thousand of its bronze glass windows to explode into a furious hailstorm of shrapnel. Those unlucky enough to not have been instantly vaporized or crushed by the falling debris were split in halves by flying, jagged, glass blades that sliced fluidly through skulls, bones, ribs, torsos. Several of the X-shaped support braces that coated the John Hancock Observatory bounced straight down Michigan Avenue as well, plowing through buses and cars and grinding one person after another into bone dust. Many of those in their path had sunk into the sticky, molten, tar ponds all over the street and could only wait helplessly for their turn to be stamped out of existence.

The rest of the John Hancock Observatory, including its twin antennae, was completely sucked up into a swirling aerial coliseum filled to capacity with electrical wires, telephone poles, train tracks, train cars (some still with people in them who sat in their seats with blackened eyeballs and tongues hanging down to their necklines), tree trunks, rooftop spires, chunks of skyscrapers, and entire portions of streets torn right from their asphalt beds. Gallons of wind also gushed down from the mushroom cloud, drowning out the sounds of gas lines snapping and hundreds of buildings rupturing from their foundations from the uncorked gas pressure in millions of stoves and heating ducts, surging through brick, steel, and stone. Buildings immediately blasted off into the sky and became residential missiles, striking at the few remaining skyscrapers left standing.

Entire office floors were gutted and their workers pulverized into fleshy mounds of teeth and hair as the steel-and-stone-filled missiles delivered their payloads. The Smurfit-Stone building, with its trademark, unevenly slanted, diamond-shaped roof, was split completely down its middle by the only remaining and airborne support column from the former IBM Plaza, which had nearly been disintegrated seconds after detonation.

Even the colossal Trump Tower, whose foundation was canti-levered in 420 million-year-old limestone bedrock, gyrated in the steel-murdering blast winds until being weakened so much by its flailing contortions that the ground puked up every single one of the skyscraper's stilt support pillars and caissons. North Wabash Avenue fractured into thousands of asphalt islands as the tower was jerked from its metallic socket in the earth and floated in slow motion above the nearby demolished frames of both the Wrigley Building and the Tribune Tower.

In what could be considered the final crescendo of the bomb's catastrophic first act, a tsunami-like blast wave tore through the Trump Tower, eviscerating it and sending the top half somersault-ing in the air towards Wrigley Field almost four and half miles away. The whip-crack sounds of each rotation it made before crashing into the ballpark's Boston-ivy-covered outfield walls drowned out the countless screams of helpless Chicagoans witnessing the death of their beloved city.

Seul Bi could barely hear herself coughing over the laughter of both her parents as she tripped over her own feet while running down the Kona beach and fell face-first into the hot sand. She couldn't breathe from the suffocating pile of dirt, salt, and seashells that were shoveled into her mouth as a result of her clumsy spill. Despite this, seeing her parents was almost enough to keep her from spitting the sand out and returning back to consciousness. She knew she was dreaming, but as her coughing persisted to the point of uncontrollable retching, she had no choice but to obey her body's involuntary reflexes and rush back to her nightmare. Seeing her father's chiseled grin and the splintering glint of humor spread across her mother's stoic face was the last thing she saw before closing her eyes.

Come on, Mom, lighten up. I'll be coming back soon. I promise. I promise the both of you. Wait for me. Wait...

When Seul Bi's eyelids forced themselves to open, her parents were both gone, along with the Kona beach line and the cradling, Pacific waters. She awoke lying face-first in a pile of ash on the sidewalk, where, only minutes ago, she had been standing near the street by her apartment and answering Mark's phone call. She coughed over and over again. Black spittle dripped down from her lower lip. The cesspool of ash in her mouth tasted both rancid, yet familiar. She recalled the soot storm that had rained down while working the graveyard shift at Rainbow. It made her wonder if what had happened that night was not a dream or an overexertion of her imagination (which she had settled on as the most logical answer for why she saw snow outside the next morning and not mounds of ash), but a tangible premonition of what had just happened?

Suddenly, a thought crossed her mind that made her stomach churn more than the flecks of ash which had found their way down her throat: What had happened to everyone at work? What about Morris, or Mary, or Sarah, or the residents at Rainbow, and especially poor Marisa? Were they all dead? Or were they all safe in a shelter somewhere?

Seul Bi looked around for any building that was still standing, but all she saw were the stone skeletons of apartment complexes. Her complex had burst into flames and disintegrated into cinders within seconds. Everywhere trees were either chopped in half or engulfed in flames, cars with fresh, charcoal-colored paint jobs rested on the rooftops of caved-in houses, power lines crackled while having seizures on the ground, and telephone poles were bent backwards in a permanent game of wooden limbo. The sidewalk and street, both of which had once been flat, had been sucked right out of their former places and transformed into a winding rollercoaster full of hills and dips. It was barely comprehensible to her.

Oh my God, what's happening? Is anyone I know alive? Wait…

"Beverly! Aunt Debbie!" Seul Bi coughed on the words. Dirty flecks of saliva fell from the corner of her mouth and onto her chin. She wasn't sure why the first thing to pop into her mind was if everyone at work survived, but perhaps it was because the thought of her cousin and aunt being killed by what just had happened scared the living shit out of her more than anything else. *Then I'll truly be alone*, she realized. She had to somehow get to her cousin's house *now*.

She forced her still shell-shocked body to stand up, but no sooner did she take one step than her knees slammed into the concrete, and she was back on the ground once again. She hadn't paid attention to the fact that she had been lying on part of the sidewalk that had become a steep slope.

"Damn it!" she yelled. Greased with frustration and fear, her words formed much easier this time around. She rubbed her knees and made sure they weren't broken or bleeding (which they weren't, but she could feel them already puffing up from bruising), then stood up and attempted to sprint down the incline towards a level part of the street, but only managed a few wobbly hops. It was like she was in a three-legged race with gravity, and gravity wasn't being a very cooperative partner.

Her heartbeat was racing like a train. She decided instead to walk in what she believed to be the direction of her aunt's place. She didn't really know if it was the right direction or not. It was impossible to see very far through the thick curls of smoke billowing out of every smooshed home. Thankfully, several piles of trees that had accumulated from the initial blast wave had all caught on fire and created an illuminated path through the forced sheen of night blanketing Evanston, or rather what used to be Evanston. To Seul Bi, though, it was like walking among rows of lit funeral pyres.

She stumbled through the smoke plumes and tucked her face into the only clean spot on her T-shirt, sticking a hand out in front of her in case she fell again or was about to run into somebody... or something. *So this must be what it feels like to hop around on the surface of the moon*, she surmised, in an attempt to de-escalate things. A humorous image is useful when the air becomes tense. It was her counselor reflex kicking in like it always did whenever she needed it the most.

Still, to be surrounded by the threat of suffocation if she breathed in the air, even for a moment, in that vacuum of uneasy silence, it made her wonder if she actually *had been* plucked right off the planet. Loneliness started to squeeze her pain receptors more than her engorged kneecaps with every step she managed to take; there wasn't a person in sight. She pulled her T-shirt closer to her face and trudged onward, coming finally to what resembled the street that her aunt lived on. The air was less heavy here, probably due to the fact that her aunt lived a few blocks closer to Lake Michigan than she did, and a merciful breeze carrying tiny pellets of lake water had also made its way down the street. This wasn't enough though to stop the fire that jiggled in between rooftops and yards and was busy devouring many of the homes within eyesight. Everything was burning.

Seul Bi walked slowly down the street, careful not to tread through a medium-sized lump of congealed ash piled right in its middle, until she spotted a familiar set of purple shutter boards and matching vinyl siding on one of the inflamed houses. It confirmed a homing instinct in her that got her this far so quickly (which she felt suddenly grateful for as well), but if it was her aunt's place, there wasn't much left of it. The roof had caved in, and every visible window had been blasted out. The once disgustingly bright purple siding had melted into purple ash streak taffy with trash-encrusted PVC panels sticking out in every direction. By the time Seul Bi was standing a few feet away, she also noticed that her aunt's place was tilted sideways. The front door was crumpled onto its side, and the rhombus-shaped doorway was sunk halfway into the porch. She didn't see any movement past the dark threshold.

"BEVERLY! AUNT DEBBIE!! ARE YOU IN THERE?" She shouted, removing her shirt from her mouth just long enough to taste the smoke-stuffed air. It made her throat ache from its uncomfortable warmth. Sweat was pooling underneath her eyelids as well, or was it tears? She couldn't tell the difference.

"BEVERLY!!! AUNT DEBBIE!!! HELLO?!"

No answer.

Seul Bi hoisted her shirt up completely over her mouth and nose and leaned forward, sliding her relenting feet in front of her until she was at the four planks of wood and concrete that, on any other day, might resemble steps, but now had become V-shaped balance beams. She tiptoed across each one of them. At the top, the potholed porch didn't look any safer than the steps. She emitted a muffled cry from underneath her shirt.

"BEVERLY!!!! HELLO!!! BEVERLY, IF YOU ARE ALIVE, SAY SOMETHING, PLEASE! AUNT DE—"

She didn't get the chance to finish calling out. From somewhere behind the smoke walls encapsulating her aunt's street, a tremulous explosion sent her reeling face-first into a scarce patch of clean wall beside the doorway. She bounced back a step, and then, without thinking, twisted herself around so that she could brace her back against the wall and grip a splintered section of the door frame. The whole street shook for at least twenty seconds, maybe more. Her arms and legs shook in sync with the pavement. She did her best to prepare herself in case the porch caved in or God knows what else, but fear bear-hugged her and was not letting go. She clamped her eyes shut.

"Oh my God, please..."

Not even an hour earlier, there had been only one fireball in the sky that had poked through the winter clouds in an unexpected but welcome visit. Now there were two that were making not just the snow melt, but skyscrapers, houses, trees, streets… people. Why? Seul Bi wanted to know the answer to this question as much as finding her aunt and cousin. The only logical conclusions she could come up with was that it was either a terrorist attack or the beginning of World War III. Or the end of the world.

Seul Bi listened for a moment. A distant but deep rumbling was getting louder, and with it came the high-pitched screams of people dying. *Something is headed this way*, she thought to herself. With the stifled death rattles came gusts of hot wind that crowded the slightly cooled air on her aunt's street, saturating everything in a wretched balm.

It was time to move. She opened her eyes and pushed herself away from the side of the house, using the momentum to swing herself into the rhombus-shaped doorway. She barely missed the crooked top section, which, if her forehead would have smacked against it, would have knocked her out for sure.

Almost instantly the darkness inside the house blinded her, but it took only a few seconds for her eyes to adjust. When they did, she saw that where the foyer and adjacent living room once stood now resembled a raided tomb. Strewn everywhere were the remains of clothes, cups, plates, books, dvds, lamps, pieces of furniture (including the seat backs from the Ektorp sofa, her favorite), picture frames without pictures. All covered in glass and plaster. All worthless.

An unsettling thought ran through her mind: *I called this place home once.*

"Beverly!" Seul Bi shouted. She scanned her surroundings, searching for any kind of movement other than the unsteady frame of the house rocking back and forth. She hoped that maybe if her cousin was hurt and couldn't speak, at least she could signal for help. She was about to yell again, despite feeling like she swallowed an entire campfire, when she spotted the unmistakable glow of a cell phone's LED display coming from what she judged was about ten feet in front of her. The light was emanating from underneath one of the broken arms of the living room's chandelier, which once hung from the ceiling proudly but now had become floor detritus. As she made her way over to the cell phone, she could see the outline of a body curled up next to it.

"BEVVVVVERRRLLY!!!!"

Long, brown hair doused in layers, curls thrown in for good measure, familiar yoga pants that Seul Bi had once joked made her cousin's butt look like stuffed chipmunk cheeks... there was no doubt it was Beverly lying there on the floor, squeezing the phone to the side of her face. A sheet of grime covered her eyes.

"Bev, are you okay? We gotta get the fuck out of here right now."

Seul Bi tossed the chandelier aside with ease. She was surprised by how light it was.

"Bev, you hear me? BEV!"

She knelt down beside her cousin and shook her arm. It warbled like a sliver of rubber. Other than needing a comb to get the hair igloos off her face and a good long bath to take care of how filthy she was, Beverly appeared to be in one piece. Seul Bi shook Beverly again, this time her legs. "Listen Bev, I don't know what's happened but I think a nuclear bomb expl—"

Beverly suddenly coughed.

"BEV! Hey, you okay?"

"Marrk's not ... ansherring ..."

"What?"

"Marrrkk's nnnnnot ... ansherring..."

"Okay, okay, I gotcha. Here, let me help you up. Can you walk?"

"No... don't."

Seul Bi pretended not to hear her objection. She stood up, leaned down, and tucked her arms underneath Beverly's whole body, using what was left of her strength to lift it. Beverly was limp all over, except for her hand that was still pressing the cell phone firmly against the side of her face. Seul Bi could only manage to hoist her gelatinous cousin up for a mere two or three seconds before dropping right back down to the floor. Beverly crumpled into a fetal position next to Seul Bi and once again moaned her objection to being moved, this time without any doubt in a loud enough voice for anyone to hear.

"God damn it! Sorry, cuz. I didn't mean to hurt you. I'm gonna find a way to get you out of here, all right?"

Seul Bi considered her options. She could find two pieces of wood to use as crutches, or try upstairs for a blanket to wrap Beverly's body with and then drag her out of the house. But where outside was safe? The explosions were getting louder, which no doubt meant that more destruction was coming their way. She tried to concentrate, but was distracted by the sweat beads dripping off the top of her head onto Beverly's cell phone.

That's it! Beverly's cell phone, Seul Bi thought to herself. There might be some chance she could call for help, or at least call her aunt's phone. *Maybe I'll get lucky, and Aunt Debbie won't be too far away. Then she could help me with Bev. That could work.*

It was the only thing she could think to do. She attempted to wiggle the cell phone out of Beverly's grip, but the more she tried, the harder her cousin seemed to press it against her face.

"Beverly, let go of the phone. I have to call for help," she petitioned.

"Ple... as... e, dooon't," Beverly mumbled. Her voice sounded fuzzy, like the background noise on a tape recorder.

Seul Bi was too scared to ask why Beverly didn't want to let go of the phone. She continued to pry at it, anyway, finally managing to jerk it out of her cousin's hand with one quick, upwards thrust. She was about to thank her cousin when suddenly a sound like wires snapping in two rang out.

"OH MY GOD!!!" Seul Bi screamed, nearly choking on her unspoken words of gratitude.

In the spot where the phone had just been, pieces of Beverly's cheek flesh were bouncing around like sprung coils. A yellow, slushy substance leaked from them, staining Beverly's tan skin a dull brown. On the flesh that was still wrapped taut against her cheekbone, globs of pus fell into a blood puddle that seemed to float in the air. Seul Bi wanted to believe that her eyes were playing tricks on her in the darkness, but then again, all of this was so unbelievable that she couldn't be entirely sure if this was real, or a dream, or something else?

No, this was really happening. All she had to do was take a long, hard look at the phone in her hand. At least ten or twelve skin strings dangled from it, some still attached to Beverly's face, some ripping apart in mid-air and flinging into the invisibility granted by the muted shade, which threatened to slip an opaque hood over everything.

Seeing this was all the proof she needed. That and having another stomach-freezing moment after inspecting her cousin's wound a little further. She discovered that the lower half of the cell phone's keypad was burned into the side of Beverly's jaw. The numbers 7, 8, 9, and 0, along with the * and # symbols all seemed to illuminate upon inspection. Their crimson colors were separated by waffle-thatch lines, as though somebody had tried to play a game of mandible tic-tac-toe macabre.

Seul Bi shifted her gaze away, catching a glint of bright white coming from outside somewhere. She carefully set the phone down and brushed her cousin's hair away from the face wounds. Beverly's eyes flipped opened, but they gave no indication that there was any life behind them.

"Beverly, I'm sorry, I didn't know. I'm so, so sorry."

Seul Bi's apology echoed softly inside the house. She cradled her cousin close to her chest, rocking back and forth. Maybe she could stay here a while, wait for Aunt Debbie to show up, and together they could seek some kind of refuge in a bomb shelter. Definitely someplace that was nowhere near Chicago. She assumed by now that the first gigantic explosion in the sky was a nuclear bomb, and that meant there would probably be some kind of fallout with poisonous, radioactive winds. They would need to get far away from the city as quickly as possible. That much she knew for certain, but the problem was determining where they would be the safest.

Seul Bi recalled something Zoe had once told her at a dinner table discussion. The subject of nuclear war had come up for some reason (she couldn't remember why), and Zoe reminisced about how in elementary school, her teachers would make all the children do "drop drill" exercises. First, a special series of bells would go off. Then they were instructed to dive under their desks, face away from the windows, and crouch down with their arms over their heads, and their heads pressed against their legs. Zoe had found these drop drills absolutely hysterical. She told Seul Bi that every time they did them, she would always get in trouble from laughing so much.

Seul Bi remembered feeling scared at Zoe's story and had asked what she should do if a nuclear bomb really did get dropped on Chicago or Evanston. "Honey," Zoe had said while grinning, "if you see a bright explosion in the sky and then you see buildings blow up and fires everywhere, go take a bath, 'cause water is the only thing that's gonna help. Hiding underneath a desk isn't going to do nothing to save you. Find some water, jump in, and pray." Zoe had said this half-jokingly, of course, but Seul Bi could tell she was half serious as well.

I wish Mom was alive, Seul Bi thought to herself. *She would know what to do.*

Suddenly, Beverly started shouting.

"Mamammma, maaammma!!"

"Hey… shhhh, it's okay. It's okay," Seul Bi said, snapping out of the past and back to the present. Beverly raised her arms and flailed them around in the air, spewing blood from her lips while her legs shook with spasms. Her torso was stone stiff, and her eyes, although still open, were quickly morphing into dilated black holes.

"I want… wa… wannnnt… Mooooooommmmmm… y… Mommmmy," Beverly groaned. Before Seul Bi could tell her that she wanted the same thing, Beverly vomited up enough blood and black bile to fill a bucket. Seul Bi swallowed back a scream, then wrapped her arms tightly around Beverly's body, trying not to vomit herself.

"Oh… sweetie, it's okay. Everything's going to be all right," Seul Bi said, unconvincingly. "Just tell me where your mom is at, and I'll go get her."

Tears slid out of the black holes. "O… ov… vvvv… er… tttth-hheere." Beverly poked her fingers in the direction of the door-way. Her arms and legs refused to remain calm, as they shook and shook and shook and shook.

"Bev, calm down, and tell me what I can do to help you."

"Noooooo…"

"No?" Seul Bi asked. "No what?" Beverly answered her by thrashing around like a mental patient receiving ECT.

"Bev, listen to me, you need help. We gotta get you out of here. Let's go."

This was going to be hard. She tried to convince herself that somewhere inside of her was a reservoir of strength, but the truth was that she was running on adrenalin and fear... and little else. Assuming she could even get her cousin to her feet, how would the two of them be able to walk without falling down every five seconds? Seul Bi began rationalizing that the right move here would be to go outside and look for help first. Not do this on her own. She was already carrying too much as it was...

NO! There was no way in hell that she was going to leave without Beverly! But as she attempted to lift her cousin, another explosion caused the floor to implode around them. Both girls were flung off their feet and right into the backside of a smashed up television stand. Surprisingly, Seul Bi didn't let go of Beverly, even after they landed in a newly made bed of broken floor boards. It seemed like she was the only one who hadn't let go, however.

Beverly had stopped shaking, stopped moving, stopped breathing.

"Bev.

"Bev.

"Bev!

"BEVERLY!!!!!!! NOOOO!!!

"GOD DAMNIT, STAY WITH ME!!!!!!"

Her screams were useless. Beverly arched her back in a ninety-degree angle, followed by one last wordless breath sucked in and pushed out, and then her body slammed back onto the floor into a limp pile of limbs. A cloud of crimson mist was visible for a few seconds right above Beverly's mouth, and then, like Beverly, it was gone.

The ground rocked back and forth from the endless explosions. Chicago and Evanston were experiencing their final death spasms before the raging fires consumed every building and person still left standing. It was only a matter of time before every single beating heart in both cities would have the oxygen and blood squeezed out of them by the nuclear heat beast. Seul Bi didn't... no... couldn't care about what was happening. She sat there propped against her cousin's body and rocked back and forth in sync with the quaking earth. The pain in her soul had caught up with the excruciating clubbing in her knees, and she remembered how, one time, a long time ago, it was Beverly that had tightly spooned her tear-damp body while whispering that "Everything would be okay." Seul Bi decided to borrow these ancient words and return them to her cousin.

"It's okay, it's okay. Everything will be all right," she whispered over and over again, hoping to offer some post-mortem comfort. Thoughts stumbled forward, thoughts about how one time during eighth grade, she and Beverly had skipped almost every day in the month of May and rode the "L" to Macy's for all-day shopping and eating sprees. Or how, another time, she had dragged her cousin to the Art Institute of Chicago Museum and attempted without success to explain the importance of Monet's "Water Lilies" to her. "I don't get it," Beverly had said, adding that "They look like something our grandmother would have hanging up in her bathroom." Or how her cousin had grown distant while dating Mark but still found time to torture her with girly things like manicures, spa treatments, and facials. Whether it was because Beverly enjoyed watching her squirm under a feminine yoke, or because Beverly simply had no one else to go with her to these pampering sessions, Seul Bi had secretly enjoyed the reprieve from her loneliness. She felt that, in many ways, Beverly was like the center of gravity, balancing what small relationship she had to the world with her much larger mental inner space.

Now she's gone, Seul Bi thought, *and all I have left is a family of memories.*

Well, there was still one more family member left—her Aunt Debbie, who was unaccounted for. Seul Bi didn't want to imagine what had happened to her, but she owed it to Beverly to search for her mother. So she mustered the energy to care just a little more. For her cousin's sake. She kissed Beverly's forehead and then stood up with all the awkwardness of a baby taking its first steps. Her leg muscles had cramped while holding Beverly in her lap, so she waited for several minutes before attempting to walk towards the doorway, fighting the urge to buckle under what felt like hundred-pound dumbbell weights chained to her legs and knees.

Finally, she forced her feet to move, but no sooner did she take one step, than there was the metallic sound of something scurrying across the floor. Her eyesight had grown accustomed to the darkness, so she immediately recognized what it was: Beverly's cell phone. She had just kicked it across the floor.

Every step seemed to become heavier as she propelled the weight of her body towards the glow of the cell phone's LED display a few feet ahead. Outside, something that sounded like squealing brakes seemed to pierce the sound barrier right as she scooped up the cell phone. She instinctively crouched down, but much to her surprise, nothing happened. Whatever it was must have belonged on somebody else's tragedy soundtrack. Relieved, she stood back up and looked at what was on the cell phone's display screen.

It was a recorded video from earlier today.

She pressed play, hoping that the date in the bottom left-hand part of the display was incorrect, but the video began with a clear image of sky and something dropping down from it. A whistling noise grew louder and louder in the recording. Beverly's voice, or rather a robotized version of it, suddenly boomed out of the half-melted internal speakerphone. Seul Bi jumped backwards a few steps, staring in the direction where Beverly lay dead on the floor, and wondered if her cousin had just come back to life to perform a morbid ventriloquist act.

"Mom, check this out," Beverly said. The back of Debbie's head sprang into view, followed by Debbie walking down the porch steps from where Beverly must have been filming.

"What's that noise?" Debbie said, her voice also a tinny version of itself. She continued to walk past the sidewalk and into the street.

"That's what I'm saying, Mom, it's so strange. I gotta call Mark. I wonder if he's seeing this at all. Maybe I'll text him."

"Honey, I don't got a good feeling about this at all," Debbie replied. She was in the middle of the street now, cupping her hands over her eyes so she could gaze up at the sky to try and spot the mysterious source of the whistling. Some of their neighbors walked out to join her.

"Yeah, me neither," Beverly agreed. The whistling had become deafening at this point in the video. Beverly took a few steps back and stood in the doorway. "Mark's on his way over, anyway. Maybe I'll just wait to talk to him."

"Didn't you tell me he's picking up Bee first?"

"Yeah Mom, he is. Seriously, what the hell is that noise? No, I'm gonna call Mark. This could be bad, and I don't wanna—"

End of video.

"There's gotta be more," Seul Bi said. She replayed the video twice, but each time it ended with the screen turning white, followed by the "end of video" message flashing across the screen. She knew what this meant, but it didn't give much of an explanation about what had happened to her aunt. Just that the explosion had occurred and her aunt was in the middle of the street when it had happened…

The middle of the street.

"Oh my God," Seul Bi whispered. *It couldn't be.*

It can't be.

She dropped the phone and limped outside, making her way carefully down the broken porch steps and into the street. A velvet sheet of orange fire had replaced the sky. The super-heated air was melting everything in sight, including the street, where in some spots the asphalt and tar had already become pits of black, bubbling quicksand. Seul Bi almost stepped in several of these sticky death traps as she hurried to reach the spot on the video where her aunt had stood. Breathing was next to impossible, so she wrapped her sweat-heavy shirt collar around her mouth and nose and sucked in the moisture to keep hydrated and safely ventilated. She hadn't taken more than four or five deep breaths before seeing something that forced the air from her lungs completely:

The lump of congealed ash.

Earlier, she had walked right past it without even a second look, but now all she could do was stare in muted horror at what had to be Aunt Debbie's broiled remains. There was also no doubt she had been fried alive, cooked by her own menopausal layers of glistening fat. Her face must have been burned off, too, save for what looked like an eye socket and half a nostril. The entire upper torso resembled the backside of an overcooked steak on a grill, and where there should have been arms and legs were instead two sets of engorged, brown stumps. A pudgy sheen that preserved the outline of a body was the only indication of the ash pile once being a human being. Well, that and a razed, pink, Burberry Cashmere scarf that was lying prostrate on the ground beside her/it. Seul Bi knelt down to pick up the scarf but shrunk back instead. Her Aunt's initials were embroidered on it. And there was no doubt in Seul Bi's mind that this was the scarf she had given as a Christmas gift to her aunt a few years ago.

I'm alone.

"Again," Seul Bi uttered, her voice softened from lack of energy, or maybe out of a need for solemnity. Sadness barricaded her from getting past this fact. She was tempted to lie down in the street next to her aunt or go back inside the house and hold Beverly. Either way, she would burn up in the fire cyclone that was undoubtedly barreling through Rogers Park's wasted borderline by now, its hellish course set for Evanston. For Seul Bi, however, thinking about being incinerated alive was still better than thinking about a future without Beverly or her aunt. They were the only family that hadn't abandoned her, that hadn't died. Her parents had died at the bottom of the Pacific. They'd died together. Buried in the same watery grave together. And she was about to end up cremated in a charbroiled city tomb, without her parents or Beverly or her Aunt Debbie by her side. Ironic? Maybe. Unfair? Yes. Reversible? That depended on whether or not Ariel's time machine was real and hadn't been destroyed yet.

Losing one's parents does funny things to a person's soul. Seul Bi failed to truly connect on any level with those around her, but in the back of her mind, she'd always felt there was some purpose or justification for her existence. Call it guilt, along with the idea that she should do something meaningful with her life. And it was a combination of this guilt and self-awareness that had propelled her to counsel others and propagate the concept of self-preservation to those who systematically and sometimes abruptly removed themselves from functioning in society. Yet she still felt she was an enormous hypocrite for teaching her patients to love themselves when she barely loved herself. She also had never been in a serious relationship that could have given her definition. She had finally received her only real confirmation of purpose from Narumi's drawings, and that was also taken away without explanation. Zoe and Jimmy were probably shaking their heads in disappointment, wherever they were.

The prospect of dying does funny things to a person as well. Seul Bi clung to her life at this point out of fear of a painful death. It was nothing more than a primal urge to survive, and she figured it was the only real explanation as to why she was now picking up the cashmere scarf, wrapping it around her face, and swiftly limping towards Lake Michigan, which could be seen from a clearing in the smoke two blocks away. Auto-pilot had taken over. Her body craved an escape from any more suffering. How exactly going to the lake would offer this, she didn't know, but at least she could get something to drink and possibly cool down in the water. At least she was doing something besides waiting to die.

"Time to jump in, take that bath, and pray," she quipped to past and present ghosts.

Lake Michigan was getting closer. Seul Bi stopped limping and began running towards it with a delirious momentum. Her legs threatened to buckle from exhaustion, but she didn't stop. Purpose or no purpose, she pictured herself surviving this day at least a little while longer.

When she reached the beach, however, surviving suddenly felt very, very overrated.

CHAPTER 47

NOT A DROP TO DRINK

"Water, please, somebody... water."

It was such a strange thing to hear when there was so much water right in front of them all, but Seul Bi guessed they didn't want to drink any of it because of the bodies floating near the Lake Michigan shoreline. There were thousands of them, piled together like sticks that, from far away, looked like a beaver-built dam. Some bodies were nothing more than black beach balls inflated with sour blood and kelp. Parts, including hands, some torsos, and more than a few heads, bobbed up and down next to the corpses that hadn't yet sucked water into their deflated lungs by the gallons and still retained their human shape. Other pieces of random flesh drifted out towards the horizon, leaving crimson kite tails across what had become a human oil slick. Above the lake hung the smell of rot.

"It hurts!"

"Help! Help!"

"Somebody, please..."

"Oh my God!"

"Water! WATER!"

"I'm so thirsty..."

While the waterlogged dead were tossed back and forth by the tides, the living huddled together in groups by the hundreds on the beach, moaning and screaming into each other's bomb-blasted ears. Seul Bi had passed through the wall of smoke separating her aunt's street from the beach entrance when she first heard these complaints. She mistakenly thought that a triage center had been set up on the beach, and she could join whatever survivors there were, maybe help care for the wounded and find ice packs for her knees and a comfortable mat to rest on while waiting to hear some kind of official report about what actually had happened. It was perfectly understandable that she let herself believe such a preposterous scenario. Her brain was shutting down from exasperation, and it craved some kind of a return to order. Yet when she collapsed on a tree stump only a few feet away from the beach and took a minute to catch her breath, she realized what she already knew was the truth: no matter how hard she tried to escape it, only pain lie ahead. It was written in charcoal on the faces of those wandering among the sand.

She sat hunched over the stump and let out a half-moaning, half-wheezing sound. Pangs of exhaustion consumed her body, causing her to almost fall face-first into the ground. She wanted so badly to just go to sleep and get this horrible fucking day over with, already. Come to think of it, this all seemed to confirm even more her suspicion that this was all just a bad dream. Maybe if she closed her eyes for a little while, she would wake up underneath an avalanche of bed covers, and winter would still be finger-painting her apartment windows white. Winter wasn't her favorite time of the year, as the cold didn't nip at her skin but tore at it with a frostbitten sickle. But if she could imagine herself back in bed a few days ago, back when the snow hadn't been evaporated by a nuclear-inspired heat wave, she would have welcomed blizzards and ice storms and sleet and all of winter's children. Anything except this.

The bruises were growing. Seul Bi fumbled at massaging the flesh puffing out from underneath the ripped parts of her jeans. Her hands were shaky. She had to keep adjusting the scarf on her face so it wouldn't fall off and expose her to the dubious flat winds sky-walking towards Lake Michigan from the south. She gave up after a few minutes and forced her body back into an upright, standing position. She realized that sitting down had accentuated her tired-ness, as she took a couple of steps forward and onto the beach but had to fight an intense urge to sit back down again. Perhaps it was the bland warmth of the sand penetrating her shoes, which conjured up childhood summers spent on the beach with her mom and dad or the possibility of death by radiation poisoning if she remained idle for too long in one place, but she wasted no time wadding up the scarf against her mouth and pushing forward into the crowd.

***

Vomit and burnt hair. These two smells burrowed deep inside Seul Bi's nose and refused to leave. The scarf was too thin. She pinched it against her nose, anyway, and did her best to fight off waves of nausea, trudging past pools of stomach bile and crowds of people with faint steam rising from their bodies. Their hair follicles, she noticed, were singed to a breakable crisp. One by one, these people dropped to their knees or nosedived into the bile pools, adding crimson splotches from where their heads hit that made Seul Bi think of decaying rose crochets pinned on the lapels of tuxedo-wearing cadavers.

Others had it worse. Far worse. Seul Bi could see, for what felt like miles, rows and rows of victims with skin drooping off their bones and unspooling onto the ground in oily piles. Their eyes bloodshot or missing from their sockets, clothes reduced to dirty strips that clung to fractured sternums and in some cases, acting as cloth baskets for intestines that bulged out of stomach wounds. Almost every single person was in a state of shock, pain, and involuntary androgyny, for it seemed there weren't any males or females present—only sexless bodies decaying into pieces of coal.

"Oh my God," Seul Bi whispered.

She realized that there was no helping any of them. Their cries for help and for water would go unanswered, and she couldn't do a single thing about it. By the time anyone would find these people along the beach, it would be too late. The thought of finding help herself crossed her mind, but the idea of heading back towards scorched, empty streets made her stomach fold into nausea-pretzel knots. The last thing she needed was to feel even more helpless, and wandering around Evanston certainly wasn't going to serve any kind of purpose other than to escape the horrors here on the beach.

It reminded her of working at Rainbow. So many times she had been assigned patients, developed a good rapport with them, and then, little by little, it became obvious that there wasn't anything she could do or say to erase their paralyzing memories of physical and sexual abuse, molestation, rape, debilitating mental disease. She felt after listening to their stories that she had been victimized, too. All she could do was listen to their chorus cries for help and join in their refrain of unanswered "whys."

Back to work.

Seul Bi's arms and legs had become heavy and uneven. A slight tremor coursed through her body from what she guessed was the result of a stuttering heartbeat. Was there anything she could do? She wondered. Maybe there was. She sifted through the walking dead and searched for anyone to save. At least this kept the guilt at bay. The guilt of being alive and not quite as fucked up as those around her. Yes, stay moving, purposeful, alive.

A cluster of crying children crouching together near the shoreline caught her attention. Seul Bi moved towards them, licking her lips to create enough saliva for speaking.

"Hey, hey, it's okay now. Where are your parents?" She asked. She sat down beside the children, but none of them even acknowledged her presence. They seemed to not hear her question, either. The satisfied buzzing of flies, which were obese from the abundance of human dinners everywhere, was making it difficult to hear anything at all.

There were four children: two teenage girls who clung together and a small boy beside them, holding another child's body in his arms. Both girls were whimpering and crying in a language that sounded vaguely familiar to Seul Bi. Korean, maybe? There was so much black muck on their faces, and their hair, though jet black, was so matted and covered with dirt flecks that she couldn't make out if they were Asian or not. The young boy said nothing. He rocked back and forth, his face also pancaked in grime, and expressionless.

"Hey, are you all right?" Seul Bi reached out and cupped the boy's neck in her hand. It felt clammy, tense. He swiveled his head towards her but didn't look at her or say a single word. His eyes were shrunk far back into their sockets and fixed on a spot far off in the distance. Seul Bi sensed he was in a state of shock. She rubbed the back of his neck.

From where she was sitting, it wasn't immediately obvious to her that the child the young boy held in his arms was corpse-rigid. There was also something wrong with the child's head. She leaned over the boy to get a better look. That's when she noticed that the head was so bloated, it looked like a purplish-red piñata, threatening at any moment to explode with guts. She gasped and quickly turned away from the hideous sight, accidentally squeezing the boy's neck in the process.

"I'm so sorry. I didn't mean to grab you."

"Please… water. I'm thirsty. I'm so thirsty," the boy uttered in response. His words ripped right through her. It was like a mantra without prana. Did this mean the boy would die soon? Seul Bi was scared. Anyone on the beach who said they were thirsty seemed to no longer need water after a while, but a coffin.

"You're thirsty, huh? Let me go look for some clean water. There's gotta be some around here, right? What's your name, sweetie?"

"Kalin."

"Kalin? That's a nice name. So tell me, Kalin, how old are you?"

"I'm eight."

"Eight years old? Do you know what happened to your parents or where they're at?"

"I dunno. We were walking down the street by our house, and then everything turned white, and I couldn't find them anymore. My sister was gone, too. I was… I was… alone."

Kalin closed his eyes after saying this, and when he opened them back up, they were replaced with tears.

"Hey, now. It's okay, it's okay," Seul Bi said in the most reassuring tone she could muster. A part of her wanted to cry for the boy's apparent loss and for the loss of her own family. Then again, she was so parched with thirst herself that she wanted to lick the tears right off his face. She pushed this stupid thought out of her head and instead, wiped away his tears.

"Sweetie, I'm sorry to hear that. Look, I'll try and get some water, and then we'll go find your parents and your sister, okay?"

Kalin's eyes crept away from her and towards the body in his arms.

"I found my sister," he said.

"Oh… right. I'm sorry." Seul Bi couldn't say more than this. She continued sitting beside him for a moment of stunned silence before finally standing up.

"All right, Kalin, listen to me. It's gonna be okay. I'm sure your parents are still alive somewhere, and they're probably looking for you as we speak, so I'm going to find us some water, and I'll ask around and see if anyone has seen them, okay?"

"All right." Kalin didn't seem to welcome her thin optimism. Apparently, neither did the two teenage girls. They had stopped whimpering at some point during Seul Bi's conversation with Kalin and were now engaged in a rapid-fire exchange of foreign words between them. It sounded like they were protesting the fact that she was about to leave, but Seul Bi didn't really know what the hell they were trying to say.

"Kalin, do you know these two girls?" Seul Bi pointed at them.

"No, they were here before me."

"All right, then." Seul Bi walked over to the two girls.

"Excuse me, um… do either of you speak English?"

They looked like sisters, or at the very least close friends. As they wiped dirt from their faces, their eyebrows wrinkled in unison at her question. They inched closer together before answering, and except for one of them having a cut on her cheek that was already scabbing over, Seul Bi felt like she was seeing double.

"A little," the duo answered simultaneously. Their accents were hard for Seul Bi to decipher, especially between the flurry of coughing and sniffling both let out while speaking. She looked from one to the other of them, inspecting their faces a little more closely.

"Are you two sisters?" She asked.

They both nodded affirmatively.

"Are you two hurt at all?"

"Hurt? No, not hurt."

"Maybe you both are just scared. I know I am," Seul Bi said while smiling compassionately at them. The girl with the cheek cut attempted to smile back, but only managed a clumsy wince.

"Do you know where your mom and dad are?" She asked. This time neither one moved at all except to lower their eyes. She didn't even want to ask what happened to their parents after hearing and seeing what happened to Kalin. Right now, she had about all she could take of family being lost. She decided to take a different approach instead.

"Are you thirsty?"

Cheek Cut answered. "Yes. Do you know where to find water?"

"No, I don't know where there's water to drink. I don't think anyone does. The water in the lake is probably bad, too." Seul Bi pointed in the lake's direction. The two girls solemnly stared towards the lake. Every lapping wave they could hear was mocking their thirst. Seul Bi drew in a deep sigh before continuing to speak.

"Like I just told Kalin, I'm going to look for something we can drink. Maybe there's some bottled water in the houses that haven't been burned up or destroyed. Can you watch him for me?" She didn't point this time but instead flicked her eyes towards Kalin. The gesture was lost on the girls. They didn't say anything and continued their sniffling parade.

Kalin also didn't react to being talked about, nor paid any attention to what was going on. His head hung low above his sister's corpse. He looked like a toy sailboat lost at sea, threatening at any moment to capsize from bullying waves.

"Um… you know, can you watch him, keep him safe, do you understand?"

Both girls muttered to each other an undecipherable string of foreign words before Cheek Cut answered with a monotone "Okay." Neither seemed happy with the request, but Seul Bi couldn't worry about their feelings right now. She had to get moving. Fast.

"I'll be right back."

It didn't take long for Seul Bi to find what she was looking for. All she had to do was look up.

Without even so much as a rumble, water started to pour down from the sky. Seul Bi was soaked in a matter of seconds. The rain brought cries of relief from those whose lips weren't burned beyond usage. Everyone who was conscious collectively opened their mouths to drink. Seul Bi also filled her mouth, which felt like a gravel road, with the downpour. Her thirst was pushed down into her stomach, reminding her that she hadn't drank anything since this all started. She sensed an oppressive force lift off her and those around her as well. People were still dying, but at least they were able to say their goodbyes to each other and not succumb to constant choking fits. Everywhere down the coastline she heard loud outbursts of gratitude to God.

But the celebration was short lived. Seul Bi's taste buds registered a taste that was awful yet familiar.

Ash.

She remembered the strange night at Rainbow when ash had fallen from the sky, caking the outside windows of the residential apartment complex. Grey flecks had replaced the snow on the ground. The mezuzah guarding the door had turned into a black hole. Soot blanketed everything, including the patio in front of the doorway. These things she was sure had happened, but the following morning, there had been no trace of anything at all out of the ordinary. Had this been history's attempt to warn itself about today, its newest day of infamy?

The rain droplets were like grenades filled with soot shrapnel, exploding all over the beach. Lake Michigan swayed back and forth with bodies and blood inside its contaminated waves. There was water, water, everywhere, and not a drop to drink.

Seul Bi threw up the ash that had already found its way down her esophagus. It wasn't enough to get rid of the grime still leeching onto her taste buds, so she shoved the scarf that was clutched between her hands deep into her mouth. She wiped at her teeth and gums until it became impossible to breathe, then pulled the scarf out and along with it, a bone-shaking cough. She stood hunched over, making sure no more filth was inside of her. The saliva-covered and newly dyed jet black scarf slipped from her hands.

"God fucking damnit," she spit out, along with blackened mucous and saliva. Had she just drank out of a heavenly urn filled with the cremated remains of the damned? Another question immediately began to swirl around her mind like piss that wouldn't flush: *what if the black rain is contaminated or radioactive?* If this was true, then anyone who drank it would probably die from radiation poisoning. She wiped away the leftover spittle caking her lips and tilted her head towards the scattered crowds. All around her people were gulping down as much of the polluted rain water as possible. The strange thing was that no one's face was distorted with discomfort. If anything, expressions of pacifism were spreading among those engrossed in insistent prayers and parting conversations. Seul Bi expected at least one person to come to their senses and recognize the danger of swallowing what could likely be contaminated ash, but nobody seemed to care. Blissful ignorance had overtaken them all.

There was a very real possibility that she had doomed herself to the same fate as everyone else by drinking the rain, despite throwing up immediately afterwards. The nagging question in her mind became whether or not she had done irreversible damage to her insides.

Better to change the subject.

Seul Bi scanned the opposite end of the beach from where she stood. She hoped to spot a house or an apartment complex that was safe to enter and look for water. Unfortunately, there weren't any within view that didn't have flames shooting out of their windows or downed power lines snapping around in their yards. The only promising option seemed to lie about fifty yards away, past the beach line. It was the fenced-in perimeter of a tennis court. Seul Bi surmised that a water fountain or vending machine would be found somewhere around there. That is, if they hadn't yet been blown away or melted. The chance of finding either a water fountain or vending machine or even a bathroom with a working sink intact seemed high, considering there weren't any flame clouds or signs of destruction anywhere near the court. At least none that she could detect from her vantage point.

Suddenly, a memory sprung to her defense, alleviating any doubt. A few months back, during an unusually humid fall night, she had watched Beverly and Mark play tennis together at this court. They had goofed off and never took a single set between them seriously. Their tennis game that night was just an excuse, anyway, to share a shower afterwards and go at it. Why Seul Bi went along and played third wheel to their stupid dating ritual she couldn't recall, but one thing was flashing in bright carnival lights: at some point, both Beverly and Mark had asked her to get them something to drink, and she had acquiescingly gone off to look for what they requested. She hadn't gone more than ten feet before finding a fountain. Next to it had been a dispenser filled with V-shaped cups.

Ahh, that's right, Seul Bi thought. *Those damned cups and their leaking tips. I had to put three of them together, one on top of each other, just so they would hold the water long enough for one good swallow. God, I'm so thirsty. If there's another dispenser like that with V-cups, I swear I would drink every spoiled drop of water that falls to the ground.*

Time to move. Seul Bi breathed hard, propelling herself in the direction of the tennis court. Thunder clapped in the distance, or maybe it was the reverberation of explosions in wasted Chicagoland. Whatever it was shook the ground with every step she took. She squinted upwards at the sky, protecting her eyes from the ash rain with a steeple made of fingers, and worried that, if it was thunder, lightning would be next. She pictured in her mind what would ensue: lightning zigzagging in between storm clouds and tree tops, and then a rogue bolt of electricity strikes her at 140,000 mph. Instantly her insides liquefy. Her body cooks rotisserie style, her scorched vertebrae serving as a skeletal spit. Of course, she had never seen or known anyone who had been struck by lightning. The odds were... what were they? Something like one in a million of getting zapped? Yet this now seemed to be as normal a way to die as having a heart attack or getting cancer, when compared to people evaporating in a nuclear bomb blast, being melted, torn apart, or any of the other six million ways to die that still remained to be experienced.

Another ear-splitting thunderclap; this time it was much closer and accompanied by flash bursts almost directly over the beach. *Focus*, Seul Bi thought. *Gotta focus. Gotta hurry up, too.* She tried to hurry her pace, but hadn't walked any more than ten yards before the combination of the tremors rippling beneath her feet, dehydration, and her muscles burning through what felt like barrels full of lactic acid caused her to lose her balance and fall directly on her ass. She surprised herself by jumping right back up like a bouncy ball. The furnace slush falling on her from above was getting thicker, blacker, and staying down on the ground meant she would end up buried under a pile of ash like her Aunt Debbie had become. No question about it.

If she could see herself in a mirror, she imagined that she would look like some kind of war refugee. She felt dirty, destitute, very Third World. And what felt like fingernails scraping against her throat wall every few seconds reminded her just how badly she needed something to drink. So she kept her balance up and her head down and continued moving forward.

She only made it a few more yards before colliding into a roaming pack of death-marked souls.

The downpour had become so murky and the sky so overcast and busy with doom that Seul Bi didn't see them coming. She wasn't able to get a very good look at anything while her head was down. The few times that she did manage to lift her head, her gaze was directed solely towards the fenced-in perimeter of the tennis court. It was her only priority. She figured that, as long as she walked in the direction of the fence line, she couldn't wind up in Lake Michigan, or worse, go in the opposite direction from a possible working fountain. She realized this was a blind expectation, much like an infant expecting her mother's nipple to always be close by, ready for suckling, but it was all she had to go on.

What she didn't expect was to be engulfed by skin peeling zombies. Every time they bumped into each other, off came a chunk of forearm flesh or tufts of hair, or a kneecap slipped off and exposed bone. Their hair stood straight up, and their shredded clothes couldn't hide the broken ribs poking out of them or the sucking chest wounds that collected black rain in their defilades. The tribe of wounded held onto each other in a single-file line, staring in cemetery silence up at space or the ground or nothing at all.

One woman, who was crawling on all fours, looked like she had been dunked in a vat of used car oil. Her lower jaw was missing, too. What remained on her face was a crusty blood outline of where the jaw once was. An incomplete blood sketch. The woman kept pushing her tongue into what was left of her mouth, but it kept slipping out of her fingers and pasting itself to where the neck usually meets the chin.

Several others who stumbled by Seul Bi looked like used-up matches. Their eyebrows were singed off completely, like they had leaned over a grill for too long. They even had that post-cookout smell pouring off their bodies. All charcoal and lighter fluid. And their faces dripped down to their necks with melted flesh, exposing cheekbones, gums, corneas. From their heads down to their limpy knees, each wore a grayish muumuu woven with dust from collapsed buildings, bone shards, skin flakes.

Perhaps worst of all, a man, or at least what resembled a man with a taut face (which was the only part of his body not absolutely drenched in blood), limped a little ways behind the rest of the tribe and carried in his arms what appeared to be a slender serving tray. As the man passed by Seul Bi, she realized that he wasn't carrying a tray, but a little boy. The boy's arms were glued to his sides. They didn't dangle in the air but kept horizontal, along with the rest of his body, and his neck was like a steel pike driven through his head.

The man whimpered softly, clutching the boy close to his chest as his limp turned into a clumsy stagger. Yet the man repeatedly stopped himself from falling forward. His legs were incredibly long and could easily be mistaken for red flagpoles swinging back and forth in hurricane winds. The boy had on muddied jeans and a few fabric strings for a shirt, revealing a hole where his stomach should be. Intestines flopped around in the hole, occasionally spilling onto the boy's lap where there was already a puddle of congealed blood. Seul Bi racked herself with a repeating thought of the man turning around, heading straight for her with his human tray, and offering a serving of stomach soup.

Still, Seul Bi couldn't move, couldn't think, couldn't do anything as the damaged souls swarmed around her. She was caught in the middle of their sojourn to nowhere. With each person who trudged past her, numbness spread throughout her body like a virus. It occurred to her that maybe her own injuries were catching up to her; that her legs were simply too sore anymore to cooperate with what she really wanted to do, which was to run fast back to a reality where nuclear bombs didn't drop from the sky without warning. Where her parents weren't dead and she wasn't twice an orphan. But that reality had been stabbed to death a long time ago, its kingdom of happy promises overthrown by the surreal. She was stuck on a broken bridge that wasn't going to lead her out of this nightmare anytime soon.

Could this fucked up *coup d'état* of the world's logical order be over if she just closed her eyes? It was worth a try. She lifted a hand to her eyes, limiting any vision to the inside of her blood-stained palm. She also held her breath until what was left of the tribe passed by. The lack of oxygen made her feel lightheaded and unbalanced, so she eventually filtered tiny breaths through her semi-pursed lips. For almost a minute, she resisted the urge to fall down or suck swells of air into her lungs, but that was all she could manage. She couldn't deny reality any longer. She sluggishly opened her eyes and bent over, bracing herself with both hands on the scarce parts of her upper legs that didn't feel bruised or knotty from exhaustion. She inhaled sharply several times, then stared at the muddy sand beneath her feet.

A strange sensation flooded her nerves.

It wasn't the delirious feeling of air returning to her lungs or of regaining her composure, but something… different. At the same time, though, her nerves registered familiarity. A faint, metallic smell wafted up into her nostrils along with the odor of cooked flesh.

It wasn't coming from the tribe. By the time she had uncovered her eyes, they had continued on their path to nowhere without her. She was certain then that the air she currently breathed wasn't infected with their decay. It wasn't the man carrying the dead boy, either. He had vanished along with the rest of his wounded kin. There was only the sand she concentrated on and her shoes, which held two very tired feet.

She stood straight up, pushing behind her ears wisps of hair that had fallen onto her face from bending over, and sniffled. She wiped ash off her face, then looked towards the perimeter of the tennis court. It was still visible, but barely. The rain had become a velvety, black curtain. She knew that she needed to hurry before it would completely envelop everything. She took a step forward and immediately noticed the smell of burnt flesh intensified.

Where was it coming from? She clasped her hands together over her eyebrows and squinted to see if there was anyone coming her way.

Nobody.

Suddenly, fear rippled Seul Bi's blood. With her feet soldered to the sand, she pivoted her head and body around to see if anyone was behind her. Somehow, she knew even before turning around there would be.

"No… not you," she said, aghast at who it was.

He had a drilling stare. This surprised Seul Bi. His face could easily be mistaken for charred meat on crumpled tinfoil, yet his stare was full of disgust and obvious hate. At the same time, that's exactly how she knew even before turning around that she would see lips covered in syrupy egg yolk pus that leaked from popped blister sores around his mouth. Dust-covered clothes that clung to burned, eschar skin that accentuated the bone fragments sticking out everywhere like pins in a meat cushion. Boots that floated in a mutating puddle of slime that was continuously sliding down its body. A face that hid any sign of a nose, ears, or hair. Two eyes stuck in gooey tissue, and that toothless mouth, which still did not offer any explanation or reason for attacking her two nights ago. That twitchless mouth was a terrifying absence of words and reason.

In his hands, he gripped the shovel that had inflicted so many bruises on her body. Bruises that continued to tie-dye her skin teeth-clenching blues and purples. The shovel's bright, metallic hue was muted by the leaking gray and black sky, but Seul Bi could clearly see the bright, red color of blood outlining its rusty blade.

She tried to scream for somebody to help her, but choked the words back down her throat and instead exhaled a wordless plea. She remembered yelling for help two nights ago and nobody coming to the rescue, so why would it be any different now? The only difference this time was that the thing hadn't attacked her first. He seemed to be waiting for her to make the first move. But she refused. Except for the tremors of fear that travelled up and down her extremities, she didn't dare move an inch. She didn't want to provoke another assault. She could still taste the dirt and worms in her mouth from their last encounter.

I gotta do something though, Seul Bi thought to herself. *It's fight or flight, and I'm—*

The thing twirled his shovel and took two slow heavy steps towards her. In an instant, all guessing about what would happen next vanished. He was there to finish what he started two nights ago, no doubt about it, but Seul Bi had no intentions of getting the living shit beat out of her again. Realizing it was a mistake to just stand still, she ran as hard and as fast she could in the direction of the tennis courts. The only problem with her escape was having her back turned to the thing, but she had to concentrate on where she was going. Nothing was visible in front of her except splattering rain and ash.

She was also surprised at how fast she could run; the uncooperative sand beneath her feet threatened to yank her down into a permanent mud coffin. Which was worse, though? Not looking ahead or not looking back? She crossed what she thought were at least fifteen yards before finally deciding to look over her shoulders, but she instantly regretted doing so. The thing was right on her heels, raising the shovel over his head to swing at her. There was no way he could miss. He towered over her, and thanks to his daddy-long-leg arms, he could easily smash the shovel directly down on top of her head. He took aim, thrusting his weapon with murderous intent, but Seul Bi turned around at the last moment. She instinctively lurched forward and veered to the right, away from the parting air behind her back.

Her quick thinking had saved her—or had it? She was sure that her head hadn't been split in two. The thing had missed with his deathstrike, yet she could feel something terribly cold and heavy running down her backside, and it definitely wasn't the bulging rain that had thoroughly poured down on her and everyone else within sight. No, that felt like warm and dirty bathwater. She thought for a moment that it could be her blood, but the temperature was all wrong for this to be true. Whatever drenched her backside had quickly penetrated her skin and chilled her bones and blood vessels. What the hell was it? She didn't want to risk taking another look behind her and possibly slowing down again enough for the thing to try and decapitate her with another swing. All it would take would be one good smack against her head with the sharp end of that shovel, and goodbye, cruel world. And she didn't need to look back to know the thing would be chasing her. The way this day had already turned out, it wouldn't make sense if it wasn't. She decided her best bet would be to just keep running straight ahead and worry later on about this new icy form of torture.

She didn't get far. About twenty feet into her sprint, her shirt and pants froze to her skin. Her legs wouldn't listen to her anymore, no matter how many times she told them to keep running. A cold and heavy liquid pierced both her front and back sides, kicking at her shins and knees while stabbing her chest with what felt like disintegrating icicles. She reflexively turned sideways. It was impossible to lessen the engulfing onslaught's sting. Her only defense in fighting this invisible enemy seemed to be running back in the direction that she just came from, but she didn't know which direction that was anymore. Thanks to a new palette of black shadow tones that consumed the sky in solid darkness, all visibility had been reduced to zero. Even if she could somehow find her way back, the thing was still chasing her. Not moving forward meant her head would be like a baseball perched on top of a tee. All the thing had to do was swing. He wouldn't miss again.

Where the fuck are you? Seul Bi anxiously wondered. No doubt he was out there. She sensed his presence nearby. But for some reason, he had stopped pursuing her. *Why did you stop following me? Are you waiting for something to happen? Maybe for me to die of hypothermia or radiation poisoning or God knows what else? Or maybe you're just toying with me, biding your fucking time because you know you could kill me at any time. Is this some kind of sadistic ploy?*

She swayed back and forth, question after question unsettling her thoughts. If she could make it to the tennis court, would there be others there who also went searching for clean drinking water? She could join them, look for a car that hadn't been destroyed, and get the hell out of Evanston. But what about Rainbow? If there was a chance it was still standing, shouldn't she at least try to see if there were any survivors? Weighing other people's lives with her own was never a strong suit. She wanted to save everyone she could. One of the initial reasons she had wanted to become a counselor was to help others save themselves. It was cathartic somehow, given the fact that she couldn't save her parents from dying horribly. She wanted, no, *needed* to save somebody today, because right now she hadn't saved a single soul. Not Marisa, Mark, Beverly, Aunt Debbie… nobody. Could she even save herself? Right now it didn't seem like she could do anything except wait until her eyes became acclimated to the freezing darkness. She bit her lips and shivered uncontrollably.

Another question proved to be more disquieting than all the others: *why do I keep sinking into the ground the longer I stand here?*

Several minutes passed. Seul Bi's teeth clacked against each other so loud it sounded like a thousand tap dancers in her ears. She couldn't hear anyone or see anything moving, but something else had started pulsing around her. It was a constant, churning noise, mercifully silencing the world's death throes, but also block-ading any other sounds as well. Sounds like the whooshing of a shovel right before it cracks her skull in two, for instance. She had no choice but to wait in the deafening void until her pupils grew large enough to see once again. When they finally did, she under-stood why the thing wasn't trying to kill her anymore, why she was numb from head to sinking toe, why she was hearing thousands of distorted cramp rolls, riff walks, and paradiddles.

She wasn't on the beach any longer, but inside the drooling, bloody mouth of Lake Michigan.

Waves chopped at Seul Bi's waistline. They were getting larger. As she pushed herself forward into the stampeding current, she could faintly see ahead of her several black, liquid mountains. She would have to climb them. It was either that or trudge back to the beach, but the burnt man was there. There wasn't a doubt in her mind that he was there, waiting for her, licking the spot where his lips used to be in hungry anticipation of her death.

She passed through a gap in a planetary ring-like row of corpses, chunks of cement, and other debris floating near the coast-line. Immediately the smushy ground outside the ring became an underwater galaxy of empty space. She halted her advance, as the water now lapped at her breasts, and taking another step meant having to swim into this misplaced cosmos.

The water temperature had spiked around her as well. She needed to rest, so she lowered herself and marinated in the unexpected warmth. The muscles in her arms and legs began to loosen as her blood circulation improved. The water felt good. So good, in fact, that she considered the possibility of drinking it, but she quickly shook that thought out of her head. Most of the bodies floating in the lake were bloated buoys of flesh engorged with water, not viscera. Their guts and blood and bile and excrement had become part of the lake's slick, tarp surface.

Seul Bi also considered the reason for the sudden temperature increase might be from cooked human fat. It made sense; the world had been stuffed into a microwave and set on high for the past several hours. And the dead didn't have a chance to cool down in the lake. That much was clear to her, judging from the boiled skin that was barely clinging to each corpse in the ring.

Suddenly she didn't want to stand where she was anymore, near the dead in the water, the dead on the beach, the death waiting for her at the lake's threshold. She didn't know or want to imagine what waited for her out in the black nothing in front of her, but it was guaranteed death if she stayed right where she was. She was a target standing still. A target for disease, radiation, the falling ash… the burned man on the beach.

Seul Bi flung herself into the oncoming waves.

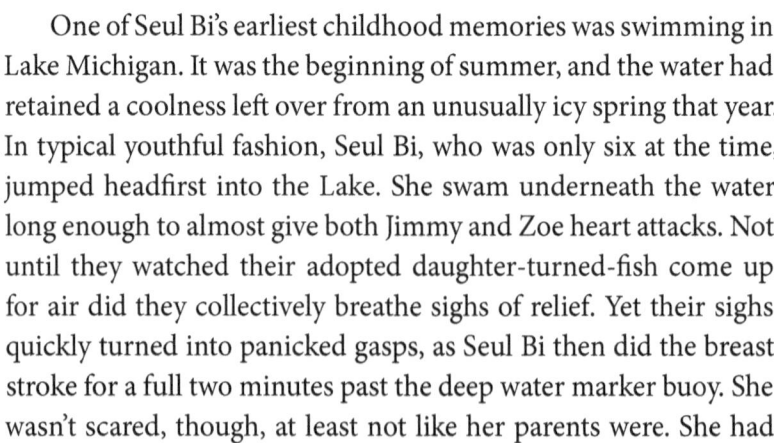

One of Seul Bi's earliest childhood memories was swimming in Lake Michigan. It was the beginning of summer, and the water had retained a coolness left over from an unusually icy spring that year. In typical youthful fashion, Seul Bi, who was only six at the time, jumped headfirst into the Lake. She swam underneath the water long enough to almost give both Jimmy and Zoe heart attacks. Not until they watched their adopted daughter-turned-fish come up for air did they collectively breathe sighs of relief. Yet their sighs quickly turned into panicked gasps, as Seul Bi then did the breast stroke for a full two minutes past the deep water marker buoy. She wasn't scared, though, at least not like her parents were. She had meant to swim that far, and the only fear that inhabited her was the kind of fear with a built-in expectation of safety, like waiting in line to ride a rollercoaster.

Was there something waiting out there for her? Perhaps an answer that would explain why she had felt out of sync with the world, like a rogue moon that desperately roams the sky searching for its original orbit. Or a reason for the incubating loneliness that would later completely surround her heart. From as far back as she could remember, these feelings of displacement existed. But where did they come from? It wasn't from being adopted—that much she knew for certain. When Jimmy and Zoe explained the reason why her eyes were slanted and her skin bore a darker hue than theirs, it didn't explain the constant feeling that she was living somebody else's life. Maybe she was too young to understand the disparity between her natural insecurities stemming from adoption and this... *other* irresistible force that was responsible for slinging her unexpectedly into deep water.

Yet as she treaded the water, trembling more from the exhilaration of what she had just done than from the thawing lake, this force pushed her to go farther out still—to risk her life in achieving a purpose that didn't seem to belong to her or anyone else.

Seul Bi never did get the chance to find out what was waiting for her in the middle of Lake Michigan. Jimmy had jumped in and swam out to her immediately after she had passed the deep water buoy. He proceeded to latch onto her arm so tightly that he instantly broke the spell which had come over her. Then he scolded her and forbade her to get back into the water for the rest of the day. So much for finding answers.

There was no Jimmy or Zoe to stop Seul Bi this time, and that strange force once again took over and drew her farther and farther away from the beach. Was this the reason why her arms and legs were able to withstand the pummeling waves?

On and on she swam, unable to make out what was more than a few inches in front of her face other than black water. The entire lake was a gigantic inkblot. And behind her, the rooftops, skyscrapers, and people of Chicago continued to melt away. A series of conflagrations sprung up right after the blast's initial impact wave and hadn't stopped burning through everything in sight, including most of Evanston. Some of the taller buildings in Evanston that were on fire created reflecting blades of oranges and reds that occasionally cleaved through the lake's surface. Seul Bi stopped swimming through the dark water to take a break and unintentionally found herself right in a spot where this eerie radiance was in full bloom. She couldn't believe it at first. She thought her mind was playing tricks on her, that perhaps she was so tired and physically exhausted and dehydrated that she was hallucinating. A part of her supposed this was what it would be like to go spelunking in a cave deep in the earth without a flashlight or lamp.

Total blackness.

One step in the wrong direction would bring instant death.

And seeing light miles below the earth was a nasty lie that offered false hope of a nearby safe surface.

Such light shouldn't be wasted, then, she thought to herself. *Even if it isn't real.*

The blackness had receded around her faster than expected. While using her right hand and legs to stay afloat, she shook her left hand in the air to air dry it as best she could, then wiped off her face. It was time for a better look at how far she had swum, and if possible, assess the situation on the beach. The rain still sputtered forth from the sky, which made it hard to see anything clearly, but she stared anyway at everything illuminated by the bright hues.

The beach was nowhere in sight. A mushroom cloud tinted orange and red hovered over Chicago. It looked like a matte abstract painting, hanging above clouds of smoke and flames palpitating in every direction. She looked away from the awful exhibition and towards her left and right instead. It was just in time: two prodigious waves were steamrolling towards her from either direction, threatening to drown anything caught on their downwind side. She scooped at the water in front of her as fast as she could and managed to avoid being caught in the trough between them, but that didn't prevent her from being dragged under in a twisting current. She frantically thrashed her way back to the surface, but when she did, the air she sucked into her lungs went back out as fast as it went in. Things had, without any warning or reason, suddenly become much, much worse.

She was now spinning around and around in a maelstrom.

There was no escape. Churning water tentacles wrapped themselves around Seul Bi, dragging her down towards the gaping black hole at the bottom of the maelstrom. She attempted to swim against the cross currents and reach the diminishing crestline above her, but it was pointless. Her arms and legs didn't work anymore. Her backside seemed to also be magnetically fastened to the spinning, liquid walls surrounding her. The mutant whirlpool wasn't letting her go. And not just her, but everything else as well: driftwood, chunks of stone from blown-out buildings, fish, and bodies that were more like meat balloons waiting to be popped than actual human carcasses. All were doomed to be sucked into the bellybutton of the beast.

Seul Bi managed to free both her hands from the turbulent water and clasp them over her ears. The roar was like being suspended inside a gargantuan waterfall. With her hands dulling the noise, something else rang in her ears; something she had been ignoring since jumping into Lake Michigan. It was the voice inside her that had warned of something like this happening. *Hey! This is why the thing on the beach didn't come after you. He wasn't afraid of the water. He wanted you to swim out here. He was ushering you towards this. It was all part of his plan. Why didn't you see that earlier? You should have swum back and took your chances with him. How could you be so stupid? That thing missed on purpose.*

She spun faster and faster as she approached the black hole. Vertigo was starting to set in. Soon her gray matter wouldn't matter. But what were her options? She couldn't swim to the top, as she had sunk so far below the crestline that all she could see above her were thrashing waves. Neither could she plunge backwards into the twirling chaos; the cross current seemed so powerful it might rip her to shreds. She considered holding her breath while inside the black hole. If it emptied out into the bottom of Lake Michigan, then maybe she could swim to a safe place topside.

Except her stamina had all but vanished. *So I can either drown above or drown below*, she thought scoffingly. *No fucking way. There's gotta be something else I can do, something that makes more sense than this. How can this be it when everything I've been through I—*

Her thoughts were interrupted by something she never expected to see again. A solid beam of light suddenly appeared beneath the black hole. It was exactly like the light beam in Kona ten years ago, the one that drew Jimmy and Zoe to their deaths. She didn't want to believe it. Perhaps it was a last-minute hallucination to accept drowning more acquiescingly? But the light beam wasn't exactly a welcome sight. It reminded her of how she didn't have the courage to help her parents when they had drowned or were killed or… whatever had happened on the Pacific Ocean floor to cause their deaths. Here it was again, only a few feet away. And she could do nothing, it seemed, to escape from being pulled into the black hole, which still had all the glassy luster of a fixed and dilated pupil, despite the water beneath it bathing in a soft translucence.

Her heart went into overdrive as she imagined what was about to happen. Her epiglottis would involuntary close all airways, depriving her brain of oxygen. Her body would shut down, and she would then faint while her body convulsed right before cardiac arrest claimed her life. Without consciousness or direction, she would eventually drift lifeless over some underwater cliff. Her hands and arms would wash ashore afterwards, as the undercurrent would be so strong it would tear her up like paper and scatter pieces of her everywhere. Most of her body would never be found or even looked for, since everyone who cared about her was dead already.

Well then, why didn't I die with my parents if my life was going to end up exactly the same as theirs? That was the one question that worried her more than dying. She was afraid of never finding out the answer for her permitted existence. People die every day for no apparent reason, though. Thinking she was different than somebody on the news who had been hit by a car walking across the street or diagnosed with a terminal disease was a lifelong mistake she had made. She was sure of that now. As tears made bee-lines all over her face, she could do nothing but wait to be sucked into oblivion.

The strange thing was that the light seemed to be waiting for her as well. It didn't zap through the hole like a laser, or burrow through the watery walls surrounding her. Instead, it lingered calmly below, like a lens flare on the last mental snapshot she would ever take.

She closed her eyes, not wanting to see what exactly was waiting for her, just as the waves behind her jerked her entire body downward with a megaphonic cackle. She breathed in and out as hard as she could while water tried to rush down her throat and up her nose.

Please God, save me! I'm so scared. I don't want to die.

What's going to happen to me? Will I see Mom and Dad?

Are they waiting for me? Is everyone going to be there?
Bev, Aunt D., Mark, Marisa...

my other mom and dad?

Oh God, please let me live.

Please let me find a way out of this.

If I can just hold my breath, maybe I can make it somehow...

maybe I can swim back to the top and get back to the beach. I need to get back to Kalin and those two girls.

Need to find water to drink.

Need to get the hell away from this fucking nightmare!

I'm so thirsty, so, so thirsty, and the water tastes good in my mouth right nowsssasdadd dssssssso good. Swallow mooore. If I sawalllow litttttllleeeee

biiiitiittttt

I'mmmmmm

wooooottt

dabbbeeada

bfdaweg

ibos

bfll

in

e...

The things you think of before you die.

PART FOUR

The Hibakusha claw at the metal latches,
and we can only hear their whispered release.
Redemption is simple.
The hard part is acting like you have been redeemed.

"Hello?"

Darkness surrounded Seul Bi along with a stale smell reminiscent of decomposing clothes, the kind found in Goodwill graveyards. She wasn't sure what had happened (the last thing she remembered was sucking water into her lungs and passing out), but one thing seemed certain: she wasn't dead yet.

Her body was laying backside-up on a patch of solid ground. She ran her hands over its surface. The texture felt like cement, or maybe stone. Whatever it was didn't have much space to it. She couldn't stretch her legs without hitting a wall of some kind. And when she swiped her hands in the air around her, she discovered walls on either side of her, too. Had she been mistaken for dead and buried alive, stuffed inside a coffin too small for her body?

"Hello? Is anyone there? Please, can anyone hear me? Help!"

It hurt to yell, or to move around, for that matter. Her knees were throbbing with pain, and running her fingers over her arms, face, and neck revealed scratches that were starting to scab over. Breathing was also difficult. Like coffin difficult. She had to find a way out fast.

She tried listening first for clues as to where she was exactly but couldn't make out a single sound except her own stertorous breathing. Maybe she really *was* buried alive. Maybe the gravediggers hadn't dug a full grave. Maybe the grave was only deep enough to put her box out of sight. A stack of makeshift boxes filled with thousands of "as yet unidentified" victims. Too many "maybes" stacked one right on top of the other on top of her.

"Please... ANYONE!" She yelled.

Nobody answered her pleas. She started to cry, unsure of what to do next, but her tears were quickly flushed away with the faint but unmistakable sound of a car engine somewhere in the distance.

Seul Bi turned staccato, suspended in between inhaling and exhaling the stuffy air surrounding her. A car? Her first thought was that her mind was playing tricks on her, that this was a delusion born from wanting hope. Yet as she closed her eyes, concentrating on the blackness beneath her eyelids instead of thinking she was going crazy, more recognizable sounds of life penetrated the tense, obsidian void holding her prisoner: a soft wind that whistled between what might be trees or buildings, the hum of an electric generator, a bird cawing.

These everyday sounds were background noises to most people—the required monotonous humdrum of living that is easily forgettable. They were rarely a cause for celebration. Yet Seul Bi felt like a buzzing dynamo because of them. It was proof that she wasn't buried alive and that her sanity was still intact. Or so she desperately believed.

It was time to find a way out. Although she still couldn't see anything, she opened her eyes anyway and pushed her hands in every direction, poking and tickling every inch of the walls surrounding her. When she stretched her arms above her head, she found two tangible promises of escape. The first was that her hands hadn't jammed into a coffin lid or wall, but a foot or two of open air. She had been fooled by the stuffiness and hadn't considered her surroundings to be anything else except a coffin or makeshift box somebody put together for the dead bombing victims. The second was something even more unexpected:

A door handle.

Rotten spit slid down her throat as she gulped from excitement. She almost didn't notice the door handle's flattened knob nestled against the wall. It barely punctured the airspace above her head.

Her excitement was marred by skepticism. *This seems too easy, too convenient, that I found this right after thinking about a way out*, she thought. She suspected this was a hallucination, another deluge to accompany the sounds of cars and wind. She expected the doorknob to be locked. One more middle finger from life before she suffocated with her eyes wide open.

"Please, God, let me open this fucking door."

Prayer answered. The door handle turned without any resistance. Seul Bi, not realizing she was leaning against the door, tumbled forward onto a thin balcony.

She didn't jump up right away. She couldn't do anything except stare in silence at her surroundings. In her mind, the phrase "WHERE THE FUCK AM I?" replayed at least a dozen times before she spoke it out loud. A wind set on vibrato answered somewhere above in the sunlit sky. At least she assumed it was sunlight brightening the dirtied gray cement that comprised the balcony floor.

The balcony had two sliding glass window doors on its left wall, which was opposite its navel-high, street-side wall. Both window doors were shut and curtained. Several towering buildings, which looked like apartment complexes, stood across from the balcony. They blocked out most of the horizon with their stone frames and rooftops. In several of the apartment windows, all of which appeared empty and lifeless behind their balcony enclosures, Seul Bi saw the reflection of an ordinary street below.

"Where the fuck..." Seul Bi said, her voice trailing off.

She slowly stood up and adjusted her eyes to being out in sunlight for what felt like the first time in years, then turned around to inspect the closet. There was nothing unusual about it. No hole, trap door, or ceiling chute that had belched her onto the closet floor. Just two cement slabs made up the back of the closet, a layer of poorly applied grout in between them, and cobwebs puckered in every corner. A perfect place to store mops and brooms.

She leaned inside the closet and searched for an answer as to how the hell she'd ended up inside of it. She ran her hands over the two cement slabs and knocked down the cobwebs in search of a crack, a trigger, the outline of a door. Nothing. She then tapped the floor with her feet. Solid as prison bars. The low ceiling inside the closet seemed to have only one purpose: cramping the storage space. There weren't any levers or knobs or strings to indicate another section of the closet might be hidden somewhere above it. She pushed up on the ceiling anyway, just in case, but it didn't budge.

Exasperated, she clenched her fists and backed away from the closet. She was mad at herself for thinking there would be any shred of a logical explanation found inside what appeared to be an ordinary storage space. Why would there be? Just because there were buildings and balconies and sunlight here, she realized it was a mistake to think that words like "logical" or "explanation" applied. Whatever this place was felt far from normal.

Normal. Seul Bi peered over the balcony at the street below. It was narrow and mostly empty, except for a few parked cars and vans. She judged that the distance between her and the street was about three floors. Sidewalks were on either side of the street, but they, too, were vacant. There weren't even visible sign posts that could offer her a clue about her surroundings. The sounds of cars in the distance faded more and more with each passing minute.

"Nyyyyaaaaaaaa!"

From somewhere behind her, a cat's unmistakable yowl startled her so much that she nearly fell over the balcony from fright. Luckily, she gripped the balcony's edge at the last second and pushed herself away from it while simultaneously twisting her body around, preventing what would have most certainly been an injurious if not fatal fall. She found her footing and was instantly met by the cat's menacing glare. It wasn't standing behind her, though, as she expected it would be, but was instead perched on a pillow behind the balcony's nearest glass window.

The curtains that covered the window were now open. Seul Bi inched towards it, wanting a closer look at what else they had been hiding. The cat, which up close looked like a milky ball of white rice, responded by flattening its ears and loudly hissing a warning to stay the fuck away. She ignored its protest and pressed her face against the glass.

There was a girl inside.

Seul Bi jerked away from the window. A girl? What the fuck was going on? She started to wonder if maybe she hadn't survived the maelstrom. Was this the beginning of her afterlife? Or could this be the moment right before the electricity shuts off inside her brain? She had heard about people who had died and were subsequently revived talking about experiencing memories they didn't know they'd had. Doctors said it came from massive brain surges right before flatlining. She considered this idea, but of all memories to have, why one with a balcony, a pissed-off-looking cat, and a girl inside a dark room?

The sunlight had receded, making visible only the outline of the girl's physique. Seul Bi leaned towards the glass for a better look. If she was going to find out the truth about what was happening, she was willing to bet it had something to do with this girl. Or at least she hoped so.

The girl was somewhere in the center of the room, surrounded by shadows. Even from outside the glass, it was obvious that she was pale-skinned and rickety thin. Short, too. She also appeared to be smiling, but Seul Bi couldn't be sure about this looking in from her position on the balcony. The girl's entire face was floating in a cup full of darkness.

Seul Bi also noticed the sliding glass door was open. *The girl must have done it*, she thought to herself. *She must have opened the door while I was looking over the balcony. But why didn't I hear it open?*

She stepped inside the room, despite the continuing clamor of hisses and growls from the feline rice ball. It assumed a pounce-at-the-jugular attack position. "Shhhhhh," Seul Bi offered in peace. "There, now. It's okay. I'm not gonna hurt you." The cat retreated a few steps in the opposite direction from her, a soft growl signifying its uneasy truce. Seul Bi crept further inside.

The room reeked of cedar. It was like a thousand cedar trees sprouted around Seul Bi with every step she took. She wondered, though, about the source of the fragrance. The room was completely empty except for several small candles burning their final minutes away. They were piled on a table in the left hand corner farthest from her. The ceiling was not that high, either. Seul Bi could jump up and probably touch it with the tips of her fingers. She realized that a low ceiling meant all smells would remain trapped in the room like apparitions, unable to float through floors or walls. *So then, the cedar smell must be from the candles,* she surmised. Their distracting and overwhelming odor had nowhere to go. It was either them, or the girl standing stoically in the shadows must have doused herself with a gallon of cedar oil.

Something else bothered Seul Bi about this room, taking over her thoughts to the point at which she almost forgot about the girl in the room completely: *no interior door.* The only way in seemed to be the sliding glass door leading out to the balcony. It was possible that this was just a storage room and that the other door on the balcony provided access to an apartment, but nothing about that made sense to Seul Bi. Why would a storage space have such large, glass windows?

Unless...

An answer loudly stomped around in her mind, one that she didn't want to believe was correct.

This room wasn't meant to store things, but people.

The girl stepped out of the lifeless shadows and into the candle-light. She wore a teal-colored shirt and blue dress pants, but her body frame was so skinny that Seul Bi immediately thought she looked like a bunch of haphazardly thin lines put together. There was a smile on the otherwise expressionless face of the girl, the same one Seul Bi had thought she'd seen moments ago while peering into the window from the outside. It wasn't a warm or inviting smile, however, but rather a forced, polite, upward curve of the lips. The kind you give somebody when their toddler vomits half-chewed-up pieces of chicken all over a restaurant floor. Seul Bi limped over anyway to where the girl was standing. She didn't care about fake smiles or even real ones at this point. Only answers.

"Hello?" Seul Bi asked.

"Hello," the girl replied in a high-pitched voice saturated with melody. Somehow it filled the entire room with an awkward calm that seemed counterpoint to the girl's perforating stare. Her cheekbones bore a translucent, pale color, while her eyes poked out of curved slits. It was hard to see them underneath the long, jet-black ropes of hair swinging in front of her face, but there was no doubt in Seul Bi's mind that the girl in front of her was definitely Asian. Definitely young-looking, too, judging from the absence of skin wrinkles and lack of thigh meat on her otherwise tiny, puked-out frame.

"Who are you?" Seul Bi asked.

The girl plunged into a deep bow before responding. "My name is Satsuki. I'm very happy to meet you."

"Satsuki... Satsuki... you're Japanese? That sounds Japanese to me."

"*Hai.*"

"So wait... where am I?"

"Japan."

"Japan?" Seul Bi's eyebrows formed half-circles on her forehead. Her mouth a full circle. "What?"

"Yes," Satsuki answered with absolute politeness. She raised an arm towards the window door behind Seul Bi. "Hiroshima, to be exact."

"What do you mean, Hiroshima? I'm confused. I mean, how is that even fucking possible?"

Satsuki dropped her arm back down next to her side but continued to beam at Seul Bi. "I'm sorry you are confused about what has happened to you."

Seul Bi studied Satsuki for a while, saying nothing. She figured that this girl knew the answers about what was happening, or would, at the very least, have some idea about the catastrophic events of the day. Come to think of it, Seul Bi wasn't even sure what day it was anymore. She had no idea how long she'd been in that closet.

"What did happen to me?" Seul Bi asked.

"You must be very tired from everything that has happened," Satsuki said, ignoring her question.

Seul Bi furrowed her brow at Satsuki. "Wait, so you know about what's happened, then? About the bomb or whatever the fuck it was that exploded over Chicago? How could you know about that unless… wait a minute." She paused to consider a name that suddenly popped into her head. "Narumi?"

"Narumi?" Satsuki repeated.

"Yeah. I was talking to a Japanese female named Narumi who liked my drawings and bought them from me, but I never got the chance to send them. She lived in Hiroshima, I think. Are you her?"

"I'm sorry. I'm not the person you are talking about."

"Well, if you aren't Narumi, who are you, then?"

"My name is Sat—"

"I know what your fucking name is! Who the fuck are you, and why am I here?"

Seul Bi's rebuke was met with the total destruction of any discernible noise in the room. The silence stood between them as though it were a novice at mediations. Neither one spoke or did anything until Satsuki finally pursed her lips and changed her expression for the first time since Seul Bi stood in front of her. A look of utter bewilderment distorted Satsuki's face, making her seem wounded, shocked, yet genuinely unsure of how to answer Seul Bi's two-part question. Satsuki decided to offer a wordless apology and another bow.

"Look, I didn't mean to swear at you or get mad. I'm not usually like that," Seul Bi relented.

"It's fine," Satsuki replied, her voice immediately returning back to a state of high-pitch bizarre cheer, given the circumstances. "I understand."

"Okay, so… at least tell me, you know, what's going on. I mean, is this real, or am I dreaming, or what?"

"Yes. This is real. This is no dream."

"So if this is real, then that means I'm actually, really, honest-to-God in Japan?"

"*Hai.*"

"But how did I get here from Evanston?" Seul Bi knew it was probably pointless to ask this but did so anyway. She still wasn't able to completely acquiesce in denying the application of logic to everything that was happening.

Seul Bi didn't wait for an answer either. She turned around to face the window. She wanted to confirm herself that she was actually in Hiroshima but didn't know much about the city other than its tragic past. All she could see were the tall, faded buildings across the street that appeared completely empty. All she could do was watch as a few wind-swept leaves scurried over the balcony ledge and spun like pinwheels into the air. There was something familiar about what she was looking at but nothing that provided any comfort or reassurance. She might as well have been looking through the window at herself.

"Did everyone you love survive, like you did?" Satsuki asked.

Her words took a moment to register with Seul Bi. There seemed to be genuine concern behind the question, but she couldn't feel anything except bitter remorse at the thought of her Aunt Debbie and Beverly dying in the horrific ways that they did. She spun around to face Satsuki before answering.

"Everyone I love? Um… no. They're all dead. Every single one of them. And I almost died, too!" Seul Bi paused. "Fucking Christ!" she exclaimed while rubbing her cheekbones and closing her eyes. "I don't understand what's happened. None of it makes any fucking sense. None of it."

"I'm sorry for your loss," Satsuki began to say, once again filling each word with a curious sympathy. "I don't want you to be afraid or upset anymore. This is difficult to understand, as you said. This doesn't make any sense to you."

Seul Bi opened her eyes but didn't respond. Satsuki continued on, exhaling deeply. "The worst part is that you have lost people in your life through unexplainable events. I know what that feels like, you see. To lose somebody who can never be replaced, for seemingly no reason at all."

Whatever intended sentimentality that this was meant to convey was lost on Seul Bi, who still didn't trust anything about Satsuki, the room they were sharing, or her claim that they were in "Hiroshima." She tried to remain calm, but looking at this young girl and hearing her high-pitched voice was just too disorienting. She wrinkled her nose in a growing disdain.

"You know what this feels like, huh? No offense, but I don't think you could possibly know what I'm feeling right now or what I've really been through. Not at all."

"Hmm," Satsuki hummed. She gazed at Seul Bi for a while, as if deciding what to say or do next. Then she glided towards the table full of candles and picked up a piece of paper the size of an index card. "There is something I want to show you."

"What's that?" Seul Bi asked.

Satsuki walked towards Seul Bi and held out the index-sized card, slightly bowing her head as Seul Bi cautiously took it from her grasp.

"*Hai, douzo*[46]," Satsuki said while gesturing with her hands that she wanted Seul Bi to read what was on the card.

Seul Bi frowned. She couldn't decipher what was written on the card. It looked like a medley of scribbled lines going in

---

46. *Douzo*—"go ahead," or "by all means." Douzo can have many meanings similar to these.

all directions. The middle of the card contained a few symbols which reminded her of something she'd seen while watching anime as a kid.

"What does it say?" Seul Bi finally asked after realizing she could stand there for a million years and probably never know what was written on the card. Satsuki folded her hands together to form an interlocking finger bridge.

"*Watashi-tachi wa minna tsunagatte iru no*," Satsuki answered solemnly.

"Huh? What does that mean in English?"

"We are all connected."

"We are all connected?"

"*Hai*." Satsuki unlocked her fingers and spun them around in a circle. "Each of us is joined together to feel everything that has ever been experienced in our lives. You hurt, I cry. I cry, it rains. It rains, floods form, and when floods form, you get hurt again. Life goes on and on and on like this, with each of us not even aware of how much everything we say or do or *think* plays a role in somebody else's happiness… or tragedy."

Seul Bi mulled this over. "I'm sorry, but I still don't understand what the fu—"

"ENOUGH!" Satsuki shouted. "YOU WEREN'T BROUGHT HERE TO UNDERSTAND!"

Seul Bi's mouth fell open. The sudden transformation of this young girl into a screeching banshee stunned her speechless. Her feet drilled into the floor with paralysis as well. What did Satsuki mean, exactly, by saying that *she wasn't brought here to understand*?

Satsuki narrowed her eyes and stared straight at Seul Bi. "These questions will only make you ask more questions and more questions. It is pointless to ask even a single question. Soon you will want to know the answers as to how you got to Hiroshima from Evanston and how I can speak English."

"Well, how are you speaking English?"

"There is no way you could possibly understand.And even if you did, it won't bring back Jimmy or Zoe, or Debbie or Beverly, or Mark, or Marisa, or anyone else you cared for who is now gone."

Jimmy. Zoe. How do you know about my parents or what happened to them? Seul Bi repeated this question in her mind until an appended version of it came tumbling out. "So… are you saying that you knew what would happen to my parents when we went to Hawaii? And you knew that Chicago would get blown up in a big fucking explosion? Was I supposed to know these things were going to happen, too? Is that what you're trying to tell me? Please just answer this one question for me… was I supposed to know what would happen to me in my life?"

"Your drawings were clues that this would happen," Satsuki replied matter-of-factly. "They were like dry rubs of the truth, but you didn't pay any attention. You just let yourself be lost in whatever moment seized you. It's the same for everyone. We ignore what is around us until it's too late. You have been alone your whole life, and yet those hands you drew were reaching out to hold you, to comfort you, but you rejected them all."

"I DIDN'T REJECT SHIT!" Seul Bi yelled. "What the fuck are you talking about?!" She stepped towards Satsuki, feeling more frustrated now than scared, but not sure of what to do next. *Enough of this shit*, she thought to herself. A part of her wanted to grab Satsuki, shake the truth right out of her, and end this stoic charade. Yet Satsuki stood completely still. Seul Bi huffed at Satsuki's indifference but decided against getting any closer. The smell of cedar suddenly grew stronger.

"I would sketch because I saw these things in my head, and they needed to come out," Seul Bi said, a new level of frustration added to her words. "I didn't know I was supposed to stare at them and think they were ever going to jump off the fucking paper and comfort me. There hasn't been anyone in my life to do that. But you know what? I don't care about any of that right now. What I care about is figuring out why I'm here. I know you're fucking lying to me. It's that, or there's something you're not telling me."

"Please, calm down," Satsuki pleaded.

"No! No, I'm not going to fucking calm down! Tell me why I'm really here!"

Satsuki redirected her stare to the candlelight flickering in the corner of the room. An uninvited blast of wind had snuck inside and was slapping the flames around, causing the epileptic shadows to seize against the walls. In the long silence that followed, Seul Bi began to breathe rapidly, as her pulse accelerated to a level that was somewhere between warp speed and extremely pissed off.

"TELL ME!" Seul Bi finally demanded, unable to control herself any longer.

Satsuki jolted her head back towards her, responding with a menacing glare. "You are here because I wanted to thank you," she said through clenched teeth.

Seul Bi couldn't believe what she was hearing. "Thank me? For what?"

Satsuki's facial expressions toggled between slight anger, hesitant joy, and muted sadness. Seul Bi couldn't tell what she was thinking or feeling. It reminded her of a television channel that's full of static and close enough to a working channel on the dial that you can hear the channel's sounds coming through the static… *but the picture is all fucked up.*

After a few seconds of hypnotic quiet that felt like forever to Seul Bi, the sound and image on the television channel was no longer a static dot pattern of haphazard emotions. It became loud and clear, as Satsuki stepped towards Seul Bi and slowly opened her mouth to speak, her voice barely a whisper.

"I wanted to thank you… for dying."

Seul Bi's eyes widened. She suddenly felt weightless, lifted into the air, and it was without a doubt the powerful arms of fear that held her up. Satsuki's words felt more like an ominous warning than an expression of gratitude.

"For dying? What… do you mean?" Seul Bi quivered.

Satsuki's cold shoulder routine continued. Seul Bi was about to ask Satsuki again to explain herself when the cat beside the window suddenly appeared beside Satsuki's feet. Seul Bi hadn't heard it move at all, which was strange, given the fact that it was so chubby, the vibrations from its movement would have easily been felt by anyone standing in the small room. Satsuki kneeled down and ran her fingers through its mane, her entire hand dissolving in the white fur. "You're such a good kitty, Chi-chan," Satsuki said. The cat purred and rubbed itself vigorously against her.

Seul Bi didn't know what to make of this. The way Satsuki was acting as though nothing was wrong, petting the cat and ignoring her questions, it all felt like a carefully choreographed distraction. But a distraction from what? She realized that, while she had been talking to Satsuki, the cat hadn't moved from the window, not even when both girls had yelled at each other. And Satsuki hadn't called the cat over to her, or looked in its direction even once the whole time…

Seul Bi felt the sudden urge to run out of the room and get as far away as possible, but it was too late.

A spiky pain grinded its way up Seul Bi's leg and spread throughout her entire body, causing her fingertips to almost vibrate right out of their nail beds. Her eyes jerked violently up into their sockets as the whole room spun out of control. Her head felt like it was on fire. Remaining vertical wasn't possible anymore. She crashed to the ground into a pool of her own blood.

Seul Bi had never broken a bone before, never even sprained or fractured any part of her skeleton, but now her tibias on both legs had been crushed. Bone splinters from the fibulas pierced the skin in at least a dozen or more places along her calves. Her brain tried to register this new form of pain, but it was information overload having so many wounds to deal with all at once. She felt woozy, lethargic. She guessed that her body was probably shutting down from the shock and that she was going to pass out. Before she did, she wanted to know who or what had broken her bones. So she gathered enough strength to prop herself up on her elbows and look down at her legs.

"NO! IT CAN'T BE!!!" Seul Bi screamed.

Two elongated arms, each resembling unwrapped fire hoses that were at least fifty feet in length, had slithered out of the balcony closet and into the room. Both arms were burned so badly that they looked like chicken bones with strips of gristle attached to them. Rot and pus oozed profusely from patches of eschar, creating a foul-smelling trail of slime underneath their scorched skin.

The overwhelming smell of cedar in the room had prevented Seul Bi from smelling their stink. This made it possible for the sinewy hands at the end of each arm to latch onto her lower legs and break them before she even knew what was happening. If she hadn't been in such brain-paralyzing pain, she might have figured out that she had walked right into a carefully planned trap by the girl who was still standing in the room.

CHAPTER 53

TEACHING SHADOWS

to ....

DANCE

Satsuki giggled through her nose as Seul Bi tried in vain to free herself from the strangling grip of each hand. The fingers on each hand had morphed into bony blades the size of steak knives and pierced Seul Bi's upper thighs. They sliced right through bone and tendon, careful to not sever any major arteries just yet. Seul Bi's face turned ashen gray. She let out a scream that punished her vocal cords, then no sound came out of her mouth, only blood.

Hyperventilating, she pried at the razor-sharp fingers, but was unable to stop them from sawing her femurs into pieces. The skin where her flesh was torn began turning dark black. All she could do was stare in horror as her legs spasmed, turning into bloody volcanoes that spewed out globs of bone marrow along with chewed up pieces of ligaments, bundles of shredded veins, and capillary debris.

"HELP! OH MY GOD! PLEASE HEEELLLPPPPPPP!"

Satsuki waded into the expanding pool of blood that encircled Seul Bi, painting her blue dress pants crimson. She knelt down beside Seul Bi and gently stroked the top of her head.

"Shhhhh, the battle is almost over. Soon it will be time to disappear," Satsuki reaffirmed.

Seul Bi continued to pry at the hands with her own shaky fingers, but they wouldn't budge. The steak knives had sliced and burrowed right through her thigh muscles and straight into the ground. The nerves connecting her brain to her legs were short-circuiting. She helplessly gyrated around like a jack-in-the-box fallen on its side.

"I… didn't… do… anything… you… please… stop…" Seul Bi pleaded. Blood gurgled out of her mouth between each word.

Satsuki continued to stroke Seul Bi's head. Chibita joined her in the pool of blood, crouching low to the ground to lap at the dark liquid with his tongue. Satsuki noticed his white fur coat had turned into a red, polka-dotted dress. She quietly laughed at him.

"Ah, Chi-chan, you're not a girl, so why are you wearing a dress? Hmm? Come here." She scooped the cross-dressing feline into her lap and immediately its entire diaphragm vibrated.

"OH MY GOD!! NOOO!!" Seul Bi watched as all ten of the bony finger blades slid out of their holes in her legs and crawled up her stomach, over her breasts, and plunged directly into her shoulders. Her entire body, not just her head, now felt like it was engulfed in a flamethrower's flame stream. And when her shoulder blades cracked into several tectonic scapular fragments, her consciousness on/off switch stopped working.

Everything suddenly began to echo. Seul Bi was jerked into a faraway daze, where the only sound she could actually hear was her heartbeat set to blast. She didn't even hear the awful popping noises when both her clavicles were torn from their arm sockets. She might have stayed in the daze, too, if it weren't for her head involuntarily smacking against the ground from wave after wave of reflex muscle spasms.

It was the coppery smell and metallic taste of blood, which had poured down into Seul Bi's mouth from her right eye, that finally shoved her back into awareness. She realized that her arms and legs had been detached from her torso, and the meaty stumps where her appendages used to be were spraying blood everywhere. It was a matter of time before she bled out and died. There was not going to be a chance to escape like before.

If she was going to die, though, at least she wanted to know her death was for a reason. Especially since it seemed like her whole life had been a huge waste of time. It was a matter of time before she bled out and died. She gathered up what strength she had left to speak, but all she could manage between crying and the lumps in her throat from dehydration and viscera stuck in her esophagus was one word:

"W..h…y…y….y….y….y…………..y?"

Satsuki leaned over Seul Bi's face. "Because your life is suffering," she answered gravely, "and you must die so that I can live and not suffer anymore. And even though it's too late for understanding, the answer to all your questions is that we are all connected. We are all connected. You. Me. Your death. My escape. *Watashitachi wa minna tsunagatte iru no. Tsunagatte iru no. Tsunagatte iru no. Tsunagatte iru no. Tsunagatte iru no. Tsunagatte iru no. Tsunagatte iru no. Tsunagatte iru no. Tsunagatte iru no.*"

Seul Bi grasped for meaning in Satsuki's explanation, sought a reason behind the repetition. Not all her thoughts were getting through, though, thanks to the endless bouts of throttling pain and sweeping numbness. She had read somewhere that losing too much blood from the body is the equivalent to drowning. Both result in death from lack of oxygen to the brain, and both were reported to have accompanying feelings of tranquility due to the brain being unable to sustain high periods of activity. She hoped for that peace to come quickly, as she was scared of experiencing any more pain, scared about not having answers, scared to die without knowing what the fuck Satsuki meant. Scared of what would happen next.

"Be brave," Satsuki said, as if she could, or rather, *was,* reading Seul Bi's final thoughts. "This is the final evolution of love."

Before Seul Bi could respond, one of the hands wrapped itself around her neck and began crushing her windpipe and esophagus in its chokehold. Her teary eyes bulged out of their sockets. Her shoulder and hip muscles bucked into the air. Her body instinctively wanted to claw and kick in protest, but her arms and legs had been torn off and were lying next to her.

"N —————————O!!!! S——T————!!!!"

Her words, which had become more like grunting noises, sank in a mouthful of blood. Dark flecks of red foam formed at the corners of her lips. Every time she tried to take a breath, her heart beat so fast it threatened to explode right out of her chest. But these palpitations did nothing to help her breathe. She continued to wheeze and try to form words from the bloody alphabet soup sloshing around inside her mouth and all over her face.

The hand around Seul Bi's neck didn't strangle her to death. It kept her alive long enough to see the other hand yank her mutilated torso towards the doorway.

Satsuki stood up and waved. Chibita leaned against her, curling his tail in front of his forepaws. Blood dripped down from the ceiling and onto their heads, the walls, the floor, deepening the crimson.

"Sayonara, Seul Bi-chan," Satsuki whispered.

Both arms slithered backwards onto the balcony, clenching tightly their prize of flesh. It was black outside. No moon or stars existed, or rather, if they did exist, they had been evacuated to a safer skyline. There weren't any eyes peeking behind closed curtains, nor cars rumbling in the streets, nor any shrill night insects buzzing around. Only wind seeped out from between the housing complexes. Like a foul henchmen to the arms, it swept up into the air a row of leaves that had been stuck in the arms' slime trails. Seul Bi couldn't feel the wind on her body, couldn't hear anything, not even her own thoughts. The arms continued to slowly retract until they had reached the balcony closet. The last thing Seul Bi ever saw was her head cleaved from her body, followed by the backside of the closet door as it slammed shut.

A-ha.

So this must be one of those theta-wave moments that Dr. Nathan was talking about. I understand now what my life has been about, why I lost two sets of parents, why I went into the counseling field, and why I had to suffer at the end.

I was born to be sacrificed.

That's it. That's gotta be it. Because I don't think I've ever felt completely happy with my life. I mean, who does really feel completely happy with their life these days? I suppose it was wishful thinking that I would be an exception or that I would find complete happiness on earth. But my life wasn't really mine to pursue. I get that now.

Stupid me, though. I couldn't see what was really happening the entire time. And besides, the only part of my life that had ever come close to being normal was with Jimmy and Zoe, but how could I have been happy as their "child" when I knew they weren't my parents? I mean, they didn't even look like me. I suppose I never did get over the adoption blues.

But then again, I was just being groomed for the slaughter, wasn't I? Like some fucking pig raised on a meat factory farm or the daughter of a terrorist who would tell me one day to blow myself to pieces for the sake of Allah. I couldn't have escaped my fate no matter what. Having memories of watching my parents grow old, of getting married and having children, of retiring and living peacefully among grandchildren, none of these things were necessary or needed to happen. My sole purpose was to be an offering on the doorstep, just like I was found that day at the monastery. Every breath I ever took belonged to her. Everything I did or said was her idea, her thoughts, her need to feel whole again, her need to seek vengeance against fate, her need to say goodbye... I guess I really did belong to her in the end.

It was August 6th. Yoshiko wasn't sure if she was going to the paper lantern festival, which was only a few hours away from beginning. It was something she did every year with Satsuki, and if the festival happened to fall on a day that Hideo didn't work, he would come with them as well. As children, every August 6th, Yoshiko and Aiko would head down to the banks of the Motoyasu River with their mother and father and send off colorful, candlelit lanterns into the water. Their lanterns would join thousands of other ones just like them in helping guide ancestral spirits on their way to heaven. They also served as floating prayers for peace. It was a beautiful tradition sacred to Hiroshima, and until this year, a tradition that Yoshiko had always been determined to keep.

Satsuki was still locked away in her room and refused to come out, but this wasn't entirely the reason for Yoshiko's hesitation. Most of the festival participants would gather on and around the Motoyasu Bridge, politely vying for a good spot to watch their lanterns drift away. If Yoshiko wanted to join the bridge crowd like she always did, it would be almost impossible to avoid the nearby sidewalk trail where, in her mind, the grass was still stained scarlet from her unborn daughter's severed arm. Just the thought of getting anywhere close to that sidewalk trail made her panicky and reluctant.

For weeks, the nervous anticipation had been maddening. Would she go or wouldn't she? Over and over she asked herself that question. It distracted her, messed with her sense of reality, and amplified everything to a million. It got so bad that she couldn't watch television, which sounded like an Omnimax theater with surround sound, or read books or magazines without having to plug her nose from the pungent odor of... paper? Yoshiko didn't understand how reading something like a magazine could make her feel so apprehensive.

The weather wasn't helping things, either. It had violently rained for three weeks straight, right up until the early morning hours of August 6th (Yoshiko had been unable to sleep and was in the kitchen making tea when the rain finally stopped pelting the kitchen window). This did nothing to cool down Hiroshima, as the city was experiencing one of its worst heat waves in decades. Plus Yoshiko knew the second she stepped outside, the humid air would be like a swarm of mosquitoes attaching themselves to every inch of her flesh, instantly sucking the sweat out of her.

I could go on and on with these excuses, she thought to herself. She sat at the kitchen table, rubbing her lower back. *But I NEED to do this because it's not just my choice anymore. I need to say goodbye to that part of my life, so that a new part of my life can begin.*

She stood up and slowly walked towards the hallway. If she truly believed what she had just told herself, then she would first need to convince Satsuki into coming out of her room. She suddenly wished that Hideo could be at her side through whatever was about to happen. He seemed to really have changed over the past several months, being devoted to the idea that their lives could return to normal. It was working too. Both were closer now than perhaps even in the beginning of their marriage. They talked a lot more, and neither one could keep their hands off each other. They had sex several times a week! Sure, they still had plenty of fights and arguments, but nothing outside what most husbands and wives go through as the result of sharing on a daily basis a bathroom, bed space, and opinions. And even though Hideo had stopped knocking on Satsuki's door a long time ago, Yoshiko believed that if he were with her now, he could provide enough strength for the both of them to endure their daughter's silent treatment.

Too bad Hideo was on a business trip. Yoshiko couldn't believe that Mazda made him work on August 6th of all days, but he had actually been gone almost a whole week. She assumed the plan was for him to return home by today, but something must have come up in his work that made this impossible. This was nothing new for her husband, or for that matter, any of the employees at

Mazda. Most Japanese salarymen were married to their jobs first and their wives second. Yoshiko never liked this inescapable fact about her husband, but at least he had made sure to call and check up on her every single day since he'd been gone. It was all the strength she was going to get from her husband, but better this than nothing.

She checked her phone. Hideo hadn't called yet, so it looked like she would have to speak to Satsuki without the advice or comfort of her husband. She hadn't told him about her decision to try to persuade Satsuki into attending the paper lantern festival. How could she? Up until right now, she wasn't sure herself that she was going to go. And would it really have mattered if she had said anything to him? Hideo's advice would probably not be anything she hadn't thought of a million times already.

There is one thing that might get Satsuki to come out, Yoshiko thought to herself. *Time to see if I'm right.*

She knocked on Satsuki's bedroom door. She heard something move, but couldn't tell if it was her daughter or Chibita.

"Sacchan, are you in there?" she asked, taking a small step back. She wanted to see if there were any shadows bleeding out from the door's bottom, but she couldn't tell if there were or not. It was too dark in the hallway, which suddenly felt much narrower than it already was. She knocked again, then backed away and crouched down, leaning against the wall opposite Satsuki's door.

"Sacchan, I don't know if you are in there, but I want to talk to you about something. Well, actually I want to talk to you about two things, or wait… that's not right. There are so, so many things I want to talk to you about, actually."

Yoshiko paused and massaged her neck before continuing. "Look, I know you're still upset with everything that happened. Maybe you're also upset with me and your father. Actually, I'm pretty sure you're upset with your father, but I don't want you to be mad at him, or me, if you are. Your father misses you. And I really miss you, too. So… I was thinking that maybe you could come with me to the paper lantern festival today. Can you believe it's already here? Do you remember how we used to go before we moved to Tokyo? You always had so much fun. You were so shy and didn't want to join most of the other children, so I would take you right up to the edge of the river and help you with your lantern. Do you remember that? I do, and I remember how you would watch your lantern float away as long as you could. You would beg me and Father to wait until it was completely out of sight. We were always one of the last ones to leave the river banks."

Yoshiko laughed, then crawled over to the door and leaned against it. "Sacchan, please come out with me. We can wait all night at the river if you want. I haven't seen you in so long, so it would be nice to spend that time with you. And look, I understand why you don't want to come out for this. Why would you want to go back to the place where everything happened? Trust me, when I thought about going back, I immediately said no myself. I don't want to be reminded of what happened that day. But what happened that day is something I can't ever forget. I doubt you will ever forget it, either. So, how about this? If we both try to help each other, then maybe we could learn to live with what happened. I want to try, because I'm not sure I can go back there without you."

Outside, several car horns beeped one right after the other. A truck revved its engine so loudly while driving down a nearby street that the balcony windows rattled for several seconds, mimicking the shaking caused by a minor earthquake. Yoshiko didn't pay any attention to this, nor did she move from leaning against the door. Instead, she pressed her ears firmly against it and listened for her daughter's breathing or movements, but no matter how hard she tried, there was only vacant silence, the kind that drip-feeds into your ears after waking up to an empty house. *Did Sacchan not hear anything I just said*, she wondered, *or does she simply not care?* She had allowed herself to be completely vulnerable in admitting she needed Satsuki's help with the healing process. Losing the baby was something that was never going to disappear completely from her reality, but if Satsuki could be returned to her, then the loss wouldn't feel as enormous, or so she hoped. One thing was clear: Satsuki wasn't going to open the door out of sympathy for her mother, nor for the sake of any shared grief between them.

This left Yoshiko no other choice; she would wager everything on the hope that her daughter might not care anymore about having a mother or father, but still cared about having a brother or sister.

"Satsuki," Yoshiko said, pausing to wipe the moisture collecting in the corner of her eyes, "if you don't want to come out of your room because of me, that's fine, but I just thought you should know that I'm not the only one in this hallway who wants you to come out." She sniffled and took a deep breath.

"I'm pregnant."

There was no denying it, although at first, Yoshiko couldn't believe it herself. Sometime right before summer was when it must have happened. Her first instinct told her that it probably happened on the night Hideo had taken her to the *jinjya*, the one where they placed their *ema* of apology for the miscarriage. It would've been an amazing coincidence, but then again, Yoshiko felt it was the karmic wheel finally rolling in her favor. Or something like that. She didn't notice anything different until the morning sickness came on in full force a month after that fateful visit. An appointment with the doctor a few weeks after the throwing up began confirmed it: a healthy child was growing inside her belly.

When she had told Hideo, he laughed, gave her a hug, and then said something about hoping it would be a boy who could help the Carps finally make the playoffs. Yoshiko had felt scared, wondering if in a few more months she would have to endure another nightmarish miscarriage. That was the biggest reason why she needed her only living child to return to her; she was absolutely sure that she couldn't go through something like that again by herself. No way in hell.

Yoshiko continued to wait for Satsuki to open the door, subconsciously holding her breath until her chest started to hurt.

When she finally exhaled almost a minute later, the force of the breath leaving her diaphragm caused her entire body to push back from the door. She slumped to the hallway floor while long, heavy tears fell fast from her eyes. They were like liquid reinforced-steel cables that caused her head to bow from their pull. She closed her eyes and dumped her face into her hands. So Satsuki really was gone for good.

Yoshiko was doing her best to avoid crying out loud. Her body instead twitched in silent convulsions. She wasn't sure how long she had stayed like this in the hallway, but just as she was about to pick herself up from the floor and go to her own bedroom and possibly shut the door for good, something touched her bowed head.

She went stiff. Whatever touched her was now starting to pat her on the head. She lifted her face up to see what it was.

A slender hand attached to a disjointed-looking arm was reaching out from behind the door, which was slightly ajar. There could be no mistake whose arm it was.

"Sacchan!" Yoshiko managed to say between her trembling lips. She slid herself over to the door and pushed it all the way open. There was her daughter, who she hadn't seen in almost a year.

"*Okaachan*[47]," her daughter softly replied.

"Sacchan! I've missed you so much!" Yoshiko wrapped her arms around Satsuki, sobbing uncontrollably.

"*Okaachan*," Satsuki repeated. "I've missed you, too."

---

47. *Okaachan*—A cute, childlike way of saying "Mommy."

The sun was a little past setting when Yoshiko and Satsuki made their way through the bulging crowds on the Motoyasu Bridge. Every arm and backside they brushed up against felt clammy, as the heat from the morning and afternoon still lingered on everything in sight. When they reached the sidewalk next to the bridge, Yoshiko grinded to a halt and subconsciously began to cradle her stomach. A thought polluted her: the last time she was here, there had been a different baby inside her stomach. That baby had died here. If she walked any farther, would the new child growing inside of her die as well? Her head and chest suddenly felt very heavy.

"*Okaasan*, are you all right?" Satsuki asked.

Yoshiko closed her eyes and nodded. "I think so. It's just that—"

"I know," Satsuki gently interrupted, "but don't be afraid." She reached her hand out to her mother for the second time today. Yoshiko opened her eyes. She wondered how long it had been since her daughter was outside in the day time like this. Almost a year? Yet Satsuki looked calm, and much more cheerful than she had expected. Whenever she had fantasized about taking a walk like this one with Satsuki, it was Yoshiko who was the reassuring one, guiding her daughter out of *hikkikomori* exile and into the world once again. She had never imagined that it would be her who needed reassurance from Satsuki that everything would be all right. Lying in that grass, blood everywhere, people gasping… the memory of that day had shut the door on Yoshiko ever feeling completely safe. But Satsuki was, in fact, the one person who truly understood. If anyone could pull Yoshiko out of the memory wreckage, it was her.

Despite knowing this, Yoshiko was still scared. She rubbed her stomach like it was a good luck charm, hoping maybe it would calm her, but her shirt felt like it had been put in front of a blow dryer set on high for hours. Her hand boomeranged back to her side.

"This damn heat!" Yoshiko blurted out while trying to shake the burning sensation out of her fingertips. "Oh, I'm sorry, I didn't mean to swear."

"Yeah, seems one of us is always swearing around this place," Satsuki said. It took Yoshiko a few seconds before she understood Satsuki's quip. She could only let out a half-hearted laugh.

"I'm sorry," Satsuki quickly apologized, then wiped her mother's face with a small towel. "That was probably a bad joke. It's been a while since I've made a joke, you know?"

"Thank you. And yes, it *has* been a while, hasn't it? You're sweet for trying to make me relax, but it's still kind of hard to move forward, you know?" Despite saying this, she slipped her hand into Satsuki's grasp. Some of the anxiety inside her disappeared as she did so.

"Come on. It's too hot to be standing still," Satsuki said while leading them both forward onto the sidewalk.

They hadn't talked much after Satsuki left her bedroom. Neither one felt it was the right time to play catch up. Yoshiko had simply asked if Satsuki was hungry, and Satsuki politely declined her mother's invitation to eat something. Then Satsuki went and grabbed a bottle of Pocari Sweat from the refrigerator, fished out a small towel from a kitchen drawer, and told her mother they should probably hurry up and leave before it ends up raining and making the humidity outside unbearable. Yoshiko doubted it was going to rain again but bit her tongue to avoid arguing with Satsuki. She wanted to savor the sweet sound of her daughter's voice and didn't want to ruin it by talking. Anyway, she imagined they would discuss everything that had happened soon enough. Satsuki walked outside, and Yoshiko followed behind like nothing had ever happened. Even Chibita came down to the *genkan* to watch them leave, as was his usual manner whenever somebody left the house. Just like old times.

Yoshiko stared ahead at the fan-shaped staircase leading to the Motoyasu River bank. It was filled with so many people that she wondered about her unborn baby's safety. She was afraid somebody might accidentally bump into her stomach. Satsuki noticed the worried look on her mother's face and thought of something fun to ask her.

"*Okaasan*, do you know if it's a boy or a girl?"

"Well, it seems to still be too early to tell, but I had Dr. Yoshimoto do a special test to find out."

"Really? What did the test say?"

"He's convinced that it's a girl." Yoshiko paused. "I can't explain it, but… so am I."

"You're having another girl?"

"I know, right? Can you believe it?"

"Looks like I'm going to have an *imouto* after all!" Satsuki squeaked, her voice cracking from excitement. Finally her life's reset button had been pushed.

Just then Satsuki had a déjà vu moment. She had already known this was going to happen. A sister was the only reason why she had decided to open the door and reach out to her mother, and she had somehow known what her mother was going to say before she had even said it. Everything was falling into place exactly as she wanted, exactly as she'd imagined it would.

Satsuki and Yoshiko purchased a floating lantern at one of several vendor tables set up for the festival. Afterwards, they weaved in between everyone until they reached the top of the fan-shaped staircase. Around forty or fifty tourists and reporters stood here, clicking away with their cameras. A much larger swarm of people had congregated at the bottom of the staircase. There were so many there, in fact, there neither Satsuki nor Yoshiko could tell where the steps ended and the Motoyasu River began. The separation between cement and water was blurred even further by several men who stood in the shallows and helped push the floating lanterns into any kind of current, big or small. They also helped many of the younger children who were too timid to set their floating lanterns into the water. A pontoon boat with several people aboard it floated near the staircase.

Satsuki scanned for any openings near the river. "There, on the far left, near where all those television crews are set up," she said, pointing to a sliver of steps with nobody on them. A row of cameras was set up on the sidewalk just above the steps. They hurried over to claim their spot. They were almost there when a man wearing a Carps baseball cap nearly stumbled into Yoshiko. He was walking fast up the steps and wasn't paying attention to her or Satsuki. When he realized this, he bowed and mouthed the words "I'm sorry," before sidestepping them and continuing to speed towards the roving crowds on the sidewalk.

Hideo? Yoshiko thought. He had looked like her husband, but no, that couldn't be possible. He was in South Korea, on business, as usual. She suddenly had an urge to call and tell him about her and Satsuki attending the festival together. *He sure is going to have a big surprise when he returns.* A wide grin was stuck on Yoshiko's face.

"See, that wasn't so bad, was it?" Satsuki asked her mother.

"Not at all," Yoshiko said, relieved that it wasn't. "Are you ready to put the lantern into the water?"

"Yeah. Can you hand me the matches?"

"Sure. I have them in my pocket. Hold on."

Yoshiko pulled out the matchbook they were given when they had purchased the lantern. They set their lantern down on the ground, and while Yoshiko held the disk-shaped votive candle that came with it in her hands, Satsuki lit the wick. Both looked at each other and counted to three before placing the candle inside the lantern.

"Wow, it's so pretty!" They both exclaimed. The candlelight seemed to completely absorb the translucent Yupo paper in a flash, amplifying the shade of pink on the lantern's walls. The pink hue wouldn't have been so strong if it weren't for the fact that the sky had turned into a dark, summer blue since Yoshiko and Satsuki had left the apartment. Satsuki crouched down beside the lantern and waved her hands in its shiny glow.

"You're the soul of my *imouto*, aren't you?" she whispered quietly to herself. Yoshiko didn't hear her but was thinking a similar thought. She bent down beside Satsuki and stared as though in a trance at the candlelight.

"It's time we let her go," Yoshiko said, her words slow and somber. She sounded to Satsuki like a monk reciting his prayers. "This past year has been terrible," Yoshiko continued to chant, "and it has without a doubt been the hardest year of my life, but I have you, and I'm grateful for that. I also have another daughter on the way. I hope you can let her go, Satsuki. I have already made my peace with what happened."

Satsuki didn't say anything at first. She wanted to tell her mother that she also had already let go. But how could she explain what she had done to make everything right? Perhaps it was best to fight and forget after all.

"Let's say goodbye," Satsuki said. Before Yoshiko could respond, Satsuki picked up the lantern and unceremoniously placed it in the river, right as a strong breeze swept across the water towards them. Considering how the summer air showed no sign of cooling down, even though it would be nighttime soon, it couldn't have come at a better time. The breeze abducted their lantern and threatened to hurry it towards the messy rows of other lanterns floating in the river. But then Satsuki pulled the lantern out of the water before it was past her hand's reach.

"What's wrong?" Yoshiko asked.

"Sorry. I forgot something."

The truth was, Satsuki hadn't forgotten anything at all. She had actually been debating whether or not to pull the folded index card out of her pocket. She hadn't brought a marker to write any prayers or well-wishes to her departed sister on the lantern's paper walls. And almost all of the lanterns she watched floating in the river were covered in writing or drawings of some kind. Goodbyes to loved ones lost, she figured. Or maybe poems, or sayings. Satsuki questioned if anyone really cared about what they wrote. Was everyone just going through the motions of attending another year's festival to remember the dead and wishing them a safe trip to the afterlife? Did they really believe in it?

To Satsuki, the Motoyasu River was a cemetery, and all the lanterns floating in it were paper tombstones. *Fuck them*, she thought to herself. *I don't care what the other festival attendees do with their lanterns or what they believe in. And why am I even questioning what I need to do, anyway? I have to add an epitaph to the tombstone I'm holding in my hands. She deserves nothing less.* She pulled out the index card, and without unfolding it or reading the message on the inside flap (where the words "We Are All Connected" were inscribed), placed it carefully inside the lantern to make sure the candle didn't catch it on fire.

"What did you put in there?" Yoshiko asked.

"My goodbye," Satsuki answered. She placed the lantern back into the water.

Yoshiko frowned. She didn't understand why Satsuki wouldn't say more about the index card. She searched her memory for what it could possibly mean to Satsuki, but couldn't think of a single thing. *Whatever*, Yoshiko thought. *Satsuki's out of her room now, and that's all that matters.* She crouched down beside her daughter and gave the lantern a little push.

Yoshiko didn't notice the bloodstains on the index card.

Thousands of people had now lined up to watch the lanterns float into the afterlife. Clusters of elderly people, including several *hibakusha*, sat in their fold-out chairs at the foot of the Genbaku Dome across the river. An orchestral theme song from some old movie could be heard playing from a loudspeaker. It invoked a mood of celebration, despite the somber occasion. Tourists, reporters, and Hiroshima citizens alike were enjoying themselves. It seemed that Yoshiko and Satsuki were the only ones besides the *hibakusha* who remained silently playing a game of catch and release with their feelings of loss.

"All those poor lanterns, I guess they aren't going to make it," Satsuki said, breaking the quiet that had crept up on them both.

"Which lanterns are you talking about?" Yoshiko asked.

"Those ones right over there." Satsuki pointed to a heap of at least a couple hundred lanterns bobbing in place. They clogged the profile of the wall across the river.

Yoshiko had noticed them, too. "Ah, *those* poor lanterns. They must be stuck against the rocks over there. I thought you were talking about those ones over there." She pointed to the thousands of colorful lanterns that were clustered together in the middle of the river, drifting as one rainbow-pixellated island while many other lanterns, including theirs, trailed behind it like a forgotten archipelago of lights.

Satsuki shook her head, then changed the subject. "*Okaasan*, can I ask you something?"

"Sure."

"Have you thought of a name for the baby?"

Yoshiko was pleasantly surprised by this question. Her face lit up as brightly as the lanterns. "No I haven't. Why? Do you have a name in mind?"

"I do, actually."

"What is it?"

Satsuki looked over her shoulder at a nearby park. The trees there were swaying back and forth, caught in the summer wind. She turned back around towards Yoshiko and grabbed her hands.

"I want her name to be ———— "